Blood Rose Angel
Liza Perrat

TRISKELE BOOKS

Cover design: JD Smith.

Published by Perrat Publishing.
All enquiries to info@lizaperrat.com
First printing, 2015.

ISBN: (MOBI) 9 782 954 168 197
(EPUB) 9 782 954 168 180
(PAPERBACK) 9 782 954 168 173

To my three roses ... Camille, Mathilde, Etienne

Take thou this rose, O rose,

Since love's own flower it is,

And by that rose,

Thy lover captive is

Carmina Burana (possibly from Abelard's pen,
expressing his love for Héloïse)

The Year of Our Lord 1334
Lucie-sur-Vionne

I

'Christ's toenails, ignore him Héloïse,' Isa chided, as I glared at Drogan sauntering towards us through the market-place stalls and customers.

'Milk-thieving bastard,' Drogan chanted, along with his as equally loathsome brothers.

'Drogan ain't never walked right because you stole his milk,' the oldest brother said, jabbing a filthy finger at me.

The third brother nodded at Drogan's legs, bowed as a barrel hoop. 'That's what our maman reckons.'

'There was no thieving,' I cried, sick of the same old taunts I'd suffered for as many of my eleven years as I could recall. 'My aunt paid your maman well for that milk.'

My aunt Isa had told me that since I was born one moon early—and of course because my mother was dead—I couldn't suckle. She'd recently midwifed Sara, Drogan's mother, and had given her coin for some of her milk, dripping it into my mouth from her spindle end.

'Maman couldn't refuse your aunt.' Drogan glanced at Isa. 'Too afraid she'd curse her with some potion or spell, like she poisoned our papa with that liniment for his bad knees.'

'We're sick to vomiting of this story, Drogan,' Isa said. 'I'm sorry your father died, but it was no liniment of mine killed him. And a hundred times I've told you, your legs are bent because your maman refused to listen to me, and swaddle you properly … nothing to do with Héloïse drinking your milk.'

'Murderin's in your family,' Drogan said, ignoring Isa. 'You even killed your own mother when you got birthed. Everyone in Lucie-sur-Vionne reckons you was born against nature.'

'A non-born what God didn't want to live,' said the taverner's daughter, Rixende, skipping by with her friend, Jacotte.

Rixende was the arse-first babe my mother had struggled to birth; the despicable girl I wished Ava had left inside her maman. Because if my mother hadn't worked so hard to save Rixende, she wouldn't have got the falling sickness and died because of having me in her womb.

'Non-born bastard ... non-born bastard,' Rixende and Jacotte sang.

I was used to Drogan and his brothers' milk-thieving torments, but what was a non-born? I was so busy staring at Rixende and Jacotte, hoping they'd explain without me asking— and looking a blithering idiot!—I jumped in fright when Drogan lunged at me.

'What's this?' His fingers reached for the talisman that hung on a leather strip about my neck—the bone-carved angel Isa had just given me as a gift from my mother. 'Some Devil's charm?'

'No Devil's charm.' I leapt backwards, shrugging off Isa's warning hand. 'And you can't touch it, or the eyes will burn you.'

But as if the angel's eyes had bewitched him, Drogan came at me again. As he touched the glittery orbs—one blue, the other green—he cried out, dropped the talisman and sucked on his fingers. 'Ah! The evil thing burnt me.'

'Told you, turd-brain,' I said, trying to hide my surprise. 'The angel's eyes will scald all who aren't supposed to touch them. So you'd do good to keep your grubby fingers away, or they'll get burned right off your hand.' I ignored Isa's gaping stare; I could hardly believe I'd invented such a lie myself. And more amazed that somehow it had come true.

Emboldened, I shook the talisman at them. 'I'll curse the lot of you cod-wits. You'll sprout horns on your faces and a tail from your arses.' I spat into the dirt, sealing my promise.

'Off with you now, children,' Isa said, giving me her warning look. 'Enough of your loitering.'

I grabbed a fistful of rotted cabbage from the ground, and flung it at them as they scurried away.

'Remember those horns and tails,' I shouted, against their laughter ringing in my ears. 'I'll do it, I will! And a murrain on your families.'

Isa gripped my hand and almost dragged me away from la place de l'Eglise.

'I know I'm a bastard who killed her own maman, but what is a non-born?' I said as we climbed the slope towards our cottage. My voice came out trembling and croaky, like an old person's. 'Did God really not want me to live?'

'Don't listen to their addled hog-rot, Héloïse. Of course God wanted you to live. You were His miracle, born the same way as a kinsman of the great Roman, Julius Caesar. A non-born cut from his dead mother's womb … a precious daughter for me and … I've always hoped, my midwife apprentice. If you'll ever come to your senses, that is!'

'I've told you, Isa, I will *never* birth a single child.'

'I know you blame yourself for your maman dying,' Isa said with a sigh. 'It's the fear that makes you shun birthing mothers. But dangerous as birthing is, a good many mothers and babes do survive despite the scores of young cut down like ripe wheat before they have a chance to grow up. Besides, with no man at our hearth, and no chance of you snaring a husband, you'll be needing a trade. Like Ava and I did.'

'Maybe,' I said with a shrug. I'd heard all this before.

'And by God's bones,' Isa said, waggling a threatening finger, 'do not *ever* try to use the talisman for spells or witchcraft. Even in jest or empty threat, the townsfolk will use it against you.'

"God's bones" was the worst curse ever, so I knew Isa was serious, but I also sensed this was my chance to get her to tell me about Ava's death. She'd always refused to speak of her twin's passing; said it was pointless moping about the past, but I guessed it was the sadness that stopped her. That and the brute who'd mixed his seed with Ava's.

'Well, if I promise never to use the angel pendant for magic,' I said, 'will you tell me the non-born story?'

***

'I'd seen Ava's condition once before, in my midwifing years.' Isa sat on a boulder on the pebbled Vionne riverbank and patted a place beside her. 'The face, hands and ankles of a woman heavy with child swelled like an unmilked cow's udder, pain tearing at her head.'

It was late afternoon, the sun's westward journey over the Monts du Lyonnais almost over, but Drogan, Jacotte and Rixende's taunts still whirled through my mind.

'I knew the only hope of cure was to bring on the birth,' my aunt said. 'But if Ava's babe came a whole moon too early it would surely perish.'

I nodded, urging her on.

'I laid Ava on the pallet, and her eyes came over all glassy, flickering about from the cauldrons hanging over the hearth to the rickety trestle table and the plants drying from the rafters. "It's like looking through mist", she said.'

As Isa spoke of her twin, it was as if I was hearing Ava's own voice coming from her lips. It felt warm and comforting, like Isa's hot chicken broth on a winter night, but at the same time a hard lump of sorrow wedged in my chest.

'I gave her a thyme and vervain brew to relieve the ache of the demons gnawing at her head … to avert evil,' Isa said. 'And some poppy-laced ale to lull her to sleep.'

She fell silent, squinting down the valley, the last sunlight like drops of gold on the rippling water, and I knew she was mustering the courage to continue her painful story.

'You know that since our maman's passing from putrid lungs,' she said, 'Ava and I had lived alone in the cottage. Midwifing and healing kept us in grain, oil and other basics, and no one troubled us much, even as their suspicion of the bastard midwife twins hung about us like a poisonous miasma. But as Ava's belly rounded, and no sign of a husband, well you should've seen those womenfolk's lips pucker in malicious delight.'

'Who was the father, Isa?'

As always when I asked this question, my aunt clamped her lips and shook her head. But she knew. I was sure of it.

'I told Ava to make an angel of it afore the brute's seed grew limbs and soul,' she began again, muttering something I could've sworn was 'his balls for trout bait'. 'I told her to banish it while it was only a river of blood and muck to wash from her loins … but she refused.'

'What happened to Ava then?'

'The poppy juice soon wore off,' Isa said. 'And Ava woke moaning and clawing at her temples. I started rubbing lavender and rose-oil across her brow, then her eyes rolled back till all I could see was the whites … no colour. Just all white.'

'How horrible.'

'Worse than horrible, Héloïse. By that time I was screaming … begging the Blessed Virgin to spare my twin—as close to me as my own soul. I'd always thought we'd go together, you see … I couldn't imagine living if Ava was gone.' She exhaled a long breath and looked down at the river; at the mountains standing upside down in the water.

'The Devil crept inside Ava,' Isa said, 'and started up a shaking as an earthquake might splinter the earth when *Dieu* was in a fury. My mind was spinning. What physick could stop the brain spasms? A potion of dandelion roots? Saint John's wort seeds eaten for forty days? I didn't have forty days, Héloïse. Not forty seconds! All I could do was kneel beside her and watch the falling sickness snatch my sister to the dark side.'

I didn't know what to say, so I just curled my hand over Isa's.

'There wasn't a second to grieve,' Isa said. 'I had to free the unborn and baptise it before it died too, or owls would devour its soul. I didn't ponder … knew I'd lose my nerve if I did. So I swiped a wine-soaked cloth over her belly, made the sign of the cross and sliced an arc clear across Ava's womb. Then I unfurled the tiniest baby from the gaping red darkness.

'At first I couldn't look at that limp, underbaked non-born,' she said, 'dragged into the world against every force of Mother Earth. But then I couldn't resist, and you know what? That little girl seemed too lovely to be doomed: pale wisps of hair, eyelids veined like a butterfly's wing, fingers curling like flower petals at witch-light.'

I gave Isa a small smile as the sun sank onto the rim of the hills in a brilliant orange rind.

'I laid her between her mother's legs,' Isa said, 'and thought I glimpsed a movement … an eyelid blinking, a fluttering so slight I could've imagined it. But it was no shadowy trick, for that girl screwed up her face so tight and bawled so loud she almost deafened me. I was bawling by then too,' she went on, 'tears of relief … and wonder! So I swaddled you, lavishing thanks on Saint Margaret for this miracle … on Ava for not making an angel of you; for giving me the daughter—the midwife apprentice—I'd never dared hope for.'

Isa was quiet, her dark eyes filling with tears. But only one leaked down her cheek. The rest she sniffed away. Like me, my aunt didn't cry or show any other signs of weakness, though telling this tale must have felt like seeing her sister; her midwifing partner, die all over again.

'Then I crossed your mother's arms over her heart and closed her eyes,' Isa said. 'Forever.'

I squeezed her hand. The sky had bled out all its light, and there were no more upside down mountains in the black river.

***

The morning after Isa told me about my non-born birth and Ava's death, I was gathering the hens' eggs when a man scurried towards the cottage waving his arms in the air.

'Midwife, come quickly ... my wife, she's birthing our child ... right now, in the field!' From his patched and worn tunic and the hemp cord gathering it at the waist I could tell he was a poor labourer hired by our *Seigneur* to work his strips of land.

'The midwife—my aunt—went to Julien-sur-Vionne,' I said, motioning towards the next village along the river. 'She'll be gone hours probably ... a difficult birth they said when they came to fetch her.'

'Who'll birth my wife then?' He looked me up and down, his arms still flapping like a bird's trapped in a cage. 'You're her apprentice, aren't you? Couldn't you do the job?'

'I've witnessed births, yes,' I said, 'but I'm no midwife apprentice. Not now, not ever.'

'Surely you know something about midwifing? There ain't anybody else. Please come, Mistress. Please?'

From the way he was blathering on, and pleading with his sad-dog eyes, I could tell the man was in a state. As much as I'd rather have rolled in the mud with our pig, I said, 'I'll come then.' But as soon as the words were out, I regretted them. Me, a midwife, after I'd killed my own mother?

Swallowing hard, trying to dislodge the stone blocking my throat, I grabbed one of Isa's baskets and took things I remembered she used for births: clean cloths, knife, scissors, some kinds of herbs. Any would do, I thought, taking vials from her shelf at random, and flinging them into the basket.

I dragged my cloak around my shoulders and hurried after the labourer, past the milking and dairy work, the weaning calves, following the screams to the small crowd gathered in the field. With dismay, I saw that this wife *was* labouring—not at weeding or sowing seeds—but at bringing her child into the world.

'Away from here, you men,' I ordered, as I'd seen Isa do. 'Only women can witness a birth.'

My legs trembling I knelt beside the thrashing girl. 'Hush, poppet,' I said, again mimicking Isa's soft but firm tone. I flipped up her kirtle that was stained with bloody fluid and gasped. I could already see a sliver of the baby's slimy head.

Oh Blessed Virgin, tell me what to do! Let me do it right.

I grasped my mother's angel pendant between a quivering thumb and forefinger, and as I spoke, Ava floated above me, as if my mother were sitting on a cloud, watching, guiding me. The words I spoke were hers. Or Isa's. I couldn't tell, with my nerves so raw and edgy.

'Good girl,' I said. 'You've already done most of the hard work, this will soon be over. You must push with the next pain.'

Her belly hardened, the girl pushed and—willing the angel pendant's powers to me—my steady hands eased out the child. As I laid the infant in his mother's outstretched arms, her screaming was replaced with a smile as sweet as spilled honey.

'A boy, a lardy boy!' cried the women, as I cut the navel string like I'd seen Isa do. Easy really, like slicing through a freshly-hooked trout.

I almost got to my feet, thinking the job done. But no I'd forgotten, still to come was that great pulpy thing Isa called the "afterbirth".

Oh God's arse, no, here it comes!

I was surprised I didn't vomit as the slimy purple mass plopped into my hands. It must've been the warmth swelling my chest that stopped my own sickness, as I watched the new mother studying her baby's face, his fingers, the whorls of his ears, his tiny nipples. She held her breath as he sighed, laughed as he yawned and giggled at his grasp on her thumb. Isa said every new mother was the same and I wondered why there wasn't a song for this moment. Maybe there were no words strong enough.

From a distance the new father struck up a great whooping. Small, bare-legged boys charged about cheering and firing their slingshots at the marauding crows trying to steal the newly-sown seeds, and other birds unlucky enough to be in the firing line.

'Not the doves,' a woman shouted. 'Le Comte will fine us if you kill his sacred doves, you frog-wits.' The boys ignored her and kept laughing and firing off their slings at those hated symbols of our *Seigneur's* power.

The new mother looked up at me. 'My grateful thanks, Apprentice ...?'

'Héloïse,' I said, 'but I'm no apprent—'

'Yes, a fine young apprentice you are,' the new father cut in, grinning as he passed a flask of ale around the other labourers. 'Done your aunt proud, you have.'

'You'll surely be the best midwife in the whole of France one day,' the mother said.

'Hear, hear!' the field workers shouted, all of them clapping.

The heat rose to my cheeks, and I wished they'd stop embarrassing me. But I couldn't help smiling too, and pressed a hand across my mouth to hide it. And the smile turned into laughter I couldn't stop, until tears ran down my cheeks.

As I skipped back to our cot, I thought about being a non-born. I sensed that mine was a life given to a child born wrongly, and that unless I did something worthwhile with it, the blood my mother had shed for me would be wasted.

As soon as Isa got home, I linked my arm through hers and told her about my first birthing.

'I know it now,' I said.

'Know what, Héloïse?'

'I want to birth babies. Not rip them from their dead mothers but real, live birthings. I want to become your apprentice.'

Isa was silent for a moment, as if she could hardly believe I was saying the words she'd always wanted to hear.

'Well of course I'm pleased, Héloïse, but it's not that simple. You'll have to commit yourself; vow to never abandon the sick, dying or a woman with child whatever the inconvenience or pain to yourself.'

'I swear, on the soul of my mother,' I said, holding the

bone-sculpted angel between my thumb and forefinger, 'to heal the sick and care for women carrying babes as best I can whatever the inconvenience. I vow to bring life, not death.' I took a deep breath. 'And I'll prove them all wrong, Isa. Everyone will know God *did* want me to live.'

Spring in the Year of Our Lord
1348
Lucie-sur-Vionne

II

The banging on our cottage door came when the moon was overhead, casting earthly things into shadow. That perilous hour when we feared her the most. I was not expecting Raoul back from Florence for months, and my husband would never knock on his own door, but still my heart thumped in anticipation. I bolted from the sleeping pallet and scrambled down the loft ladder.

But as I shone the tallow candle into the doorway my hope faded. Not my Raoul, but Farmer Donis, in calf-length leather boots and tunic drawn in with a leather belt—the garb of a reasonably prosperous farmer who owns his land rather than working our *Seigneur's* strips.

His wife was expecting her first child any day, and knowing that even unborn babies are cantankerous—often coming in the night—I was in no doubt about the reason for the farmer's visit.

'Is Midwife Isa here?' Donis's cheeks glowed pink from the cold.

'Isa no longer performs births.' I was surprised he'd asked for my aunt. I thought all the townsfolk knew I was the only midwife nowadays. 'But I've been delivering healthy infants for many—'

'I know,' Donis said, stroking his beard. 'You're Midwife Héloïse, but you sure you're as good as the old one? They say the first babe's the hardest, and so it is with my Alix ... in agony for hours and no sign of it.'

'It depends on the strength of the mother, the lie of the child and many other things,' I said. 'Now do you want me to help your wife or will we just stand here freezing in the darkness?'

'Come on with you, then. If my Alix and the child survive, you'll be paid in honey.'

'My aunt and I never accept payment unless the outcome is good. Now if you don't mind strapping my birthing chair onto your cart while I get ready?'

I left Farmer Donis hoisting up my chair while I washed my face and hands, pulled on my kirtle and tucked rogue wicks of hair beneath my cap.

I heard Morgane stir up in the loft. 'Maman?'

I climbed back up the ladder. 'Go to sleep, poppet. I have to leave for a birth but Isa will stay with you. When she wakes, tell her it's Poppa's grandchild.' I glanced across at my gently-snoring aunt. Since Isa no longer worked, midwifing and healing kept me away many hours, and I was glad she was here for Morgane, though I wished—especially during the long winter nights—that her father could be at home too.

'I want to birth the babe, Maman.'

'I've told you, my eager little apprentice … seven is too young but soon you'll be old enough to do your own midwifing.' I smoothed wisps of hair from her brow, kissed her sweet-smelling cheek and hurried out into the night.

Farmer Donis clicked his tongue and the horse clopped away from our cot, the last home on Lucie-sur-Vionne's northern boundary. I kept my gaze low, on the cloud shadows the moonlight sent scudding across the meltwater-swollen river, avoiding the slightest glance at that night orb, for fear she'd curse me or the coming birth.

Westward, the Monts du Lyonnais hills crouched like craggy behemoths and to the east, beyond the flicker of lantern light from the city of Lyon, the *Montagne Maudite*—cursed mountain—sat as a queen beneath her eternal snowy crown.

The spring air frosted my cheeks and I tugged my hood

around my face, hunching into the folds of my cloak. We trotted on in silence, swaying to the rhythmic thud of hooves on damp earth, jolting in the slush-filled ruts of the last snow. The bleat of a new lamb, the cackle of a goose and the bark of a dog signalled life amidst the slumbering townsfolk.

Just beyond the millhouse, home of Johan Miller and his twelve children, Farmer Donis reined in his horse. His was the last cot before the road sloped down towards the market-place.

'Go inside, Midwife,' the farmer said, leading his horse towards the barn. 'I'll bring your chair.'

Clutching my basket, I walked through the gate upon which stood a raven, my heartbeat quickening at the sight of that death omen. Feathers glimmering beneath the moonlight like blue-black silk, the raven fanned its tail, stretched its neck towards me and cawed what seemed a warning, 'Go, go!'

***

Farmer Donis's mother—Poppa—was Isa's childhood friend, so I'd always known the family kept bees, making candles from the wax. Isa said that even during leaf-fall and winter their home was filled with this breath of sleepy summer, and as I stepped inside, the smell of honey and thyme-scented wax engulfed me.

Inhaling the pungent smell, I shouldered my way through the gossips—the girl's relatives crowded in to witness the great moment. Women can never resist a new baby, even in the middle of the night, and they clucked around the girl lying on the beaten-earth floor like a mother partridge fussing over her brood.

'Isa couldn't come,' I said to Poppa, setting my basket on the table. 'Her hips've been bad ... and more painful at night.'

Poppa flapped away my apology, her smile puffing out her cheeks like new apples. 'I'll wager you'll do as good a job as the old witch herself.'

Alix's mother, a wrinkled woman with black teeth stumps, was dabbing a grimy rag to her daughter's forehead.

'Why is Alix on the floor?' I asked.

'We always birth like this,' the old woman said. 'When the pains come on hard, you lay your bare loins against the earth so they'll take strength from Mother Earth.'

'She'd be more comfortable on my birthing chair, or the pallet.'

'Are you certain?' said Alix's sister, the crabby-faced Nica who'd never held me or Isa in her heart. 'I birthed all my six on the ground.'

'Yes the midwife is certain!' a crimson-cheeked Alix cried. 'Please ... my arse is killing me.'

I nodded, and as the gossips heaved the girl onto the pallet, Alix wailed, 'God must hate me that I should have such pain. Women are born only to suffer ... this child will kill me, I know it.'

The first thing Isa had taught me was that fear and hysteria are the worst enemies of easy childbirth. 'Don't be afraid,' I said. 'Meet each pain with a breath and conquer it.'

As I unpacked my kit, Poppa laid out a mistletoe twig and sprinkled salt in the cradle to stop the fairies abducting her coming grandchild. Farmer Donis opened the door a crack and almost threw the birthing chair at me in his haste to be gone from a room full of women.

As the pearly dawn broke over the horizon, Alix's agonising travail continued. I got her to sit in my chair for a time, then rest on the pallet. She used the pisspot, walked around a bit.

'Drink this.' I held to Alix's lips a beaker of birthwort root juice. 'It'll make the pains work better.'

Mid-morning came but there was still no sign of the baby, so I looped my angel talisman over my head and laid it in Alix's navel dip.

'What are you about with that thing, Midwife?' Nica pointed to my pendant rising and falling with Alix's breaths.

'It can help show the child the way out of the womb,' I said.

'Won't harm the babe, will it?' Alix's mother said. 'I've heard of midwives using charms if the fancy takes them ... causing infants to come out bent and twisted.'

'Or dead,' Nica said. 'Like that one of mine your aunt killed.'

'It was a tragedy, Nica,' I said, recalling Isa's distress after that birth. 'But the navel cord strangling your babe was not my aunt's doing, and my talisman will not hurt Alix's child in any way.' I cast Nica and her mother a dark stare, resisting the urge to snap at these ignorant women. 'A midwife brings life, when she can. Not death.'

'What the Devil's balls are you on about, Nica?' Poppa said. 'Can't you see your sister needs all the help she can get? And how you can think ill of Isa's niece I don't know.'

'As if I'm the only one,' Nica sneered. 'You must go about this town with your eyes and ears shut, Poppa.'

My blood was boiling now, my hands shaky. 'Could we all just concentrate on getting this birth over with ... *safely*?' I said.

'I'm only sayin' ...' Nica started, excited voices outside the door interrupting her. A scatter of dirty boys—three of her own brood—barged inside.

'We saw men,' Nica's youngest said. 'In the woods.'

'What men?' Poppa asked.

'Look like outlaws,' another said.

'They was sat around a fire, swilling ale,' the third brother said, wiping a sleeve across his leaky nose. 'Reckon they're headed our way.'

'I did hear rumour of outlaws,' the old mother said. 'Soldiers fighting the war against those English barbarians, with no work after Crécy, and no pay from their lord.'

'And robbing merchants on the south and eastward roads,' Poppa said. 'Trundling away whole carts of wool and spices. Gold even!'

We'd all heard the terrifying stories of townsfolk ambushed, their homes looted and in the women's silence, their questioning eyes, a pall of fear rippled through the room.

Another moan from Alix snapped us back to the problem at hand.

'Outlaws or not, this ain't no place for young boys,' Poppa said to Nica's sons, as the gossips helped Alix onto the birthing chair again. 'Can't you see we're doing women's work?' She flapped her arms, shooing them outside. 'Go and help the men in the fields, where you should be.'

The boys scurried off, swiping hunks of bread from the table on their way.

'It's an omen,' Alix's mother said, crossing herself. 'Outlaws here and Alix's babe coming at the wrong time of the year. Everyone knows an infant born in the green mists of spring comes out weak and scrawny.'

'Isa brought Midwife Héloïse into this world a spring baby,' Poppa said, flinging a stout arm towards me. 'An undercooked one at that, and look how *she* thrives.'

Oh yes, Poppa. I thrived but what a price I'd made my mother pay for that. My hand, massaging Alix's lower back, stopped mid-circle as that familiar stab of guilt jabbed deep in my chest. As another throw took Alix up, her body stiffening beneath my touch, I massaged harder, faster, rubbing away the pain. And I willed, once more, the remorse and sorrow that had dogged me for as long as I could remember, to a distant cranny of my mind.

***

At last, mid-afternoon—and thankfully no sign of the outlaws—my oiled hand felt the baby's head.

'It's coming,' I said. 'Let's get Alix back onto the birthing chair. Heat water ... bring me your cleanest towels.'

Amidst grunts and panting breaths, the women hauled the exhausted girl onto the horseshoe-shaped seat and hurried about the cot, all the while chanting, 'It's coming, it's coming!'

'You must push with the next throw,' I said, sitting on a stool in front of Alix.

All strength bent on her work, Alix pushed as the next pain took her up. Tears oozed, her cheeks swelled, her face turned scarlet. She kept bracing her feet against the birthing chair and pushing, the gossips taking turns supporting her underarms from behind the chair.

'I can't go on any longer!' she cried after an hour. 'Please, Midwife, just get it out of me.'

'Ain't no other way to get it out besides pushing, Alix,' her mother said.

I heard it then. A faint and distant rumble. Like a storm brewing over the Monts du Lyonnais.

'It's them outlaws,' Nica's sons shouted, tumbling into the cot again. 'We saw 'em, riding along the ridge.' They pointed towards the northern boundary of Lucie, to the spur on which my own cottage stood—the cot where my ailing old aunt and my young daughter were, with no man to defend them.

My blood slowed, my legs faltering beneath me, and I yearned yet again for Raoul to be home with us. But he wasn't and stuck here birthing a child there wasn't a thing I could do to help Isa and Morgane. I took slow, measured breaths to calm myself, instructing Alix to push harder; to get this child out as quickly as possible.

'Can't see anything,' Poppa said, as she pushed aside the oilcloth and peered out across the fields.

We might not be able to see the outlaws yet, but I could almost smell the women's mounting fear. What chance did we have of running or hiding; of defending ourselves? Such easy prey for lawless brigands. I swiped at the bead of sweat trickling down my brow, caught my pendant between shaky fingers, and willed its comfort and powers of protection to me.

I reminded myself that whatever the circumstances, the midwife must appear calm and in control. 'Must be just a storm,' I said blithely and, as another pain caught Alix, 'concentrate and push harder.'

'Push harder,' the women said, and Alix huffed and heaved and pushed.

'Good girl, that's it.' I tried to keep the panic from my voice as I heard the sound of hammering outside. It was not the usual ox-cart rattling or the amble of cattle, but the thump of swiftly-riding horsemen.

'Get under the table, boys,' Nica said. 'And don't move.'

Crouched beneath the table, legs bent up and arms hugging their knees, Nica's sons didn't seem the least bit afraid, an excited kind of zeal shining in their young eyes. But the women's rising terror echoed my own. We all stood rigid, our breaths sharp, hesitant.

'For the love of God's blood, push,' I said when Alix's belly hardened again.

Alix pushed, seemingly—thank the Virgin!—oblivious to the approaching outlaws. Still no sign of the baby. The shouts and cries outside grew frantic. Hooves thudded louder.

'Come on, Alix,' I urged.

'Come on, Alix,' the women urged.

With the next push, the crown of the baby's head appeared and a cry of relief echoed around the cramped room.

I knelt between Alix's upraised knees and as much as I wanted to get this birth over with with, I eased the head out at the next powerful throw to stop Alix's tender skin from tearing. Then to my dismay, as the shoulders came, so too streamed the greenish-black muck.

Amidst their joy and shouts of, 'It's a boy ... a boy!' the gossips didn't seem to notice my concern, or my held breath. Nor did they realise the baby wasn't breathing.

I turned the child upside down, a finger cleaning the dangerous dark liquid from his mouth.

'Why's my baby blue?' Alix said.

I laid him flat, began blowing air into his mouth and nose, my rhythm soft and steady.

'The boy's dead, ain't he, Midwife?' Alix's mother said.

'You killed him, you witch!' Nica launched herself at me, tried to prise the child away. 'You and that Devil's curse of a talisman.'

'Let me do my work!' I shoved Nica aside with my hip, blowing more air into the baby's mouth.

'What's wrong with my baby?' Alix wailed.

As I kept breathing into those tiny airways, willing the child to breathe, I caught the first whiff of smoke from outside. My gut churned, my bowels turning to water.

'The horsemen have set fire to the miller's home!' Poppa cried from the window.

'What can we do?' Nica shrieked.

'Cutthroats like them ain't got no reason for coming here,' Poppa went on, 'only to carry off our best food and ...'

'And loot our homes,' Nica finished. 'And attack the womenfolk.'

'Oh save us, God and Your Holy Virgins.' Alix's mother crossed herself.

'Shut up, all of you!' I tried to concentrate on the baby; tried to ignore these hysterical women. And the danger outside.

Stay in control. Keep calm.

A moment later the little body began to turn pink. *Merci, Saint Margaret, merci!*

'Nothing's wrong with your son,' I said. 'A healthy boy.'

'Thank the Lord for that,' the old mother said. 'But what of those outlaws?'

'Don't worry, they'll just ride on straight out of Lucie. You'll see.' I coughed to mask the quaver in my voice.

Nica frowned at the baby. 'He might be breathing now but his head ain't right.'

The women fell silent, the boys crept out from under the table and they all stared at the child's head, which sloped upwards to a lopsided point. His eyes were swollen shut by a massive bruise that spread across his face, his nose mashed to one side.

'What's wrong with his head?' Alix asked.

'Who cares about a pointy head when we all might be clubbed to death any minute,' the toothless mother shrieked.

'I'm sure they've already left town,' I said. 'Listen, there's no more noise.'

It was true; all I could hear was birdsong. The distant thuds could be any farming noise. 'Anyway, a misshaped head is normal after a long travail. The bruising will soon clear and his head will become round again. He'll look the perfect boy he is.'

As if affirming my words, the baby shrieked as I took my knife from the basket.

'Leave that navel string good and long, Midwife Héloïse,' Poppa said, as I cut it three finger-lengths from the belly, and sealed off its raw end with cicely. 'That's what your aunt Isa said when she birthed my boys: it'll help his yard grow long, and make some girl happy one day.'

I swaddled the babe as Alix's old mother smeared honey onto her daughter's breasts to give him strength and sweeten his nature. She then placed the small bundle against Alix's breast and the tiny lips fastened onto her nipple.

As Poppa and Nica scrubbed the blood from Alix's thighs with hanks of straw, the baby's eyelids drooped, the blue of his eyes glowing beneath them like lapis through silk. Alix stroked the soft down on his head and the tiny fist folded around the fingers of her other hand as if he knew without seeing that the hand was his mother's. 'Let's pray he enjoys a long, hard-working life,' she said.

'Rather may he become rich,' Poppa said, with her wide smile, 'so we can all *stop* this hardworking life and idle away our days languishing on silken beds, wrapped in ermine cloaks, listening to the songs of beautiful minstrels with great pulsing members.'

We all giggled. Even the sour-faced Nica let out a chuckle.

Enchanted by this heavenly moment, I jumped as the door flew open. A hulking man blocked all the light, his black beard coarse as horse's hair, neck thick as a bullock's.

III

The outlaw looked on the birth scene with obvious surprise. A scowl darkened his grimy, sweat-slick face. 'Christ drowning in *merde*. What the …?' He stepped inside, a stench of smoked fish and old ale filling the room, the horsewhip he brandished in one shovel-like hand making unearthly cracks.

Despite the fearsome display, and the sword in his scabbard, a reckless courage flared inside me.

'Get out,' I ordered, jabbing a finger at the door. 'Can't you see this is a birthing room … a sacred place for women only?'

The outlaw glowered down at me. 'Bit bold for a woman, aren't you? Who might you be?'

'I'm the midwife, and I order you out of this cot now!' A drop of sweat rolled down my nose.

The room remained silent, save the outlaw's bellows-like panting, and the ragged breaths of the women and Nica's boys. The man's gaze flickered sideways, locked on the newborn. He stepped towards Alix and her baby. 'What's wrong with its head?'

'Nothing,' I said. 'He's a perfect child.'

'Yes, perfect,' Poppa affirmed.

'Looks like the head of the Devil itself.' The outlaw laid his whip over the baby's brow, stroking the tender skin with the tip, as if caressing a kitten. 'Such a monstrous thing don't deserve to live.' His scarred face puckered into a grin that could have melted stone.

The new mother shrank away, whimpering and clutching her son to her breast.

'Don't hurt that newborn,' I said, 'or God will see you straight to Hell.'

The outlaw turned his crooked stare on me. In a movement more deft than a slaughterer's knife, he wrenched the babe from Alix's grasp. Jerking the newborn free of his swaddling, he held the bawling child upside down by the ankles.

As the infant screamed, writhing like a trout snagged fresh from the Vionne, the outlaw eyed the cot wall beside him. My insides seized with sudden terror.

Oh Lord no! Blessed Virgin save him.

'Stop,' I said. 'Give me that child.' I began rocking my angel pendant back and forth before the brigand, stepping towards him until I was level with the black hairs unfurling from his tunic. His eyes widened, fixed on the talisman's glowing blue and green ones.

I knew the newborn's life—probably all our lives—depended on not showing him fear. As a woman who'd lived without a man at her hearth for almost two years, I'd learned that terror only fuelled such lawless beasts.

With the soft, low voice I'd used to sing my daughter to sleep, I said, 'If you don't hand me the baby, and leave this cottage right now, a pack of wolves will pounce on you as you sit around the fire with your friends, boasting the spoils of Lucie. They'll rip out your black heart and feed it to the Devil.'

Still gripping the bawling child, the outlaw's eyes didn't flicker from the swinging pendant.

'Give me the child,' I went on, in my lullaby voice. 'Pass him to me now.' The pendant swung back and forth, back and forth.

Still not taking his gaze from the talisman, the outlaw handed me the baby.

As he backed out of the cottage step by step, his eyes still on my pendant, everyone remained still and silent as if staked to that earthen floor. Even the baby, cradled in my arms, was quiet.

Outside, I heard the outlaw curse, remounting his horse. As he cantered away, I let out a long, relieved breath and the women struck up a babble.

From the doorway, Poppa shouted after him: 'You're the Devil's now. By his hairy arse, may you choke to death and go to him soon!'

'And a cloak of serpents wrap about your neck and strangle the life from you!' Alix's mother added.

I swaddled the baby again and as I placed him in Alix's arms I noticed the gossips had turned their gazes on me, straying to the angel pendant, then—as if they dared not look at it for too long—back to my face.

'Oh there's no need to be afraid of it,' I said, my tone glib. 'Neither my talisman nor I have the power to curse that man ... or anyone else. I only made up the wolf story to scare him off.'

Nobody spoke. No one moved.

They can't be as stupid as that thug ... surely they believe me?

'It was all lies, don't you see?' I let out a nervous half-laugh. 'To stop him murdering Alix's beautiful boy.'

'But he believed you.' Poppa's face crinkled into a hesitant smile. 'And by the Virgin's milk, truth or not, that's what counts, doesn't it? A brave heroine is our Midwife Héloïse!' Gnarly fist raised, she looked around at the women, as if inciting them to agree with her; to show their comradeship.

'Hear, hear,' the old mother said, a bit half-heartedly.

'Thank you for saving my boy,' Alix said.

'But how can we be sure it weren't no lie?' Nica's eyes narrowed, glittery with distrust. 'You know what they say ... the better the witch, the better the midwife.'

'Some people are silly enough to believe everything they hear, Nica,' I said. 'But I don't have time to waste on such rot. The outlaws might've stopped at our cottage ... my aunt and daughter are alone.'

'Yes, you get gone to them,' Poppa said. 'You'll be sick with worry, especially with no husband to protect you.'

Alix's mother slid two pots of honey into my basket as birth payment, and Poppa shoved a pie at me.

'Made with the last of our dried fruit and honey. Isa always makes out she hates my pies, but I know the old witch gobbles them down. Now off you skedaddle,' she said, flapping her arms at me.

'I'll come by tomorrow,' I said, 'to check on Alix and the little one.'

'And you and Isa will celebrate with us?' Poppa said. 'At Alix's churching?'

'Wouldn't miss it for anything,' I said, wondering, not for the first time, how a woman's childbirth impurities could contaminate her. The ceremony of thanksgiving for her survival of childbirth is certainly important, but how could God think a woman creating life is filthy? And how can He allow men's wars and brigands' attacks to destroy that life at the same time? I might worship Our Lord but there were some things about Him I'd never understand.

I hurried from the farmer's cot to Poppa's cheery wave, and Nica's burning gaze searing through my back.

IV

Alongside me, swollen with the spate of spring rain, the Vionne surged reckless and powerful, in perfect cadence with my steps as I ran along the old Roman road.

Banked by willow trees, I had more chance of avoiding the outlaws on this woodland road, since they'd been cantering along the higher, busier road that passed between the cottages, and down to the heart of Lucie-sur-Vionne.

Breathless, my hose and kirtle hem mud-splattered, I lurched into our cot, inhaling the rich, gamey aroma of woodcock, and thyme leaves.

Isa was stirring the stew, her cauldron swaying gently over the fire and casting a high shadow across the wall. Not a sign of the outlaws.

She glanced up sharply. 'What the Devil's your hurry, Héloïse?'

I was silent for a moment, a palm squeezed against my scudding heart. I placed Poppa's pie on the table and slumped onto a stool to catch my breath.

Isa poked a finger into the pie crust. 'Poppa showing off as usual ... thinking her pies are better than mine,' she said with a laugh. 'How is the old crone?'

'Poppa's well,' I said, still breathing hard, 'and thank *la Sainte Vierge* so are you and Morgane ... those brigands ...'

Since Isa was at home, I assumed my daughter was with her.

She would be in the garden weaving daisies into a necklace for her cat, Blanche.

'Of course we're well,' Isa said her brow beetling. 'Why wouldn't we be? But look at *you*, white as the baby Jesus's bum.' She placed my basket on a shelf in the herbal lean-to and hung my cloak from a wooden nail behind the door. 'What's this about brigands? What happened at that birth, is Poppa's granchil—?'

'Alix, Poppa and her new grandchild—a boy—are all well,' I said. 'It's not that. I ... I know you've always said never to do it, but I had to ...'

'Had to do what?' Isa clamped her hands on her narrow hips.

'I wouldn't have told you, only I know that tattle Poppa will, since she tells you everything. I threatened to curse a man—a brigand—with the talisman ... made out it has the power to inflict evil.' I gulped in air. 'I know I shouldn't have, but he would've killed the newb—'

'God's balls, Héloïse! How many times have I ...? What's this gabble about brigands? You'd better tell me everything.'

'Didn't you hear?' I said, my breath steadying. 'Haven't you seen the outlaws?'

Isa kept shaking her head as she poured water into another pot and flung in a handful of dried chamomile flowers. '*What* outlaws?'

'A gang of brigands rode into Lucie ... pillaging and burning cottages! I was so worried about you and Morgane.'

'I've seen no outlaws, Héloïse, but have you forgotten?' Isa stirred the herbal brew, waving the other arm in the direction of the lepers' cot. 'We're safe, living beside them. One sniff of their rotting flesh, one look at those patches of dead grey skin, a half-eaten away lip or nose, and anyone, brigand or otherwise, would gallop away as fast as his horse could take him.'

'Let's hope you're right ... so where is Morgane?'

'I took her with me to the tavern,' Isa said, pouring me a cup of goat's milk and setting the bread and cheese before me. 'Jâco's still suffering from the kings' disease. Neither the cabbage potion nor the rosemary and honey plaster of goat dung eased his pain—'

'Morgane isn't here?'

'… keep telling Jâco too much ale and rich food will—'

I sprang from the stool. 'Isa! Is Morgane still on the market-place?'

'Well yes, I left her playing cat's cradle with Pétronille and Peronelle. You know how she loves to play—'

'But that's where the outlaws are headed!' I spun about on the spot, not wanting to believe Isa; not knowing what to do. Why wasn't Raoul here? He might be a short man but there was none in this town stronger and brawnier, while we had only blunt words to defend ourselves. And false threats from a talisman that couldn't curse a gnat.

I flew out the door, hoisted my skirts and ran like a hare.

Nothing can happen to Morgane. I would never forgive myself. How would I tell her father? Two deadborn sons is surely enough of God's punishment.

The words in my head drummed to the beat of my steps as I tore back along the woodland road, fanning sprawls of violets and primroses that clung between the rocks.

Though exhausted from the sleepless night, Alix's laborious travail and the terror of the black-bearded outlaw, I didn't feel a bit tired. I was aware only of the urgent thrum welling inside me; the dogged need to find my child and assure myself she was safe.

I slowed as I glimpsed a blurred movement through the budding willow branches—a woman and a child running across a field amid frolicking lambs. A cantering horseman was pursuing them, and as the figures came closer, I saw they were Jacqueline, the miller's wife and their youngest girl, Wanda. Mother and daughter were hurtling towards the Vionne as if the river could somehow save them from their mounted attacker. Wanda clutched a bouquet of pink primroses she must have been gathering.

Trying to calm my pounding heart, I backed out of sight

behind an oak, and laid a hot cheek against the cool mossy trunk. Jacqueline and Wanda had reached the river and were splashing into the shallows, shrieking as they stumbled on wet stones.

The outlaw soon caught them. Without bothering to raise club or sword, he let his horse trample Wanda. At the thud of hooves striking her small head, sickness surged from my belly, and as the little girl fell, her bouquet burst in a shower of pink petals. I pressed a hand to my mouth to mask my scream.

Oh Mother of God, this can't be happening!

The outlaw jumped from his horse, pushed Jacqueline face down into the water and mounted her from behind, like a dog. He thrust into the miller's wife, over and over, yelling 'Yah, yah!' And when Jacqueline no longer moved, her face still underwater, he remounted and cantered off, still chanting his joyful, 'Yah, yah!'

I knew death. Every wise-woman and midwife knows it. But before now, I'd seen it only in deadborns, or in a sunken-cheeked face or fevered brow; in the festered plough and scythe wound. But this savage massacre was something entirely different, and the pain of it sliced through me colder than a splinter of ice, hotter than my burning tears. I knew the miller's wife and daughter were beyond any wise-woman's help, so I set off again, my legs threatening to fold beneath me at every step.

Once I reached the end of the riverbank road, I climbed the grassy slope away from the Vionne. I stood, panting on the crest above the swirling river, and glanced down the other side towards the larger road and the thread of dwellings that unspooled between ours on the northern boundary and Alix and Poppa's cottage at the southern end.

Apart from our *Seigneur*—when he was in residence in the castle—the shopkeeper-artisans and the priest whose homes bordered the market-place or one of the alleys criss-crossing from it, Lucie's townsfolk lived in these small thatched cots, built along the lanes leading to their strips of land.

I swiped a damp tuft of hair from my brow, ran my tongue over my dry lips as I gazed, with horror, upon the scene before me. Bowls and drinking mugs lay scattered amongst spindles, farm tools and children's toys.

A sickening volley of cries rose from the wounded, those who'd been in the outlaws' path and felled like timber as they went about their daily tasks: a child drawing water from the well, another gathering kindling, others balancing buckets of goat's milk. A wife plucking a chicken in a yard.

Amidst the expectant squall of circling crows, the outlaws were galloping down towards the market-place, shouldering their horses through scattering people, kicking at them with spurred boots. I counted twelve, but the gang bore down on Lucie-sur-Vionne with the thunder of a thousand-strong army, nail-studded clubs waving like murderous flags.

My daughter's small face loomed in my mind and, ignoring the danger before me, I took a deep breath and raced after them.

***

I found myself caught up in a swarm of bellowing townsfolk on la place de l'Eglise, their shoes clattering on the cobbles as they darted about mindlessly. Women, children and men gripped one another—anybody—heads spinning left and right. None knew where to run, what to do. Every dog was barking like a mad beast, chickens squawked and geese honked. The outlaws' horses pawed and whinnied nervously. I gripped my talisman, kneading the old bone between my thumb and forefinger as if it were stubborn dough.

The Captain of Lucie's band of sergeants was shouting orders to his men, and to the panic-filled crowd, but nobody took the slightest notice of him. Sergeant Drogan sauntered about on his bowed legs, waving his baton of office self-importantly.

'Have you seen my Morgane?' I said.

Drogan shook his head, sniffing at me as if I were a dog turd. I scuttled away from him.

Dog shit in your teeth, Drogan!

Several of the gang members scrambled from the church towards the stocks, where they'd hitched their horses. Scrips thick with looted church treasure, they remounted.

Once the brigands were gone from his church, Père Bernard loped inside. A clot of people clutching the hands of small children followed the priest's lanky figure into the sanctity of God's home. Then the arched door of Saint Antoine's slammed shut.

'Let us in!' those left outside shouted, their fists hammering on the great studded door. I shook my head in disgust, picturing our gormless swine of a priest safely inside, ignoring their pleas.

The church bell began to ring, though I couldn't imagine from where Père Bernard expected help to come. There was no time to think about help though, I had to reach the tailor's shop and find Morgane. But it was impossible to fight my way through the ragged cordon the thugs had formed about the knot of terror-stricken folk huddling around the fountain—those who hadn't been quick enough to escape into the church or down one of the lanes winding between the shopkeeper-artisans' homes.

Townsmen were pitting stones, sticks and dinner knives—anything they had at hand—against the outlaws. Even the poorest man had to arm himself with sword, knife or bow and arrows to keep the peace, but our pitiful weapons were no match for the gang's mighty swords, crossbows and nail-studded clubs. Nor their horses snorting, quivering and tossing their heads.

'Have you seen my Morgane?' I said to Jacotte, her pudgy body pressed against mine in the crowd. The blacksmith's wife shook her head and dismissed me with her usual disdain.

'Your girl was with Yolande's twins,' the baker's wife, Sibylle said. 'They ran into the tailor's shop.'

Through the dust and people, I saw the circle of horses was blocking the tailor's shop. And there was no other way in; no way to get to my child. My mouth felt baked and I ran my tongue over sweat-bristled lips.

Holy Mother, what can I do?

A boy stepped clear of the mass, and my heart leapt into my throat. It was Anselme, my friend Yolande's boy. 'Turn your horses around and leave us alone now,' the tailor's son said with more gusto than he must have felt.

Without hesitating, one of the brigands swung his club at Anselme, striking him square on the forehead. The boy's legs folded beneath him like broken twigs and as he crumpled to the ground, the people screamed louder, their mouths agape.

Yolande's family was one of the few in Lucie I could call real friends, and I ached to run to Anselme, lying still on the bloodied cobbles.

'My son, my boy!' the tailor wailed, and my chest swelled with sucked-in breath as he ran to his son.

One of the gang drew a bolt from his crossbow. As his savage black horse reared up, the point pierced its target—the core of the tailor's heart. Yolande's husband fell beside his son, casting the brigand a last look of reproachful astonishment.

Women screamed again, enfolded round-eyed children into their skirts and clutched babies to their breasts. I screamed too, but though it hummed in my throat, the husky noise didn't sound like mine. I swallowed hard and looked away from the wounded littering the cobblestones, the scarlet rivulets trickling from gashes. Grief, and help for the injured, would come as soon as I'd found Morgane.

The troop of horsemen had divided up, a handful still circling the crowd, the rest looting shops.

Please, not the tailor's. No, not that shop. Please, God … please anyone!

My eyes were smarting with tears, sweat and grit, my heartbeat racing, so I knew I was in the middle of it all, yet I felt like a ghost watching, powerless, from a distance. This must be what Hell is like.

I stole closer to the tailor's shop; closer to the jittery men and their horses. One of the outlaws—the black-bearded hulk I'd threatened with my pendant—turned towards me and through the fug of people his evil eyes bore straight through mine. My legs felt weak as old broth, but as the horses' hooves threw up the next pall of dust, I slipped from his sight through the nearest opening: the heavy tavern door.

Alewife Rixende was crouched beneath one of the tables with her four girls. Her husband, Jâco, was sprawled across its scarred top. Oblivious to the danger outside, his great gut heaved in and out with each drunken, snoring breath.

'What do you want in my tavern?' Rixende hissed.

'Nothing. I'm trying to find my daughter.'

'If anything's befallen your Satan-eyed maid you'll only get what you deserve,' Rixende said with a snaggle-toothed sneer. 'Thieving what was mine.'

'Will you ever get over that, Rixende?' I curled my fingers around my pendant and peered back around the tavern door.

To my relief, the attackers were finally turning their horses about. In a last flurry of dust, they rode off, scrips bulging with bounty.

I raced to Yolande's, stumbling on my skirts, almost falling face-down onto the cobbles. Inside the looted wreck of the tailor's shop, there was no sign of anyone.

'Morgane? Yolande?'

My chest tight, my legs feeling light and frail as wings, I hurtled back outside and up the narrow steps to the family's sleeping quarters.

Behind the pallet huddled Yolande, Pétronille and Peronelle. And, between the three dark heads, Morgane's red curls. I thought I would burst with relief and happiness.

'Maman!'

'Thank the Blessed Virgin.' I gathered my daughter into my arms and hugged her till she squealed.

'Thank Our Lady you're all safe,' I said, looking around at the frightened faces. 'The outlaws have gone ... it's safe to go outside. And we should go now, Yolande, because your Anselme is injured and needs care. And your husband ... tried to defend Anselme ... a crossbow bolt.' I couldn't get the words out, just kept jabbing at my own heart, at the place the bolt had shot through her husband, shaking my head in sorrow.

'No, no!' Yolande began wailing, stumbling down the steps, her twins following.

Gripping Morgane's hand, we hurried after them, as my usually decorous and quietly-spoken friend threw herself across her husband's bloodied body. Her scream was an iron spike stabbing through my heart. A housewife had removed her apron and was trying to drape it over the tailor but seeing it wasn't large enough, and that Yolande was in the way, she covered only the top half of him.

Yolande looked up at me, her face dust-smeared, black shreds of hair loosened from her cap. 'What will I do without him, Héloïse?' Her voice was rough with tears, and she raised both arms as if asking *Dieu* in Heaven, rather than me. 'What now?'

Yes, what now? How would the family survive without a man at their hearth? I knew the loneliness she would feel without her husband's protection and counsel; the solitude I'd known these two years of Raoul's absence. But at least my husband would, I prayed, come home.

***

The air was thick with the smell of animals, piss and straw. People smeared in dirt, dust and blood wandered about the market-place dazed, or bent over the wounded.

Now out of hiding, Père Bernard strolled about barking orders. 'Carry the wounded into the church ... the barber-surgeon will see them in turn ... all pray together ...'

'Thank the Holy Saints you're both safe.' At the sound of Isa's voice Morgane and I spun around. My aunt held her work-basket over one arm, mine over the other. 'Come on, Héloïse, snap to your senses, we've got work to do.'

Once inside Saint Antoine's, after cleansing my hands with rose-water, my first job was to apply a comfrey-leaf compress to Anselme's brow. Apart from his shallow breaths, the boy showed no signs of life.

'Hold this against his head,' I said to Yolande, 'it will help the swelling ... I'll be back as soon as I can.'

With Morgane's helping hand, Isa and I began washing cuts, staunching bleeding and packing wounds with yarrow.

'Two people can have the same injury, such as this break,' I explained to Morgane, supporting a boy's arm as I applied a datura root poultice to the crushed limb. 'But you'll treat them differently depending on whether their temperament is sanguine or melancholic, or if their pee looks different.'

'I know, Maman ... and if a person is to be well, you must make sure their four humours are balanced.'

'But remember,' I said, 'many things can send the humours awry—illness, old age, even pestilence miasmas—and your patient will sicken.'

The barber-surgeon was setting cracked limbs in his own fashion: tweaking and pulling the bone and causing excruciating pain to his patient. Or victim, as Isa and I thought of them.

'If only Lucie-sur-Vionne had a special place for treating the sick,' I said to Isa, cringing at the terrible shrieks as the barber yanked on a bent leg. 'Like a pilgrim or pauper's hospital.'

'Why would we want a deadly hospital?' Isa said. 'A filthy place no sane person, sick or healthy, dare enter.'

'I don't mean a hospital for nightly shelter,' I said, Morgane still holding the broken arm while I splinted it. 'But a place with proper beds for the sick, where they could be separated from the healthy, and treated until they're well. This filthy floor is hardly suitable.'

'Well these filthy flagstones are all we've got,' Isa said. 'So you'd best stop moaning for something we'll never have.'

'You're the one who says all healing begins with cleanliness, Isa,' Morgane said.

'Stop your cheek poppet, and hold this leg for me,' Isa said. 'Another arrow wound by the looks. That's right, good girl. See how you should cleanse it with wine, then apply lion's foot.'

'Wine? Lion's foot?'

I looked up into the scowling face of the barber-surgeon, dressed in his usual leather apron and blood-stained boots. I wrinkled my nose at the tang of blood that always lingered about him.

'In the absence of a physician,' the barber-surgeon said, 'I'm the only person in this town qualified to treat the injured, and I don't need your charlatan potions and spells making things worse. Wine, of all things?' He raised his eyebrows at his assistant, as if in horrified disbelief.

'Crossbow wounds should be treated with a poultice of dung,' he explained to the assistant, loud enough for our benefit, 'to reconnect the body to the earth ... any decent healer knows that. And he'll need bleeding to rebalance his humours.'

'Bloodletting will just worsen this kind of wound,' Isa cut in. 'As will dung. Dried and powdered lion's foot root stops all kinds of bleeding.'

The barber-surgeon rolled his eyes as if we were idiots. 'Wine will simply imbalance the humours. Dung—and dung only— should be used to clot this wound and help it heal.'

As the barber-surgeon moved away, shaking his head, I looked over at Yolande still kneeling beside Anselme. One twin on each side of their mother, Pétronille and Peronelle were weeping. As I hurried back to them, Yolande drew her son's hand to her lips, but the boy was still not answering his mother's calls.

I pushed back the wad of black hair that always hid most of Anselme's face, and lifted the compress from his brow. Rather than going down, the bump had swelled more.

'Can we have some hands here please?' I called out.

'Rather than lug Anselme up those steps to the sleeping quarters, we'll put him on the pallet in the shopfront,' I said as several townsmen helped Yolande and I carry her son to the tailor's home.

'All we can do is make him comfortable and hope he wakes soon,' I said to Yolande once we'd settled Anselme on the pallet beside the hearth. 'And have faith in Our Lord.'

'Maman and Isa and I will pray hard for your brother,' Morgane said to Pétronille and Peronelle. 'He'll wake up, you'll see.'

Isa, Morgane and I finally left the ragged square, my limbs heavy as lead as I hoisted my skirts to cross a drain overflowing with discarded offal, tinged rusty red with blood.

Climbing the slope back to our cot, I was aware only of the orange husk of sun above the westward hills; of nothing else besides the working of my body: muscles dragging tired limbs, joints flexing, blood pulsing through my veins. I folded my arms around myself as if to hold my body together just a little longer.

We neared the cot, where crows circled above the two bodies still floating in the Vionne. One of Jacqueline's outstretched arms had trapped her in the reedy grasses. The other reached out, almost touching Wanda, whose body rocked in the shallows beside her maman. Sodden pink petals surrounded the little girl like a cast-aside wreath.

'Today was an outrage,' I said, an icy finger twisting in my heart. 'Something must be done ... somehow we need to protect Lucie-sur-Vionne from such terrible attacks.'

V

'Was it you planted our physick garden, Isa?' Morgane said, sitting cross-legged beside Blanche and stroking the cat.

'Always full of questions.' I gave my daughter a smile, but inside I was still crying for Yolande. Thank the Blessed Virgin Anselme had woken, though the blow to his head seemed to have stolen his mind. Before March had blown itself out on a wet wind, and as the first few weeks of April sun dried the winter-flooded fields and summoned the scent of clover, I kept wondering whatever I would do—how I'd be—if something befell Raoul.

But there wasn't much time to dwell on misery, to yearn for my husband's warm green eyes, his broad smile and sinewy back. It seemed that almost overnight the new warmth had nursed the grain into life and budded shoots on bare branches, and we had much work tending our plants and animals.

'Well, was it you started our garden, Isa?' Morgane repeated.

With a grimace, Isa straightened from the rose bush she was tending—her most valued medicinal flower that tumbled down one whole wall of the cot. 'We don't know which wise-woman laid it,' she said, rubbing the ache from her hips with a soil-streaked hand, 'but this physick garden was old many moons afore Ava and I came to be. Even before our own mother was birthed.'

'Did my grandmother—Ava—look the same as you?' Morgane asked. 'Like Pétronille and Peronelle?'

'Didn't I say that's enough of your questions, Morgane?' I chided. I allowed myself a secret smile though, for her eagerness to suck up knowledge as a piglet sucks milk. I knew it pleased Isa, as if Morgane was making up for all those years I'd made my aunt suffer. 'Now leave that cat alone for a bit, poppet, and help me harvest these radishes.'

'Oh no, we were different sorts of twins,' Isa said, as Morgane left Blanche stretching her claws in the sun. 'Unlike your friends, Ava and I didn't come from the too-abundant seed of one man, but from the seed of two different men. Our maman never knew which outlaws' seed took root from the band that surprised her in the woods, but one gave me his darkness, and another Ava her paleness. White as the moon she was, with eyes like ...'

Isa frowned, as if trying to recall what her dead twin looked like, panic crimping the lines on her face when she couldn't bring Ava to her mind's eye.

'Ava's eyes were like a summer sky what's cooking up a storm,' Isa finally said, with a definite nod.

'Blue and grey at the same time,' Morgane said. 'Like Maman's eyes?'

Isa nodded. 'Just like your mother's. And unlike your maman,' she threw me a wry smile, 'I'm glad you want to know about the women in your life, Morgane. The more a girl knows about those who came before her, the stronger she'll be. That's how we keep our mothers' memories alive.' She made the cross sign and squinted heavenward. 'May the Virgin bless Ava's soul ... our own Maman's soul.

'The notches on the wall tell me I've lived around five and forty years,' she said as she began planting our staples—cabbages, onions, leeks and garlic. 'I'll be lucky to survive many more summers but I hope you'll keep this garden going after I'm gone, Morgane ... after your own maman is gone. Because you're only the latest in a long line of women responsible for its care.' She waved a gnarled hand towards my pendant. 'Just as you'll take care of our talisman; safeguard it to bequeath to the next daughter.'

'Where does the angel come from?' Morgane asked, reaching across to the sculpture resting against my breast, and tracing a finger around its edges. 'Why won't either of you ever tell me?'

'I asked that same question when I was your age,' I said. 'And as Isa told me, that story will wait until you're old enough to understand. But from where the talisman comes isn't important, it's how wisely you use it to help birthing mothers.'

'The angel's eyes are just like mine,' Morgane said, touching a fingertip to the pendant's glimmering orbs. 'So it should belong to me.'

'It will be yours one day, I keep telling you,' I said, recalling her birth, and her bewildering eyes: one green as Raoul's, the other blue as the Virgin's robe. Isa and I had known then, that Morgane was one of Saint Margaret's chosen daughters who could claim the talisman's powers for healing and birthing.

'But why can't you give me the pendant now?' Morgane insisted.

'You're too young,' I said. 'Now come on, help me plant this flax ... besides, I had to wait until my eleventh summer before Isa let me have it, so stop your moaning.'

'And I only gave it to your maman then to jolt the stubborn girl to her senses; so it would show her the path her kinswomen had carved for her,' Isa said, launching once again into her well-ripened tale about my rebellious childhood.

'I can still see her braids streaming like two lashing whips,' Isa went on. 'So quarrelsome, she'd argue with the birds and the trees.'

'You can't argue with birds or trees,' Morgane said. 'Besides, Maman did get a husband, and she's become the best wise-woman and midwife. So you must be telling me tales, Isa.'

'So she must be,' I said with a good-humoured smile at my aunt. 'But that's enough tale-telling about me for one day. Fetch my basket, poppet; it's time to visit our patients.'

Isa's bad hips stopped her walking any distance these days, so I'd leave her at the cot brewing and bottling physicks, renewing our decoctions, ointments and plaisters, while I took Morgane with me to gather herbs and plants, and to the homes of birthing women and ailing townsfolk.

'And on the way you'll tell me the story about where the talisman comes from?' Morgane said with a grin.

'Get off with you, cheeky mouse.' I shook my head as I opened the gate in the wooden fence enclosing our cot, and we left behind our comforting smells: the wild scent of rosemary and thyme scattered across our rushes to enhance their woody fragrance, the sweet and bitter odours of our brewing remedies. 'I'll tell you when you're ready to hear it.'

***

'My milk's dried up,' Alix said by way of greeting as we stepped inside her cot, that same sleepy scent of honey and thyme candlewax perfuming the air. From his cradle, the unsleepy shrieks of Loup, her baby son, also greeted us. 'Your brew didn't work, Midwife Héloïse.'

Despite the terrible memories of the black-bearded outlaw that still plagued my dreams—my nights even darker without Raoul's comfort—Morgane and I had returned to Alix's cot several times since Loup's birth, to examine mother and newborn. As I'd told them, only a few weeks after his birth, and the outlaws' attack, Loup's head looked as normal as any other babe's.

I'd always known that a clutch of townsfolk were fearful of the spells they believed a midwife or wise-woman could cast on their children or their chickens, so I wasn't sure that Alix's manner had taken on an unfriendly edge, or whether I was imagining it. But her frown, and her accusing tone, left me in little doubt.

'What's in your brew anyway?' Alix said, as Morgane lifted the bellowing child from his cradle.

'Anise, dill and bitter milkwort,' I said, cleansing my hands in rose-water, then checking Alix's belly was shrinking back to normal size. 'Keep drinking it and soon your milk will flow like the blessed Jordan.'

'Is that all you put in your brew?' The voice startled me, and I spun around to Nica, slumped on a stool in a shadowy corner. 'Only plants?' She fixed her sharp eyes on me as a windfucker's on its prey.

I was certain then. Nica had turned her sister's mind against me—as venomous as her own had become the day she'd birthed a deadborn and blamed it on Isa. And, as my aunt had told me, once bad is done, it becomes an incurable sickness, each new child down the line suffering.

'Only plants, Nica,' I said. 'Why, what else would you think I put in my milk brew?'

'Oh I wouldn't know anything about a midwife's potions,' Nica said. 'I'm just a humble wife, mother and beekeeper.'

'Shouldn't you be tending your children and your bees then, rather than skulking in dim corners?'

'How soft and sweet he is,' Morgane said, patting Loup's back, the child's cries weakening as she unswaddled him and began the slow and sensuous massage I'd taught her. 'I would love a baby brother just like Loup.'

As I watched my daughter's nimble fingers, that cleft in my heart deepened—the grief for my two deadborn boys. God's tiny angels now. Few of Lucie's townsfolk knew for certain their birth date, but since Isa notched the wall for each of our passing years, I knew I'd reached my five and twentieth summer. Scarcely any childbearing years left, and with a husband journeying for so long, I feared we'd never know the joy of a living, blood son; an heir for Raoul's stonemason trade, and his mark—the entwined H and R that bound us forever.

'Put Loup back in his cradle, Morgane,' Alix said. 'He needs to sleep.'

'Oh. Y-yes.' Morgane's freckled cheeks flushed pink and I

knew Alix's heartless tone had cut her, but she reswaddled Loup and laid the baby back in his cradle, beneath the garlic and rowan hung to ward off witches.

As Morgane took Alix's wrist and timed her pulse with the sandglass, Alix and Nica remained silent, though I caught their gazes straying to my pendant then darting away as if they were afraid a simple glance might cause it to curse them.

'The patient has a good steady pulse,' Morgane said, dropping Alix's hand.

Anxious to be away from the cot's frosty mood, I quickly checked Alix's privities for bad smells while Morgane packed everything back into my basket.

'We'll come again next week,' I said.

'No need, Midwife,' Alix said. 'I'm well. We'll just pray Loup doesn't starve to death.'

'As I told you,' I said, casting Nica a warning stare, and trying to steady my voice, 'keep drinking the brew and your milk will flow again before the day's out.'

Taking Morgane's hand, I marched out of the cot, my nose in the air. I remained silent, bristling inside as we stalked off beside the row of beehives.

Stupid, ignorant women!

Morgane opened her mouth several times to say something, but shut it again, obviously thinking better of it.

Of course I knew what many thought of my talisman; couldn't help but overhear their whispers—those same murmurs Ava and Isa had borne—that the angel possessed not just special birthing powers, but also the potency to welcome demons thirsting after newborn blood. Menacing the black-bearded outlaw with it had only deepened those suspicions. But why couldn't they see I was only trying to save baby Loup's life?

We walked past children picking out stones from the newly-ploughed land, men carting manure as women scattered peas, wheat, barley, oats and rye from folded-up apron fronts. I thought about the oath I'd sworn on Ava's soul, and how when I came up against this kind of suspicion I wondered if it had been worth committing myself, since my efforts often seemed only to work against me.

We passed the mill, the wheel turning in the millstream flashing bright flecks of water. Johan Miller and his remaining eleven children were building a new millhouse beside the charred remains of the one the brigands had torched. The older ones weaved willow sticks through the timber framework to make the walls, while the younger ones frolicked about in a mixture of mud, straw, animal hair and dung, supposedly mixing it into daub to cover the walls. But they simply squished the muck through their toes and flung handfuls of it at each other. Despite losing their maman and Wanda only a few weeks gone, the little ones screeched with laughter as the mess splattered onto the faces of their siblings.

In my mind's eye, I saw again the gruesome corpses of Jacqueline and Wanda, and slivers of ice rolled down my back. Our town and its people, and my cot, were still defenceless against attacks of all kind. I was still deep in thought—about the black-bearded thug, and Alix and Nica's coolness—that I barely registered the church bell echoing across the countryside.

'Maman?' I looked down to Morgane tugging on my hand. 'Come on, the priest is calling everyone.'

'Well,' I said, 'it must be something really important to summon us to church right in the middle of a working day.'

VI

To reach Saint Antoine's church, Morgane and I crossed la place de l'Eglise. The market square hummed with the squeals of children, the cackle of geese and bark of dogs, and the twitter of women with baskets dangling from their arms.

The sun glinted off the colourful picture-signs hanging above each shop: the bandaged arm announcing the barber-surgeon, the apothecary's mortar and pestle, the pig with a tankard of ale on its back boasting the Au Cochon Tué tavern's brews. The butcher's cleaver thunked in time to the jangle of the black-smith's hammer in his forge and his shouts to his apprentice to bring water.

From the stocks opposite Saint Antoine's, the woodcutter-sexton, Poncet Batier, stared from eyes yellow and sharp as a hawk's. His hair stuck out like feathers, and the rotting vegeta-bles people were hurling at him smeared across his grizzly face.

'You again, Poncet Batier?' I said, as a slimy wad of stinky radish leaves splattered on his brow. 'You were here only last week.'

'Can't help himself,' Isa said with a grin, as a band of ruddy-faced boys laughed at him, pulled faces and threw fistfuls of dog shit. 'Poppa heard he's been charging high prices for cheap coffins ... some folks are just born dishonest.'

People pushing against us, we passed beneath the vaulted church doorway, my gaze as always rising to the carving above the arch—of Devils leading roped sinners towards a flaming cauldron while angels led the fewer elect in the opposite direction. A reminder that in Hell we are nameless and forgotten; that Judgement Day loomed large and forbidding.

As well as ensuring the people of Lucie-sur-Vionne had an oven, a wine press, and a mill to grind their grain, for which our *Seigneur* charged *banalités,* Comte Renault de Fouville had to provide a humble church with a reasonably literate priest. And Lucie's church certainly had been humble, so Isa told me, when she and Ava were girls. But Isa also said that twenty and more years gone, le Comte had funded lavish renovations into Saint Antoine's in the hope, it was rumoured, of luring his favoured priest to Lucie.

Isa claimed all priests were sodomites, and the thought of Comte Renault and Père Bernard together—the thought of what they did!—sickened me. But I really didn't give a hog's arse who our *Seigneur* invited into his noble bed. I was just grateful for the church building that had brought Raoul to me.

'How's tricks, old witch?' Poppa said with a friendly thump on Isa's back.

Isa clutched her belly and mimed a gag. 'Been sick in my guts for weeks ... ever since I ate a pie some crazy crone sent home with my niece.'

It always made me smile, seeing them together, two old friends with the same quick wit, cursing humour and tough, no-nonsense ways. All the more comical since Poppa was built like a bear and Isa like a skeleton.

'I'll kill you off yet,' Poppa said, her eyes merry blue dots sunk in a face like a wide-open flower.

We turned our attention to Père Bernard, raising his arms to calm the jostling and chatter.

'Several weeks have passed since our churchyard embraced the victims of the vicious gang attack,' the priest began. He wore his usual black robes and the pinched look of a person who is always cold. 'And it gladdens me, and Our Holy Father, that we are helping each other grieve for our loved ones; banding together to banish this heinous attack from our minds. Certainly, I am bereaved for the treasures that once stood on the altar for Mass; those finely wrought pieces the outlaws will surely melt down to sell the gold.' He raised a hand, knotted with creepy green veins, to silence the mutterers. 'But there is no loss greater than the lives the brigands took. It is not for my treasures, the apothecary's expensive medicines or the blacksmith's tools that we should grieve, but for those lost souls.'

Everyone looked to the victims' families: Johan Miller who'd lost Jacqueline and little Wanda, and to Yolande and her little twins, standing on the other side of Morgane. I reached across my daughter and squeezed my friend's arm. She lifted her tear-filled gaze to me and shook her head as if in helpless acceptance of God's decision to take her husband and maim her son.

'I'll wager a flagon of my best brew,' Alewife Rixende said, making the sign of the cross, 'that someone in this town—or *something*—cursed this outlaw attack on us.'

Rixende didn't have to mention my name; it was enough that her pretty gaze turned vicious as she fixed it on me. And my angel talisman. The ground straw rustled with people and their whispers, all of them looking at me.

I opened my mouth to snap back, but felt Isa's hand, hot and shaky, on my elbow. 'Don't let that trout-brain rile you, Héloïse.'

'That's a lie,' one of the field-hands shouted. 'Midwife Héloïse did good by my wife just a week gone ... babe and mother alive and well.'

'Quiet please,' Père Bernard said. But as ever, everyone ignored him. It was always the same in church: the priest droning on like a trapped bumblebee while boys wandered in and out, flirting with giggling girls. Others chattered about the harvest or how so-and-so was getting too fat for her kirtle, or how the alewife was making eyes at every man besides her husband.

'Even if that milk-thieving midwife's Devil's charm didn't curse the attack on us,' Sergeant Drogan said, 'it *did* burn my fingers ... not to mention bowing my legs.'

'Oh here we go again,' I said in a bored tone, returning the people's stares with as much pride as I could muster. 'The same old and tired accusation.'

As always when Drogan hurled at me that impossible burning allegation I wanted to demand he show everyone his burn scar, but of course that would also reveal me as a liar.

Alongside Drogan were his two young daughters, motherless since Drogan's wife's was murdered last harvest season. But he'd taken a new wife, the young Catèlena, frail as a lark's wing, one cheek swollen with a fresh purple bruise.

'I see Drogan's been at poor Catèlena again,' I whispered to Isa. 'That's one rumour I'm certain is true: Drogan did bludgeon his first wife to death.'

'Shut your big mouth, Héloïse,' she hissed.

Since le Comte had appointed Drogan a sergeant, he had the power to arrest me on a whim, so I did shut up, and breathed hard to stem my frothing anger.

'Only what you'd expect,' Alewife Rixende said, 'of a bastard what had no name to get wed.'

'No father to beat her into obedience,' said Jacotte.

'May the Holy Virgin save us from your goat-brain, Rixende,' I said. 'And if you stopped making such a pig's foot of your own marriage, and hankering after mine, your husband mightn't drink himself silly every day and be unfit to attend Mass.'

I shrugged off Isa's warning hand as a few people smothered giggles, others muttering to their neighbours.

'That's enough now,' Père Bernard said weakly, as if resigned he'd never recall the crowd's attention.

'Speaking of curses and Devil's charms,' Jacotte said, thrusting a chubby finger at me. 'Rumour has it the midwife cursed one of those outlaws with her talisman.'

'That ain't true,' Poppa snapped. 'Héloïse only made out her pendant could curse that brigand to stop him murdering my grandson ... and thank the Blessed Virgin she did! Just ask my daughter-in-law, Alix. She ain't here today ... not yet been churched, but she'll tell you so.'

I wasn't aware my breath had caught in my throat until I tried to let it out, and couldn't. Asking a divine power to set harm or evil upon someone, even to save a newborn, is heresy. Punishable by burning.

'Héloïse is a skilled midwife,' Yolande said. 'Birthed my girls without a hitch and heavy with her Morgane at the time.' She gestured at Pétronille and Peronelle, but her twins, like most of the children, had become bored with the usual church quarrels, and were whispering and giggling with Morgane. 'Birthing twins is difficult and danger—'

'And goes against Mother Earth,' Rixende cut in.

'*And* she woke my sleeping Anselme with a potion,' Yolande went on, throwing Rixende a dignified glare. Beside his mother, Anselme remained wordless. As usual, the usual chunk of dark hair hid most of his face. 'When that savage outlaw struck him down, I thought I'd lost my son as well as my husband. But Héloïse woke—'

'Your boy awoke as idiotic as a court jester,' Rixende said. 'Wouldn't even yell if his arse were on fire.'

'After such a wound to the skull,' I said, 'Anselme just needs more time to come back to us.'

'Enough now!' The priest stamped his foot. 'I will not tolerate women's petty squabbling within the sanctity of my church. Whatever—whoever—brought the terrible attack on us, it is too late for recrimination. Besides, the reason I have gathered you all is because our *Seigneur*, his lordship le Comte de Fouville, has good news.' The priest paused, waiting until not a child whimpered; not a twist of straw rustled. 'So if you would all gather on the market-place for our *Seigneur's* announcement.'

As always before leaving Saint Antoine's, I knelt in front of the church's most beautiful statue—Raoul's sculpture of Our Lady. She was holding out a dove to the Christ child, a chubby boy clutching a bouquet of daisies. Ordinary daisies like the ones Morgane and I plucked and dried over the hearth to ward off fleas.

Of course Raoul had never seen my mother, but his hands had carved an effigy of how my mind's eye saw Ava—her strong and quiet gentleness. So I'd always thought his hands magical, bringing my mother back to me to banish my troubles, if only for that precious instant I escaped into Ava's warm and peaceful place. Beyond the clouds, the sky and sun. Far away from man and beast.

Ava's voice came from the Virgin's lips.

Be strong, my warrior.

Isa had told me Ava wanted to name me Héloïse because it meant "famous warrior". As if she sensed I'd need a warrior's strength in my battle through life as the bastard child of a bastard midwife.

With a glance at my husband's stonemason mark, the enlaced H and R, carved into the hem of Our Lady's lapis-coloured robe, I sensed him as always beneath that vast, vaulted church ceiling. I glimpsed his stocky frame, the brawny muscles tightening in his arms, his brow knotting in concentration as he chiselled his statue into shape. I thought of how his love protected me against the townsfolks' jibes and taunts and I prayed for Raoul's good health in Florence.

Bring him home safely, Blessed Virgin.

VII

'We must leave Florence immediately, Crispen,' Raoul Stonemason said to his apprentice. 'Once Toubie's ague passes and your brother's well enough to travel … we should get away from here before this pestilence strikes us down too.'

Raoul paced the room he'd rented with the apprentice brothers in the heart of the great city for almost two years now. He flicked a hand through his thatch of red curls, and glanced once more at Toubie, lying on the pallet.

'So thirsty,' Toubie said, sweat bristling his brow and upper lip. 'Throat feels like it's full of nettles.'

'Drink,' Crispen said, holding a cup of ale to his brother's dry lips. Toubie drank it all in several gulps, followed by a second cupful.

'You'll feel better in the morning,' he said, as Toubie slumped back down on the pallet.

But Raoul had the sickening feeling that Toubie would never feel better.

As most people in Florence by now, he knew a lot about the pestilence. Like a cloud of flies, it swarmed around those who caught it. If you looked into the eyes of a sick person, or displeased God, or were stuck in the eye of a malign wind, you caught it too. And you died.

He knew too, that it began as Toubie's illness; as any old ague—fever, chills, sweats and pink spots. Then the rosy rings appeared on your neck, groin and armpits, turned to black stones and could swell to the size of a goose egg. You writhed with the agony, went mad with the thirst, your stench worse than a grave dug up by foxes. And if you didn't get the painful black boils, but caught the type where you spat blood, you could be dead in an hour.

Only two days gone, the family renting the room across the street had all perished. Raoul had watched the anguished relatives tend their loved ones for the week before, then as dawn stretched across the sky, they'd heaped the four black-scarred bodies outside the front door. He'd shuddered as the red-robed and hooded *Compagnia della Misericordia* removed them, along with the other fresh corpses littering the streets.

And if Toubie's illness is not just a passing ague ....

Raoul couldn't bear to think about that, and crossed himself, praying to Saint Etienne.

The day had been stinking hot again and it was almost dark now, but another swathe of heat flooded Raoul. He flung the door wide, letting the cooler night air wash over him.

Toubie must have felt the heat too, as he sat up on the pallet, ripped off his shirt and flung it aside. Raoul stared at his apprentice; felt as if his blood had turned to mortar as he saw the clusters of pink rings on Toubie's arms and neck. Blood roses.

His heart beating so fast he thought it might explode from his chest, Raoul staggered away from Toubie.

'Oh no!' Crispen too reeled back from his brother. 'The rings weren't there before. I thought it was just an ague ... hoped ....'

Raoul also knew that whatever the type of pestilence a person caught, most of those dwelling in the same house got it too, and died, along with the animals. His instinct told him he and Crispen should run as fast as they could before the miasma took hold of them too.

'We both know the best thing is to get away from him,' Crispen said, as if he'd heard Raoul's thoughts. 'But ...'

'But you can't leave your brother,' Raoul said. 'I know, I'd feel the same.'

'I understand if you want to get away from here,' Crispen

said. 'You go home. I'll stay and take care of my brother and if we—or I—don't come back to Lucie-sur-Vionne, you'll know neither of us survived it.'

Raoul waved away Crispen's tear-stained gaze. 'I'd never abandon you or Toubie. You know both of you are my family ... as much as Héloïse, Morgane and Isa.'

He thought about that family he'd dreamed of when he met Héloïse, arriving in Lucie-sur-Vionne as a lonely, kinless stone-mason to help repair the church. Warmth, love—but mostly fear of losing it all—consumed Raoul as he recalled how he'd carved out his clan; sculpted it as meticulously as Saint Antoine's statue of Our Blessed Virgin.

'I'm going to see the wise-woman,' Raoul said, snagging his coat from the nail behind the door, 'get some of her poppy juice.'

He headed off down the street, knowing the pain-easing potion would cost him a small fortune, but with so many suffering the demand was great and the wise-woman could charge whatever she liked.

***

'I'll repay you, Raoul,' Crispen said as Toubie drank the poppy-laced ale, his face twisting with effort, pausing as a spasm of shivers racked his body. 'Anything to ease his pain.'

As Raoul shook his head, waving away Crispen's words, he thought back to the previous month, when he'd first wanted to flee this pestilence-ridden city. But he hadn't been able to let down those who were paying him and his apprentices to design the wall of the great Santa Maria del Fiore Cathedral and to sculpt its exquisite gargoyles.

I'm a dependable, trustworthy master mason ... if word got around that I'd skipped off leaving work half-done, it'd look bad for future jobs.

But then everything quickly changed. People had started

dying all around them and there were barely any workers left. Building had begun on the Santa Maria del Fiore only fifty years gone—and slowed for thirty of those until the discovery of Saint Zenobius's relics spurred on new work—and Raoul had dreamed of helping with its design and construction a little longer, but now there was nobody left to pay the workers. The pestilence had almost halted work altogether.

And now it was too late for them too. Toubie—perhaps all three of them—might soon be dead.

Night fell, and Crispen moved the tallow candle the length of Toubie's body, placing more soaked cloths over his brother's burning skin. The small circle of light revealed black spots that stained Toubie's belly and made of his face an unrecognisable mask.

Crispen whispered comforting words to his brother, wiped his fevered brow, gave him more poppy-juice. He did what he could, which wasn't much.

'The boils've grown bigger,' Crispen said, several hours later, the tallow stink overpowering in that hot, stifling room. 'It's as if they want to burst.' He looked up at Raoul. 'Maybe we could cure him if we lanced them and drained out the poison?'

Raoul shook his head wearily. From the number of pestilence deaths they'd witnessed in Florence these past weeks, Crispen must surely be aware of his brother's fate. He likely was, but Raoul sensed that his apprentice was clinging desperately—illogically—to the reasoning that while there was breath, there was hope. A few had survived it, certainly, but recovery was so rare it wasn't worth the yearning.

Many said the pestilence was God's wrath, punishing the people for their sins. Others claimed the great earthquake of January had caused it, when it carved a path of wreckage from Naples up to Venezia, collapsing houses, toppling church towers and crushing villages. The quake had spewed up foul fumes from deep inside the earth, causing a great struggle of oceans and planets. The waters then rose, and vaporised, and the air corrupted into this deadly miasma.

'Christ on the cross!' Crispen cried, falling backwards as Toubie's black sores began to split like pea pods, spewing out thick creamy pus.

The boils might have burst but Toubie did not get better. More sores grew, to the size of a walnut. His skin resembled parchment and he passed into a state of troubled unconsciousness, sweating and gasping, but lying limp and still in a kind of silent struggle, lids drawn over unflickering eyes. A silence that seemed worse to Raoul's ears than the earlier howls.

A sour wind blew up and the candles danced, almost guttering, as Crispen kept swabbing the stinking mess from Toubie's wounds, Raoul stifling his gags and clamping his sleeve tighter over his nose.

'If only Héloïse were here,' he said. 'She'd know what to do to help Toubie ... she'd have something in her armory of medicaments.' At least those sweetening herbs she burned, he thought, to mask Toubie's dreadful stench. A stink that could've come from an opened tomb.

At the blackest hour of the night, when the moon was at her peak—her most dangerous Héloïse had always told him—Toubie began crying out. 'Maman, Maman!'

Raoul felt even more pity for the boy as their maman, along with their papa, had long passed from an excess of black bile. Crispen and Toubie had been left without parents, but Raoul had seen the potential in the brothers' strong bodies and keen minds, and taken them on as his stonemason apprentices. He'd given them a chance in life, just as a stonemason friend of his father's had done when Raoul had lost first his maman in childbed and then his papa.

Raoul could still hear the mason's encouraging voice: 'You're well-suited to the job, lad ... your hands sculpting angels and animals from stone flaunt not only muscle, but art too.'

'Behind that hard mason's shell, you're just a big soft egg,' Héloïse had said with her cheeky smile that made his heart skip beats. They'd both known, too, without even saying, it was

Raoul's desperate attempt to try and replace their two deadborn sons. But he'd never regretted his decision, for Crispen and Toubie had proved hard-working, quick-learning boys.

'Calm yourself, Toubie,' Crispen said, which seemed pointless to Raoul. But what else could he say, or do, as the boy weakened and slipped further from them?

'We should call a priest.' Crispen's voice thickened with panic as Toubie began struggling to breathe.

Raoul laid a hand on Crispen's arm. 'You know there're no priests left in Florence, my boy ... none that dare touch pestilence victims at least.'

'I know ... I know,' Crispen sobbed, 'I just can't bear to think of him dying with no priest for confession, no absolution.'

'We'll pray to Saint Etienne for him,' Raoul said.

Toubie sweated. He gasped for breath, though his eyes still remained shut and he showed no awareness. In the last light of the sputtering candle, Raoul watched in horror as Toubie's head arched back, his limbs stiffening as a spasm gripped his whole body. Saliva curled from his clenched jaw, and he didn't have to hold a feather to Toubie's lips—as he'd seen Héloïse do—to know the short life of his apprentice, his son, was over.

Toubie's fingers, strong and sturdy as iron, still gripped the bedsheet, and Raoul watched with a heavy heart as Crispen gently untangled and straightened each one. He folded them across his brother's breast and laid his own on top of them as if offering a final prayer.

'I'm so sorry, Crispen.'

'There was nothing you could've done.' Crispen crumpled to the rushes stained with his brother's piss, shit and vomit, and rested his head on his bent-up knees. 'Nothing anybody could've done! He was the best brother in the world, why did God have to take him?'

He started up a bitter weeping that wrenched at Raoul's soul.

Raoul sat with Crispen, one hand gently squeezing his shoulder until the sobs died down. Then they made the sign of the cross and wrapped Toubie's body in a sheet and left it outside the door for the *Compagnia della Misericordia* to remove at dawn.

'We should go now,' Raoul said, shoving their tools and few possessions into leather satchels, looping their water flasks over his shoulder. 'Run for our lives. Let's get home to safety in Lucie-sur-Vionne.'

VIII

Once everyone had shoved their way out of Saint Antoine's, Morgane and the twins skipped off to play at the tailor's shop while Isa, Poppa and I turned our attention to our *Seigneur*.

Le Comte de Fouville tilted his head like a falcon on the hunt. He gazed down his hooked nose at us, his nostrils flaring with those of the great war horse upon which he sat. He held the reins in one hand, and in the other, the cane he'd walked with since an arrow from an English longbow pierced his hip at Crécy.

Isa nodded at the man beside le Comte, sitting astride a shiny black stallion, and elbowed Poppa. 'Corpus bones, what's Physician Nestor doing back in Lucie?' Wearing the crimson and blue robes and black cylindrical cap of a physician, he carried himself with the same arrogant air as le Comte. 'You told me he was in Lyon lining his pockets on the ailments of rich merchants and nobles?'

'He was, till he turned up yestermorn at the castle,' Poppa said. 'I ain't found out why ... yet.'

Poppa didn't keep bees or make candles; that was Alix and Nica's side of the family. She worked at *le château* as Chief Washerwoman each day, and brought down all the castle stories each evening at curfew.

'Who's Physician Nestor?' I asked, and from the mutterings across the market-place, it seemed others were wondering the same thing.

'The youngest Fouville brother,' Isa said. 'A monk-physician.'

'Following this heinous brigand attack,' Renault de Fouville began, his booming voice silencing the townsfolk, 'and the threat of the English ever close, all towns are being walled. And I am pleased to announce that King Philip has approved our petition to build such a wall of protection about the heart of Lucie-sur-Vionne.'

'Hear, hear!' People shuffled about, punched fists into the air, and an excited chatter sprang up.

He raised both arms in a dramatic gesture to quieten the crowd. 'This wall shall be called the vingtain,' le Comte said, 'and in my duty to the inhabitants of Lucie, la Comtesse Geneviève and I shall be residing permanently here in the castle to oversee building of this fortification, along with repairs of the existing curtain walls.'

Renault de Fouville owned most of the land and many of Lucie's homes, as well as those in the nearby villages of Julien-sur-Vionne and Valeria-sur-Vionne. He spent much of his time travelling about between these estates, so we didn't often see him.

As le Comte turned in his saddle to face his brother, I saw how he'd aged in the two years since he'd fought for the King. The battle-scarred skin of his face, tanned to leather by sun and wind, now sagged from crimson jowls around a veiny, purple nose. Clods of belly fat hung over the horse's saddle, his arse spreading right across the beast's flanks.

'And I have appointed my brother, Nestor as my personal physician,' he went on. 'A fine medicine man who shall forthwith reside with us here in *le château de Lucie.*'

'Protector, Satan's arse,' Isa hissed. 'A man like Renault de Fouville will no more care for his people than his haughty monk-physician brother. The promises of that useless bit of flea-*merde* are hollow as a whore's.'

'I'll bet my ears Nestor's feeling smug as a cat what's pilfered the ham,' Poppa said with a cackle, 'now big brother also limps with a cane.'

'But Nestor will have forgotten that Renault got his limp

heroically, as a knight fighting for King Philip,' Isa said, 'while his own limp *stopped* him becoming a knight and fighting for the King.'

'Why smug?' I said.

'Nestor's always hated Renault and his other brothers,' Poppa said. 'Right from when they were boys, teasing Nestor about his inturned foot. Which is why the father shovelled him off to the monkhood as soon as Nestor turned seven.' She waved an arm in the direction of the monastery, on the furthest edge of Lucie's fields.

'Nestor got to be Chief Infirmarer,' Isa said, 'afore he was packed down south to Montpellier University for his physician training.'

'And didn't that stink of rumour?' Poppa gave a knowing nod. 'Renault sending young Nestor away from Lucie over some scandal or other.'

'Well all I know,' Isa cut in, 'is now le Comte's no longer fit to fight, he's got nothing better to do than skulk about in the castle supposedly protecting us and overseeing the building of some piddling wall.'

She nodded towards the castle that towered above Lucie-sur-Vionne, blocking out the westbound sun and casting an early shadow over the market-place, its shops and homes. And to its fortifications, crumbling like the frayed hem of a working girl's skirt, which would now be repaired.

'Too right,' Poppa said. 'Renault only wants the quiet life now with his personal physician on hand for his every medical whim.'

'So there'll be less work for us now Lucie has a physician?' I said. 'And for the barber-surgeon too?'

'We'll not starve from lack of work, Héloïse,' Isa said. 'Nobody can afford what Nestor charges. And most know we're more skilled—and get better results!—than that hog's turd of a barber-surgeon.'

'Not forgetting you only ask for payment as each can manage,' Poppa said. 'While everyone knows that neither the barber-surgeon nor the physician will budge without the chink of coins.'

'Why's this wall called the vingtain?' Pierro Blacksmith called, over the crowd's noise.

'Because,' le Comte de Fouville said, his thundery voice snapping us all back to attention, 'the wall shall be built and maintained via a tax—an exceptional tax—of one twentieth, *un vingtième*, of your revenues.'

'Will this *exceptional* tax become permanent?' asked Sara, Sergeant Drogan's mother, as a collective groan rose from the crowd shuffling about again on the cobblestones.

'As it usually does?' Jacotte added.

'More taxes?' Alewife Rixende said.

'We're already bled dry,' cut in her husband, Jâco. 'How're we supposed to afford more?'

'Do you want a strong wall to protect us from outlaw ambushes?' le Comte said, pushing his nose into the air. 'Not to mention those plundering English?'

'Yes, but—' Jâco started.

'You've no choice but to pay up then. Besides,' Renault de Fouville added with a haughty smile, 'complaints against ving-tain payments are considered treasonous. So, to avoid future assaults, upon alert from the lookouts all those dwelling outside the bourg will gather their valuables and their children and run to sanctuary within the vingtain.'

'How will this wall be built?' Pierro Blacksmith asked.

'Alesi Stonemason is the Master Mason.' Le Comte nodded at a thickset man. 'In charge of its construction.'

'The vingtain wall will simply be an extension of the present castle curtain wall which shall be repaired,' Alesi Stonemason explained, bowing in acknowledgement to his *Seigneur*. 'This will mean more work, but our lord is anxious to provide us with maximum protection.'

'Hear, hear,' the crowd shouted.

'Keep out the brigands,' the butcher said.

'And the English barbarians,' Drogan added.

I stole a glance at the sergeant. His new wife Catèlena was looking straight at me as if she was trying to ask or tell me something. But as soon as I met her gaze she looked away, with a fearful, rabbity glance up at Drogan.

'The vingtain will encircle both the castle and the buildings of Lucie's market-place,' the mason said. 'The rear of these shops and homes will serve as the back of the wall, with extra stones mortared to join them into one continuous fortification.' He motioned towards the Monts du Lyonnais. 'Stone will be taken from the same quarry used to rebuild our church ... lots of work for willing hands.'

'If only Raoul was here,' I said to Isa and Poppa. 'He would've got this Master Mason job. His work is better than Alesi Stonemason's.'

'For you, there's no greater stonemason than your Raoul,' Isa said, and I couldn't help smiling at the sound of his name, the thought of his soft touch that seemed impossible from hands so rough. And his voice—loud and raspy from years of inhaling dust and shouting over building noise.

'At least your man'll be assured of work,' Poppa said.

'How will the vingtain keep out thugs?' Jacotte asked.

'There will be only one, east-facing gatehouse,' the Master Mason said, 'with a great oak door, secured by heavy drawbars. In the event of attackers, it will be as if we are all safe within the castle—without actually being inside it. No evil will be able to reach us ever again.'

'Another advantage of the vingtain,' Renault de Fouville cut in, 'is that we shall charge a toll for merchants entering the town on market-day to pitch a stall ... any outlander in fact. Thanks to our market, Lucie-sur-Vionne is already a rich town, but the vingtain shall make us prosper yet more!' Le Comte's smile implied he felt solely responsible for this wealth.

As the crowd started twittering about this vingtain tax, Poppa waved us off and slipped away back to her washing at the castle.

Others too began returning to their work.

Drogan strode ahead of his two daughters, Catèlena trailing behind. She caught my eye again and threw me a brief smile. I smiled back, still sure she wanted to tell me something.

'Well, I wonder how much of this new market toll will benefit us?' Isa said, as Catèlena scampered after Drogan and his girls like a small and obedient dog. 'More sous to line le Comte's silk pockets, I'll wager. Though the Devil only knows why he's so determined to stuff the Fouville coffers even more, what with la Comtesse Geneviève barren every one of her thirty years, and ripe for the change. And since the other Fouville brothers, apart from Nestor, are all dead in King Edward's war, there's still no heir.'

'La Comtesse Geneviève should've dropped ten babes by now,' I said. 'I'm surprised le Comte hasn't shunted her off to a nunnery and taken on some young and more fruitful wife.'

'Poppa reckons he blames their lack of a child on la Comtesse,' Isa said as we headed towards the tailor's shop to fetch Morgane. 'Says her womb is slippery, or overheated, or burns his seed, or whatever other reason he can dream up. But if le Comte does prefer lying with the priest, mayhap he's not even attempting to mix his seed and hers. All these years and Poppa's not heard of a single mistress or whore. We've always thought poor old Comtesse Geneviève was just a front for his buggery.'

'And if they don't get an heir,' I said, 'what will happen to their wealth?'

'I know not, Héloïse. All I know is what good a person could do with all those riches.'

***

'If the goats are milked and that pig fed,' Isa called to Morgane, 'you can fill a bucket for the lepers.'

The unexpected church summons had made us all late with

our chores, and Morgane scurried from the pig's enclosure, scattering squawking chickens, the geese and Blanche, who was toying with an almost-dead rat. Into a leather bucket she began scooping the rich russet soil from the ant-hill, known for its curative powers of the lepers' crippling, unsightly illness.

The lepers were dead to the Church, to the world really, and Isa and I were the only townsfolk who approached their cot, taking them barley cakes, cheese and herbal potions. Despite what the townsfolk believed Isa had taught me long ago that their disease was not so easily caught.

Those lepers who weren't too disfigured were allowed down to the market-place for supplies as long as they wore their covering cloak and rang their bell. But they were so shunned—more even than Isa and me—that they never ventured far.

'Then fetch the reaping hook, poppet,' I said. 'We'll gather more rushes while Isa's with the lepers.'

We set off towards the lepers' cot, built on the same spike of land as ours—a fair stride from any neighbouring ones. A clutch of Lucie-sur-Vionne's townsfolk might be wary of living too close to us, but they all still hastened to our door for comfort and cures, or for us to midwife them.

Throughout my childhood with Isa, ours had been a draughty tumbledown cottage, the moss-laden thatch like a hat slung carelessly across a brow. But my husband's deft stonemason hands had transformed it into one of the finest dwellings in Lucie, and I suspected that when people came seeking cures, their envy of our comfortable home did nothing to soften their suspicious minds.

The lepers too, were tending their garden, and as we approached, several raised a hand in a wave, smiles puckering their scarred faces.

'*Bonjour!*' we called cheerily as Isa pushed open their gate. With a wave, Morgane and I continued on, slithering down the gold-green riverbank slope.

Far from the market-place filth, the Vionne waters surged

unsoiled here, smoothing boulders as soft as baby's skin. The dry whistle of the breeze through the rushes was like a welcome call, blackbirds preening on greening boughs, and across the field a mighty oxen team dragged a plough through damp soil.

'Remember, poppet,' I said, catching my breath as I waded into the cold shallows, 'normal grass won't do. We need these long rushes for the cot floor.' I hooked one by its underwater roots. 'See how much thicker and sturdier it is?'

Morgane soon got bored piling rushes onto the pebbly shore. 'It's so hot,' she said, her freckled cheeks already pink. 'Can we go to our magical pool?'

'The sun might be warm, my sweet, but as you can see, the water's still too cold for swimming. But why not, I'm glad enough of a rest.'

I wedged our rushes against the hollow of an oak trunk to retrieve on our way back, and we scrambled over rocks and pebbled shore until we reached the place where the Vionne cut into the hillside folds; where foaming torrents of snowmelt roared like a hundred clashing voices into a deep pool.

'The summer your papa and I were wed,' I said, helping Morgane remove her smock, 'I would bring him to this pool.'

'I know. You tell me that story every time we come here. Is Papa coming home soon?'

'This summer ... if all goes well with that cathedral in Florence.'

'But then he'll leave us again, to journey for more work?'

'You know masons have to follow the building work,' I said, as she splashed about in the silver-flecked shallows, 'often many leagues away. But your papa should stay a long while this time, building Lucie's vingtain and repairing the castle.'

The tops of my thighs and my nipples tingled, just imagining the pleasure of Raoul's hands on my body, and I stole a furtive smile.

'So no more bad people can attack us?'

'That's right, poppet.' I rinsed her smock and draped it over a bush to dry. 'With a strong and high wall surrounding the town, no more evil can reach us.'

Sitting beside our enchanted pool, and dreaming of Raoul's body pressed against mine, I thought of that first week we met, when the young Raoul Stonemason was sculpting Our Lady as part of Saint Antoine's rebuilding.

At the chime of the curfew bell—and against the enraged glare of Rixende—I'd taken the stonemason's hand and led him through the band of willows lining the riverbank road, until we reached this magical spot. From here, we'd climbed part way up the slope to the secret cave Isa's maman had shown her and Ava, hidden from view even if you knew where to look.

Rockslides partly filling it, the cave was small, nothing like the great tunnelled cavern it must've been when the Romans mined it for gold. Surrounded by centuries-old smoke-blackened walls, the rock crystals gleamed like stars as we lay upon the sweet-smelling fleece I'd plucked from my basket.

Amidst marbled rock pillars that rose around us like protective limbs, Raoul's hands slid through my hair, cupped my face, wandered across my shoulders, and then, oh, on my breasts and belly.

I leaned into his embrace. How could I not want what came next, terrifying and exciting at the same time? He unknotted the drawstring of his breeches. I moved my lips against his, hungry and demanding. He didn't hurry or push and I hooked my arms around his back and pressed into his chest. I melted into him, and didn't cry out when he took me.

Afterwards, when we lay still, Raoul touched a finger to my wet cheek.

'I hurt you, Héloïse.'

'There's no pain in these tears,' I said, the swift arrow of love impaling my heart, and settling, finally, my soul at peace. 'Just tears for the first real happiness in my life.'

The piping of a skylark jolted me from my dream.

'What're you smiling about?' Morgane said, as the brown bird took flight and soared away.

'I was thinking of your papa ... about him coming home to us.'

I dried my daughter off with wads of grass, rebraided her hair—Raoul's red-gold waves—and my breasts swelled at the thought of bathing with him again, cascading water caressing our sun-kissed shoulders. And feeling him lean into me as the sun dried our skin, and tell me I smelled of the river. Once Raoul was safely home, my family—my life—would be complete again.

As we trundled back to the pile of rushes, I was still amazed at all that had passed between us in those first few silent breaths in Saint Antoine's. I didn't tell Morgane that if she ever confessed such a ridiculous thing as instant love, I would laugh out loud, or scold her for being so witless.

IX

'Thank the Blessed Saint Etienne that terrible pestilence isn't here in Lyon,' Raoul said, the relief lightening his heavy heart as the stonemason and his apprentice stepped from the barge onto the quay in the great city.

Raoul and Crispen had taken a boat from Genoa to Marseille, then a barge up the Rhône through Avignon. The eastern sky wore a flush of gold, the rim of sun rising over the *Montagne Maudite* as they mingled with the bustle of trade.

Though still mourning Toubie's death, Raoul did feel a glimmer of happiness as they walked amongst the healthy travellers and merchants; the businessmen clothed in velvet and satin swishing into the goldsmith's, strutting from the spicemonger's or a silk merchant's emporia. The heat, the flies, the piled-up corpses they'd fled in Florence seemed so distant, almost as if that horror had existed only in some nightmarish nook of Raoul's imagination. Except that Toubie was missing, his absence constantly jolting Raoul back to the reality of his apprentice's grisly death.

'Yes, a great comfort to see normal, breathing life,' Crispen said, 'and all this buying and selling, instead of streets littered with the dead.'

Raoul caught the sound of Crispen's choked sob and laid a hand on his apprentice's forearm. 'Come with me, I'm going to show you something as magnificent as the Santa Maria del Fiore will be one day ... if the pestilence leaves Florence, that is. As much as I'm itching to get back to Lucie, we can't pass up this opportunity of seeing this architectural marvel.'

Amid the pressing crowd, Raoul and his apprentice gazed with a stonemason's wonder and interest at Lyon's grand cathedral dedicated to Saint John the Baptist. 'Building started about two hundred years ago,' Raoul said, cocking his head to one side as his mind did the calculation. 'But it's probably only two-thirds finished.'

From his leather satchel, Raoul pulled his notebook made from paper, the new smooth writing material popular in Florence, through which the ink didn't bleed as on parchment.

'I hope Lucie-sur-Vionne will know such beauty one day,' he said, sketching the details that interested him. 'And after the experience I gained on the Santa Maria del Fiore, I hope too that you and I will design and build it, Crispen!'

Stashing the notebook back in his satchel, he and Crispen set off along the dusty westward road out of Lyon.

The crowds, and the shambling carts and packhorses overtaken by the occasional galloping King's messenger, slowed them, though Raoul felt they were safer in company. But the further west they travelled, the smaller the roads became and the quieter, until there was nothing to hear but birdsong, the creak of farmers' cart wheels and the trickle of a stream. Threads of lilac smoke from the cottages filtered from cracked-open doors and holes in thatched roofs, the spring air heaving with burned tallow, sweat and old ale.

The sun rose higher over the fields, strips of land stretching before them in a promise of bread for the coming year. The florins clinking in his pocket quickened Raoul's step as he imagined the bright year ahead with his precious family, his table boasting abundant loaves.

Raoul and Crispen rested in the sparse spring shade of an oak, swigging ale from their flasks, and tearing off bites of the bread and cheese they'd purchased in Lyon.

Crispen remained wordless. He didn't look at Raoul, his gaze alternating between the little wooden cat he'd started carving while they were on the boat, and some faraway place over the horizon. He'd barely uttered a word the whole journey from Florence, his eyes tear-glazed every time Raoul tried to console him about Toubie. But Raoul understood his pain; couldn't imagine the heartache of losing the very last soul of his family— those worth more to him than a hundred pots of gold. So he left Crispen to his silent grief and his wood-carving, and thought about Héloïse.

Only two years away but it feels like a hundred. Has she thought of me as often as I've thought of her? Or has she taken a lover, some townsman or passing traveller enchanted by her innocent air, her nurturing sense, the charm of her sharp tongue and her quick temper when riled?

Raoul chuckled to himself, his spirits lifting as he smelled her breath when she kissed him, sweet as strawberry wine, her long pale-brown hair loosening from her cap and caressing his face as they made love. And her eyes when she set her mind to something—sharp and blue-grey as a stormy Vionne. He breathed deeply, tried to ignore the hardness of his yard pressing against his breeches.

He pictured Morgane too, skipping about with that cat of hers, her strange, different-coloured eyes bright in her freckled face—his firstborn, with hair the same coppery hue as his, a nimbus around skin so clear he could see the veins pulsing at her temples. He'd immediately thought of her as his little Flamelock.

A two-wheeled cart clattering towards them interrupted Raoul's thoughts and frightened the birds into silence. It was the rickety type used to transport dung, wood or hay, rather than the four-wheeled wagon of a wealthy merchant.

As it reached Raoul, the driver leaned down from his seat. His beaver-fur hat with its glinting Saint Christopher medallion, his boots made from ordinary tanned leather, rather than the newly-fashionable pointy shoes, confirmed to Raoul this man was a small-time trader.

'God give you good day, sirs,' the driver said. 'What brings you to tramping this road?'

Raoul and Crispen tipped their hats. 'Greetings to you too, sir,' Raoul said. 'We're looking to rent passage to the market town of Lucie-sur-Vionne.' Raoul waved an arm towards the Monts du Lyonnais, jingling the coins in his pocket. 'I can pay you for your trouble.'

The trader threw him a suspicious look. 'Why haven't you got your own horse, sir, or even a donkey?'

'Oh I might've been able to afford a cheap hackney or nag,' Raoul said blithely, not wishing to tell a stranger he could have afforded a whole stable of palfries. 'But I wasn't sure it'd make the four or five leagues to Lucie. Besides, I'd have had to lay out more sous for saddle, halter and spurs … expensive things I have no need for at home.'

Crispen remained wordless and Raoul added: 'We're stone-masons, arrived in Lyon this morning from Florence where we've been sculpting an exquisite cathedral.' He held up his calloused hands as if that was proof enough.

'I've come from Lyon too,' the trader said, 'set to board a barge, and travel south to replenish my stocks of cloth and wares from the merchant ships coming from the east. But a friar coming off the barge warned me that a pestilence—a well-water or a swine pestilence, nobody's certain which—is loose in the east, and the south. He told me the captain of a Genovese hulque said many have fallen ill with painful black swellings in Sardinia, Corsica and Sicily. The friar said the Church is calling it "God's Wrath" … doubtless caused by witches.' The trader crossed himself and rolled his eyes heavenward.

'I was lucky enough to purchase a supply of exotic fruit and spices from a merchant coming off another barge,' he said. 'Said he felt too ill to sell his produce and was keen to offload it for a reasonable price rather than it all rotting. So,' he said with a smile, 'as well as cloth, I'm now trading in oranges, dates and pomegranates.'

A frown crinkled the trader's brow as if something had crossed his mind, and he drew back from Raoul. 'But if you hail from Florence, sir, you'll surely have heard of this new pestilence?'

'Well all I can tell you,' Raoul said, adopting a glib tone, 'is that some sort of disease-laden cloud of air is hovering over Florence. Rome too. But we left before this miasma caught us.' He glanced at his apprentice, hoping Crispen would do as he'd advised, and mask his grief over Toubie's illness and death. He'd warned him that if people knew about the contagion they'd fled, they might think he and Crispen were sick too, and shun them. Like this trader, who would be frightened, and refuse them passage. Crispen knew too, not to say a word to Héloïse either. Raoul didn't want to worry her, or worse, have her force a hundred different "prevention" medicaments down their throats.

'I assure you we're in perfect health,' Raoul said, as he noticed the trader looking them up and down. 'Besides, isn't it safer to travel in a group?' He gestured towards the thicket surrounding them on both sides of the road. 'Priest's robes and pilgrim badges might put off outlaws, but even ordinary travellers can help deter thugs.'

He hoped his garb of a prosperous craftsman: quality leather belt, laced calf-length boots and new hat would allay the trader's fears that he might be one such cutthroat.

'Welcome, good sirs,' the trader finally said, helping them up onto the seat beside him. 'Merlin Lemarchand is my name.'

'Like the sorcerer?' Raoul said with a laugh, as Merlin clicked his tongue and the horse clopped off. 'I'm Raoul Stonemason … master mason, and this is my apprentice, Crispen.'

'It is true that trade from the east has fallen off these last months,' Merlin said after several minutes. 'I suppose traders aren't going to those places until they know for certain if there *is* pestilence, or it's some other catastrophe, because there's been flood, famine and earthquake in those parts. Anyway, let's pray this pestilence is only a disease of outlanders, many leagues far from us where no one's heard of Jesus Christ.' He crossed himself again. 'Those ports are seething with heathen outlanders you know, sirs ... and I've heard it's them who're dying. And if our men in those ports are also perishing, that's because they've been rutting with outlander whores and boys, and only deserve what they get.'

'So, what takes you towards Lucie-sur-Vionne, sir?' Raoul said, keen to move the conversation away from the pestilence.

'The Spring Fair.' Merlin twisted his head and nodded towards the cartload behind them. 'As I said, I have beautiful cloth to sell ... and now this rare fruit too. And since building has started on the vingtain, there will be even more at the fair—builders, blacksmiths, carpenters—'

'Vingtain?' Raoul beetled his brow.

'You didn't hear? Yestermonth, a gang of outlaws ambushed Lucie. Looted and burned homes and killed several townsfolk. Violated women too, so they say.'

An icy bolt splintered Raoul, then a scalding heat burned his insides.

'They're now building a wall of protection around the town,' Merlin said, 'to keep out brigands. Not to mention those smelly English if they decide to come this way.'

Raoul's gut heaved, and he clutched the side of the cart, fearing he might faint and fall to the ground.

Killed and violated townsfolk! Blessed Saint Etienne, no! If Héloïse and Morgane are dead, I want to die too.

Since the day he met Héloïse, Raoul had grown into her, flesh and spirit. If she suffered, he did. If she bled, so did he. He didn't think there had ever been such a burning of two into one ... a marriage so complete as his.

'Demon stolen your tongue, sir?' the trader said.

'I'm worried for my wife and my child.' Raoul still gripped the side of the cart.

'No matter,' Merlin said, with a wave of his hand. 'If something's happened to your wife, you'll just get another. God makes more women every day, as He does children.'

'Not ones like Héloïse.'

'Sounds as if you love the woman,' the trader said with a startled look.

Raoul said nothing; just gave Merlin a small smile.

'A man marrying for love,' Merlin said, 'how odd.'

Merlin Lemarchand was an easy travelling companion, and as the cart rattled along in the sun-baked grooves of so many other wheels, Raoul found himself chattering on to him. He sensed it was more to stop himself worrying about his family, rather than wishing to tell a stranger about his life. Besides, Crispen was still hunched in silence, and Raoul felt he should make up for his apprentice's lack of conversation.

'After the birth of our daughter, my wife was brought to bed of two deadborn boys,' he said. 'But, Our Lord willing, we'll soon have a living son … one I'll teach the building art, like my apprentice here.' He gave Crispen's thigh a friendly slap, but the boy didn't flinch. 'So, along with Crispen, when I'm too old to wield a chisel and scramble up scaffolding, he'll carry on my trade. My future son, and my wife and daughter, are my hope.' He felt himself blush, and looked away from the trader.

'No need for embarrassment, sir,' Merlin said. 'I don't think you weak-spirited to love a woman so much. Rather lucky I'd say … must be a rare symmetry of your stars.'

'So how long have you been apart from your family, Raoul Stonemason?' Merlin asked as they stopped to rest the horse. He drank from his flagon and passed the ale to Raoul.

'Best part of two years. I knew it would be hard, but I couldn't pass up the opportunity of the money—and experience—building fountains in Florence,' Raoul said, thinking with delight of the large sum of gold florins sewn into his undershirt. He passed his bread, and strips of smoked pork, to the trader and Crispen.

'It's certainly comforting to know the wolf will stay in the woods over winter if God punishes a town with a poor harvest,' the trader said. 'Or any other calamity.'

***

Through the late-afternoon haze, Raoul's first glimpse of Lucie-sur-Vionne was the castle sitting high on its rocky knoll. Then, huddled beneath it, along the web of small roads leading to the central market-place, the homes came into sight. But when he saw Saint Antoine's, the pride swelled his chest.

'These hands helped rebuild that church.' Raoul pointed to the spire cresting the western hilltop; at the pointed arches that had replaced the rounded ones. 'That man can carve out such beauty,' Raoul went on, studying his hands as if seeing them for the first time, 'sculpting the folds of a saint's gown, the wings of an angel, and pillars rising to an almost invisible vault. And know that to be our work in honour of God. That, good sir, makes an artist of the least man.'

'I envy you your pride, and your love, Raoul Stonemason,' Merlin Lemarchand said, giving Raoul the kind of smile he'd have reserved for an indulgent child. 'Sadly, we merchants and traders can't boast the same of our trade, which has such a poor reputation.'

As Merlin Lemarchand's cart approached la place de l'Eglise market-place, the wooden scaffolding, the pulleys for raising stones, and the abundance of workers told Raoul that building on this vingtain wall was well underway.

'We'll go to the Mason's Lodge straight away and ask for work, Crispen,' he said, but as Raoul watched the labourers transporting stone blocks from the quarry on oak planks, he recalled the church renovations—and the day he met Héloïse—and his mind filled with thoughts of her, and his child. 'After we've seen Héloïse and Morgane, that is.'

A strange mixture of excitement and fear overcame Raoul, and his stomach churned again as if he was about to vomit.

Merlin reined in his horse and as the beast drank thirstily from the drinking trough, Raoul's gaze skittered across the throngs of market-goers. Héloïse and Isa weren't amongst the gossiping women. Morgane wasn't with the gaggle of children playing with a kitten. He couldn't see them anywhere, and tried to calm himself with slow breaths.

What if they died in this outlaws' siege, or were violated? I couldn't bear it.

'Come on, Merlin.' Side-stepping pecking chickens, Raoul took the trader's arm, Crispen trailing behind. 'You must meet my wife.'

Market day transformed Lucie-sur-Vionne into a clamour of trade, news and gossip, and the crowds jostled them as they walked passed the stalls lining the streets. All the shops were open too, the lower half of doors hinged down as display counters, the upper half propped up to shelter the goods.

They passed the smithy, where the apprentice was holding a horse's head while Pierro Blacksmith, clad in his grimy apron, hammered nails into the beast's foot.

The stink of slaughtered animals' blood and viscera flared Raoul's nostrils as they neared the butcher's shop. The apprentice had cut the throat of a suckling pig and its blood spurted onto the boy's leather apron and into the pail beneath it.

Raoul called out a greeting over the rhythmical *thunk, thunk* of the butcher's cleaver striking the chopping board. The butcher looked up from his meat-laden counter, carcasses dangling from hooks in the shop behind. He slopped a pile of entrails into a bucket, and squinted at Raoul, pressing a bloodied hand to his brow to shield his eyes from the sun.

'Is it really you, Raoul Stonemason? Welcome home!'

As the butcher thumped a chunk of meat onto his scales, balancing it with metal weights until he, at least, was satisfied he was getting a good deal, Raoul almost asked him about Héloïse. But his tongue was stuck to the roof of his mouth.

They moved on through the people, and the sunlight glimmering off the merchants' silks, towards the raucous crowd overflowing from the Au Cochon Tué tavern.

'Out of my tavern!' Alewife Rixende screeched. With all the

vigour of a man, she shoved a drunken customer out onto the market-place. 'I don't need the likes of you pissing and chucking up your meal on my clean rushes. If you want charity, go to the monastery.' The alewife spat a glob of yellowish spittle at the man. 'And don't come back till you can pay your debts!'

No doubt the customer had lost his money in a dice game, but Rixende was familiar with the tricks of thieves, pedlars and ruffians and hadn't the slightest qualm about hoisting them onto the street without their possessions, or even their clothes if that was the only way to make up her losses. Raoul smiled to himself. Alewife Rixende might look fragile, but she was still lithe as a green cornstalk and deftly handled her rowdy clientele.

'You're back!' Raoul spun around to Héloïse's willowy friend, Yolande, her apron flapping in the breeze. 'Héloïse will be so happy.'

'So she is … they are …? I heard of the outlaws' attack.'

'Héloïse, Morgane and Isa are safe,' Yolande said, looking from him to Merlin and Crispen.

Like a scented bath after a dusty journey, relief washed over Raoul, but the shadow that darkened Yolande's face, and the tears that clouded her eyes, puzzled him.

'This good trader was kind enough to bring Crispen and me to Lucie,' Raoul said, giving Merlin's shoulder a squeeze. 'He's looking for lodgings.'

'Oh, the tavern's bursting with vingtain workers,' Yolande said. 'There isn't a single room, floor or stable in the whole town. And being market day, there are even fewer places available.'

'Never mind,' Raoul said, beaming Merlin, 'we'll lodge the good trader in my cot.'

'Lord have mercy,' Merlin said, scratching at his ankle as Raoul led him and Crispen on through the crowd to where Héloïse and Isa usually had their stall. 'This spring damp has brought a devilish outbreak of fleas, and they love to feast on me.'

'My wife's the midwife and healer here in Lucie,' Raoul said with a laugh. 'She'll have a potion to ease your flea bites ... Héloïse has a cure for everything!'

X

'**For fresh breath, tell** your patients to chew aniseed and fennel seeds,' I said to Morgane. 'Clean-smelling breath is important because, like dirty bodies, foul breath carries disease.'

Morgane gave an exaggerated sigh. 'I know, Maman, and tell people to clean their teeth every day with rosemary ashes.'

The market was almost over, that last part of the day when people haggled for the best prices, and I'd left Isa at our stall to go and buy supplies of our own. Amid the thrilling eastern scents of sandalwood, paprika and patchouli, and the pungent saffron and cinnamon, I negotiated a good price for a dram of cloves, and cumin seeds for healing wounds.

Morgane and I cast last longing gazes at the mysterious sack-cloths of peppercorns, cardamom pods and brown sea salt, and continued on, weaving through the clutter of stalls and people.

I glanced up at Alix and her sister Nica, selling their aromatic beeswax candles. Their firm-set lips and suspicious glances felt like an army of spiders scuttling down my back.

Alewife Rixende was sweeping out the main tavern room, her daughters scouring the bench tops with river gravel, and flicking water at each other in fits of giggles.

Rixende's heart might be blackened with jealousy, her tongue as forked as a viper's, but she was a hard worker, I had to give her that. The Au Cochon Tué tavern had been in her family as long as anyone remembered and at sixteen summers, on her parents'

83

death, Rixende had taken it over without hesitation. As well as cooking, cleaning and making up beds, she brewed all the ale, which her fanfarolle of a husband, Jâco swilled as fast as his wife could ferment it.

Rixende caught my eye and leaned on her broom, her curvy body angled, as always, to attract the attention of passing men.

'Whatever Père Bernard reckons, I'll wager it was you what cursed us with that outlaw attack.' Her upper lip hitched, exposing the lustful gap between her front teeth.

'Oh yes that makes sense,' I said, my voice loaded with sarcasm, 'a midwife-healer who destroys and kills. Really, Rixende, your witless slander makes you look not only evil, but dumb as a headless chicken.'

'Devil-eyes, evil-eyes, Morgane got the Devil eyes,' Rixende's oldest daughter, Pina, began chanting. Her sisters, seeing a chance to shirk their cleaning duties, scurried off behind the woodpile, their braids lashing like whips made of flax. 'Devil-eyes, evil-eyes, Morgane got the Devil eyes,' Pina went on.

'And it seems your daughter's growing up to be just as stupid,' I said, with a look at Pina. The sisters reappeared then, each dangling a glossy black rat's corpse, and squealing in delight as they swung the rats back and forth before Morgane's eyes. 'Devil-eyes, evil-eyes, Morgane got the Devil eyes.'

As I stepped forward, raising a hand to slap the girls' faces, Pétronille and Peronelle skipped across to us.

'Come and play hoodman's bluff.' Pétronille took Morgane's arm and I almost pushed her off with the twins, thankful to send my daughter away from the hurtful taunts. Though their venom seemed to bother me far more than it did Morgane.

'You gotta laugh at the harmless games of children, eh Héloïse?' the alewife said. Snowy tapers of hair that had escaped her cap whipped about her face, and if her smile hadn't been so malicious, I'd have had to admit Rixende was still as beguiling as that morning I'd met Raoul.

It was on la place de l'Eglise, a sun-soaked day of my

seventeenth summer, when Yolande told me a church worker had injured his hand. I'd hurried across to the din-filled scaffolding, towards the sound of chisels on stone, the hammering on timbers and the workers themselves: marble-cutters, painters and glassmakers, carpenters and smiths, all hired by Comte Renault to renovate Saint Antoine's church.

Rixende hovered like a persistent wasp as I bathed the stonemason's injured hand. It was nothing serious, but gave her an excuse to flirt with him—something I could understand as I had to lower my own gaze to stop staring at this splendid man: his stout frame, the muscles of his sun-gilded arms straining his chemise and his waist-length coppery curls tied back with a length of cord.

I smiled to myself, recalling that neither he nor I spoke as I massaged in the almond-oil and honey mixture to soothe and help healing. But I'd shuddered with a strange kind of coolness, and heat. We kept silent as I took a strip of linen cloth from my basket, and as I bandaged the stonemason's hand, I sensed he was studying me. Finally, I couldn't help myself, and lifted my gaze to his face; his eyes as green and clear as the Vionne in spring. His smile widened, and he started telling me about his statue of the Blessed Virgin, and how it was the piece he would submit to the guild to become a master mason.

When there was nothing else I could do for his injury; no more reason to hold up his work, he thanked me. I saw myself walking away from him, and Rixende snagging my arm, telling me to keep my whoring hands off the stonemason; that he'd be her husband. That they were practically promised to each other.

I was convinced the stonemason's warm smile had just been one of thanks, and I'd imagined something more—the fantasy of a girl with no chance of marriage. After all, I was plain as a common daisy beside Rixende, the rose of Lucie-sur-Vionne in full, petulant bloom. With hair as fair as flax, the lecherous tooth gap and nipples pressing like crossbow bolts against the rough cloth of her kirtle, she could surely hook any husband she desired, and I'd given up all thoughts of Raoul Stonemason then and there.

'And, as I was sayin',' Rixende said, startling me back to the present. 'Before you rudely interrupted ... I got reason to think you cursed us with this outlaw attack. Jacotte reckons so too. After all, you did curse your own girl.' She nodded at Morgane, skipping around the old Roman fountain with Yolande's twins. 'If a midwife can blight one of her own, why not others?' She spat three times on the back of her hand. 'Whelp shoulda been drowned at birth, before she turns into the same witch as her mother, cursing all what cross her path.'

'She's only a girl—' I started.

'She might be only a girl,' Jacotte said, lumbering over from the blacksmith's like a palsied old maid, 'but the Devil can be at work in many innocent-looking ones. Ain't that so, Rixende?'

'Gormless slug-brains,' I hissed, my temper brewing as darkly as storm clouds. 'Spouting nothing but *merde*, straight from your arses.' I swivelled around to leave, and barged straight into the solid wall of a man.

I couldn't speak at first; couldn't believe it was Raoul. I felt the rush of my quickening pulse, my heart leaping into my throat. How long had I waited for this? How many chilled and lonely nights? In that instant, as I fell into my husband's arms, Rixende and Jacotte's taunts soared from my mind.

'Where's my little Flamelock?' Raoul said in his gravelly voice when I finally released him, and held him at arm's length, looking him up and down. Still the same Raoul. There was something though ... something different about the warm, green eyes. And that muscle was dancing in his neck—the one that jittered when my husband was disturbed or unsettled. Or angry.

'Morgane's around, somewhere ... she'll be so happy to see you too,' I said, 'but where's Toubie?' I looked at the man standing beside Raoul and Crispen, who was nothing like Toubie. Nothing like a stonemason's apprentice.

'Sadly the boy fell from high scaffolding,' Raoul said. 'He ... he died.'

I couldn't help noticing the flush to Raoul's cheeks, the way he lowered his gaze. After two years away, my husband still hadn't learned how to lie convincingly.

'So sad,' Crispen said. The boy's face might be taut with grief, like Raoul's, but he too was a hopeless liar. Crispen pulled a little wooden cat sculpture from his pocket. 'I carved this for Morgane ... I know how much she loves cats.'

'It's beautiful, Crispen, and I know she'll treasure it,' I said, sensing now wasn't the time to probe for the truth or the reason for their falsehoods.

'And this is our trader friend,' Raoul said, changing the subject far too quickly. 'Merlin Lemarchan—'

'Midwife!' I spun around to the urgent shout; to the hawk-eyed woodcutter-sexton, Poncet Batier, who'd been in the stocks twice in the same week. His beard was slimy with grease, the hood covering his head crawling with lice.

'You'll have to come,' he said. 'The wife's having a hard time of the birthing ... babe refuses to come out. In a bad way, is Jehanne. I can pay you in wood or beans, take your pick.'

I looked from my husband to the woodcutter—a ferocious-looking man with whom I wanted no business. All I wanted was to race back to our cot with Raoul, tear his clothes from him, wrap my legs around his back and feel him deep inside me, filling me up with two years' worth of love.

'I ... I'll have to go, Raoul, but I'll try and be home quickly.'

Raoul dropped my hand, and let out a sigh.

I touched his shoulder. 'Don't be like—'

'Midwife, you gotta come now!' Poncet Batier said.

'Go,' Raoul said, with a wave of his hand, his voice more scratchy than usual. 'I suppose a birthing woman needs you more than a husband who's been away two years.'

XI

𝕱**rom the moment 𝕴** stepped into the woodcutter's lowly cot I could see the labouring girl was in a bad way, her grime and sweat, mixing with that of her gossips, curdling the cloying air.

The fire was banked down with turfs to save fuel, and only flimsy threads of warmth filtered into the tightly-shuttered room that served for cooking, living and sleeping. Damp seeped up from the beaten-earth floor and in a corner a goat bleated, a chicken fluttered its feathers like a fretting housewife and a scraggy dog sniffed at a bucket overflowing with piss.

Thrice the summers of his wife if my guess was correct, Poncet Batier stamped around the room flinging his hairy arms into the smoky air.

'No men allowed in a birth room,' I said, shooing the woodcutter-sexton outside, along with the animals. 'And empty that as you go.' I indicated the latrine bucket. 'Then you can fetch my birthing chair from my cot … it will help your wife give birth more easily.'

I set my basket on the floor and washed my hands with rose-water, as the wild-haired man muttered something inaudible, but left with the bucket. I opened the shutter, flapped out some of the smoke, then turned my attention to the girl lying wide-eyed, crazed with pain, on blood-sogged straw.

'It's Jehanne, isn't it?' The girl looked no more than twelve summers, and was clutching a daisy chain. Jehanne nodded, her yellowish hawk-eyes the same as Poncet Batier's telling me there was truth in the rumour that had soiled the market-place air like nine-day pottage: the husband was also the girl's father.

'What's happening?' Jehanne said. 'Am I dying?'

'Jehanne's my niece,' said a stout woman who was crouched beside the girl gripping her hand. 'Been this way half the night and no sign of the child.'

The other gossips, a pasty-faced neighbour and a woman as bony as a herring, nodded in grim agreement as another pain seized Jehanne.

'That's why we sent for you, Midwife,' the pasty neighbour said, over Jehanne's shrieks. 'Or we coulda birthed it ourselves.'

'Birthed it?' Jehanne's yellowy eyes filled with tears.

I looked, in amazement, at the gossips. 'Jehanne doesn't know she's with child?'

'We thought it best not to frighten her,' the stout aunt said.

'With ... with child? Jehanne said.

Her father's lustful cruelty sickening me, my heart softened for the girl and I clapped my hands to jolt the women into action.

'Change this soiled straw. And get Jehanne onto the pallet. She's in no state to give birth lying on the ground like a dog.'

'Mattresses are costly and precious,' the aunt said. 'She'll soil it.'

'Do you want to help your niece?' I said. 'Or make it worse?'

The woman scowled, but in a flurry of skirts and grime-stained hands the gossips hauled Jehanne onto the pallet.

'Am I dying?' the girl asked again, still gripping her daisy chain.

I sat beside Jehanne and spoke softly, close to her ear, brushing damp wicks of hair from her scarlet cheeks.

'Not dying, Jehanne. You're going to have a baby, but don't be frightened, I'll take good care of you. Relax and breathe slowly, and the baby will come.' I mimed deep in-out breaths and smiled encouragement as the girl did the same.

I bent over Jehanne's belly, and placed an ear against the taut skin. Relieved to hear the *boom, boom* of the baby's heart, it wasn't beating as rapidly as I'd have liked.

With the gossips' help I shifted Jehanne onto her side and, my hand slick with almond-oil, I reached up into the girl's womb.

'The baby hasn't reached the door yet,' I said.

As the hours went by with no sign of Poncet Batier or my birthing chair, I helped Jehanne with her breathing. I heated mint-scented oil over the fire and massaged her belly and legs.

The gossips chanted prayers. The aunt stuck her head between her niece's legs and shouted into the birth passage, 'Infant, come out! God calls you to the world!'

'Perhaps you can sneeze the child out?' the herring-thin woman said, shoving pepper under Jehanne's nose.

The pepper didn't work. Nothing worked.

I hooked my angel talisman over my head, and placed it on Jehanne's navel dent, willing its strength and power to her. And to the unborn child of this child.

'We'll pray to Saint Margaret,' I said, 'protector of women in childbirth.'

'Dear Saint Margaret,' the aunt began, 'please help our Jehanne come to bed safely of a healthy babe. She's a good girl and is doing her best.'

At moments like this, notions of my own mother wandered into my mind. Ava, whose hands had guided so many souls into the world but who had died doing this one thing she did so well. How unfair. Isa's words chimed in my mind.

Life is not fair, Héloïse, though we want it to be.

'Jehanne's too young, that's the trouble,' the aunt said. 'It's what I told him from the beginning.' She snarled at the door, as if at the husband, but Poncet Batier was likely finding solace in the tavern, as did most men whilst their wives laboured to birth their offspring.

'A girl at her first blood ain't supposed to get with child,' the bony woman said.

'Oh it can happen,' I said.

Twilight darkened the westward hills. Each of Jehanne's throws seemed harder than the last, wringing the girl out like a scrap of cloth and leaving her terrified of the next one. And as a vicious wind sprang up outside and the moon rose in the sky— her powers of choosing life or death heightened—Jehanne's pains ceased altogether.

'Why's it all stopped?' The aunt's voice was spiked with panic.

I closed my tired eyes for an instant as I bent an ear to Jehanne's belly again. Not a single beat of the baby's heart.

The gossips stared at me, waiting to see what I would do next. But this midwife had no other tricks. I swallowed hard, tried to clear my exhausted mind, to remind myself of Isa's teachings.

A good midwife and wise-woman must not let herself feel their pain or grief.

The baby was likely dead; there was only one thing left to try and save the mother. I withdrew the little casket of dark powder from the bottom of my basket.

'What's that?' the aunt asked.

I didn't tell the gossips this was the ergot powder, about which Isa had warned me.

The angel powder is a dangerous secret to know, Héloïse. It can expel unwanted babes from the womb. But at the right time, and with good luck, the angel potion can bring life. Although simple to make, from rotted rye, be wary of using it, for it can bring madness, death and evil tramping in its wake.

'Jehanne's losing strength,' I said, mixing the angel potion with a little spiced wine to mask its bitterness. 'This will bring on the pains again.'

The women clucked with worry as Jehanne sipped the brew, then slumped back into their arms.

'Get her upright,' I said, strong pains seizing Jehanne again. The women dragged the exhausted girl to her feet, and I massaged her belly, pushing the baby downward.

I reached an oiled hand into the womb. 'The baby's head's at the opening. I need you to push now, Jehanne.'

'I can't,' Jehanne wailed, her head lolling to one side. 'No more ... let me die. Please ...'

'You must,' I urged.

Finally, against a wind baying like a boar stuck with arrows, the baby came. It was indeed dead.

In one horrified hiss, the gossips gasped at the lifeless little boy with the oversized head.

'A changeling!' the aunt shrieked. 'Stamped with the hoof-mark ... marked out for the Devil himself.'

'And it's part spider,' the pasty neighbour said. 'Covered with black hair, just above its Devil's mark.'

'Spiders bring death,' the thin woman hissed. 'Death and pestilence.'

'Or the midwife's been practising dark arts ... witchery.' The aunt's voice was shrill, accusing.

'Magic and charms perhaps,' I said, boldly meeting her scornful eyes. 'But witchcraft? Never!'

Jehanne wouldn't have heard their cries of horror, or their accusations, for her boy had arrived in a river of blood I couldn't stop. No amount of wool I packed into the girl's battered womb staunched the flow, and within minutes of her deadborn babe, Jehanne too, faded from life.

Flooded with sorrow for mother and child, I took my talisman and as I relooped it over my head I saw, still clutched in Jehanne's fist, the wilted daisy chain.

***

The woodcutter's cottage was chaotic, the gossips crying and cowering in a corner, and shielding their eyes from the changeling. And from my angel pendant.

Poncet Batier must have heard the commotion, for he flung open the door, a gust of wind scattering leaves across the stained straw. The husband-father didn't seem to notice the deformed and lifeless child, staring only at his dead wife. His mouth drew tighter than a miser's purse string.

'What the Devil's yard have you done, Midwife?' He lunged at me, grappling at my neck, trying to wrench away my pendant. 'I've heard the talk about this evil talisman. You cursed Jehanne—killed her—with it. You'll pay for this, witch! Women are dangerous creatures, but you're the worst … Devil's monster.'

Spent after the long hours working to try and save mother and child, I couldn't hold my tongue.

'You're the monster, Poncet Batier. You who calls himself a girl's husband, when you're her father. I hope your evilness withers you like wheat in a drought.'

The woodcutter flew at me again, the hawk eyes specks of flame burning in the scarlet blotch of his face. Grimy hands reached about my throat. I gagged on his grip, his stench of dirt, onions and old ale.

I struggled to breathe, the air clotting inside me as I tried to prise his fingers from my neck. But his grip was strong as a windfucker's talons and the blood pooled in my cheeks, my eyes straining to pop from their sockets.

Against the wind keening through the poplars, and through the mist of my panic, I caught the gossips' shouts.

'You're the monster, Poncet Batier!' cried the aunt, the women encircling the woodcutter. 'Planting your vile seed into your daughter at her first blood.'

Together, the women wrenched the man's fingers from my neck and wrestled him to the ground.

Gasping for air, I reeled from that tangle of skirts and the struggling man they held to the floor.

'No wonder the babe weren't right,' the pasty neighbour said. 'It goes against Mother Earth, mixing your seed with your own girl's.'

'You don't give a damn for your dead son,' the thin woman said. 'Your only grief is losing the plaything you call a wife. Who'll midwife us and cure our sickness if you kill her?'

'I hope you pay in purgatory for what you did to Jehanne,' I said, my hands trembling as I threw my kit back into my basket.

'Be gone, shrew!' the husband flung an arm at the door.

The woodcutter's resentful gaze scalding me like a flaming rush, I hurtled outdoors into the darkness; into a wind fierce enough to pluck a chicken.

My exhaustion, coupled with the woodcutter's attack, brought on a giddiness and I swayed, almost losing my footing. I righted myself on a fencepost and set off, lowering my hood against the dust, tears of frustration and sadness stinging my eyes.

I should've stayed away ... gone home with Raoul as any good wife would have done. I should be by my husband's side, rather than suffering the assaults of lunatics like Poncet Batier, and trudging about in a cold, bleak wind.

Dragging my cloak around me, I clutched my pendant, its sharp edges cutting into my palm. As I hurried through the creaking moonlit trees, bare branches waved like skeletons whispering into the ear of the wind.

How quickly people can turn against you, they breathed. *How fast the river of suspicion can drown you.*

***

I hung my cloak on the nail behind the door, and almost tripped over a man snoring on the pallet beside the hearth. It was the trader; Raoul must've brought him to lodge with us. Beside the trader, Crispen too, was snoring.

I stored my basket in the lean-to Raoul had built off the main room, where, apart from our medicaments, we kept rope and candles, and grain in sacks sturdy enough to defy the most persistent rodent.

Exhausted and famished after my long day and the gruelling birth, I ladled some of Isa's hare stew from the hearth cauldron into a bowl. The hare had been a birth payment—one likely hunted illegally on le Comte de Fouville's land, but that never bothered anyone, as long as they didn't get caught.

My whole body ached, screamed to lie down, but I took a moment to wash away my grime and cleanse myself with rose-water.

I struggled up the ladder Raoul had installed when he built our sleeping loft. Isa would have been asleep for hours, turning in as she always did just after twilight, and Morgane's excitement at seeing her papa must have calmed as my daughter slept deeply, curled around Blanche in a ball of elbows, knees and furry cat.

'Finally.' Raoul's whisper croaked into the darkness. 'Come here.'

I couldn't bear to relive the disaster at the woodcutter's cot; craved only to collapse onto our soft, hay-stuffed mattress with Raoul, and forget all of it.

But melting into my husband's arms awakened my hunger for him. Raoul too, was eager, and our hands moved like frantic ants over each other. I shook, felt Raoul's trembling body as he pressed against me, hard and urgent. Any doubts that my husband's love might have waned over the last two years vanished like a drop of water hissing into a fire and I clung to him, my legs hugging his back, my arms crushing him to my chest, my face nestled in his sinewy neck.

I wanted to cry out; to shriek with the pleasure; the relief of satisfying a long, parching thirst but aware of Isa and Morgane, I pressed my lips together.

'Only the Blessed Saint Etienne knows how I've missed you,' he said as we finally lay still, and panting.

'Weren't you glad to be away from your wife's razor tongue?' My fingers twined through his mane of hair, stretching curls to my nose, inhaling its scent of dust and stone. 'Like most husbands?'

'I'm sure you'll make up for it,' Raoul teased. 'And now I'm home, you won't have to leave the cot as much, to go out midwifing and healing ... being away most of the night, like you were tonight.

I remained silent, trying to drink in my husband's words; to get my mind around their meaning.

'After you left the market-place with Poncet Batier, I went to see Alesi Stonemason,' Raoul said. 'The Master Mason's hired me to work on the vingtain wall and the castle repairs. I earned well in Florence, but it's a good feeling to know there's more coming in ... and that you won't have to work yourself silly. Isa told me you've been at it like a slave.'

'I like being busy, Raoul ... less time to think how much I was missing you.' I jabbed a finger into the russet hair curls matting his chest. Besides, I can't stop doing my work. The townsfolk need me especially since Isa's no longer working and I'm the only midwife and wise-woman. Except that charlatan Rixende ... though she's useless and only sells her so-called medicaments to spite me.'

'I'm not asking you to stop altogether.' Raoul took my hand, thread his fingers through mine. 'I understand your calling ... really I do, and the oath you swore on Ava's soul. All I'm saying is I'll be needing a hearty meal after working on that vingtain all day, and a wife's warm and welcoming body on my sleeping pallet.'

'I'll try,' I said, 'but it won't be easy.' I kissed Raoul's brow and snuggled against his strong body. In the tiny space between us, I made a small sign of the cross, and thanked the Virgin for this miracle of my husband's love, still as strong as when he'd left for Florence.

It is ... isn't it? It has to be. I couldn't bear to think there was slightest crack in our rock-hard love.

'What really happened to Toubie, Raoul?'

I heard Raoul's hesitation, felt the heavy silence between us, and thought maybe he'd fallen asleep.

'I told you, Héloïse, he fell from scaffolding ... so tragic. But you know our trade's a dangerous one.'

'Oh I do know the stonemason's job is hazardous.'

Why was Raoul still not telling me the truth about his apprentice?

'That's why I've been working so hard. Not only did we have

to survive while you were gone but there was always my fear you wouldn't come back. As a girl, Isa kept telling me: get a trade, don't depend on a husband. She taught me that women need to support themselves.' I took a breath. 'Well, like you, Raoul, I've mastered my trade. I'm good at it and I can't stop now. Look at poor Yolande ... not knowing how they'll survive without the tailor.'

'Speaking of the tailor's family,' Raoul said, 'I've taken on Anselme as my second apprentice. After the Mason's Lodge, I went to see Yolande. I'll pay him two sous a week, since he'll eat with his mother and sisters, rather than with us. After a week's trial we'll establish the contract.'

'So Anselme will come to live in our cot?'

'No,' Raoul said. 'Yolande's happy he'll become my apprentice but since those thugs murdered her husband she feels safer having her boy live with them.'

'But he might never be ... be right in his head.'

'It's true, Anselme will never have the fine skills to follow his father's tailor footsteps,' Raoul said, 'but he's a strong and willing lad, and I want to give him this chance. Besides, as you said, the family will need an income. You can't always rely on the guild to look after you.'

'Just what I was saying, Raoul. A woman needs to look after herself, and her family. Anyway,' I said, stroking the skin on his palm, thicker than the hide on a man's heel, 'maybe that will bring Anselme back to himself.'

'I'd forgotten your smell ... such a green smell of peace,' he said, pressing his nose into my hair. 'It makes me think that with you in my world it will always be a peaceful place. And with our future so bright, I'm sure God will give us a son soon.'

'Let's ask Him tomorrow,' I said. 'It's Saint Ava's day and Isa and I bought Masses for my mother's soul.'

Raoul was soon asleep but, exhausted as I was, my eyes refused to shut. Raoul wanted me to give up my trade. He'd not said it outright, but I feared that's what he meant.

XII

𝕴 **woke on the** morning of the Spring Fair, several days after Raoul's return, with the chill of a wraith walking by. I thought of Ava and grasped my pendant.

Raoul slept on, his throaty breathing steady. I caught Isa's wheezy breaths and Morgane's quiet ones, and down by the hearth, Merlin Lemarchand and Crispen snored loud enough to wake the Devil. All was well in my cot, and I couldn't imagine why Ava's spectre would haunt me on this morning of our greatest fair, celebrating the height of spring. Maybe it wasn't Ava, but the terrible deaths of Jehanne and her child still gnawing at my heart.

I shook off the shiver, disentangled myself from my husband's limbs and laced up my kirtle. I climbed down the loft ladder and washed my face in the basin of water.

Feeding in sticks, I fanned the fire's dwindled night embers, flame shadows soon dancing on the wall. Besides its warmth, we kept the fire going to make draughts, so the air was always smoky, but sweet-scented with the rosemary we kept burning to purify the air of any sickness ailing people might bring to our cot.

I opened the shutters, inhaled the scent of drenched earth and loam, and once I'd broken my fast I took the leather pails out into a morning wrapped in a fine mist. In the frail grey light, cottages, barns and trees looked like ghosts, and all who were tending livestock seemed anxious to finish their chores. The Spring Fair was a well-earned break from the harsh toil of our daily work and a bit of threatening weather wouldn't dampen anyone's spirits.

'This rain won't last, Midwife Héloïse,' one of the lepers called, as I lifted an arm in a wave to them. 'You'll see, we'll have as fine a Spring Fair as any yet.'

I smiled back, but sighed at the injustice. The lepers had never been allowed at the fair.

As I returned from the well with our water, Merlin sat up on the pallet shivering as I set the kettle on the trivet to heat.

'You're cold,' I said, 'I'll heat some pottage to warm you.'

'Yes, cold.' Merlin hugged his arms around himself. '... and hot too.' He tried to stand, stumbled and fell back down. 'Oh and ... and giddy.'

I touched a palm to his brow. 'You've got a fever ... a touch of ague. Best you stay in bed today.'

Merlin looked startled. 'No, no. I can't miss the Spring Fair; can't miss this opportunity to make a bit extra.'

The noise must've woken Crispen with a start, as the apprentice leapt from the pallet. Staring at Merlin, his eyes wide and filled with—was that fear?—he sprang away from the trader, towards the cot door.

'Whatever is wrong, Crispen?' I said.

'N-nothing ... m-must've been in the m-middle of a nightmare.'

'A terrible nightmare to make you stammer like that.' I eyed him warily as I filled a beaker with boiled willow bark cordial.

'Here Merlin,' I said, 'something to ease your fever.'

A fit of shivering gripped Merlin as he took the beaker with a trembling hand and drank thirstily, slopping the liquid onto the rushes around him.

'*Merci*, Mistress.' He slumped back onto the pallet. 'I'll be well soon, I'm sure ... can't miss the fair.'

'Well let's hope it's only a touch of the ague,' I said, sprinkling fleabane and alder leaves over the rushes. Merlin was scratching at his flea bites again so I hung dried fleabane from a rafter too, for extra protection.

'Odd, isn't it,' I said to the trader, as I clambered down from the stool, 'how those little black soldiers find one person so flavoursome and another not at all?'

Merlin Lemarchand seemed in such a hurry to get to the fair, he wasn't interested in talk of fleas or anything else as he threw on his breeches, splashed water over his face and gobbled down some bread and ale.

As Merlin scurried out through the door, Crispen, still staring wide-eyed, jumped aside, a palm over his heart, and I wondered what ever could have made the usually calm and happy lad so jumpy.

'What's wrong with Merlin?' Isa said, lumbering down the loft ladder.

'Just a touch of fever,' I said, as she broke her fast on cheese, bread and ale while I started shelling the peas, setting aside the pods for Morgane to feed the pig.

Isa took her wolfsbane liniment from the lean-to where we kept our medicaments in clay jars, from which I replenished the laced bags in my work-basket. These moist spring mornings gnawed hard at her joints, and she eased herself onto a stool, her brow creasing as she massaged her hip.

I threw the peas into yesterday's stew along with garlic and began stirring as the liniment worked its magic to ease Isa's pain—the same magic it should have performed on Drogan's father's knees during my eleventh summer. But instead the man had fallen down dead. The weaver might've died of a hundred other things but since a wise-woman's remedies were the usual target blame had naturally fallen on Isa. And that had sealed the weaver family's hatred of mine.

***

'I want to see everything!' Morgane said to her father, jigging about and adding to the frenzied air of fair excitement as townsfolk and outlanders flocked into the meadow. 'And remember the pie you promised ... I'm starving.' She pulled a face as if she'd not eaten for days.

'Thank you again for my beautiful cat,' Morgane called after Crispen as he loped off to join some other apprentices. She waved the wooden carving in the air, Crispen returning her wave, though the lad's charming and easy smile was still missing. Soon I would find out; I would make it my business to learn what he and Raoul were keeping from me.

'That lad will be a fine father one day,' I said, as Isa and I unpacked our baskets, spreading herbal decoctions, balms, ointments and cordials on an old woollen blanket.

'Yes, he'll make some girl a good husband,' Raoul said, 'as Toubie would have.'

A shadow darkened Raoul's face, his gaze darting away from me, and in his green eyes, which had always revealed to me the things my husband could not voice, his pain and grief for Toubie was clear.

But just as quickly his face brightened and our daughter squealed as he lifted her off the ground and twirled her in circles, her braids lashing about like sparks of fire. 'Don't worry, my little Flamelock, we'll see all the fair.'

Amidst the coloured booths and the flying pennants, small-time traders like Merlin Lermarchand—and rich merchants— were plying every kind of thing: pearls, sweet Spanish fragrances in stone bottles and tusks from animals they called elephants. They sold perfumed soaps, violet-scented sugar, olive oil for beautiful hair and vine stem ashes boiled in vinegar to dye grey hair blonde. All rare and wondrous things we only saw at the Spring Fair.

Amidst girls selling flowers and jongleurs chanting their latest verse, Raoul hailed a vendor hawking pies and sweet pickled herring.

'Best pies of the fair, soaked in wine, stuffed with nuts and currants,' the vendor boasted, as Raoul handed him two deniers. 'Nothing like the first bite of fair food is there, good sir?' he said, as Raoul handed the pie to Morgane.

'Take thou this rose, O Rose,' a bard spouted, swooning passed them. 'Since Love's own flower it is, And by that rose, Thy lover captive is.'

Raoul turned to me. 'My O Rose.' He mimicked the bard's tone, a hand over his heart in a dramatic gesture, his brow knotted in the pantomime of heartache. 'Thy lover captive certainly is! See you soon my sweet rose,' he said with a raspy laugh, grasping Morgane's hand. Isa and I laughed and waved them off as the first drumbeat rang out and a circle of strutting horses began their parade.

'Herbs for all your ailments. Congestion, gout, dropsy,' Isa called to passersby. 'Balms for tired eyes, potions for all types of ague.'

'Soothing rose-water,' I said, 'for irritated skin, sore eyes … calming bad nerves.'

As our leper friend had predicted, the drizzle stopped. The morning wore on and the pale glow of the sun heightened over the meadow humming with people bartering and haggling, settling old arguments and looking for new ones. Labourers looked to be hired, girls looked for husbands and thieves looked for purses to cut. A black-robed Dominican friar preached to a circle of admirers, dogs barked and children squealed loud enough to wake Satan in Hell itself. Messengers, musicians and pilgrims also swelled the numbers, trebling the population of Lucie-sur-Vionne for this one festive day.

Rixende's business was lively, the alewife pouring cup after cup for men who swilled the ale, threw dice and sang out of tune songs about lusty women.

'Stop gulping all the ale, you sheep-brained oaf!' Rixende screeched like a barn owl, waving a fist at her husband.

Jâco laughed her off, his crimson cheeks puffing, veiny

nose purpling as he carried on drinking and joking with their customers.

Isa nodded at the alewife. 'Ava told me Rixende's hands were fisted when she pulled her bum-first from her mother's womb.'

'Same fists it seems she'll keep clenched her whole life,' I said with a laugh. 'The ones that will box Jâco's ears tonight for drinking all her ale.

The townsmen of Lucie were always teasing Jâco for not giving his virago of a wife a proper beating. Women were born to work for, and obey, a husband. But no beaten man could take his wife to court, for none would sympathise with a man so feeble he couldn't defend himself against his own woman.

'Merlin's ague must've eased,' I said, nodding across the crowd at our trader friend, amidst the other travelling merchants displaying their treasures.

'Hopefully,' Isa said, packing two vials of rose-water into a customer's basket. 'We wouldn't want every fair-goer catching it.'

Mistress Ariane, the shoemaker's daughter, sidled up to us. 'I need a brew to stop me throwing up,' said the thin girl, her doe-eyes more sorrowful than usual. 'Since those outlaws murdered my brother and sister I've been sick in my guts.'

We gave Mistress Ariane some ginger root, and to a girl having trouble with her courses, I sold a brew of mugwort, ginger and lion's foot. To the baker's wife, Sibylle—with child yet again—I gave our special raspberry brew.

'It will help stop the seed from slipping out,' I said, with a silent prayer to Saint Margaret. More babes than I could count had slipped from Sibylle's womb. There was never much I could do for the distraught woman, save soothe her sobs with comforting words, bid her drink camomile and geranium cordial, and cleanse her womb with our special mixture of garlic, mint and vinegar.

'And rose-water to soothe your nerves,' I said, slipping a vial into her basket.

'*Merci*, Midwife Héloïse, and you'll come to the bakery again soon to check me, won't you? You said you'd come every week. And you must because—'

'Of course I'll come,' I said with a smile knowing that even thrice daily visits wouldn't calm Sibylle, so agitated that she spoke incessantly and I often had trouble edging in a word.

'You should do something about Rixende,' Sibylle went on, nodding in the alewife's direction. 'She's not only selling ale, but medicaments too. I know she's no wise-woman, and just sets herself up in competition to spite you, Héloïse, but surely there's something you can do to stop her?'

'We know what Rixende's doing,' I said, 'but there's nothing we can do.'

'If people want to buy from an ignorant charlatan, that's their problem,' Isa said.

'Well I just thought you should know—' Sibylle started.

'I'll have some of your mixture for my husband's bad digestion please,' the butcher's wife cut in. 'The last batch worked wonders for him.'

I gave the butcher's wife juniper berry mixture, and bade both women a good day as Yolande approached. Pétronille and Peronelle skipped along beside their mother, Anselme trailing behind with his slow, measured gait.

'Where's Morgane?' Pétronille asked.

'With her papa.' I nodded in the direction of the entertainers. 'Probably waiting for the jugglers and acrobats.'

Pétronille took her twin by the hand and the girls scampered off, their black braids swaying as they zig-zagged through the crowd.

'Will my boy ever come back to me?' Yolande said. 'He still hasn't spoken a word. It's like that brigand ... as if he stole Anselme's mind.'

The usual wedge of dark hair covering one eye, Anselme was gazing at some place yonder with the intense stare of someone who is not quite right in his head. The lad had been Raoul's apprentice only a few days but my husband kept assuring me, and Yolande, that though he didn't speak, Anselme carried out his instructions with care and inherent skill. 'A born stonemason,' Raoul had said.

'Anselme's mind is still wounded, deep inside him,' I said. 'It just needs more time to heal.'

'Our rose-oil might help your boy, for its feeling of wellbeing,' Isa said, packing a vial into Yolande's basket, and waving away my friend with her offer of a coin.

'And we'll keep praying to the Blessed Virgin,' I said.

'Thank you both,' Yolande said, 'and thank Our Lord for your husband, Héloïse. I'm grateful he's taken on Anselme … to see my boy learning a good trade instead of hanging about the shop, unable to help me continue my husband's trade. Neither of us will ever be the fine tailor he was,' she went on with a rueful smile. 'People can tell the difference … can see tailoring isn't what *Dieu* intended for us.'

'As Anselme seems to have found his skill for masonry,' Isa said, 'one day God will let you know what He meant for you too, Yolande.'

'That's just it,' Yolande said. 'He has. I think I'd do well learning your midwifery art.' She looked at me, her dark eyes the brightest I'd seen them since before the outlaw attack. 'That is … if you'll teach me, Héloïse?'

I clapped my hands in glee. 'You'll start immediately, Apprentice Yolande … at the very next birth.'

Sergeant Drogan's wife came then, with a sore throat. Catèlena also had a new bruise beneath one eye, for which she didn't ask any treatment.

I gave her blackberry brambles boiled in wine for her throat. 'And some fresh goose salve,' I said, slipping it into her basket. 'For your face.'

Catèlena nodded, so afraid her husband might catch her buying from us that she dashed off in such a hurry she almost collided with Johan Miller.

'Poor girl. If that savage Drogan kills her too …' I said.

'Have you got something for them?' the miller said, standing before us, shoulders sagging, bags hanging beneath his eyes, the sorry-looking arc of his children all coughing.

I placed a honey drop into the children's outstretched palms. 'This should help their coughs … and even tastes sweet.'

'You could bake up a few mice too,' Isa said, 'to build their strength.'

Johan Miller nodded, his cheeks flushing as he asked his next question. 'Have you got anything for me too? A potion for … for the sadness? Since those thugs took my Jacqueline and my little Wanda, I can't … '

'I'm sorry, good miller,' Isa said, 'the only potion for grief is time.'

'Perhaps a new wife would help?' I said.

The miller swept an arm across the curve of his children, all sucking on honey drops. 'Yes, I hope to find a new one today … my brood could do with a mother.'

'Strange isn't it?' Isa said, as the children dawdled off after their father into the crowd. 'A woman can live her whole life without a man—providing she has a trade—but a man can't survive five minutes without a woman about his hearth.'

Business continued briskly and Isa and I had soon sold everything, with a healthy pile of deniers to show for it.

'Let's find Raoul and Morgane,' I said, folding our blanket.

'And get ourselves a tasty morsel of that pig.' Isa's face crinkled like a dried apple as she sniffed at the air.

'I should see how Merlin is first,' I said as we made our way towards the middle of the meadow where young boys were cranking the great spits, kicking away dogs that jumped and snapped at the roasting hogs. 'Just to be sure he's fully recovered.'

***

'Still not well, Merlin?' I asked the trader, slumped on a low stool and not looking at all well.

'Your cordial helped, Midwife Héloïse,' he said, mopping

his pale and sweaty brow. 'But I'm still hot and weak, and now these strange marks.' He pushed up his shirt sleeve to reveal rosy rings flourishing on both arms. And when I looked closely, I saw them too, on his neck. 'Do you know what they are? I've not seen them before.'

'Nor me,' I said, my fingertips tracing the circles, feeling for bumps. I stretched his arm out to my aunt. 'Isa?'

Isa squinted at the pink rings, and shook her head. 'Could be a rash from some plant or food, I don't know … not seen anything like it before.'

Further discussion of Merlin's rash was cut short as the black-smith's wife, plump as one of Poppa's best pies—accompanied by her daughter, Tifaine—shouldered Isa and me aside.

Jacotte's hair was tied up in a grubby handkerchief, circling a face that sagged in pudgy pockets. 'Make way, Mistress Tifaine and I have important business,' she said, her gaze roving hungrily across Merlin's display of silks in shades of saffron, lavender and apricot.

Marriage to Pierro Blacksmith had turned Jacotte from a beautiful young girl into a fat old woman before her time, and I was glad I couldn't say the same of my life wedded to Raoul.

'This one's pretty, Maman.' Tifaine pointed to a bolt of emer-ald silk glimmering in the sunlight.

'Not green, you dolt.' Her mother waved a flabby arm. 'Green's bad luck for a bride.' I recalled then, that Tifaine was to marry Sergeant Drogan's oldest brother at the next haymaking.

Jacotte's gaze came to rest on the lapis-coloured cloth. 'Now this, Tifaine, will be perfect for your bridal gown.' She looked up at Merlin. 'What's your best price for an ell, merchant?'

'You shall have it good and cheap,' Merlin said. 'Four sous for the ell, if you please.'

'Four sous?' Jacotte said. 'Nothing but thievery.'

Isa and I left her and Merlin haggling, and continued on through the mass of fair-goers. As I sidestepped to avoid a rowdy tangle of small boys and dogs, I stumbled over my skirts, and almost fell right onto our *Seigneur*. Renault de Fouville and his wife, la Comtesse Geneviève, along with several servants, were standing before the stall of a pock-marked pedlar.

Even bent over his cane, wads of fat sagging from his backside, our *Seigneur* commanded authority and power in that single look he turned on me.

'Pardon my clumsiness, *Sire*,' I said, bowing and holding up a palm as I backed away.

With a twist of his gilded cane, le Comte flicked imaginary dirt from where I'd brushed against his ermine-trimmed mantle. He lifted and shook a goatskin boot, which I'd not even touched, and went back to sniffing the *le camelot*'s potions.

Isa's shrewd, blackbird gaze was fixed on la Comtesse Geneviève, a woman with high cheeks, who wore a steeple headdress atop braids wound into coils over her ears. We'd not seen la Comtesse since they came to reside in *le château* to oversee the vingtain building and castle repairs, and my aunt wasn't the only person goggling at her, for we rarely saw such finery: the kirtle caught by a wide belt embroidered in reds, greens and yellows, her soft leather shoes dyed a sombre green to match her kirtle. But behind that noble garb, in the constant knotting of her handkerchief through fingers adorned with gold rings inset with gems red as glowing coals, I sensed agitation. It seemed la Comtesse's mind didn't know what her hands were doing.

Isa laid a quivering hand on my arm. 'By the hair of dead pigs, la Comtesse is with child.'

'We both know it can happen to an old woman we thought past her childbearing years, Isa. Why are you so surprised?'

It was common knowledge our lord's wife was no snip of a girl, and that her womb had stayed barren for all the seventeen summers she'd been wed to Renault de Fouville.

'La Comtesse will give birth to my heir this haymaking season,' Renault de Fouville was saying to the pedlar, as if to confirm our observations. 'I must ensure his safety.'

'And what of la Comtesse's safety?' Isa hissed.

'I understand, *Sire*,' the pedlar replied, a smile lighting his withered face. 'I have just the thing to ensure his safe passage into this world.'

From the rows of miracles stoppered in jars or hidden beneath cloths, the pedlar plucked a small wooden box, and pulled out a tiny ampoule filled with whitish liquid. 'The milk of the Virgin Mary,' he said. 'La Comtesse must keep it beside her in the birthing room. Demons will flee the moment they catch sight of it. And for you, my good lord, at an excellent price.'

Le Comte de Fouville hesitated, frowning and stroking his chin, one palm patting his belly as large as his wife's.

'Come now, *Sire*,' the pedlar said, 'what price would you put on the life of your heir?'

'We'll take the milk,' la Comtesse Geneviève said, removing several coins from a silk-covered purse.

'*Merci*, la Comtesse.' The pedlar bowed his head. 'And may you be delivered of a fine, healthy boy.'

'This is surely her last chance to birth an heir,' I said, my gaze following the elegant sweep of le Comte and his wife, the bustle of people parting to let them through. 'Without a living Fouville child it's no wonder they're desperate for the babe to survive. But placing their faith in a pedlar's trinket—surely the milk of a goat—rather than in the care of a good midwife? That I don't understand.'

'Oh but she does have a good midwife.' Isa and I swivelled around to Poppa's bright blue eyes and broad grin. 'I came to tell you just that, Isa. Le Comte installed some fancy midwife from Lyon in the castle yestermorn. She's to stay till after the heir's born.'

'By the Devil's balls, is that so?' Isa's voice dripped with scorn. 'Of course he'd never let Héloïse or me—Lucie's own midwives—near his heir, even though we're as skilled as any fancy city midwife, mayhap more skilled!' My aunt hesitated, as if to say something more, but pressed her lips together.

'Who cares?' I said with a shrug. 'We've got more than enough townswomen to birth. And I've no wish to put one foot in that gloomy-looking castle, and certainly not to birth le Comte's heir. Can you imagine what he'd do to me if something went wrong?'

In my mind's eye I saw myself being hanged until I was almost dead, then disemboweled, or burned at the stake.

As Poppa filled in Isa on the rest of the castle news, I glanced over the wares of the pedlar who'd sold the milk ampoule to la Comtesse Geneviève.

'Relics. Get your holy relic ... protection against all evil,' the man was calling. 'Fragments of Saint Catherine's fingernail, a piece of the bush from which the Lord spoke to Moses, the Angel Gabriel's feathers fallen in the Virgin's chamber during the Annunciation.

'Ah, good Mistress,' the pedlar said, catching my eye. 'I sense you're in need of my blessed water, collected myself from the Jordan.'

I glanced at the pedlar's frail and twisted legs. He'd have trouble walking out of this meadow, never mind getting anywhere near the Jordan River. 'If fools buy your so-called relics, sir, that's their business but I'm not so half-witted to be taken in by pretty stories only a child believes ... or a lord desperate for an heir.'

'You don't strike me as half-witted, Mistress. Besides, what a person *believes* he's buying is the important thing ... you should know that, as the wise-woman and midwife of Lucie.'

'How did you ...?' I stopped short. He could have spotted Isa and me selling our wares, or anyone could have told him.

'That's true,' I said with a sly smile, thinking of the spiced wine we'd sold only this morning as a hysterical sickness potion. 'But why do I need your holy water, sir?'

The pedlar's face darkened, his voice lowered as if he were sharing a great secret. 'Death stands behind you, Mistress. The crown of his head gleams in the very light of day in which you stand. You'll soon be questioning your faith and have great need of my holy water.'

'Is that so? Look about us, dear sir.' I gave him a sarcastic smile, waving an arm at the swarm of fair frolickers. 'The sun's shining, people are happy, having fun. I can't imagine a single reason to question my faith.'

'How about a lock of Mary Magdalene's hair then?' the pedlar went on, ignoring my arguments. 'Or drops of the water she used to wash Jesus's feet?' He held up a cork-stoppered clay vial.

'And I suppose that's the hammer that pounded the nails into the cross?' I gestured at a plain wooden hammer.

Le camelot smiled. 'No, Mistress, that's what I use to repair my old cart. Now, my last—and special—offer, just for you. A fragment of bone from the innocents slaughtered in Bethlehem.'

As the pedlar ran a gnarled thumb over the sliver of smoothed bone, I grasped my angel pendant between my own fingers. 'Thank you, sir, but this talisman is the only bone fragment I need for protection.'

Squinting at my pendant, *le camelot* reached out to touch it. 'Hmm, a fine piece of workmanship. The eyes gleam like … like …?'

'One is lapis, the other malachite,' I said, snatching it away from his fingers. 'But if you touch the eyes, they'll burn you. Only Saint Margaret's chosen ones … the women who can use its power to heal the sick and help birthings can touch them.'

I hoped the pedlar didn't notice the flush I felt rising to my cheeks; the blush of that lie I'd fabricated on the market-place when I was a young maid and Drogan had tried to take my pendant. A falsehood whose effectiveness still amazed me.

'Might then,' the pedlar said, his watery old eyes eager, 'your talisman be blessed by a saint? Or … oh!' He pressed a palm to his heart as if it were failing him, 'might it *be* a holy relic? The bone of a true saint?'

'Holy relic? Bone of a saint?' Alewife Rixende shrieked as she tramped past me, her daughters in tow. 'More like the bone of some dumb ass.'

I returned the alewife's sneer with an equal measure of scorn then, my voice whispery with mystique, I said: 'If I told you, or anyone, where this pendant comes from, that tale would travel faster than the wind. I'd be open to attack and theft wearing such a talisman. And if anyone ever stole it from me I'd feel … feel I'd lost my mother's protection.'

'*Oui*, Mistress, you're wise not to reveal the story to a soul,' the pedlar said, as if in absolute agreement with my reasoning, but failing to mask his hope that I'd reveal all. 'And if it truly *is* a holy relic, especially don't let that priest of yours know.' He gestured towards the black-robed Père Bernard, speaking with Renault de Fouville and his monk-brother, Physician Nestor in a tight little circle, all brandishing mugs of wine. 'Religious relics are such pilgrim pullers, the priest would claim it for his church. *Oui*, you're right to guard secret its value and identity, Mistress.'

Le camelot took a breath, eyes still agog. I almost couldn't resist his curiosity, but managed to turn around and wave him off with a small smile, leaving unquenched his meddlesome thirst for the legend of a bone-sculpted talisman.

XIII

As Isa and I wove through the gleeful crowd, I gave no more thought to the pedlar's ridiculous vision of Death hovering over my shoulder. Some people will spout any old rot just to get a sale.

'Hot sheep's feet! Cheese … fresh cheese!' the vendors cried, strolling about with their trays of food. 'Tasty pies stuffed with pork and raisins!' My nostrils quivered with the pungent smells.

Amongst the forest of booths I spotted Morgane's cinnamon-coloured braids and Raoul's horse-like mane. Raoul was looking over an array of gleaming knives while Morgane admired coloured ribbons and combs of polished ivory.

'They're so lovely, Maman.' Morgane picked up one of the combs as Isa began negotiating a price for leather flasks. 'Can I have one?'

'Certainly not,' Isa snapped, before I had a chance to say anything. 'Only rich nobles have the sous for such expensive objects.'

Tears filled Morgane's eyes and, with a broad wink, the merchant placed one of the combs beside Isa's leather flasks. My daughter drew in her breath, staring at the merchant as if she couldn't believe her good luck.

'With those magical eyes, little maid,' the merchant said, 'you're sure to have a handsome husband in a few years, who will buy you whatever your heart desires.'

Morgane's freckled cheeks reddened at his mention of her mismatched eyes, but she thanked the merchant, and held the comb—along with Crispen's wooden cat—to her chest as if fearful the man, or Isa, might snatch it back. In her other hand, she grasped Raoul's, and tugged us towards the entertainers and the roasting hogs.

We sat cross-legged on the grass with Yolande, Anselme and the twins, all of us tearing through the sizzling pork loin served on trenchers. Even old people like Isa, their teeth worn down to rotted stumps, sucked greedily at the pork crackling seasoned with garlic and rosemary.

Savouring this rare extravagance of fresh meat, the juice dribbling down my chin, I licked the delicious fat from my fingers as we watched the minstrels. Dressed in gipons of scarlet and black, with open sleeves over red chemises, they took up fife and drum to call everyone's attention.

More musicians took up lute and gittern and began singing those famous melodies in their strangely-accented voices. As they sang my favourite—the one about Arthur and Guinevere—I leaned across and kissed my husband's cheek, my lips leaving shiny grease traces across his sun-baked skin.

'How beautiful and tragic, isn't it, my strong and handsome King Arthur?' I winked at Raoul and we both smiled at Morgane—our fairy girl who took her name from that same tale.

'Your strong and handsome King,' Raoul said with a mock bow of his head, 'granting his queen her every wish.'

'A son then please, handsome King.'

'Ah, a son ... a son. Should we go and join them?' Raoul nodded at the young boys and girls holding hands and giggling as they headed for the shade of the woods, oblivious to the disapproving frowns of their parents, and the priest.

'Maybe there's already a son in here,' I said, patting my belly, my heart dancing at the thought that Saint Margaret might've answered my prayer. 'The moon was right, the night you returned from Florence.'

Raoul's smile warped the sun-dappled pattern on his cheeks and his lips met mine in a slippery kiss. Amidst the meadow's honest fragrance of spring flowers, I inhaled his scent: sweat, lingering dust from the building site, vestiges of ale and rich garlic pork.

Scarlet-clad jugglers came next to hold the crowd's eye, mischievous young boys darting about trying to distract them and bring their clubs crashing down. Dogs jumped through hoops and walked on their hind legs. They begged for coins, and bowed their thanks.

Acrobats turned dazzling wheels, and Morgane, Peronelle and Pétronille squealed with glee when the magician pulled a rose from behind Morgane's ear.

'My cat must be magical, Maman,' she said, waving about Crispen's little sculpture. 'And *he* made the flower go behind my ear.'

'Your cat can do whatever you want, poppet,' I said, Raoul and I both grinning like fools. 'If you believe it.'

A man who could fart at will, his arse emitting every imaginable animal noise from a frog to a boar, was met with squalls of laughter.

As we held our sides, aching with mirth, I glimpsed Alesi Stonemason striding towards us.

'Sorry to drag you from your family, Raoul,' the Master Mason said, 'a section of the vingtain wall has collapsed ... would you mind taking a look at it with me? It shouldn't take long to find the problem.'

'Of course,' Raoul said, jumping to his feet with a squeeze of my hand.

'Come back soon, Papa,' Morgane said, 'or you'll miss all the fun.'

With a tweak of his daughter's braids, Raoul strode off with Alesi Stonemason, and the patter began—the jokes and stories which the entertainers shrewdly interrupted before each punchline to collect coins.

Whilst all this was going on, the players had been setting up a small stage, and suddenly a little wooden Noah on strings appeared. The twittering crowd fell silent as a white-clad God floated down onto the stage, and the play began.

'You must build an ark, Noah,' God commanded.

'Why should I need an ark, God?'

'Because great wickedness has come to the world,' God said. 'So I have decided to wipe mankind from the face of the earth. You must build this ark for your family, Noah, to escape the catastrophic flood that will destroy every living thing on earth.'

'Every living thing, God?' Noah said. 'But then it will be the end of the world.'

'That is right, Noah,' God said, 'now I command you to bring into your ark two of all living creatures, one male, one female.'

God disappeared and, as Noah started hammering at bits of wood, his wife bounced onto the stage.

'What the Devil's arse are you up to, Noah?'

'Can you not see, wife? I am building an ark to escape the end of the world that God is sending us, in the form of a great flood.'

'But you haven't finished bringing in the harvest, Noah. Or repaired my kitchen stools. I forbid you to build an ark till you have finished your jobs, you cod-wit. End of the world or not!'

The audience laughed as Noah and his wife began slapping and punching each other.

Lightning appeared—a great slash of yellow as wide as the whole stage—striking down Noah's wife who collapsed in a tangled heap of strings.

The curtain closed as the crowd cheered, whistled and applauded. Even the cold-faced Père Bernard clapped together his spidery hands from where he sat in a high velvet chair with le Comte, his wife and Physician Nestor.

'The end of the world,' Isa said with a sigh. 'By the Devil's blood, I hope I'm not still on this earth to witness that.'

***

The roasted pigs were gnawed down to bone, the shadows long, and people started gathering reluctant children and dogs and straggling off home. 'Can't see Crispen anywhere,' I said, hooking my basket over one arm and helping Isa to her feet.

'Don't fret, he's a grown boy and will find his own way home,' Isa said, her words trailing off as a man staggered towards us. My heart lurched as I realised it was our trader friend. Merlin stopped a little way from us. He swayed, sank to his knees and fell face down onto the grass.

People started walking around and over him, muttering.

'Ha, traders can't hold ... drink ...'

'... blame Alewife Rixende ...'

As Isa, Morgane and I hurried towards the crumpled figure, those same passersby shrank from the trader, gagging and clapping their hands over their noses. Once we reached Merlin, I understood why: his smell wasn't that of an unwashed drunk but the sickly sweet stench of rotted apples.

'Help me turn him over,' I said to Isa and Morgane, 'so we can see what could be wrong.'

'Might be the strawberry tongue sickness,' Sara said. 'But it sure don't smell like it.' Drogan's mother wrinkled her nose and covered her mouth.

'The Devil's pointy ears!' Poppa said. 'That ain't no strawberry tongue illness.'

The crowd began chattering, each offering his own diagnosis of Merlin's affliction.

'Trader ... ague from foreign land ...'

'... ate something rotten ...'

The barber-surgeon stepped forward. 'Suppose I'll have to help,' he said, with a great sigh. 'Before you charlatans kill the man with some useless potion.'

'Useless pot—?' I began, the barber-surgeon's words flaring my temper.

'Let's just get this man onto his back,' Isa cut in.

We each took one of Merlin's arms, the barber-surgeon lifting his legs, but as soon as we tried to turn him, the trader screamed so loudly that we dropped him.

'The Devil's piss pot!' Isa cursed, 'I never smelled such a sickness.'

'Nor I,' the barber-surgeon said, crossing himself.

'I don't dare touch him again,' I said, 'and cause him more pain.'

The people gathered around us were still babbling on, but keeping clear of Merlin's rotten-apple stench. Père Bernard seemed unusually lost for words, the priest's lips more pinched than ever.

Amidst the trader's pitiful shrieks, Isa, the barber-surgeon and I managed to roll him over and, where the rosy rings had been, Merlin's neck and arms were now stained with boils the colour of aubergine.

The crowd flinched and gasped as one. Mothers pushed small children behind their kirtles, as I pulled a vial of rose-water from my basket, soaked a cloth and dabbed it across Merlin's sweaty brow. The barber-surgeon had disappeared and Isa and I stared uncomprehendingly at each other, then down to the writhing Merlin.

'Stay quiet, Merlin,' I said, 'we'll take care of you.'

'What're those black boils?' Sergeant Drogan said.

'Never seen anything like them,' his mother said.

'Looks to me as if something, or someone, cursed this trader,' Nica said, her hooded stare piercing mine.

'Whatever ailment has struck this man down, Nica,' I said, 'I need to get him back to our cot so we can take proper care of him.'

'Make way!' a voice boomed, and I looked up to the stern face of Nestor de Fouville, barging—as best a person could barge with an inturned foot—through the knot of people.

'Move aside, you two.' The monk-physician flicked his cane at Isa and me. 'I am the physician here ... by far the most qualified.' Holding a silk handkerchief over his mouth and nose, Nestor stared down at the groaning Merlin.

'What ails him?' someone asked, and everyone looked to the physician.

Physician Nestor's brow knotted in a frown. 'Mmn,' he muttered. 'Malalignment of the planets ... stars ... imbalance of the humours ...'

It was obvious the physician had no better idea of Merlin's sickness than we did.

'I've not seen it myself,' said a big man I recognised as the leader of the group of players. 'But we've heard from other travellers that a deadly pestilence has reached our southern shores.' His strident voice—and fearsome words!—silenced the people.

'It's not swine plague, well-water plague or white plague,' a woman player said, 'but a pestilence marked by these angry-looking black swellings.' She pointed to Merlin. 'It's said they grow to the size of a pigeon's egg.'

'There's rumour this miasma comes from the lands of Arabia,' said another player, an old man with silvery threads of hair. 'And a death toll so great that all India—half the world—is gone.'

'They reckon it stinks worse than sun-rotted corpses,' a young acrobat chimed in, gesturing towards Merlin. 'Just like him.'

'Are you certain these are not just simple carters' tales?' the priest asked.

'Well I can't be sure,' the players' leader said. 'But many holy men over the seas—men such as yourself, Père, the wandering friars, preachers and pardoners—are supposedly relishing this destruction. They're saying God has sent His angels to wipe the wicked from the earth.'

'The Pope's physician has urged him to flee Avignon,' the wispy-haired old man said, 'but our Holy One refuses to leave his palace.'

'I too have heard of a pestilence from far to the East,' one the merchants piped up. 'Rumoured to come from the Mongols, into the merchant city of Caffa.'

'They say this miasma will keep spreading north on the winds,' the player woman said. 'And once it reaches Paris, France will be King Edward's for the taking.'

'Those barbarians won't take our soil,' a farmer cried. 'France will never have an English king.'

The fair-goers, so cheery just an hour gone, were stunned into terrified silence. How quickly things can change.

'Seems le Comte de Fouville has vanished, along with his wife,' I said, nodding towards the tall chairs where they'd been sitting.

'The barber-surgeon, and Nestor too,' Isa said, over the people's yammering. 'Some physician that one is.'

'Are you sure it's this pestilence they're talking of?' Poppa asked as we struggled, with the help of several fair-goers, to lift Merlin into his own cart.

'No,' Isa said, without a trace of the wry banter with which she usually addressed her friend. 'We don't know for certain this pestilence has come to Lucie ... yet.'

May-June in the Year of Our Lord
1348
Lucie-sur-Vionne

XIV

'**Merlin's dead!**' **I cried**. Raoul was still away at the vingtain site with Alesi Stonemason so Isa, Morgane and I had taken the trader's horse to reach our cot, hitched to the cart in which his fresh corpse now lay.

But there wasn't a moment to think or grieve over Merlin Lemarchand, as the tortured cries coming from the cot splintered my skin like shards of ice: the same cries as Merlin's.

'Who the Devil's arse is that?' Isa said.

'It's Crispen!' Morgane said, as we hurried inside.

I knelt beside the pallet and the writhing Crispen.

Blessed Virgin, not him too!

'He hasn't got Merlin's black boils,' Morgane said, 'but he smells the same.' She wrinkled her nose. I handed her and Isa strips of cloth, which we tied across our noses against his stench, and Isa set more rosemary and juniper burning to sweeten the terrible odour.

'Try and calm yourself, Crispen,' I said, wiping damp cloths across his face. 'We're going to take care of you.' But Raoul's apprentice, yelling, sweating and gasping for breath, showed no awareness of my words.

'Not in all my years have I smelt such a ghastly thing,' Isa said, as Morgane built up the fire. 'Like fish left for days in a hot sun. Give him a little poppy-juice, Héloïse; I'll boil up some Saint John's wort leaves too, for his pain.' She set the kettle on the trivet to heat as I wiped away the blood that had begun trickling from his nose. Another drizzle of blood appeared. I wiped again. And again.

'Merlin didn't have this nose-bleeding,' Morgane said. 'Is it the same sickness, Isa?'

Isa's brow beetled as she stirred the boiling leaves. 'Satan's blood, I have no idea what ails him.'

I lifted Crispen's head and tried to get him to drink the pain-easing poppy juice, but before anything could pass into his mouth, a stream of blood shot from it.

I gasped, recoiling from the apprentice as Raoul strode into the cot. He looked down at Crispen, stopped still and inhaled a sharp breath. He held it in, his eyes wide, as if his own mallet had struck him down.

'Blessed Saint Etienne help us ... not Crispen too.' Raoul gestured outside, to where we'd left the trader's body in his cart. 'I saw ... saw M-Merl ... black boils ... '

His face turned the hue of bone, Raoul grabbed Morgane with a quivering hand and shoved her towards the open door. 'Get outside, Morgane ... away from Crispen.'

'What's wrong with Crispen?' Morgane sobbed. 'He was laughing with his friends just this morning at the fair.'

'Héloïse, you and Isa must get away from Crispen too.' Raoul ignored Morgane. 'And don't look into his eyes.'

Startled at Raoul's panicked voice—louder, coarser than ever—I stepped away from Crispen. 'What ... but why? Raoul, we don't know it's the same sickness as Merlin ... we're not even sure what ailed the trader.'

'You know we can't ignore a sick man,' Isa said. 'Especially not your apprentice.'

'The pestilence! Get away, now!' Raoul was screeching like a lunatic.

He breathed hard, ploughed one hand through his rampant hair, still restraining Morgane with the other. 'Take Blanche to the barn and stay out there with her,' he snapped, more harshly than I'd ever heard him speak to his little Flamelock. 'I need to speak to your mother.'

'But I'm Maman's apprentice, Papa. I want to help her and Isa care for Crispen.'

'Do not disobey me!'

Morgane scooped up Blanche and, clutching the real cat and Crispen's wooden one, she ran outside into the rain that had started to fall in slow, fat drops.

'Satan's forked tongue!' Isa cursed, as more blood spurted from Crispen's mouth and the boy went stiff, his head arched, his eyes rolled back. Spit leaked from his rigid jaw, and we all looked on in helpless horror as, seconds later, Raoul's apprentice fell limp and breathed his last. We'd not even had a chance to think about fetching the priest.

Isa and I covered our masked mouths; Raoul's was still agape, his eyes brimming with the terror of someone who's come face to face with an unearthly monster in the woods.

'We need to get him outside,' Raoul said. 'Get rid of the contagion.'

'You think this is the same as Merlin's sickness, Raoul?' I said. 'But how do you know about it?' Tying a strip of linen across his nose and mouth, and rummaging about in the lean-to for an old blanket, my husband still ignored me. 'Raoul, explain please, rather than just barking orders at us.'

'I will, Héloïse ... but let me get Crispen out of our home first ... away from us.' Without touching Crispen, he rolled the blanket around the boy's body, and I was shocked at the lack of love and grief he showed for the apprentice who'd been as akin to Raoul as a son. It was so unlike my tender and kind-hearted husband.

'Can Isa and I help?' I said.

'You keep away!' Struggling and panting, pearls of sweat rolling down his furrowed brow, Raoul dragged Crispen outside into the steadily-falling rain.

'Satan's blood, what is this sickness?' Isa said, when Raoul finally came back inside, and I handed him a rose-water-soaked cloth to cleanse his face and hands.

Raoul took the jug of ale, his shaking hand filling three beakers. He motioned for Isa and me to sit with him around the table.

'Before we fetch the sexton,' he said, 'I need to ...' He exhaled a long breath. 'To gather my wits ... and to explain.'

He swallowed the ale in one gulp and poured himself another full beaker.

'I didn't tell you the real reason I left Florence early,' he began. 'Or how Toubie really died, because I didn't want to frighten you unnecessarily.'

He looked from Isa to me, taking my hands, a rough thumb stroking my clasped ones, his eyes bright and shiny in the hearth flames, like a mad person's. 'I've been praying—as Merlin Lemarchand prayed—that this pestilence was only a disease of outlanders; that it would stay in the south and never come this far north to Lucie-sur-Vionne.'

'When Merlin fell ill at the fair,' I said, 'the players spoke about a pestilence in the south.'

Raoul nodded. 'The same terrible pestilence that killed Toubie, Merlin and Crispen. The sickness that came to Florence after the winter.'

As Raoul released my hands, a worm of worry uncoiled within me, and I grasped my pendant, rubbing the angel between thumb and forefinger.

'Florence was already weakened by yesteryear's famine, when half its citizens perished,' Raoul went on, 'which is why I found work so easily, but still ...' He swallowed more ale. 'They're calling it the Great Mortality, a new pestilence so deadly it might be caught by a simple glance, or—since it flies through the air—just stepping into a victim's house.' He took a quick breath. 'And if the fever comes on you, you'd best make your will because Death comes swiftly. The soothsayers predict this miasma is so deadly there won't be a single soul left on earth.' He finished his ale. 'The people of Florence were dying without last rites ... buried without prayers! Can you imagine their fear, dying like that?'

My throat tightened as the pedlar's words clanged in my mind like the passing bells.

Death stands behind you, Mistress ... the crown of his head gleams in the very light of day in which you stand. You shall soon be questioning your faith ...

'But Crispen had no black boils,' I said, as the rain fell harder, heavy unrelenting drops that slashed at the thatch and ripped the leaves from tree branches. A fast drumming that beat in time with my heart.

'Some don't get the black boils,' Raoul said. 'But another kind, where the miasma takes hold quicker, and everything—breath, sweat, blood, piss and black shit—smells just as foul.'

'Blessed Virgin have mercy on us.' Isa made the sign of the cross.

'The talisman will protect me ... protect us all,' I said, still gripping the little bone angel.

Raoul let out a high-pitched cackle. 'Don't fool yourself, Héloïse. Your talisman might comfort women in childbirth, but you can't believe it has any special protective powers, surely?'

'It does,' I said, 'if you believe in it strongly enough.'

'The ancients from Egypt believed malachite has protective powers,' Isa said, gesturing at the pendant's luminous eyes. 'Their slaves mined it and never caught plague.'

'Well I'd rather not trust my family's lives to old charms and legend. And if you and Héloïse have any sense, nor will you. That's why,' Raoul said, lifting the ale jug again, but seeing it was empty, thunked it back onto the table, 'I'm asking you, Héloïse, not to go near or treat any more pestilence victims. Because *Dieu* only knows there will be many more like Merlin and Crispen.'

'Who cared for Toubie, Raoul?' I said, my steady gaze holding his. 'You and Crispen would've had to be near him; touch him. How is that different to me treating townsfolk?'

'We didn't know Toubie had the pestilence till it was too late,' Raoul said. 'I could hardly throw my son, the very last of

Crispen's blood family, onto the street.'

'You might be right to fear this contagion,' I said, 'but no decent wise-woman can ignore the sick. For two years, while you were away, I had to make sure we had an income, so how can you blame me now for wanting to do my job? And not forgetting the oath I swore on Ava's soul.'

'Maybe you're right, and all the blame should be mine,' Raoul said. 'For seeking work so far from home, and forcing you to work hard; to become so ... so unwomanly. For that you can reproach me but this is different, Héloïse.'

'Yes, this pestilence seems a deadly ailment,' Isa said, a gnarled hand twining through the silver braid that had slid from beneath her cap. My aunt spoke softly, as if talking about it too loudly might make it real. Because it didn't seem real, rather some unbelievable outlander story Raoul had brought home. But Toubie had died. Then Merlin. Now Crispen. 'Besides, if it spreads, as pestilences are known to,' she added, 'the work ahead will be beyond any of our powers or treatments. And certainly beyond the powers of our angel talisman.'

'I can't believe you're taking Raoul's side,' I said. 'You swore the same vow as me, Isa.'

'There are no sides,' Raoul cut in. 'I'm loath to go against the oath you took on your mother's soul; on your life's calling. But to save my family I'm forbidding you, Héloïse ... that's if it's not already too late.'

I flinched. 'What do you mean too late?'

'I'll wager you both tried to care for Merlin?' Raoul looked from me to Isa and back to me. 'And since you brought Crispen into our home too, this pestilence is likely already here. And it will kill us all.'

'But it was you who brought Merlin into our home,' I said, my pulse quickening, the blood in my veins heating. 'And Crispen.'

'But I didn't know—' Raoul started.

'After the death of poor Jehanne and her babe I swore never to have anything more to do with the woodcutter-sexton,' I said, snagging my cloak from the hook and motioning towards the corpses outside in the rain, 'but we should get Poncet Batier to remove them.'

'No, I'll go,' my husband said. 'I won't have you going out in this downpour.'

I looked at Raoul. So he had understood me; how Isa and I could never ignore a sick person. My taut shoulders relaxed a little; my spirits lifting.

'Any decent husband would protect his wife from brutes such as Poncet Batier,' Raoul went on. 'As any good wife would protect her family from sickness.'

And as he opened the door and stomped outside into the rain lashing like a punishing switch, I saw I'd been wrong—there wasn't a trace of understanding in Raoul's iron-hard eyes.

XV

'**I**'m away to the building site, Héloïse.' Raoul climbed down the ladder from the roof where he'd been removing moss from the thatch as he did every spring. He looked over to me, planting our beets, carrots and beans. 'The Master Mason's keen to restart work on the vingtain. Besides, there's more work than we thought, since le Comte wants not only the crumbling curtain wall repaired, but the entire castle.'

'At least you'll be assured years of building work in Lucie,' I said.

'*Voilà*,' Morgane said, 'so you won't have to leave us and go journeying for work.'

The rain, falling steadily all week since Merlin and Crispen's terrible passing, had stopped the building, but this morning the sun had broken through the clouds. It shone the plashes in the fields a dull pewter, and burnished the slurries on the road.

'Thank the Virgin Noah's Great Flood isn't for us after all,' Isa said, resting back on her ankles from where she knelt planting parsley, chamomile and mint. She tilted her wrinkled face heavenward and left earthy dabs on her brow as she crossed herself.

'Neither Noah's Great Flood, or a pestilence, it seems,' I said, glancing at Raoul as he filled his leather water flask from the pail. 'No one else in Lucie has been struck down with Merlin or Crispen's sickness, thank the Lord, so maybe they were just two unlucky ones, and we'll see no more.'

Neither Raoul nor I had mentioned our rough words of the day they'd died. I put it down to our mourning for Crispen and Toubie, which left us with little heart for dispute. I didn't say to Raoul I was quietly relieved—a little triumphant even—that his fear of this pestilence spreading through Lucie-sur-Vionne seemed unfounded. Raoul said nothing either, but of course no man would admit to his wife he might've been wrong.

'Oh there will be more victims, Héloïse,' Raoul said.

In deference to his heartache for Crispen and Toubie; the deep grief that had made him so curt and cold this last week, I didn't answer back, but like the first gust of a north wind, the coolness blew up between us again.

I kept my gaze low, and began tending our sprouting dye-plants: the weld, the woad to make blue dye for our kirtles, and the madder whose prickly leaves faded Morgane's freckles, and from which we made red dye and a tonic to ease childbirth.

'That Godless pestilence won't get us, Papa,' Morgane said, deheading the daisies she'd plucked from which we'd make fever-cooling tea, or dry for fleabane. She laid Crispen's wood-carving beside her, while Blanche crouched on her other side, sharp eyes alert for fluttering or scurrying creatures. 'Maman's talisman and Crispen's cat are protecting us.'

'*Pfft.*' Raoul turned his palms skyward and threw her a despairing look. 'Don't trust your life to charms and pendants, Morgane … whatever your mother says. The only way to avoid the pestilence is to stay away from it.'

'Yes, Papa,' Morgane said, and I thought her far more dutiful than I, as Raoul's words chafed me like the roughest cloth.

Once my husband strode off along the woodland road, his satchel, which I'd packed with bread, boiled eggs and goat's cheese, slung over one shoulder, I went to the barn to hitch Merlin's mare to the cart. 'Fetch my work-basket from the lean-to, Morgane,' I said, 'we must visit our patients.'

'And be a poppet and put some cheese into my basket,' Isa said. 'I promised it to the lepers.'

As Merlin's horse clopped along the higher, busier road along which the other outlying cottages stood, Morgane and I waved back to Isa standing amongst the white-seeded poppies from which we made the pain-easing juice—the potion that had done little to relieve Merlin and Crispen's pain. No, something far more potent was needed, if such a medicament even existed, to ease that unspeakable agony.

Despite the sun's warmth I shivered, as we passed the workers clad in their homespun cloth bent over weeding, and the farmers' cows put out to pasture, recalling their terrible suffering and harrowing deaths. I crossed myself and sent a prayer to Our Lady that I'd never again witness such a sickness. Since Raoul's tales of the pestilence in Florence I'd tried to imagine the same disaster happening here in Lucie but my mind just couldn't hold it.

In Alix's garden, her toothless mother was sowing beans. Nica's oldest girls were helping, while the smaller children charged around playing hide and seek. Swaddled to his mother's back, baby Loup slept, whilst Alix and Nica captured wild swarming bees for their own skeps.

After Nica's milk-sapping allegation, I'd not returned to see Alix or the baby but Poppa assured Isa that the mother was well and baby Loup was thriving on an abundance of milk.

'A fine mare you got there, Midwife Héloïse,' Farmer Donis called, from where he was marking his sheep.

'Her name's Merlinette,' Morgane said. 'After our friend, Merlin who died.'

'Since the poor trader died in our home,' I explained, ignoring Alix and Nica's stares that seemed to accused me of killing Merlin just to get his horse and cart, 'we inherited his belongings. I'd never seen the need before, but after only a week, I wonder how we ever got on without a horse and cart.'

Once on la place de l'Eglise, I hitched the horse to the Roman fountain post, and as Merlinette drank from the trough, I stood and watched my husband at his work. Amidst the noise and dust, and apprentices transporting quarry rock and mixing mortar, Raoul's strapping body tightened as he and Anselme guided a large stone into place to raise the vingtain wall. His brow knotted, and I could see he was explaining to his new apprentice how to choose each stone depending not only on size and thickness but also on colour, luminosity and the way it matched neighbouring ones. I recalled that wondrous glimpse of the stonemason sculpting Our Lady and felt again that first flicker of our love—strong as the protective wall he was building.

Just as seamless ... not the slightest fissure.

'Come and play the flea game, Morgane,' Pétronille cried from the tailor's shop. 'See how much better I am than Peronelle.'

My daughter might be eager to learn the healer-midwife skills, but the chance of playing with friends won every time, and she skipped off towards the twins.

Yolande was sitting on the bench below the tailor shop's scissors and needle sign, struggling to run a fine-tooth, delousing comb through her daughters' raven-coloured hair. But the twins kept tugging away, more interested in seeing who could pick off the most fleas the quickest.

The previous week's rain had brought an infestation beyond any I could remember, and from the trail of maddening welts, it was evident they'd feasted on the tender flesh of Pétronille and Peronelle's arms.

'How many did you catch?' Pétronille asked, as Morgane sat beside them on the bench.

'Ten at least, probably more.'

'Only ten?' her sister said with a sneer. 'I got twice ten. How many have you got, Morgane?'

'No fleas at all,' Morgane said. 'Maman washes them off me all the time.'

Pétronille giggled. 'You're a silly-wit. Even if your maman washes them off, they just jump back on straight away.'

'And so she washes them away, again and again. Maman's always washing me ... she says a clean body and clean clothes means less sickness.'

'Then your skin will peel right off you,' Peronelle said, and the twins exploded in giggles. 'Everyone knows that happens if a person washes too much.'

Peronelle pulled up her smock, where she found three more fleas crawling up her leg. One of them she caught, but the other two leapt away.

'You are so slow,' Pétronille said in the mocking tone she often used with her twin, as if thirty extra minutes of life had given her a world more knowledge. 'You let two get away.'

'My fleas only got away because they're so strong … stronger than yours,' Peronelle said. 'And since they've been sucking on my blood, that means my blood's also stronger than yours.'

'You're not only slow, but stupid,' Pétronille chided. 'My blood's the same strong … er, strongness as yours … it has to be, because twins have the same blood. Isn't that right, Midwife Héloïse?'

'I know all about twins,' Morgane chipped in, proud as always to show off her midwifing knowledge. 'Twins are made because there's too much of the man and woman's seed for only one child so when the stars shine in the right place, it's mixed to make two babes … two babes with the same blood.'

'Told you,' Pétronille said to her sister. 'Same blood, same fleas, same everything.'

With indulgent smiles, I left the girls debating blood and twins, and headed with Yolande, my new midwife apprentice, for the baker's shop to see Sibylle.

***

Sweat glistened on the baker's reddened cheeks as he pumped on the bellows, his sleeves rolled up. Inhaling the warm and floury scent, Yolande and I plucked loaves from our baskets and handed them to the baker's apprentice, who slid them into the oven.

'Thank the Blessed Virgin you're here, Midwife Héloïse,' Sibylle said, scuttling into the shopfront.

'What's happened?' I laid a palm on her slight belly mound. 'You're bleeding?'

'Nothing's wrong,' Sibylle said. 'But after so many slipping from me, I'm sick with worry, all day long.' As always, the baker's wife barely paused for breath, her words spilling from her like ale from Rixende's tankards. 'Each time the blood started I knew I'd lost it but still I tried to hold it inside me. But none of them wanted me, Midwife. Will this one reject me too?'

Before I could reply, she kept on: 'You know my husband and I've prayed for a live babe eight long years but God refuses to give us one. Just one!' Her eyes glistened with tears. 'If God intends this for me, I wish He'd stop quickening me then taking it away ... it just makes the mourning worse.'

'I'm sure our Lord doesn't want to punish you,' Yolande said in her soft and steady voice, which seemed to soothe Sibylle a little; to stop her gabbling on like a frightened goose.

I'd tried every remedy I knew, including a little-known tincture of bee pollen and another of powdered boar's testicles. And whenever I came across a mandrake root, I'd pass it to Sibylle with a wink. But even the effigy of an aroused husband hadn't helped her womb hold a babe.

'People don't think you've had a child,' Sibylle went on, wringing her white-knuckled hands. 'But I can tell you, mine were no less than infants who drew breath ... I gave them life, nourishment ... held them in my womb just as if they were in my arms. But they were buried as easily as the rags of monthly courses.'

'That's enough now, Sibylle,' I said, delving into my basket for the sage and wild tansy. 'You're well over the most dangerous time when a babe is apt to fall out, but this might reassure you. Drink a small amount often and I'll have every reason to believe you'll birth a healthy babe not long after the haymaking.'

'I pray you're right this time,' the baker's wife said, as she and

Yolande made the sign of the cross. 'It's good of you to worry for me ... and visit me so often. I don't care an empty eggshell what the mean-spirited folk say, I don't believe you've a shadow of badness in you.'

'Just try not to worry so, Sibylle,' I said. 'Your moods will affect the babe.'

I stopped myself telling her that a distressed mother could cause malformations or unsightly birthmarks, which would only cause her even more torment.

Yolande opened the bakery door and as we made to leave, I caught the sound of moaning from the blacksmith's shop next door.

'Someone's in terrible pain?' Yolande asked.

'Sounds like Jacotte,' I said, 'I'll go and see what ails her.'

'The blacksmith's wife's been poorly for two days,' the baker said. 'Some belly thing ... ate bad fish maybe.'

'I'd stay away if I were you,' Sibylle said, gesturing at the gleaming black stallion tethered to the fountain post beside Merlinette. 'Since the barber-surgeon came down with the fever yestermorn, Physician Nestor's been coming to treat Jacotte. And we all know what physicians think of the medicaments of a healer woman, especially ...'

Sibylle's unspoken words hung in the air like the stink of the butcher's rotting pigs' feet.

Especially the medicaments of a non-born bastard.

'A physician as highly-trained as Nestor de Fouville charges hefty fees,' Yolande said. 'I'm surprised the blacksmith can afford him.'

I made a sour face. 'I suppose some folks would pay a small fortune to avoid calling me.'

'If people are stupid enough to waste their hard-earned sous,' Sibylle said, 'that's their problem. But I reckon there's not much sickness up at the castle for Nestor to treat ... he'd be eager for work down here in the town.'

Another agonising cry pierced the air. I recalled those same cries of Merlin Lemarchand and Crispen and a shiver scurried up my arms.

***

'What do you want here, Midwife?' Pierro Blacksmith's stare, through the edged-open door, was icy as winter.

'I know your wife's never liked me,' I said, 'but I've come to offer my help.'

'We don't need your help, Physician Nestor's here.' Jacotte let out another scream, and the blacksmith turned and hurried back into the shop's dimness.

Cloud had shrouded the westward hills in a fog as thick as pea broth, and I was about to leave when, around the physician's bulk, I caught a glimpse of Jacotte lying on the blacksmith's work table. Her sweat-drenched smock clung to her large body, which spilled over the table sides. Tifaine held her mother's limp hand. In their concern for Jacotte, nobody paid me any attention.

I glimpsed Tifaine's dress for her marriage to Drogan's oldest brother, cut out but swept aside to make room on the table. Merlin Lemarchand's exquisite lapis-coloured silk now lay heaped on the dusty blacksmith's floor.

As Physician Nestor stepped aside to reach into his bag, I winced. Jacotte was covered in twitching leeches, their sucking parts embedded in her dense flesh. Then I clamped my hand over my mouth to stop myself crying out, for her neck and arms were spotted with the same rosy rings as Merlin's.

'Your wife is a large woman, so I must take a decent amount of blood to draw out the poison and restore the balance of her humours,' Physician Nestor was saying. 'And being born under Aquarius today should be ideal for leech-bleeding. But to determine when your wife might recover, I need to study the position of the planets at the time she fell ill.' The blacksmith kept his place beside the physician, nodding deferentially.

'If she is not improved by nightfall, you must purge and fast her,' Nestor said as he removed and rinsed the engorged creatures and dropped the writhing lobes into his leather pouch. 'Here's a receipt for a bowel-opening tincture.'

When he began packing his bag, the blacksmith and Tifaine thanking him profusely, I ducked back onto the market-place. By the time the physician came limping on his cane, out to his horse, fat splotches of rain had started to splay the dust of the vingtain worksite.

'Move out of my way please, Midwife. I must be gone.' Nestor de Fouville dismissed me with a wave of an embroidered glove.

'We've seen this same illness recently, Physician Nestor,' I said. 'You remember the trader who fell ill at the Spring Fair, and died not long afterwards? I believe it's a pestilence.'

He placed his good foot in the stirrup as leverage to hoist up the crippled one. A physician of high status, the sumptuary laws allowed him extra luxury but I was certain Nestor only wore such finery—the silver threaded belt, golden spurs and purple gown with fur-trimmed hood—to detract attention from his inturned foot.

The saddle leather creaked as he settled his rump, and wheeled his horse so carelessly that a rain-dampened dust clod splattered my kirtle.

'The rosy rings on Jacotte's body are the same as on that trader,' I insisted. 'It's the same pestilence; the one they say comes from the East. I'm certain of it.'

'Are you saying I don't know my profession, Midwife? Ten years of study at the renowned medical faculty of Montpellier University? *Ten years* and you claim to know better?'

'You might've read a hundred books,' I said, defending myself boldly, 'and studied a thousand cases, but you've barely touched a living patient compared to the many I have cared for. Your job might be preventing illness, but mine is curing it.'

With a shake of his head, Nestor flicked the reins and trotted off across the market square at such a pace he almost ran down a knot of vingtain workers heading into the tavern to take cover from the rain.

An icy sweat broke out on my brow, beads of it—mixed with raindrops—coursing down my cheeks. I stroked Merlinette's muzzle, more to calm myself than the mare that, despite the drizzle, was quite serene.

As I hoisted myself up onto the cart, I began to shiver. Was Raoul right, and the pestilence *was* spreading through Lucie? Should I heed his warning and stay away from its victims, or follow my calling and my vow, and try to help them?

I grasped the horse's reins in one hand, my pendant in the other, willing to me its strength, comfort and counsel.

XVI

'Hear those screams?' Raoul heard one of the carpenters say. 'Same pestilence has struck the blacksmith's wife as what killed Raoul Stonemason's trader friend and his apprentice.' Raoul turned towards the carpenter and this talk of the pestilence, which was crackling the tavern air like the summer lightning cleaving across the town.

The Au Cochon Tué tavern was the oldest of Lucie-sur-Vionne's buildings apart from the church. But whereas the newly-renovated Saint Antoine's stood tall and proud with its straight lines and angles, the tavern was a low thing squatting beneath its thatch. The timbers were bowed, its front as protruding as the bellies of the men—and Alewife Rixende's husband—who took too much ale there.

'Keep paying, keep drinking,' Alewife Rixende said with a lusty grin. The vingtain workers threw down handfuls of deniers as she thumped tankards of ale onto the large tables.

As Raoul took in this news of Jacotte's sickness, the tavern's stench of rotten food and dog piss rising from the rushes—something he'd barely noticed before—overcame him.

How cramped we all are, he thought; the same closeness that had spread the miasma in Florence, and Raoul felt his breath short and sharp in his throat as if he couldn't get in enough air. He suddenly wanted to be out of the tavern but there were so many workers crowded inside, sheltering from the storm, he'd have a struggle to get through them. Not to mention the clusters blocking the doorway

'Jacotte's got the same black boils as your trader friend,' the baker said to Raoul. 'And stinks as bad as he did at the Spring Fair ... so bad Sibylle and I could smell her from the bakery all this morning.'

'Squealing like a hog at the slaughter, she is,' the butcher said. He pressed a fingertip to his ear. 'Listen, you can even hear her over the rain.'

Raoul certainly couldn't ignore Jacotte's screams. They seeped in through the cracked-open tavern windows and his chest tightened with the same terror as the day Toubie had fallen ill. Then Merlin and Crispen. Beside him, Anselme remained silent, though Raoul sensed the lad could guess his thoughts. His heart beating fast, he signalled to his apprentice and they stood, and started trying to push their way through the wall of bodies towards the door.

But after only a few steps, Raoul knew escape from the tavern was useless, and he and Anselme squashed back onto a bench.

'Not a thing that fancy physician can do for the smithy's wife,' the baker said, as another scream pierced Raoul's ears. 'Been at the blacksmith's these last two days but Jacotte doesn't sound one bit recovered.'

'We must pray hard for her healing,' Père Bernard said.

'Reckon she'll be needing more than a prayer,' the carpenter said with a sly wink at the men behind the priest's back. But Père Bernard must have noticed, for he scowled at the carpenter.

'I must say though,' Alesi Stonemason said, 'no one was that surprised at the death of your trader friend, Raoul.'

'Not surprised?' Raoul frowned, feeling giddier by the minute at being hemmed in.

'We all know those merchants and traders are under contract to the Devil,' Alesi Stonemason said as Pina, Rixende's oldest girl, doled out portions of eel pie. Raoul refused the food, just the thought making him want to vomit. 'They're just like the

Jews and moneylenders ... all that buying and selling, they think they're better bargainers than ordinary folk, and get so confident they reckon they can outfox the Devil. Well all I'll say is that your trader friend learned the hard way that nobody can win against the Devil.' The Master Mason looked around at his workers. Shovelling pie into their mouths, they nodded in agreement.

'Merchants are like that,' Jâco said. 'Money sticks to them worse than soggy leaves. And a human working for the Devil can steal a hundred souls, so we can only hope he hasn't damned every last soul in Lucie!'

'By its very nature,' Père Bernard said, licking juice from his chin. 'A merchant's enterprise violates our Christian beliefs in the evils money can cause. *Homo mercator vix aut numquam potest Deo placere*—a man who is a merchant can scarcely or never please God.'

'Merlin Lemarchand was a good man,' Raoul said. 'No money-hungering merchant but a simple, honest trader.'

'You hardly knew him,' Alesi Stonemason said, dabbing at a spot of blood trickling from his nose. 'How could you know an outlander in just a few days?'

Raoul watched, with rising horror, as Alesi wiped away another splodge of blood. And another.

Blessed Saint Etienne ... no it can't be!

He'd not told the priest the true cause of Crispen's death, for fear he—and his family—would be made outcasts.

'Ha, the Master Mason can't hold his ale,' a carpenter sniggered, along with several others, as Alesi's face turned white as bleached linen save for the green hue shadowing his cheeks. He lurched upright, and staggered about on the spot. Probably thinking he'd vomit all over them, the men all parted to let him through to the door. Raoul wanted to follow him; to reach the open air too, but he laid a warning hand on Anselme's arm.

'Let Alesi get well away first.'

'Whatever you all say about this pestilence,' Rixende was saying as she stowed another fistful of deniers in her apron pocket. 'It's plain to me as the dick on a rutting stallion. Something, or someone, has cursed us with this sickness. What, or who, the Lord only knows.' She wiped her hands on her apron and crossed herself. 'Perhaps you could ask God, Père Bernard? And while you're at it, ask Him what we need to do to stop it spreading to more of us.'

Once Raoul had seen Alesi leave, he laid a hand on Anselme's shoulder. And as they tried again, in vain, to get out of the tavern, he caught the alewife's gaze darting to him, her tongue flickering against the gap in her teeth, jutting a hip at him as he stepped around her. He wondered if she'd spared a single thought for Jacotte, her sick friend.

Rixende's blatant ploys for his attention had never flattered Raoul; the lavender-oil with which she doused herself to entice him simply brought on a pounding in his head. No, he felt only pity and distaste for the alewife, trying to take Héloïse's place. Nothing—nobody—would wrench him from his wife, and Raoul realised that he'd taken to praying more; pleading with God and Saint Etienne not to let this pestilence take hold of Lucie and rip apart his family as it had done so many in Florence. But judging from Alesi Stonemason, it seemed the Lord had ignored Raoul's pleas.

'All we can do is pray hard,' the priest said. 'And keep coming to church.'

'If you say so, Père Bernard,' Rixende said with a pout. 'But since you got no idea what to do with those who curse us, you could at least come out back to my kitchen and bless my cauldron. There's a demon in it what's burning my food, and my husband has threatened to leave me if any more of his meals are ruined … and you know what'll happen then—first my husband, then my customers.'

'You been threatening your wife, Jâco?' the baker said with a grin. 'Best joke I've heard today.' He let out a guffaw and the men's laughter bounced off the tavern walls, ale slopping across the scarred table tops.

Jâco laughed along with them, though Raoul sensed it was only to cover his embarrassment. But Raoul was in no mind to think about Jâco living under his wife's heel. For, as they finally reached the tavern entrance, they barged straight into Alesi Stonemason's young apprentice standing wide-eyed in the doorway.

'He's dead, my master's dead!' the boy cried. 'Just now, in the Mason's Lodge. Keeled over and died.' The trembling, white-faced lad looked like he too might keel over and several labourers took him by the shoulders, sat him down and pressed a mug of ale to his lips.

'Alive and healthy one minute, dead the next,' the apprentice said, after he'd gulped several mouthfuls. 'What could've killed him so fast? I don't understand?'

With a fearful glance at Anselme, Raoul crossed himself.

'Maybe it was this pestilence?' the butcher said. 'The one Jacotte's got; the one even Physician Nestor can't seem to cure.'

'Or Midwife Héloïse,' Rixende said, and Raoul felt her gaze searching out his again. 'I heard she tried to worm her way into the smithy's home; to curse my poor friend with one of her poisons ... till Pierro threw her out, that is.'

Rixende's words felt like a chisel blow to Raoul's skull.

Don't go near, or treat, any pestilence victims.

How dare she disobey me ... put my family in danger?

His hands fisted, Raoul breathed deeply, trying to calm his mounting rage as he marched back to his cot.

***

The cot door flew open and Raoul stamped inside, sending the plants Isa and I were bunching scattering across the table. Every trace of warmth and love bleached from his eyes, I was almost afraid, but not quite.

'Is it true?' Raoul asked. 'You've been treating the blacksmith wife's pestilence?'

I recoiled from this unexpected fury; the spittle his words sprayed; that muscle quivering at the side of his neck. 'I never touched Jacotte.'

'You would have, Héloïse, if the blacksmith hadn't thrown you out.'

I glanced at Isa, who gave me a slight shake of her head as if urging me not to argue with my husband.

I laid a tentative hand on his forearm. 'Raoul, I didn't ... please—'

'Weren't you listening when I forbade you to go near pestilence victims?' He shook off my hand. 'You might be trying to help others, Héloïse, but to me you just seem selfish and reckless ... aren't you worried about your—*my*—family?'

'I *am* worried.' The pressure of unshed tears pained my eyes. 'But I didn't know that Jacotte had the pestilence until I saw her and ... and it's not easy for a wise-woman to ignore an ailing person's screams. Then there's the oath I swore too, my mother would be unhappy if—'

'She would not, Héloïse. Ava would understand this is different. Besides, she's dead and gone.'

His words lanced my breast like the sharpest sword. 'She's not dead! She's still alive, in here.' I kept jabbing a fist against my breast until I felt I'd thumped all the air from myself. 'Anyway, after Merlin and Crispen, you said we'd all get it but none of us did.'

Raoul's voice softened and I thought he'd understood my quandary. 'Look Héloïse, I accept God's calling for you to heal and midwife, but it's only luck we haven't caught this pestilence yet. I told you it spread like an inferno in Florence, and it's already scattering its poison across Lucie: Merlin and Crispen, Jacotte—and now—Alesi Stonemason. And it will get worse.' His voice rose again, until he was almost shouting. 'I'm telling you, ordering you, to keep away from the stricken, or you'll get it too. Then your family. Dead, all of us!' He turned and strode towards the door.

'Don't go off like that, Raoul. You're right … I know you are. And from now on, I'll keep right away from the pestilence.'

'Papa, why were you shouting at Maman?' Swamped beneath Blanche's white fur, Morgane stood in the doorway. 'Why are we all going to be dead? Because of Merlin and Crispen?'

'We're not all going to die, poppet,' Isa said. 'Now come inside, it's too late to be playing in the garden.'

'I'll be at the Mason's Lodge,' Raoul said gruffly, ignoring his daughter. 'With Alesi gone, there's a lot to discuss.'

Once Raoul's steps faded, Isa spoke into the heavy silence. 'Raoul has cause, Héloïse.'

'I know he's right, but don't you feel the same as me? How can a healer turn her heart against suffering? How it's hard for me to ignore the vow I swore to Ava?'

'I swore the same healing and midwifing oath as you, Héloïse. I breathe the same nurturing air. I can understand your recklessness, but Raoul can't. Besides, you know women are born to serve men and comply with a husband's orders. So by Satan's black prick, if you want to keep this man, you'd best yield to his every wish and command.'

XVII

'That'll be for Mistress Tifaine and her brothers,' Sibylle said, as the passing bells rang. The baker's wife was lying on the pallet, my practised hands showing Morgane how to feel the lie of her babe. 'The whole family came out in the boils after Jacotte died, except that lout Pierro Blacksmith,' the baker's wife went on, at her usual breathless pace. 'We heard that when Jacotte's boils appeared, Physician Nestor ran from the smithy's fast as you can with a crippled foot. Though anyone would understand his fright after seeing your trader friend. Smelling him too!'

Naturally we'd heard of Jacotte's passing several days gone, and that her children, along with Mistress Tifaine's fiancé, Sergeant Drogan's brother, would likely follow her to the churchyard soon after. The pestilence had struck down others too: the butcher, the barber-surgeon, and their entire families. God had also called home our apothecary and his family. Against my heart, I had heeded my husband's orders and not gone to any of them. But news of their passing, and the care I had refused them, weighed me down like stones in my apron pocket.

'Is it still holding on in there?' Sibylle said, glancing down at her belly.

'Holding on perfectly,' I said. 'And growing so well he'll likely be running before the year's out.'

I finally managed to calm Sibylle's chatter, and Morgane and I slipped back out onto the market-place. After another week of steady rain, work had once more resumed on the vingtain and I watched Raoul for a moment. My husband caught my eye, gave me a quick nod and turned back to Anselme.

'Have you something in your basket for my girls, Héloïse?' Yolande called, from the tailor's shop.

'Where are the twins?' Morgane asked. After a week of rain confining them indoors, I too was surprised Pétronille and Peronelle weren't playing outside.

'Inside.' Yolande's voice was softer than usual, her gesturing hand betraying the slightest tremor. 'Both complaining of bellyache.'

But one glance at Pétronille and Peronelle slumped over, clutching their stomachs, their brows dotted with sweat, and an icy claw gripped my heart. No wormwood syrup, mint or rose brew would help this bellyache, for the little girls' arms were covered in rosy rings.

I looked at Yolande. Surely she'd seen them?

'Those pink rings,' she wailed. 'They didn't have them before. Oh no, no!'

'Go home now, Morgane.' I pushed my daughter away from the friends she was trying to comfort.

'I want to help make them better, Maman.'

I knew I too should hurry away from this pestilence house. But leave Yolande alone at such a time? I just couldn't think of it.

'Go now, don't argue.' I flapped my daughter towards the door.

'Get better soon,' Morgane said to the twins as she stomped from the tailor's shop, her fire-shot braids whisking about her scowling face. 'Because we need to finish our game of queek.' But as I soaked cloth in our cleansing rose-water, I saw the girls were in such discomfort they wouldn't have noticed Morgane's presence. Nor, I wagered, could they recall a half-finished game of queek.

'This should cool their fever,' I said as we lay the twins on the pallet and began bathing their faces and necks.

Throughout the afternoon, we wiped off the sweat, changed

their sodden linen, and gave them peppermint brew for their aching bellies. Yolande remained silent, as if the shock of the pestilence creeping into her home had stolen her tongue. Or perhaps she thought that once voiced, her daughters' illness could never be reversed.

Dusk fell, and with it the clang of the curfew bell, and Yolande and I watched in helpless dismay as the girls' blood roses turned from crimson to violet, and purple-black. We tied lengths of linen across our faces to fend off the stench, and bathed their skin—cool as mildewed stone—with herb-sweetened water.

As they cried out with soul-piercing shrieks, I gave them sips of poppy juice. It soothed them a little, but I could see the life was abandoning their flesh inside, the putrefying pulp bursting its way from their small, floundering bodies. I crossed myself and prayed, but it seemed I was speaking into God's deaf ear.

Anselme came inside and tears filled his dark eyes. But the lad didn't utter a sound as he lit a fire and heated the pot of broth. He looked at me and his mother, pointed to the broth. Yolande and I shook our heads, and the boy hovered in agitated silence.

As if it were Death already announcing its arrival, the knock at the door startled me.

'Héloïse? Come out here, now!' I recognised my husband's voice, and shuddered at its crackle. 'You too, Anselme.'

As soon as I stepped outside, Anselme cowering behind me, Raoul grabbed my arm roughly. That taut muscle on the side of his neck jigged about, as always when he was troubled or angry.

'Morgane told me about the twins' rosy rings, Héloïse. Why are you treating them, risking your own life and that of our family? You promised ... "From now on, I'll keep away from the pestilence." That's what you said only a week gone.'

He looked at his apprentice, still standing behind me, shoulders stooped, the wad of dark hair obscuring half his face. 'And you're coming home with me too, Anselme ... I'm very sorry to hear about your sisters, but I can't allow my apprentice in a pestilence home, any more than I can my wife.'

'Please Raoul,' I said staring in disbelief at my husband, so different from the kind and loving man I'd waved off to Florence two years gone, feeling my heart would splinter with sorrow.

Or had he always been like this, and a bastard girl's thankful and blind love just hadn't seen it? Maybe I'm the one who's different? Maybe Raoul being away so long has changed me?

'Yolande is my closest friend,' I said. 'We've shared everything since we were girls: haymaking, harvests, feasts ... secrets. How can I leave her alone now? As I said before, you and Crispen didn't abandon Toubie. You mightn't have known he had the pestilence until it was too late, but you still must have touched him. Don't you see, Raoul?' I took a quick breath and carried on before my nerves failed me. 'We can't escape the pestilence, and we can't avoid everyone who comes in contact with it, or catches it ... especially not the midwife and wise-woman.' I touched my pendant, trying to keep the tremble from my voice. 'Can't you have faith in this, as I do?'

'You're such a fool, Héloïse.' His voice warbled uneasily. 'You can have all the faith on this earth, but as I already said, how can a bit of old bone stop you falling ill?'

'Maybe you're right, and it is just is a bit of old bone,' I said, kneading the pendant between my thumb and forefinger. 'But with no cure, it's all we've got ... that and our rose-water to keep clean and stave off sickness. Just as you appeal to your martyred Saint Etienne, I have faith in this talisman.' I was silent for a moment, willing him to consider my words.

'Perhaps I am being selfish and reckless, Raoul, but I can't abandon Yolande or her twins. Won't you make an exception for them? I'm being so careful, wearing a mask so I don't breathe in the miasma and washing—'

'I understand your nature to heal ... you know that,' Raoul said with a great sigh, against the girls' agonising shrieks echoing across the market-place, and Anselme looking from Raoul to me and back to Raoul again. 'And that you don't want to abandon

Yolande, but for your safety—for ours—I must forbid it. Besides, I had some good news for you, but seeing your stupidity; your stubbornness, there doesn't seem much point telling you.'

'What news, Raoul?'

'Since Alesi Stonemason's death, I've been appointed Master Mason for the vingtain wall and castle renovations. But what use is a higher wage and status if we're all dead?'

'You deserve to be Master Mason.' I leaned forward to kiss him, but he pulled away as if I were a pestilence victim. 'Please, Raoul … this is such a terrible time for Yolande.'

Raoul fell silent, stroking his chin. 'You'll follow me home, Héloïse … now or never. You too, Anselme.'

My husband swung away, but Anselme kept standing on the market-place, shaking his head.

'Anselme?' Raoul called over his shoulder. 'No? Well consider our contract terminated.'

I watched him stride off across the market-place, shoulders bowed, thick hair thumping against his taut back. In the tavern doorway, Rixende leaned on her broom, her mouth hitched at me in a gleeful sneer.

Yolande stepped outside. 'You should listen to your husband. Obey him. Go home with Raoul, Héloïse … away from this sickness. *Dieu* already called home my husband, and if He takes my girls too, I'd rather be dead myself.'

'You still have Anselme,' I said.

'There's nothing more I can do for him in this life … his future's in your husband's hands.' She looked up at her son. 'You go too, Anselme … Héloïse isn't the only one who must obey Raoul's orders.'

Anselme shook his head again.

'I can't leave you, Yolande,' I said. 'Just as you wouldn't leave me. Raoul doesn't understand … those who aren't called to help the ailing can't make sense of it.'

'Your husband's as good as threatened to throw you out of the house if you disobey him. He'll probably beat you if you stand here much longer.'

'Raoul's never hit me.'

'Never hit you?' Yolande's voice trailed off, and she fixed her harrowed gaze on me. 'I don't want you here, Héloïse ... don't want the guilt if you and your family fall sick.'

'But ...'

Since we were girls growing up together, I'd always given the orders and Yolande had followed them unquestioningly. Maybe that's why I loved her so much: someone who did what I asked without question. Unlike my husband.

'Go,' Yolande repeated. 'Do as Raoul says, and keep away from pestilence victims.'

I'd never heard my softly-spoken friend speak so sternly, and I meekly took my basket and hurried off across the square, without Anselme.

XVIII

The following dawn, Anselme rapped on the cot door, but the boy didn't have to attempt a single word for me to know the short, sweet lives of Pétronille and Peronelle were over.

'There's no more pestilence risk now, since the twins are gone,' I said to Raoul. 'Will you at least allow me to go to Yolande and mourn with her?'

Raoul said nothing but gave me a small nod without looking at me. I walked outside and stepped straight into a muddy puddle that dragged at my boots as if trying to suck them off my feet.

Outside the houses bordering la place de l'Eglise, rivulets of water trickling between the offal buckets and kitchen rubbish carried the stench of rotting food. Overhead, a crow flapped lazily between the upper storey sleeping quarters, already darkened by the overarching jetties, and that shadowy agent of the Devil sent a shiver across the back of my neck. The louring clouds made gloomier the criss-cross alleys leading off the market-place, and in the parts where arches touched buildings on both sides of the street, holding apart the tilting homes like Rixende intervening in a tavern brawl, it was especially sombre.

It seemed Yolande hadn't moved from where I'd left her, kneeling beside her girls on the pallet. But she had, as Pétronille and Peronelle's hair was combed and braided, the girls dressed in clean muslin shifts. Their church clothes.

She looked up at me. 'Oh *Dieu*, oh Heaven, why am I still living?' She tried to expel her grief with lamenting sounds, but it seemed her sorrow was so deep it wouldn't let her weep.

I shook my head, unable to think of any fitting words. I took a clutch of thyme from my basket and sprinkled it about, so the souls of Pétronille and Peronelle would take shelter until we could bury their bodies.

'I keep thinking they'll wake any second, demanding to break their fast before they skip off outside to play,' Yolande said, as the hawk-eyed woodcutter-sexton arrived, his cart bearing two coffins.

'Just one coffin,' Yolande said. 'My twins came into this life as one … they'll leave it the same way.'

'So the other just goes to waste?' Poncet Batier said with a scowl, bringing one of the coffins inside. His lice-filled hood dropping from his head, he lifted both girls into it, pushing Peronelle's cross, which had fallen to the ground, back between her interlaced fingers.

The neighbours and other mourners arrived, each face taut with grief. Sibylle brought a fresh-baked cake from her husband's oven. The shoemaker's wife had cuts of ham. Poppa, unusually subdued, thumped a pot of honey onto the table. Even Rixende—who despised Yolande purely because she was my friend—came with a jug of ale.

I set juniper branches to burn, the fragrant smoke known to dispel melancholy as well as deadly miasmas, and the mourners began to wail. I sobbed too, but the howling voice was Yolande's.

The smell of Death lingering on my skin, I was suffocating in that cramped, smoky air, breathing only the smell of all of us, imagining it soon mingled with our own deathly stenches.

Giddy and fearful of passing out, I flung open the door and stumbled onto the market-place. Inhaling deeply, the salt of sorrow rasping at my throat, I crossed over to the presbytery to tell Père Bernard that the bodies of Pétronille and Peronelle were ready.

***

The vingtain workers halted their pulleys and laid down their tools to attend the Mass for Pétronille and Peronelle. Amongst them, Raoul met my painfully swollen eyes with a wary look, as if he didn't trust me to keep my promise. Or maybe it wasn't mistrust but dread; terror, like my own, that this vile illness would strike down his family—the only earthly ones Raoul could call his own?

I *would* keep that promise, I wanted to tell him, if only he'd come and stand beside me on the church rushes, rather than with his group of workers. But he'd barely spoken a word to me since our argument last evening outside the tailor's shop, muttering a simple *yes* or *no* or shrugging if I asked him something. His gaze was as chill as the flagstones of Saint Antoine's on which Anselme and Poncet Batier placed the single coffin. And as I looked about me, it seemed that Raoul wasn't the only person who'd changed.

Masked beneath their grief for Yolande's twins and the other souls we'd lost to the pestilence, I sensed a difference in the people; something deeper than the flagrant, fearful panic. It was like the cusp of a season; a change you're not aware of until you look outside one morning and see that the trees are naked, their leaves rotting on the ground.

'Why did Pétronille and Peronelle go to Heaven so soon, Maman? We hadn't finished playing our game of queek.' I looked down to see Morgane standing beside me, with Isa. I didn't know how my daughter had come to be here, but it was a comfort to fold her small hand in mine. In her other hand, she clutched Crispen's wooden cat.

'I don't know why God called them to Him so soon, Morgane. The Lord's wishes are sometimes … are often beyond me.'

'Think to our garden, Morgane,' Isa said. 'Which flowers do we pick first?'

'The most beautiful ones,' she said solemnly.

'People are eyeing each other suspiciously,' Isa said to me. 'Worried who might be carrying the miasma.'

Many too, were pointedly not looking at their neighbours, but fixing their gaze instead on the painted church walls—reminders that the eternal torture of Hell is the only alternative to salvation. The damned hung from trees of fire by their tongues, the impenitent burned in furnaces, the unbelievers suffocated in smoke. Wicked men and women fell into a bottomless well, sinking to a depth proportionate to their sins: fornicators up to the nostrils, persecutors up to the brow. Monstrous fish swallowed some, demons gnawed others. Yet more were tormented by serpents or fire. Candle smoke had already begun to darken the colours, so bright just a few years gone, when Saint Antoine's was rebuilt.

Père Bernard lit candles around the coffin, then, holding the chalice in one hand and the silk-covered ciborium in the other, he began chanting: *'Requiem aeternam dona eis, Domine, et lux perpetua luceat eis*—Grant them eternal rest, Lord, and may everlasting light shine upon them.' And as he spoke, our Lord Jesus, affixed to the large crucifix hanging on the wall above Pétronelle and Peronille, seemed to struggle and writhe with each candle flicker.

As usual in church, people began whispering amongst themselves, and there was no denying the sharp edge of fear.

'... pestilence ... spread ...'

'... all of us ... perish ...'

'Fairest Jesus greets them,' Père Bernard went on, crossing himself and bowing his head, the hair ringing his tonsure falling over his face. 'The angels will sing for them. The Holy Virgin weeps for them ...'

Once the priest finished blessing the twins, everyone made the sign of the cross.

I kept glancing at Yolande, who was gripping Anselme—no longer Raoul's apprentice since he'd refused to leave his sisters—and couldn't stop shaking my head. How could Pétronille and

Peronelle, Yolande too, deserve such punishment from Our Lord?

'Most worshipful friends,' Père Bernard went on, 'after so many deaths in such a short time, there can be little doubt that the wrath of God is visited upon us. In His divine judgement He has sent us this pestilence as chastisement for our sins, punishing us the same way God washed away Noah's sinful world with the Flood.

Père Bernard didn't deliver a sermon at every service. Often there were simply messages from the King about war victories or losses, royal births and deaths, or taxes. But now our priest's sermons were only about the pestilence, all of us desperate to grab whatever holy defence we could against an illness that had struck at least one in so many families.

'The vast majority of us will be eternally damned,' Père Bernard said. '*Salvandorum paucitas, damnandorum multitude*—few saved, many damned. But,' he shook a fist in the air, 'no matter how few are chosen, the Church offers hope to all sinners. For sin is an inherent condition of life which can be absolved by penitence. "Turn thou to me and I shall receive thee and take thee to grace," saith the Lord.'

'Surely we're no more sinful than other people?' I hissed to Isa. 'How can God be so cruel as to send us such a punishment?'

'Watch your loose tongue about God,' Isa said, jabbing an elbow into my side. 'Especially in church.'

'Some say this pestilence doesn't come from God,' the baker said, 'but from strange weather. I heard that last autumn in the Orient, they had three days with rains of frogs, serpents, lizards and scorpions. And rains of fire and lightning, and stinking smoke falling from Heaven.'

The level of chatter rose to a low, constant din.

'Silence,' the priest said, raising both arms, thin fingers splayed like a spider's legs.

'Some are saying the miasma comes from mountains in a faraway land,' the blacksmith said, 'that spewed fire and hot rivers.'

'Forget rains of insects and fire-spewing mountains,' Sergeant Drogan said, the feeble-looking Catèlena standing by his side, her face lowered to try and hide her husband's latest blows. 'I heard it's the Jews what brought this pestilence.'

'*Voilà*, the Jews are poisoning the wells with the miasma,' Drogan's mother, Sara, chimed in, 'to kill and destroy all of Christendom and have lordship over the world.'

A gasp rose from the crowd, and the noise of cloth brushing against peoples' legs seemed loud and scratchy.

'Silence, *please*,' Père Bernard said.

'But I heard good news too,' Drogan went on, 'they've started lynching the Jews ... in Narbonne and Carcassonne, throwing them onto bonfires.'

'Oh yes, it must be the Jews ... once again,' Isa said, her voice heavy with sarcasm. 'The outsider we Christians have been taught for so long to despise.'

'Well it is the Jews what—' Sara countered.

'Not forgetting that the Jews always have the most property,' Isa said, 'which seems handy for looting, if you ask me.'

'Nobody's asking you,' Sara said.

'I understand, dear brothers and sisters,' Père Bernard almost shouted, over the noise, 'that your fear leaves you vulnerable to rumour. Yet in His infinite wisdom it is most certainly God who has sent us this trial. He has sometimes spoken to His people by visiting unspeakable things upon them, this venom in the blood being one of the most terrible. Naturally we all fear it. Who would not dread such painful carbuncles, or walk in terror of crossing Grim Death's path?'

The priest dropped his voice as if to let us in on a great secret. 'All of us have, at some time, taken Satan's bait, enticing us away from God.' Père Bernard's gaze moved over us until, I was certain, it seared straight into mine. 'There is none amongst us who has not fallen. So, as the baker tends his oven, the farmer tends his crops, the physician tends the sick, God cares for us. Let us not fail Him!'

'That's all well and good, Père Bernard,' Rixende said, 'but how do you keep yourself safe from the pestilence? There must be medicaments or spells? Some must know how to cure it, but refuse to share the remedy with the rest of us.' The alewife darted me a glance.

Surely Rixende can't truly believe I have a remedy? If only I did!

'The only way is by loving God and begging His forgiveness,' Père Bernard said, 'by turning from the Devil and all his works.'

'Amen!' Sergeant Drogan cried, and a scattering of amens followed.

As everyone crossed themselves, my fingers too jerked into that long-time reflex, but something stopped me. When Raoul was helping rebuild the church I recalled imagining the new one as a palace, or something as grand as Heaven itself. If man could raise such a building using only his faith and his skilled hands, I thought he could achieve anything he wanted. Now I understood how small and powerless man was, and I wondered if God's church really was the sanctuary we all believed it to be.

As if my hand was working separately from my mind, it refused to make the cross sign and fell instead to my bone-carved angel.

The talisman's warmth seeped into the icy nooks of my body as I stared at Raoul's statue of Our Lady, solemnly looking down on the congregation, her hair rippling from beneath her crown. Her pale and polished features seemed like living flesh, and her eyes, which caught the glancing flickers of light, shone as if alive.

Blessed Virgin, please ask God to banish the pestilence from Lucie; not to take anyone else. Am I right to ignore its victims; to obey the husband I respect and love ... the man I feel lucky to have, who saved me from the living Hell of my bastard status? Deep inside, I know he's right and only wants to protect us, but what of the voice urging me to honour my vow, and Our Lord's calling to care for the sick?

Anselme and Poncet Batier carried the coffin to the freshly-dug grave. Amidst the churchyard mourners, I exchanged another cool glance with Raoul. Our gazes darted away just as quickly.

Light rain began to fall as the sexton lowered Pétronille and Peronelle into the ground, the breeze scattering pink and white blossoms across the coffin as if Mother Earth were adding her own gift to our rosemary and thyme offerings.

'... so may Thy mercy unite these children above to the choirs of angels,' Père Bernard chanted, sprinkling holy water, his black robe flapping in the wind like a crow's feathers. Beside me, Yolande looked up to the sky, her lips mouthing thanks to the Lord for giving Pétronille and Peronelle—who had been so thirsty—one final drink.

As Poncet Batier began shovelling quicklime into the open grave Yolande fell to her knees. 'Wait!' She inhaled deeply, as if trying to breathe in courage.

'I felt your heartbeats when you were growing in my belly, and I still feel them.' She hammered a fist against her breast and her voice, which had been shaky at the edges, began to break. 'I'll always hear your chatter, your laughter, your songs. I love you both. Never will I forget you.' And Yolande, a meek and dignified woman, lay slumped across the earth, the nakedness of her grief spread out for all to gape at. She let out a heart-wrenching sob, leaning so far into the grave it seemed she wanted to topple into that gaping maw of earth and be buried with her girls. High in the trees, crows cawed, and the breeze bent down to sweep the little twins up to the sky.

I held my friend by the back of her kirtle, strangled sobs erupting from the crowd. Tears flowed, people dabbing at eyes and noses and averting their faces so she could mourn in privacy.

Once Yolande's sobs subsided, Père Bernard's outstretched arms held us in silence for a few moments, before he spoke again.

'If all of you would please assemble on la place de l'Eglise,' he said, 'our Captain has an important announcement from le Comte Renault de Fouville.'

'Can't imagine whatever could be more serious than this

pestilence,' Isa said, hooking one bony arm through mine, the other through Yolande's.

***

'In an effort to vanquish this pestilence,' the Captain of Lucie's team of sergeants began in his booming voice, 'our *Seigneur*, Renault de Fouville, has ordered all the cats in Lucie be rounded up.'

'Round up the cats?' Alewife Rixende said, against the din that had struck up. 'What will you have us do with all the mice and rats then? Unless Captain,' her tongue worked the gap between her teeth, 'you're thinking of rounding them up too, and having us bake them into pies?'

That was met with a few half-hearted laughs, and more chatter.

'How does le Comte know it's the cats what're spreading this pestilence?' said Pierro Blacksmith.

'Our *Seigneur* can't be sure it's the cats,' the Captain said. 'But as our protector, he wants to do everything within his power to fend off this vile sickness.'

'Doomsday must be coming!' someone cried.

'Lord save us,' Yolande whispered, pressing the back of one hand to her brow.

I thought she'd cried all her tears, but her eyes filled again, darker and hollower in her face as pale the Virgin's. I clasped her hand, which was hot and clammy, as the Captain carried on.

'You will bring all your cats, and any stray ones you can gather into sacks, and these symbols of the Devil will be put to the torch.'

'What's "put to the torch", Maman?' Morgane said.

'It means they're going to burn all the cats, you Devil-eyed dimwit,' Rixende's daughter said with a snigger. Pina's blonde braids jiggled as she laughed. 'All the cats, including yours.'

'I won't let them,' Morgane said. 'They'll never burn my Blanche!'

'I need to lie down, Héloïse,' Yolande said, her palm now pressed against a reddened cheek. 'I don't feel well ... need a drink ...'

I looked at Yolande; at the beads of sweat dotting her face, at her pale lips parted in thirst, and at the clusters of pink rings on her hands and wrists.

I dropped her hand and reeled backwards, Raoul's words a warning drumbeat in my mind.

I forbid you ... forbid you ... protect yourself; our family. Senseless. Reckless.

Cold sweat snaked between my breasts as I nudged Isa, and motioned to Yolande's blood roses. My aunt moved Morgane to the other side of her, further from Yolande.

'I should take her home,' I whispered, trying not to attract attention; trying not to incite terror and panic.

'You can't touch her,' Isa hissed. 'Raoul will have another fit of rage.'

'I can't just leave her here on the market-place!'

Anselme must have seen what was happening, and hurried towards us. Without a sign, he bent his long legs, lifted his mother and carried her, like a child, back to the tailor's shop. As I trailed behind them, I caught Raoul's stare, his green eyes—sharp as unripe grapes—darting between Anselme and me.

XIX

By the time I'd seen my patients it was late, but I rode Merlinette home slowly, partly from fatigue and sorrow but also to put off facing my husband. The rift between Raoul and I already gaped cold and lonely, and I had no mind for more dispute.

As I swayed to the mare's rhythm, I held my pendant, soothing the ache in my bones and my heart. With little else besides luck and faith to cling to, I prayed the talisman would indeed protect us.

It was drizzling when I reached the cot and I almost felt sorry for the pig, huddled miserably beneath the eaves. Wind flurries moaned at my door, rustled the leaves of the fruit trees and swayed the wicker-basket that hung beneath our cherry tree. There was only one young pigeon in the basket, so I supposed Isa had taken its mate.

I lingered in the barn, brushing and feeding the mare, changing her water. I spoke soothingly, though Merlinette was as calm as ever.

I stepped cautiously inside. Raoul was sitting at the table, whittling a stick, his neck muscle juddering. He didn't look up at me but I sensed—and smelled—his simmering anger. And I knew he was watching me as Blanche watches a rat, just waiting for it to come close enough to pounce.

Isa and Morgane too kept their gazes low, on the pigeon from the wicker-basket that was struggling in Isa's hands.

'I left Yolande in Anselme's care,' I said, breaking the taut silence. 'It seems he loves his mother more than his future as your apprentice.'

'Anselme does what he thinks best,' Raoul croaked, 'but I can't have anyone on my work site coming from a pestilence home.'

'I gave him medicaments for his mother,' I said, 'and then I left the tailor's shop.'

'Not immediately you didn't, Héloïse. I have it on good word you stayed quite a time with Yolande.' His voice was rough as the stones he cut.

'No … not long! Raoul, try to understand. It felt like my soul was being wrenched from me, leaving her without proper care. Anselme has good intentions but not the slightest skill of a wise-woman.'

I didn't mention that Yolande had ordered me once again from her home; forbidden me to remain near her pestilence-stricken body.

Apart from Raoul's gravelly breaths, I could've heard a mouse scurrying across the rushes. Wordlessly, I placed my basket on the shelf in the lean-to, my cloak on the nail behind the door, and began chopping the rosemary and marjoram bunched on the table.

'Don't be mad, Papa.' Morgane's freckled cheeks flushed as she stroked the terrified bird. 'Maman said she didn't touch Yolande.'

'Hush now,' Isa murmured, taking the pigeon and smoothing down its fiercely flapping feathers. The bird calmed in her grip, one bright black eye blinking at me, and I imagined its tiny heart thumping beneath the soft feathers. She kept stroking the bird, and it almost fell asleep in the fireside warmth.

'Say something, Raoul,' I said. 'I *am* obeying your orders … I didn't stay with Yolande. But just so you know, since the barber-surgeon is dead and Poppa says Physician Nestor refuses to leave the castle, there's no one else in Lucie to treat the sick.'

'What kind of physician ignores the sick, I ask you?' Isa

said, as her wrinkled hand moved up to the bird's neck. In one deft movement she twisted and pulled sharply and the pigeon flopped limp in her lap.

'That monk-physician has the right idea isolating himself,' Raoul said, the stick so sharply whittled it was down to a point. 'That's the only way to escape the pestilence ... to keep away from the sick.' He raised his cool gaze to me, but I turned away and made a big job of adding the rosemary and marjoram to the iron pot that already bubbled on the hearth.

'Poppa says the lot of them would've fled the castle to one of their outlying estates by now if it weren't for la Comtesse Geneviève,' Isa said, plucking the young bird whilst Morgane reached out to catch the soft feathers drifting into a mound about my aunt's feet. 'Apparently the *Seigneur's* wife is having a hard time carrying the heir. Losing blood, Poppa heard, so the midwife has ordered her to bed and forbidden travel.

'But the pestilence will dog them into the hills of their iso-lated estates,' she went on, slitting open the bird's belly with her knife. She pulled out the guts and tossed the carcass into the pot as Morgane fanned the hearth flames. The sweet scents of the herbs filled the room, mixed with the smell of feathers, onions and blood on Isa's red-raw hands.

'There's no escaping it, Raoul,' I said. 'Not for us. Not even for nobles. And people can't run from their homes because most are either too poor or have nowhere to go. They have no choice but to stay. And a wise-woman,' I added, 'never flees her patients ... no matter how much she fears a sickness.'

'But what you are doing is madness, Héloïse!' Raoul waved the pointed stick. 'If you go into pestilence homes you'll surely bring it here. How can I allow that as protector of this family?'

'I know you can't, Raoul.' I was treading on the thin edge of his temper but I couldn't stop myself. 'And I do feel your frustra-tion, so why can't you see mine?'

'I can! But I've had it with your idiocy ... your hollow prom-ises.' In one quick movement, he leaned towards me, raised a hand and brought it down hard against my cheek.

'Christ's blood!' Isa gasped. Morgane gathered the frightened Blanche into her arms and began to cry. I was so stunned I couldn't move or speak but I felt flayed, red and naked.

'How dare you, Raoul? I did not disobey you!'

It was only a small lie but I almost believed it, so why not him? A hand pressed to my smarting cheek I ran outside, back to the barn.

'It's enough that you try to,' he cried after me, 'that you can't see sense ... that you make me live in fear for my family.'

I buried my face in Merlinette's mane and sobbed hard for all I'd lost: my friend and her beautiful girls, my husband's love, my family's peace and goodwill.

Later, as I trudged back inside, Isa ladled out the pigeon and bean stew. 'Let's call a truce while we eat, leastwise,' she said. 'And thank the Blessed Virgin we're all still well.'

'But for how long?' Raoul said.

I was so exhausted I almost fell asleep over my supper, but I'd begun to suspect the tiredness wasn't just from the pestilence worries, or the frostiness of my hearth. My tender breasts and urgency to use the chamber pot, the sickness in my belly, told me a babe might have taken root in my womb. I'd not told Raoul, not before I was sure; waiting for my husband to be more agreeable and to welcome such happy news.

Raoul had no bedtime story for Morgane—no *Reynard the Fox* tale, *The Wolf and the Lamb*, or *The Dog and the Sheep*. There was no fireside laughter. He did not bid me a good night or kiss me, and his glare, as icy green as the Vionne in winter, plunged deep into my breast.

I dragged myself up the loft ladder, cast aside my clothes, pulled on my sleeping chemise and collapsed onto the pallet.

By my side, Raoul turned his back to me once again. I brushed aside his curls and touched a finger to his shoulder.

'Raoul, please.' A gentle squeeze of that rigid shoulder. 'I'm ... I am ...'

'What, Héloïse?' he hissed into the darkness. 'You're sorry you keep putting our family in danger?'

'N-nothing.'

After several moments filled with Raoul's heavy sighs, I said, 'I can't keep on like this. While I knew you loved me I didn't care a stitch about vicious townsfolk gossip; about non-born bastards not entitled to live or get wed or people's suspicions about my angel pendant. But now you've turned against me Raoul, I can't bear the sadness. I feel so alone. I know you're right to forbid me to care for pestilence victims, I ... I'm just ... it's hard. Especially now Yolande has it. But I won't ... I promise—'

'Just keep your word and stop going into pestilence homes, Héloïse ... stop hankering to go into them and everything will be good between us once again.' Raoul flicked his shoulder angrily and I dropped my hand, tucking it beneath my still-smarting cheek. But as I gripped my talisman, I wasn't sure if things could ever be right between us.

Tired as I was I couldn't sleep, thinking of Raoul's fury and of Yolande; how I couldn't be with my friend when she needed me most.

And outside—in the wicker cage hanging beneath the cherry tree—the lone pigeon cooed all through the night, waiting for its mate's answering call. And when no answer came, I listened to it singing sorrowfully from its tiny, hollowed heart.

XX

'You'd just prefer I didn't have a job at all, wouldn't you Raoul? This pestilence is simply a good excuse to forbid me to work?'

'You know that's not true.' Raoul stuffed bread and strips of dried meat into his satchel as quickly as he could, anxious to be away to the work site; away from me. 'I respect your calling in life, and your vow to Ava, even if there's no need for you to work.'

It was almost the end of May, over a week since the twins' death and since Yolande had caught the pestilence; a torturous time that had stretched like a hundred years, and the air in our cot still taut as Raoul's plumb line.

'Please move aside, Héloïse, I must get to work.' Raoul strode past me, ensuring he didn't touch a single hair of my body.

'At least let me go to the tailor's shop, just one quick visit, to see how Yolande is.' I followed him outside, kneading my scrunched hands. 'I know Anselme tries to tell me when I ask him, but since he can't speak a word, I only worry more.'

As I scurried after my husband, willing him to look back; to acknowledge me, I glimpsed a figure—Anselme?—hurrying along the Roman road towards us, waving his arms. I knew immediately what he'd come to tell us, and a shock of ice crushed my heart.

Raoul stopped still before his apprentice. I ran to both of them.

'She's well ... my mother is recovered,' Anselme said. 'I came straight away ... knew you'd want to know, Héloïse.'

His voice, exactly as it was before the outlaws' attack—and the words he spoke!—shocked me so deeply I couldn't speak for a moment.

'What did you do?' I said. 'What happened?'

'Nothing different from what you did with my sisters,' Anselme said. The sun shone his hair a deep midnight blue, as lovely as his smile. And his voice.

'Fully recovered ... you're sure?' Raoul asked. 'A few came through it in Florence, but it was rare.'

'She's a little weak, and thinner,' Anselme said. 'But not the least fever, thirst or rash. And since I have no sign of the blood roses, I was wondering, Raoul, if you'd consider ...?'

'Your mother's recovery, lad—and hearing your voice again—is the best news I've had in a long time,' Raoul said, thumping Anselme on the back. 'Yes, of course, I'd love to have my willing and capable apprentice back.'

My husband even afforded me a smile, and as the birds trilled from the willows and the Vionne waters pirouetted beneath the sunlit breeze, I glimpsed Raoul's love wakening again.

On impulse, I bent down, plucked a cluster of tansy and crushed the bright yellow flower. Its fragrance rushing at me, powerful and bewildering, I knew now was the right moment.

'I'm with child, Raoul,' I blurted out. 'I feel—hope—it's a son to carry on your trade ... to inherit your stonemason's mark.'

Raoul's face broke into the warm smile I'd so longed to see, and my heart brimmed with happiness. 'A son!' He picked me up and twirled me around as he did with Morgane. 'Saint Etienne must've had an ear open.'

'Ah! You're making me dizzy, put me down.' As my toes touched the ground, his firm kiss on my lips tasted like the best castle wine. 'Besides, I need to go and see Yolande.'

Raoul, Anselme and I set off for la place de l'Eglise, fat lambs gambolling in the lush grass, sunlight gilding their fleeces, green blackberries almost plumping before our eyes. And down along the Vionne the croak of frogs rose up like crazy laughter.

'You can speak again, Anselme!' Raoul was still grinning; still shaking his head in disbelief.

'Surely a miracle,' I said. 'Oh I can hardly believe Yolande's well … she's truly recovered?'

Anselme couldn't stop nodding and smiling, and flinging the black arc of hair from his face.

Yolande, the first in Lucie to catch the pestilence and not die. My dear friend's recovery—one small triumph over the vile sickness—splintered the hard nut of my despair.

***

'What could that priest want with us now?' Isa's brow pleated into frown lines as the church bell summoned us yet again.

As always in early June, our garden was fragrant with the sharp tang of blossoming lavender, and beneath a morning sun that turned frowsy cloud wisps a pale pink, Morgane and I picked the last cherries.

'Yes, what could be more urgent than the pestilence?' I said, flinging another handful into the basket.

'The bell will have no ring left if Père Bernard doesn't stop using it,' Morgane said, and sucked her cherry-stained fingers.

My aunt let out a chuckle, from where she knelt amidst the clump of flowers that looked like tiny blue helmets—wolfsbane or, as Isa called that dangerous plant from which she made liniment for her bad hips, Devil in Monk's Disguise. The same ointment Sergeant Drogan believed had killed his father.

'And if there's no more bell, whatever would our priest pull on then?' Isa said, throwing me a wink and a cackle.

Thankfully that joke was lost on my daughter, but Morgane did give us a small smile, the first I'd seen since we buried Pétronille and Peronelle.

'Now why don't you catch that cat and put her in the barn,' Isa said, pointing to Blanche, stalking the garden for tiny creatures. Morgane had refused to give up Blanche for burning with the rest of Lucie's cats, and Isa and I hadn't insisted. Even Raoul had thought burning the cats was a ridiculous notion. While we were home, we could hide Morgane's cat quickly if anyone came, but if someone wandered up for a remedy when we were out, they might catch sight of Blanche. And I knew a few townsfolk who'd take delight in telling Sergeant Drogan about one cat that had escaped the funeral pyre.

We'd also managed to keep Morgane away from la place de l'Eglise, where the Captain had incinerated the cats in sacks hung from a post over a blazing fire. Smoke had risen from the pile of charred corpses for days, giving off that stomach-churning stench of flesh burned alive.

I stored our baskets of cherries in the lean-to, to sell at market, hitched Merlinette to the cart and Morgane and I hoisted Isa up onto the seat.

After a rain-soaked May, summer had arrived swiftly, our world bursting into beautiful bloom: larkspur, meadowsweet and gillyflower. It was hard to imagine the pestilence's poison-ous seed could flourish in the midst of such a heavenly garden.

The farmers' toughest season—the haymaking—was in full swing, with every pair of available hands put to work. Despite the clanging bell calling us to Saint Antoine's, the teams of workers still moved down the fields cutting the grass with long-handled scythes. Cloth strips bound around their heads against the dust, the women followed with pitchforks, turning the grass so it would dry evenly. Older children gathered it into large piles, stacking it to form sheaves to shed water and keep the inside dry.

Gruelling work but also a time when people spent long hours together after curfew, when work was prohibited as nobody could see to perform properly: barns crowded with harvesters toasting bread and cheese and telling stories around fires, and sleeping and rutting in the hay. This season, the thought of all those people crowded together sent a shiver scudding down my back.

The bell was still chiming as we hitched Merlinette to the fountain post and joined the townsfolk. They were not gathered in the church as was usual, but on la place de l'Eglise. I sought out Yolande, and squeezed my friend's hand, sending more silent thanks to Our Lady for the miracle of her recovery.

'By now we have all heard the terrible stories from the south,' Père Bernard began, above the din of the vingtain workers who were laying down tools and hurrying to the edge of the crowd. 'Entire families gone, bodies rotting in streets littered with crying orphans; of animals decaying along the roadsides of ghost towns.'

People began muttering, and the priest raised his arms to call for silence.

'I have begged to know what unthinkable sinning has brought this pestilence upon Lucie-sur-Vionne,' he went on. 'But God, who is showing us His displeasure with His sinning flock, has not revealed Himself to me. So I must believe that your sins are so horribly beyond anything I have feared. Because,' he said, jabbing a forefinger into the air, 'where righteousness blooms, blood roses cannot! We must work harder; repent more to banish ourselves of every last sinner.'

'I thought we'd done that?' Isa said. 'When we burned the cats, but the pestilence is still killing us.'

'It stole my husband,' Poppa said, her voice heavy with sorrow. 'Who are we to blame now, Père Bernard?'

The foul miasma had also claimed many others, including Sergeant Drogan's remaining brother; so many dying in such a short time that Père Bernard had taken to holding collective burials.

'In burning our cats,' Sibylle said, a palm held protectively across her belly mound, 'the *Seigneur* took our best mousers and ratters, so the rodents are now breeding like fleas.'

'Hear, hear!' the baker said, crossing himself. 'Rats've almost taken over my bakery.'

'You told us the pestilence punishes the wicked,' I said. 'The English barbarians and the heathens. But what reason could God have for punishing Yolande's little twins, and all the other children who've perished? Surely they didn't live long enough to know such sin?'

'What sins have we all committed,' Poppa said, 'that our fathers before us, and their fathers before them, did not?'

'They were punished too,' Père Bernard said. 'With a famine. Rain drowned the crops and murrains killed the beasts.' He lowered his voice to a whisper. 'People were so starved that the rotting corpses of hanged men would disappear from the gibbets ... human flesh was sold at the market.'

A sob drifted from a woman at the back of the crowd, which came alive with fear and murmuring. And I could see in their drawn faces, the way they held themselves stiffly, that they were all asking themselves the same question as I was: who would be the next to sneeze, to bleed from the nose, to break out in the black boils?

I rubbed my hand in small circles on my belly.

Will this little one ever feel the sun's warmth? Will his young eyes feast on the leaf-fall colours, the greens of spring, the white of winter?

The blacksmith then asked the words I was certain hovered on everyone's lips: 'Are we all going to die, Père Bernard?'

'Our Lord is inflicting a special punishment on us,' the priest said, his gaze flickering across the crowd, and—did I imagine it?—lingering on me. 'And we should not be questioning His chastisement but asking ourselves which of our sins deserves such punishment.'

'But we're doing everything asked of us by God,' Sibylle said. 'Praying hard, attending church often ... and still not obtaining salvation.'

I took a breath, voicing the doubt that had started to tease my mind. 'What if God isn't punishing us at all?' I shook off Isa's warning hand. 'What if, instead, He has abandoned us?'

'Satan's black blood, Héloïse!' Isa cursed, beneath the crowd's chatter. 'The priest will burn you like those wretched cats if you don't shut your mouth.'

The people looked at me, making sounds somewhere between murmurs and groans, but I held their stares.

'Midwife Héloïse is right,' Sibylle said, 'it does seem God is either being unfair or is ignoring us.'

'Everywhere in the world heretics are saying God is not so unjust to punish the righteous with the guilty,' the priest said. 'But these heretics who question the hand of God in this pestilence—who question the authority of God's holy church—only increase the danger of damnation to the rest of us.' He paused until he had our full attention. 'And there are heretics like that in this very town.'

Wild chatter struck up again, people shielding their eyes from the scalding sun, and the vingtain site dust that swirled up from their shuffling feet.

'We must be vigilant against such heresy,' Père Bernard went on. 'Remember, only our Lord can cure sickness—through prayer, confession and punishment.' His voice rose again. 'Heretical cures are blasphemous, and will just make matters worse. For, if God sends us penance and we try to escape it, are we not defying His will?' He crossed himself again. 'I warn you, magic charms and spells, and heathen incantations, are all heresy. And anyone in Lucie-sur-Vionne guilty of such practices will be punished.'

Many in the crowd began weeping, their sobs leaden with desperation, but my breath seized in my throat. For there was no mistaking to whom the priest's words were directed. Isa's fingernails jabbed into my forearm.

'Your words are starting to sound like banging on hollow drums, Père Bernard,' Poppa said. 'Besides not sinning, we want to know exactly what to do to stop this pestilence killing us all.'

'Hear, hear!' shouted several others.

The priest turned to Poppa, where she stood with her son, Farmer Donis, and the other farming folk. 'You know a good crop comes not without toil and suffering. Cry thee now for this blighted crop, yes! But pray harder for a better next season. Place your trust in God!'

More whimpering came from the crowd; they weren't the words we'd hoped to hear.

'Only way to avoid catching the pestilence,' the blacksmith said in the drunken slur that had become his usual manner, 'is to leave town.'

'Or shut yourself inside, and have everyone who comes to visit vetted for sickness,' Rixende said, flinging an arm in the direction of *le château*. 'Like le Comte up in his castle.'

'But the rest of us ain't got a castle to hide away in,' the blacksmith said. 'And can't afford to run. And even if we could, where would we go?'

'No point running,' Isa said, 'the pestilence only runs faster.'

Père Bernard raised an arm again, wiping the other hand across his brow beaded with sweat. 'Dear friends,' he said, 'even if we had the means to flee this pestilence, we must not. For if we do, our only companions shall be loneliness and fear. Here we must stay, and accept this cross. Let us bear it in His holy name! Stay, and I vow that while I am spared, no one in this town will face death alone.'

Several amens followed, but many more *humphs* from those like me, I supposed, who were unconvinced.

'Wait, I am not finished,' Père Bernard shouted, against the chatter, as the people started dawdling away. 'I have a further, more serious, announcement.'

'What other midden-rot could he possibly spout?' I hissed to Isa.

'It has come to my knowledge,' Père Bernard began again, 'that the lepers—greatest and most flagrant sinners of all in Lucie—have joined the Jews in their devious pact to poison the wells with the pestilence miasma.'

People shuffled, sharp breaths rising from their dust, sweat and grime.

'As I said, if we are not zealous in ridding every last sinner from our midst,' the priest went on, 'we may face the loss of *all* our lives and our souls. As such, the leper sinners will be put to the flames ... this very eve.'

Wild chatter erupted; not out of compassion for the lepers, since every townsperson aside from Isa and me saw their disease as divine judgement for their sinful lives; their suffering as an opportunity to atone for their sins and purify their souls before death. No, it came more from their shock at the enormity this pestilence had already taken on.

'Quiet please.' The priest's frown and bowed shoulders made him look as he always did. Cold.

'But if we send the lepers to the flames,' I said. 'And it's not them—like it wasn't the cats—wouldn't that be committing the sin of murder?'

People began talking again and the priest rattled a fist. 'Silence! God demonstrates His wrath in sending us this pestilence through the Jews and the lepers. That wrath must be quelled.' He ran his tongue over his bluish lips. 'Besides, the order to offer the leper sinners to the flames comes from our lord and protector, le Comte de Fouville ... our *Seigneur* who must be obeyed. And anyone,' he went on, his gaze searching out and resting unmistakably on Isa and me, 'any person warning the lepers of their punishment, or helping them to flee will suffer the same sanction.'

'He won't really burn our leper friends,' Morgane said. 'Will he?'

'No, surely the *Seigneur* can't be serious?' I said, gripping her hand, and Isa's.

'Le Comte de Fouville might seem a bit of a bumbling fool,' my aunt said as we moved away from the knot of people still talking around the fountain. 'But he's not known for idle jokes.'

XXI

The bloody eye of the sun sank towards the western hills and the haymakers finished up their long, hot day's work: men and their sons scything the last stalks, wives and daughters following wearily, tying them into sheaves. Others were already trudging home, weed hooks, hoes and rakes slung over sagging shoulders. A farmer sat outside his barn, sharpening his sickle. Women washed out churns, licking the sweet butter from their fingers.

As I made my way home after visiting my patients, I didn't understand at first where the stream of people was trooping to, along the woodland road. Then, approaching our cot, I realised they were headed for the lepers' home and my chest constricted as if someone had punched the place between my breasts.

They carried small children and baskets of food, Lucie's team of sergeants keeping a watchful eye on the lepers' hut. And on our cot.

Despite the priest's threat, Isa had warned the lepers what was coming, but they'd merely said: 'Flee? Wherever would we go?' And, as le Comte de Fouville's men-at-arms ordered the thin and ragged lepers outside, and prodded them forward with their pikes, I knew there was no escape for them.

A young leper man with a ravaged face held up his small girl, setting her on his shoulders as if to say: how can you burn an innocent child, you monsters? But the crowd paid no heed to the little one as they cried, 'Burn the sinners! Burn the sinners!'

'Why do the priest and le Comte think the lepers brought the pestilence, Maman?' Morgane said, as the men-at-arms herded the trembling huddle into an oversized cage they'd hauled in. 'Where did it come from? And if the earth is a ball like Père Bernard says, won't the pestilence just roll over the top and then come back around to us again? So we'll never be rid of it?'

'I don't know, poppet,' I said, flicking one of her cinnamon-coloured braids nervously through my fingers. 'But what I do know is we don't want those sergeants to catch sight of Blanche, do we? You should lock her in the barn, and stay there with her, so she doesn't get lonely or frightened.'

'Why can't I watch the burning?' Morgane said. 'Other children are watching.'

'I don't care what others let their children do,' I said, 'this is no sight for a young girl ... no sight for anyone!'

'Papa would let me watch ... I bet he would,' she said with a scowl.

'Well your father isn't here. He's had to stay late at the Mason's Lodge ... again.'

Still pouting and gripping Crispen's wooden cat, Morgane dawdled off to the barn.

'The Church has already declared them dead to the world,' I said to Isa. 'So why burn them? How can you execute dead men?'

'So the flames will cleanse their *supposed* sins,' Isa said, through tight lips.

'And what if the lepers aren't the sinners everyone believes? What if leprosy isn't cast by God's hand, but just a sickness like any other?'

'That's something I've asked myself more than once,' Isa said, shaking her head.

The townsfolk had started hurling rotten vegetables and pebbles at the trembling lepers, and I winced, sucking in my breath as the hard clumps bruised their flesh. Squashed in the cage, naked save for loincloths, some cried mournfully. Others moved their lips faintly, perhaps in a last beseeching prayer to a deaf God. The rest trembled in silence.

'This is madness,' I said, 'the pestilence has turned us into lunatics.'

'Our priest might try and convince us all that divine punishment is the source of this sickness,' Isa said, 'but in their misery, people will always look for a human to blame. When we can't vent our anger on God, we must vent it on someone.'

'But it's all so wrong, Isa. How could the lepers have poisoned our wells? And with what Jews? There aren't any that I know of in Lucie.'

'Not a single one, but we humans have always devised Satan's blackest pain for each other.'

'I can't bear to watch this heartlessness any longer,' I said, as the cruel snap of switches hit the lepers' bare flesh. But try as I might I couldn't avert my eyes, or close the door. I still couldn't believe Renault de Fouville would go through with his order and actually burn our friends.

But burn the wretched souls our *Seigneur* did.

His men lit the kindling surrounding the cage with the spark from the flint-and-steel, the wild-eyed lepers crying out as the first flames singed their feet, fingers clawing frantically at the iron bars. Flames snaked from those bare feet up legs, their lips moving in fiercer movements, until their howls deafened me.

The crowd kept up its chant: 'Burn the sinners! Burn the sinners!'

The flames licked the piled-up wood hungrily. Smoke swirled about the lepers, choking their screams. I pressed my hands to my ears, but I could still hear them. On and on they wailed. The crowd still chanted for their death.

Their loincloths smouldered, caught fire. As flames leapt up their backs the screaming rose to a hideous peak. I smelt that same dreadful stink as the mound of burned cats.

The flames caught their hair, heads igniting like infernal

wreaths. Cinders and shreds of blackened cloth scattered the ground about the cage. The crowd looked on in gleeful, fascinated awe.

The pyre burst into full flame, quick and fierce as the blacksmith's furnace. Since people were usually executed by hanging, this was the first burning I'd witnessed; the first time I'd smelled scorched human flesh, heard human fat sizzle into the fire. Never before had I seen heat split apart a man's foot or heard his bones popping.

How did they feel as they burned? Could they smell the stench of their own flesh and hair, devoured by the flames? Did their screams echo in their heads, or was the pain so terrible they felt nothing, and screamed only in terror?

As I glimpsed the white of bone through the orange curtain, I turned away, clutching my heaving belly. But it was not the child in my womb making me gag.

'Why is it taking so long, Isa?' Tears spilled down my cheeks.

Speechless, her tanned face turned pale, Isa covered her own ears.

Finally—praise the Blessed Virgin—the screaming faded, and eventually the flames died around a blackened crust of corpses.

The crowd cheered and clapped as I stared at the roasted bodies, and held a strip of cloth over my mouth to stop the vomit from rising.

The Captain set alight the lepers' cottage. 'To be certain we're completely rid of the miasma they've been spreading,' he proclaimed.

This new blaze took vicious hold, the reedy thatch setting a fiery crown upon the cot, fingers of flame stealing down the timbers; orange frames around the clay daub between.

While the cot burned, the men-at-arms pushed away the charred remains of the cage. They dragged the corpses from the pyre with long sticks, and raked over the still-glowing ashes. They then broke up the lepers' bones with their pikes, so that nothing of their sinner bodies would remain to befoul the earth. I no longer wept. I frothed now with rage, and with misery, as the people packed up their baskets and their children. The thrill over, they began dawdling off home to bed.

'Such brainless boneheads they are,' I said to Isa. 'To think the wrath of God—sending us this pestilence through the lepers—is appeased; that it won't kill more of us.

'It's not finished you slug-brained idiots,' I shrieked at the departing crowd. 'The pestilence is still here ... it will still kill us.'

They laughed and grimaced, and pulled lunatic faces at us. And as the last one disappeared along the old Roman road, the wind picked up the pale dust of the lepers, carried it away, then let it fall, soft as snowflakes, on my own head.

***

Several hours later, an impatient rapping on my door startled me from sleep. The place beside me on the pallet was empty, so I guessed Raoul was still at the Mason's Lodge. Maybe he'd stay there all night—not to work, but to drink ale, play dice and avoid his wife. I clambered down the loft ladder and opened the door to Rixende's daughter.

'Maman says you gotta come now ... my papa's ill.' Pina said. 'Is it the pestilence?'

The girl gave me a quick nod and looked away, as if embarrassed her mother had been forced to summon me to care for Jâco.

I recalled then, that I hadn't seen Rixende at the lepers' burning, and it was not in the alewife's habits to miss such gruesome entertainment.

'How sick is your papa?'

'He just fell down, some hours ago,' Pina said, 'blood coming out his mouth and nose.'

The blood-spitting kind of pestilence ... even more catching than the black boils type ... kills more quickly.

The stink of the lepers' burned corpses still thick in my nostrils, the townspeople's clapping and cheering loud in my ears, it all sickened me; fouled me on the inside. I glanced up at the night sky; at the stars shining like dew on the Heavens. Perhaps they weren't stars, but the lepers' angels winking down at us, safe, finally, from our torture.

'I'm sorry, Pina, there's nothing I can do for your father.'

'But Maman reckons you can cure it ...' The girl's voice trailed off as I shook my head in disbelief and shut the door.

I climbed back up the loft ladder wearily but, my thoughts churning like the Vionne in spring, sleep refused to come.

I must've dozed off eventually, as another banging on the door woke me again with a jump.

In the candlelight, Alewife Rixende stood before me, fists and mouth clenched, threads of blonde hair stuck to her sweat and tear-stained face.

'Jâco's dead ... why didn't you come when I sent for you?' Her tongue snapped at the gap between her teeth. 'What kind of wise-woman turns her back on the sick?'

'I'm sorry about your husband, but I knew Jâco was beyond my help. There was no point—'

'I'll wager you could've saved him ... if you wanted.' Her glistening eyes lowered to my pendant. 'That talisman can do what you want—birth babes or kill them, curse murderous outlaws and cure the pestilence. You cured Yolande, didn't you? It's just your hatred for me that stopped you saving one of mine.'

'No, no, you're wrong. I wish it could, but my talisman can't do any of those things. And it's you who's always hated me, ever since you decided I stole Raoul Stonemason from you. All I do is try to defend myself.'

I reached towards her, my hand hovering over her forearm, thinking Rixende and I might call a truce to our battle, which suddenly seemed so trifling against the great pestilence war raging around us.

'Spoken like the Virgin Mary herself!' Rixende sneered, and

shoved me so violently that I fell over backwards.

Oh Mother of God, the baby ... if she's hurt Raoul's son ...

I picked myself up off the floor, brushing stray bits of lavender and rosemary from my hands and my chemise. I furled a hand over my belly, praying the watery womb bed was protecting the child.

'You'd best go, Rixende ... just go home, there's nothing I can do for you.' Reasoning with her was as useless as trying to warm stone in snow.

'You could, if you wanted,' she shouted, stamping off into a night more sombre than the back side of the moon.

I was right to heed my husband's warning; not to rush off to help the dying Jâco. Why care for the likes of Rixende and her family, putting my own at risk ... for no more thanks than vicious insult? Raoul was right—I must've been mad to want to help any of these ingrates.

XXII

𝕵oﬤan 𝔐iller's silﬤouette eclipsed our doorway. 'They're all ailing,' he said by way of greeting.

It was almost a week since the lepers' burning, but the stench of their charred flesh still lingered in the air around the cot. 'All eleven of my children after ... after those brute outlaws stole my Wanda and my Jacqueline.'

Raoul was sitting at the table sharpening his tools, and his gaze lifted to me, as alive as a creature poised to strike. Morgane was fishing boiled eggs from the pottage, and looked from me to her father and back to me again.

'What's wrong with them?' I said.

'Oh it's not the pestilence,' the miller said with a nonchalant wave. 'Not that, no ... can't be that ... don't know what they've got ... not the pestilence.' The man barely took a breath, his words tumbling from quivering lips. 'Can you come ... help them? It's not the pestilence ...'

No, it couldn't be ... not all eleven of them.

My mind split in two: one part screaming at me to obey my husband and send away Johan Miller, the other—the healer voice—pleading with me not to ignore the sick.

'I'll come right away,' I said, flicking my cloak from the nail. We might be at summer's peak but a chill skidded across the nape of my neck. I went to take my basket from the shelf but Raoul's grip on my wrist stopped me.

'Wait for me in your cart,' I said to Johan. 'I'll be out shortly.'

'The miller says it's not the pestilence, Raoul, and I *have* been obeying your orders, ignoring all the victims it's struck down this past week. I thought ... hoped ....' I laid a palm against my still-flat but churning belly. 'After Yolande recovered and you took back Anselme, I thought you were happy ... that our love was strong again?'

'You know it's surely the pestilence.' Raoul's neck muscle started twitching. 'For our sakes, for the sake of my unborn son, don't go there.'

'Let me at least see what's wrong with those poor children, Raoul. You heard Johan ... he insists it's not the pestilence.' I tried to shrug off his arm, but we just kept turning around and around like two people doing an angry dance.

'It is, Héloïse! And there's not a thing you can do to help them. True, a few in Florence survived it—not the blood coughers, only the swelling kind—but here in Lucie it's killed everyone except Yolande.'

'Mayhap the miller's children do have another sickness,' Isa said.

'And Maman can help them get better,' Morgane said.

Raoul turned to his daughter. 'Go to the barn and play with Blanche ... this is between your mother and me.'

'But—' she started.

'Go, now!' Raoul raised a hand as if to slap her.

Tears glistening her eyes, Morgane scuttled outside.

'Even if the miller's children have got it,' I said, stepping around Raoul's sturdy frame blocking the doorway, 'we both know by now that staying at home won't help. The miasma's here in Lucie ... in the air, on the market-place, everywhere. The only way to escape is to run away, and none of us can do that.' I took a shaky breath. 'I swear to you, on Ava's soul, that I won't go into the millhouse if it is the pestilence.'

But as I stepped up into the cart beside the distraught miller, I sensed my words were just a feeble poultice I'd laid over the wound that still festered between us.

The miller's horse clopped along past the naked and vacant

fields, the frenzied haymaking activity finally over, and everyone's hay sitting in the tithe barn for each family's share to be reckoned. As if he were alone in the cart, Johan Miller stared straight ahead. An owl hooted a mournful cry into the silence.

I felt trapped in a cage like the woeful lepers, the bars closing tighter around me, until soon there would be nowhere left to go. And then this black miasma—for I imagined it as a poisonous cloud—would seep under our door, and coil up the ladder to our sleeping loft. And there it would smother us all as we slumbered.

Once we arrived at the miller's newly-built home, I could see from the doorway that his children were gone. All eleven of them. The look and smell of the corpses told me they'd been dead for at least a day.

Of course it was the pestilence, what else? And once again, here I was, acting as if other families were more important than mine. This vile sickness was sending me insane too; stopping me from thinking clearly.

I cupped a hand to the miller's elbow, mustered my most tender voice. 'You didn't think to come for me earlier?'

The miller looked at me, but his eyes appeared unseeing, turned deep in on himself. 'Johan?' I squeezed his elbow.

'Something to fix them ....' He tugged at my basket. '... cure them ...' His feeble, shaky fingers kept pulling at my basket.

I took the miller's horse to fetch the sexton, oversaw the grisly task of removing eleven small corpses, and gave Johan Miller a sleeping potion.

Almost collapsing with fatigue and misery, and shaking with the terror of facing my husband again, I trudged back along the Roman road, my head full of the children's stink; the stench their poor father hadn't seemed to notice. Or had ignored.

Like a helpless cow that needs milking, bellowing with the pain in her teats, I wanted to scream; to smash the miller-gone-mad in the face, to take Isa and Morgane and Raoul and get as far away from Lucie and the pestilence as we could. But, as Isa kept saying, running was pointless.

But when I got home, the cot was silent, aside from Isa and Morgane's gentle snores from the loft. The only light coming from the red glow of fire embers, I climbed the loft ladder and saw our pallet was empty. No Raoul curled in slumber, facing the wall. No Raoul anywhere.

***

'Isa?' I leaned across the sleeping Morgane and gently shook my aunt. 'Is Raoul at the Mason's Lodge?'

Isa sat up blinking, silvery feathers of hair escaping her night cap. 'Is it morning already?'

'No, only just night ... I'm back from the miller's but Raoul isn't here.'

'Was it the pestilence, Héloïse?'

'Yes, but it had already killed every last one of them.' I tried to keep the sob in my throat as I caught Isa's gasp. 'I know ... an unspeakable tragedy for the miller.'

'Unthinkable,' Isa whispered. 'But Raoul ... after you left with Johan Miller, he sat brooding by the hearth for an age. Never even bid Morgane and me a good night.'

'So he's sleeping at the Mason's Lodge again to avoid—or punish—me?'

'Raoul doesn't tell me what he's doing, Héloïse, but look at this through his eyes. Besides us, he hasn't got a single soul in this world ... no parents, no siblings, no other family. Of course he wants to keep us safe. I've warned you about your disobedience,' she was wide awake now, 'your insistence at putting your work before your family. Every man has his limits, and mayhap Raoul has reached his, and he's left you.'

'Left me ... surely not?' I couldn't begin to think of such a thing. 'You know a husband doesn't leave his wife ... he throws *her* out. Besides, he'd never leave his beloved Flamelock, and he'd never abandon his Master Mason job. He told me this vingtain is no simple wall, but a work of art seen by all who pass through Lucie ... said he'd be spoken of in years to come as a good—or bad—stonemason. No, Isa, he'd never give up that!' Even as I spoke the words I knew I was trying to convince myself more than my aunt.

'You're not thinking right, Héloïse ... Raoul wouldn't have to abandon his Master Mason job, to leave you.'

'Well, he'll be spending another night in the Mason's Lodge,' I said, my stomach twisting into a knot. 'I'll go down there in the morning ... try and make our peace ... again.'

'*Humph.*' Isa gave a small snort. 'It mightn't be that simple to get back on good terms with your husband.'

'I can only try.' I wriggled into my night chemise and slumped down on the pallet. But weary as I was, I tossed about, gasping for every breath, suffocating in this airless pit that had trapped Raoul and me; buckling beneath the great dent in the armour of our love I'd thought so solid. I hugged my arms over my belly. The last time we'd made love was probably when this babe was seeded. Would I ever feel the warmth of our passion again, his tender words and caresses?

But on the edge of my yearning for my husband's love, a simmering resentment began to roost. As Raoul hadn't known Toubie was afflicted with the pestilence before it was too late, I too, hadn't been certain about the miller's children. Besides minor breaches, I was obeying his orders, but Raoul was ignoring the oath I'd sworn on Ava's soul and my calling to do my work properly. And how dare he not tell me where he was spending the night, making me worry so I wouldn't sleep at all? I gave up trying, crept down the loft ladder and lit a candle. I sat by the hearth, staring into the dying embers.

Unlike Alix and Nica's sweet-smelling beeswax candles, ours made from Vionne rushes dipped into melted tallow always left our hair and clothes reeking, but now it seemed such a stench, it made me gag. The bard's words from the Spring Fair rang clear and sorrowfully in my mind.

Take thou this rose, O Rose ... love's own flower ... by that rose, Thy lover captive is.

The stinking candles dimmed, guttered and died. There remained only a wisp of candle smoke, warm hearth ash. Cold ashes. Then nothing.

XXIII

The following morning I whisked through my chores. I left Morgane with Isa tending her rose bushes, and rode Merlinette down to la place de l'Eglise.

'Hurry up,' a vingtain labourer said, glancing at the sky, as the sweaty workers mixed together lime, sand and water, the building site humming with sound and movement like a hive of bees. 'We need to finish this mortar before it rains or it'll be wasted.' Raoul had told me that was a tough job, the lime burning your skin and your throat and I noticed they were all coughing, and stretching their shoulders constantly.

I scanned the workers' faces, couldn't see Raoul's. But what I saw was cold, raw fear. People were avoiding those coming out of miasma homes too: Yolande, Sergeant Drogan's mother and his wife. As the shoemaker's only surviving daughter stepped from the shop, a vingtain labourer caught his breath and leapt aside. 'God keep you, Mistress Ariane,' he murmured, guarding his gaze low.

They were all eyeing me too, more warily than usual. They must have thought me ill myself or, since news and rumour whipped through Lucie like a north wind, they'd learned of the rift between Raoul and me.

'Did you hear about Johan Miller?' Yolande said, nodding over at the churchyard, lumpy with fresh graves, as if a frantic mole had spent the night digging mounds of earth. Amidst the small group of mourners, Père Bernard was chanting his prayers for the dead.

'What other tragedy could that poor man possibly suffer?' I said, swatting at gnats biting the skin around my eyes.

'None ... now,' Yolande said. 'At dawn, a trout fisherman found his body floating in the Vionne. Everyone's been talking about the heavy stones that fisherman found in Johan's pockets, but the story Père Bernard got was some garbled tale about the miller losing his footing in the shallows. The pestilence hasn't quite sent us all crazy, Héloïse ... it seems people do understand the miller's grief, and nobody wants him damned for all eternity; denied his place in Paradise.'

Yolande motioned again towards the sorry-looking churchyard. 'They're burying him now, along with his children ... and several farmer and labourer families too, struck down after the haymaking.'

In a fenced corner of the presbytery garden, Père Bernard's pig lay on its side, panting. And below the graveyard, the Vionne flowed a murky grey, rubbish and animal bones scattered across its banks. And in the bushes littered with entrails, rotting meat and knots of fly-riddled shit, a skinny dog rooted around. Two shirtless men lifted a barrel of excrement from a cart and emptied it into a spot on the water where lush green grasses and reeds sprung from the richly-fertilised earth. I was thankful we lived far from this town refuse, where our water streamed a clear, unsullied green.

'Well I suppose we should all keep doing what Père Bernard says,' Yolande said, 'and continue praying to God ... thank Him for sparing some of us, at least.'

'Pray to God?' My hands bunched into fists as I fought to stave off the mounting anger. 'How can you pray to a God—love a God—who mercilessly stole your twins, Yolande? Innocents wrenched from life before they'd had a chance to truly live it? I certainly couldn't. And haven't we had enough of praying to God and seeing not the slightest result?' I pressed a fist to my lips.

'You should watch your blasphemous mouth, Héloïse.' Yolande spoke in the same warning tone of Isa's so familiar from my childhood. 'You already said too much in church ... saying God has abandoned us.'

'Oh you mean when our God-fearing *Seigneur* and priest decided to murder the innocent lepers?' I said. 'Can you truly still think God has our interests in His heart? Has He given us a reason to believe He is really working for us?'

'God works for us everywhere,' Yolande said. 'How can you doubt that?'

'And what if He doesn't? What if that's just a story we've made up to comfort ourselves? When this vile sickness took your little girls, I already had doubts. But now I'm convinced He does *not* work for us ... and that the Church, God's house, is certainly no haven from Hell.'

Yolande's high brow pleated in frown lines. 'You never could stop your tongue running away from you. And perhaps these troubles between you and Raoul are making your tongue even *more* reckless?'

'I am more edgy,' I said, as a group of girls walked by, Rixende's oldest amongst them. 'But I still think this pestilence has changed everything ... changed us all. And I'll wager I'm not the only person in this town questioning the workings of God and the Church. Anyway, speaking of my husband ... I need to see him right now.'

'Where's the Devil-eyed girl then?' Pina said, as I made to walk off to the Mason's Lodge. 'You curse her too, with the pestilence ... like Maman reckons you cursed my papa, and refused to cure him?'

'Hold your tongue, you nasty little wretch,' I snapped, the girl's jibes angering me more than usual. I glanced at Yolande who arched her thin, black eyebrows.

'I'm the nasty little wretch?' Pina jutted out her chin, hands clinched on her hips.

Her smile, the identical mocking grin of Rixende's, made my

arms erupt in freezing bumps. The girl resembled her mother so much I might've laughed had I not been so enraged. 'I heard you just then ... how you don't reckon God or the Church is real. Maman's always saying you're a heretic, so why should I listen to anything a heretic says?'

I could scarcely believe the girl's insolence and slapped her hard, on the cheek. 'Be gone, you little horror,' I hissed. 'And keep away from my daughter.'

As Pina sauntered off into the sweltering heat, and Yolande drifted away, I glanced across to the tavern. Rixende, sharing a mug of ale with the blacksmith, had witnessed the whole thing.

The alewife threw me a vinegary smile. 'Perhaps a Jew took your husband?' she said. 'That's what they do ... take our Christian people then torture them and drink their blood so they'll look like Christians too.'

As she doubled over in raucous laughter at her own jest, I could only stare in disbelief. I'd thought Rixende's mourning might soften her edges, but the alewife was still hard as a crone's tit, and not so drowned in grief apparently. Tattle had it that the very day after Jâco's passing, she'd taken to spending her nights with Pierro Blacksmith.

'Or maybe your husband got sick of your disobedience,' she went on, 'and came crawling into my bed, instead? Her tongue flicked between her teeth. Her face was haggard, with grief I supposed—drink certainly—and her once cornflower blue eyes were sunken into red-rimmed hollows with the unnatural brightness of a person on the cusp of lunacy. 'Then again, maybe Raoul Stonemason just dropped down dead somewhere, from the blood-spitting pestilence ... the type what you cursed on my Jâco? Ain't that right, Pierro?' She nudged the blacksmith's elbow, and Pierro's face slid from where it had been propped in his hand, and thudded onto the table. 'After all a proud stone-mason like Raoul would never abandon a Master Mason job, would he?'

'Don't be stupid, Rixende, as if I could curse Jâco ...'

My voice trailed off. The alewife's words might be the rantings of a drunken buffoon, but still a scalding heat shot through my body. I'd not thought of that: the sudden, silent killer felling Raoul.

But no, that couldn't be! He was surely in the Mason's Lodge. I breathed deeply, trying to calm my nerves; asking myself why I was wasting time sparring with the alewife instead of making peace with my husband. I stamped off once again towards the Mason's Lodge.

'Midwife Héloïse!' The urgent whisper came from the weaver's shop. 'Please come … quickly.'

'Catèlena …?' I started, as Drogan's wife glanced about, pulled me into the shop and closed the door. This was a pestilence home but I could not find it within myself to ignore Catèlena's miserable, pleading look.

'What is it?' I said, rummaging through the cloth and leather pouches in my basket. 'I have some of that goose salve I gave you at the Spring Fair, which works miracles.'

'No goose salve.' Catèlena's voice was still quivery. 'Please, give me your midwife's herbs … the ones I've heard cast out unwanted babies. I thought I was with child before, and almost asked you then. I wasn't, but this time I'm certain.'

My gaze lowered to her belly. 'Does Drogan know?'

'No, and the Virgin willing, he and his mother will never find out.' Catèlena crossed herself. 'My husband is a liar and a vicious man. It was no intruder who hammered to death his first wife, and I'd rather die than give that savage creature another child. And if it was a maid I'd only drown her before she's old enough to suffer at his hands, as I, and his two little girls, already suffer.' She took a quick breath. 'Please can we do it now? Drogan's gone for the day—up to the castle for I don't know what reason—and if he finds out he'll kill me, and damn me straight to Hell.'

I bade Catèlena lie on the family's sleeping pallet, and pressed my fingers against her belly. 'How many courses have you missed?' I said, realising that Raoul and the Mason's Lodge would have to wait.

'Just one.'

'Won't Drogan's mother be home soon?'

'Mère Sara is at the river with Drogan's girls,' Catèlena said. 'They'll be gone hours, washing all the clothes, and their hair. When I saw you passing, I knew this was my only chance. Please, Midwife Héloïse.'

'As reluctant as I am to do this without good cause, it won't be dangerous or difficult, since you're still in the first moon. The soul doesn't enter the unborn child until much later, so it's no mortal sin to banish it.'

'There is good cause!' Catèlena's eyes brimmed with tears as she laid a palm against the swollen purple mass on her cheek. 'You know—as everyone in Lucie knows—that Drogan beats me far more than is normal for a husband to hit a wife, and now he's started on his girls ... blaming them for not being sons. Please, you must help me.'

I nodded, took the angel potion from my basket and added water from the kettle.

'I'll wait with you until it's over.' I settled on the ground beside the pallet as Catèlena drank. We sat in silence for a few minutes. I itched to get to the Mason's Lodge but I'd abandoned far too many patients these past weeks, and since Catèlena showed no pestilence signs I felt I should stay and comfort her.

'You've been lucky in marriage, Midwife Héloïse ... Raoul Stonemason seems a good, caring husband.'

'I do think myself lucky,' I said, feeling my face flush as I thought, in dismay, of the shredded mess that loving marriage had become. 'Especially as a bastard non-born who many think had no right to wed.'

'*Tsk, tsk.*' Catèlena clicked her tongue. 'Pay no attention to the viper-tongued townsfolk, or Alewife Rixende, who will never forgive you for marrying Raoul Stonemason, even though he wasn't ever hers if I remember?' She frowned, her tiny hands moving to her belly.

'It's working already?' I asked.

'No, just a twinge. Please, tell me how Raoul chose you over Rixende. An amusing love story will lift my sad heart and ... and stop me thinking about what I'm doing.'

'Well,' I said, 'a week after I'd treated Raoul's injury, I went back to the building site ... with the excuse of checking his hand.' I gave her a conspiratorial smile. 'He'd removed the bandage, and the wound was well-healed. Then I felt his fingertips on my elbow, guiding me to a shadowy corner, and thought I'd faint on the spot.'

Catèlena smiled. 'Your first kiss?'

I nodded. 'A week later he said he wanted me for his wife. And if he was accepted as a master mason, his mark would be an interwoven H and R.' I let out a giggle. 'Neither of us has ever learned any letters apart from the H and R, and that's enough for me.'

'I've seen that mark,' Catèlena nodded, 'on the new vingtain blocks.' Her eyes filled with tears. 'If only mine was such a romantic story to tell my children one day ...'

'I don't know why Raoul chose me,' I said. 'Perhaps he'd looked past my plainness and seen something deeper. Or I wasn't as plain as I imagined. But that was the moment I'd thought would never come, my chance for a family name, a clan. Then I remembered my status ... told him I was sorry but marriage had no place for a bastard like me.'

'What did he say to that?' Catèlena ran her hands over her belly.

'He said a woman might wed in the name of her father but that he cared nothing of my tainted birthright; that there wasn't a single other woman with whom he wanted to build a family.'

'Rixende must've been mad as a nest of wasps,' Catèlena said.

'Madder! She was already misguided by townsfolk rumours of the bastard midwife and her bastard aunt and mother, but I'm sure that sealed her hatred for me; when she swore to make me pay for thieving the man she'd claimed as hers.'

'You're so lucky, Midwife ... not to have to live in terror of your husband.'

'Why did you marry Drogan then?' I said, blinking away the smarting tears when I thought of Raoul's slap.

We'd all heard the stories about the villeins of olden times, but nowadays, whilst not everyone owned their own land or home, and rented from our *Seigneur*, every person was free to go where he wanted, and marry who he desired, except nobles of course.

'Because he seemed so charming at first … his good looks enchanted me, and I thought how blessed I was, such a small and plain mouse, to be marrying a man like him. Now I know he only wed me because feeble mice are easy prey; they never make a fuss or hit back, like Alewife Rixende used to beat Jâco.'

'I could hardly believe it when le Comte de Fouville appointed your husband one of his sergeants,' I said. 'A suspected wife murderer!'

'Oh that's exactly why he appointed him,' Catèlena said. 'Our *Seigneur* believed Drogan would be a good strong arm to discipline rowdy townsfolk. Besides, if you believe the whispers, le Comte de Fouville always has an eye out for handsome men like Drogan to lure into his castle chamb—'

Drogan's tall and rugged frame, his clear almond-coloured eyes and nest of dark curls flitted into my mind, then vanished as quickly, when Catèlena gasped and doubled over, clutching at her belly.

As the angel potion took effect, I squeezed her hand, felt her nails digging into my palm as the great ripping cramps invaded her body. I thought of the babe inside me.

Don't let me lose this one … Mother of God, please no.

Frail and small as she was, Catèlena remained stoic, for fear of alerting the neighbours I supposed. Even as the blood began to flow, clotted and dark, she didn't cry out.

Several hours went by, the blood still running, and both of us praying to Saint Margaret. Still Catèlena made no sound, her tears spilling silently down her cheeks.

I kept cleansing my hands in rose-water, and packing wool into her womb until the bleeding finally ceased.

'If Drogan, or your mother-in-law, suspect you were with child, just tell them it simply fell out of you before taking root,' I said, helping Catèlena change into fresh clothes. 'I'll wash these and return them in a few days.' I shovelled the bloodied clothes and linen into my basket. 'So you won't have to explain anything.'

As I took my basket and made to leave, the weaver's shop door opened and Drogan's mother bustled inside, her grand-daughters in tow.

***

'What business you got in my home, Midwife Héloïse? Sara's gaze darted to my basket overflowing with the bloody linen. 'And what in the Devil's *merde* is wrong with Catèlena? Why's she lying on the pallet?'

'Your daughter-in-law has lost the babe she was carrying,' I said.

'Oh.' Drogan's mother seemed, for an instant, stumped for words. 'But why are her soiled things in your basket?' Her voice thickened with suspicion, her eyes narrowing. 'Looks like the actions of someone hiding something.'

Catèlena seemed to freeze with her fear and didn't move, or speak.

'What are you suggesting, Sara?' I said. 'Mother Earth simply doesn't let some babes take hold in the womb, and probably for the best, since those ones are not meant to be. Catèlena told me you were washing today, at the river. I knew you wouldn't wash again for a week, so I took the soiled linen to help out Catèlena, and you.'

Sara stared at her daughter-in-law who remained speechless and cowering on the pallet, tears streaming down her cheeks. I silently willed the girl to keep her mouth shut.

'I happened to be on the market-place,' I went on, 'when Catèlena called me inside, the pain in her belly terrible, the blood already flowing. I stayed to comfort her until it was over. Now I must go to my other patients.'

And see my husband!

'I hope your discomfort and your sadness pass soon, Catèlena.'

'I ... I'm sorry, Mère,' Catèlena said in a shaky voice. 'Sorry the babe is ... is gone.'

As I reached the door, I turned back to Sara. 'Give Catèlena warmed chicken broth. That's the best thing at a time like this. Then let her sleep.'

Sara gave me a curt nod, but her sharp eyes followed me outside, and I didn't breathe easily until I was well away from the weaver's shop.

My heart heavy with Catèlena's misery, I finally trudged across to the Mason's Lodge. It was empty though, and there was still no sign of Raoul on the vingtain site. He and Anselme might be up at the castle planning repair work, but I certainly wasn't going up to that bleak place. Making peace with my husband would have to wait until the end of his working day.

I rode Merlinette home along the woodland road, thinking what I'd say to Raoul tonight after curfew; how I'd try to make up with him—to reignite those first sparks of love that speaking with Catèlena had made me hunger for even more.

In the distance the field workers were hunkered over, harrowing the newly-sown seed with soil to protect it, the horses dragging along the bundles of brushwood harrows tied to their tails. They worked quickly, their faces tilting skyward, looking anxiously at the gathering swags of magenta clouds.

I'd felt the chill of the coming storm; smelled its pungent zing, but the first crack of thunder still startled me. Fat raindrops spattering my shoulders, I urged Merlinette on, trying to calm the rush of my heartbeat; to convince myself Sara had believed our story, and that Catèlena wouldn't speak of my angel potion to a soul. Because if Drogan found out, he'd not hesitate to have his wife—and me—hanged on the gallows.

Isa had taught me that the mixed seed has no soul at such an early stage, but God and the Church still regarded our act of banishing it as a mortal sin. I'd seen too many women suffer and even die at a husband's savage hand, and if the angel potion was the only way I could help them, so be it. God understood that, surely?

As a splinter of lightning lanced the leaden sky, more thunder pursuing, the wind whipping my kirtle about my legs, it seemed God had not understood. Perhaps He wasn't even listening.

XXIV

Morgane stood on a stool, hanging the star-shaped flowers above our doorway. 'Why's it called Saint John's wort, Maman?'

'Because today is Saint John the Baptist's feast day, poppet … the four and twentieth day of June, when the fully-bloomed plant can ward off evil spirits.'

'See how the yellow petals resemble a halo?' Isa said, 'and the red sap signifies the blood of the martyred saint.'

'Well, while the Saint John's wort is keeping *away* evil spirits,' Morgane said, 'maybe it will bring *back* a good spirit … bring Papa back home to us? Doesn't he love us anymore?'

'Of course he does,' I said. 'Your father will always love us … whatever happens. He's just busy with his work, and will come home when he can.' I ignored Isa's raised eyebrows and tried to keep my voice chirpy, as if my husband's sleeping at the Mason's Lodge for the last week hadn't bothered me a gnat's wing; as if I didn't feel the weighty sorrow, like I was carrying one of Raoul's granite boulders in my heart. 'Now hurry off to that well, poppet … I'll need water if I'm to brew any ale before the day's out.'

'Are you going to try and talk to Raoul again today?' Isa said, as Morgane skipped off with the pail. She placed her bundles of twined herbs on the table for me to hang from the lean-to rafters.

'What's the point?' I said, laying out squares of cloth for

Morgane to fashion lavender bags later. 'He's rebuffed me every day for the whole week he's been gone. I just keep praying to the Virgin he'll forgive me for going to that sorry millhouse, and to Yolande's home when she fell ill. As far as I know, he's not aware I've been in the weaver's pestilence home to care for Catèlena so he can't be bristling about that at least!'

Once I'd hung the herbs to dry, I took the pestle and mortar and began crushing together thyme and parsley. 'I've been worried sick about Sibylle and her unborn, but since her husband came down with pestilence I've kept clear of the bakery too. Although they say he's well now ... another miraculous recovery.' I wiped the back of my hand across my sweat-streaked brow. 'Raoul will surely come around soon ... once he sees I really am heeding his wishes.'

As Isa raised her dark eyebrows again, the horse whinnied from the barn. Better than a dog Merlinette was, her noise always alerting me to approaching strangers, human or animal. I assumed she was neighing at Morgane, coming from the well with the ale-brewing water, but as Morgane skipped inside the mare kept up her noise.

'It must be those hens,' I said, 'fussing to be let out.'

I'd locked them in the barn for the night after a fox slipped in yestereve and carried off one of our best layers. Although the squawks had sent me running, I was too late, glimpsing only a fiery tail vanishing under the gate.

'I'll really have to go and let them out,' I said, as Merlinette whinnied again, louder, more urgent. My hand on the pestle fell still then, as I caught muffled sounds outside. 'Bring Blanche, poppet, we'll lock her in the barn with Merlinette.'

'Why, Maman? Who's outside?'

'Nothing ... I don't know.' My scalp went cold, as if my hair was being stretched from it. 'Just get Blanche, now.'

But before my daughter could grab her cat, the door burst open, and Sergeant Drogan sauntered in, as well as someone can saunter with bent legs. His great shoulders jostled our hanging pans, his long boots casting gobbets of dirt over my clean floor rushes.

'Why are you barging into my cot, Sergeant Drogan?' I grabbed my knife from the table, my fingers tightening around the handle.

'Why wasn't that cat burned with the others?' he said, as Morgane scuttled past him clutching Blanche to her chest.

'Don't take Blanche.' I pictured Drogan's cruel satisfaction as he gleefully torched Morgane's beloved cat. 'That cat's been her greatest friend since she lost Pétronille and Peronelle.'

'I don't give a pig's fart about a stupid cat. It's you I've come for, wife of Raoul Stonemason.' Sergeant Drogan waved about his baton of office, and wrinkled his nose as if our cot were a midden. 'Stinks in here like the Devil's own hearth … the very air tainted with heresy.'

'Well if you say burning rosemary is heretical,' Isa said, flinging an arm at the smoking herb, 'you've gone as mad as some others in this town.'

'Why have you come for me, Sergeant Drogan?' I still held the knife aloft as a fist of terror struck me: he'd discovered that I'd got rid of his and Catèlena's unwanted seed.

'Don't be afraid,' Drogan said, the almond-coloured eyes lighting with his smile, as he removed his cloak, the damp wool stinking in the summer heat. He sat by the hearth as if it was his own.

'I'm not afraid of you,' I lied.

'Well that knife shaking in your hand certainly makes it look like you are.' Drogan twisted a large amber ring on his finger—a ring I'd never seen before, and something that large and shiny I would definitely have noticed. 'Besides, since the pestilence took the old captain, and half our sergeants, it's Captain Drogan now.'

Captain Drogan? Oh save us, Blessed Virgin!

'I'm not afraid of you,' I repeated. 'I just don't like you … any more than you like me.'

As Isa was always warning, I knew I should keep my thoughts

to myself. Taunting Drogan, especially if he really was Captain now, would only make things worse, but I did enjoy seeing his smug smile fall away.

'Who do you think you are, talking to your Captain that way?' he said. 'And put that knife down.'

'You think I might stab you, Drogan?'

'Who's to know what someone like you might do ... now put that knife down.'

With an exaggerated sigh, I boldly met his gaze, and placed the knife on the table. 'I'll ask you again, what do you want with me? Surely not to insult me with some new and ridiculous accusation you've thought up to replace the milk-thieving, leg-bowing farce?'

'Oh but I'm here for exactly that reason, wife of Raoul Stonemason,' he said, his brawny figure looming over me. 'I'm arresting you on charges of misconduct.'

'Misconduct?' I laughed out loud, to mask my relief. Catèlena hadn't told him; he knew nothing. I kept laughing, right in Drogan's face. 'Is this a bad joke?'

'Misconduct?' Isa said. 'Your accusations are unfounded and ridiculous, Serg—Captain.' She thrust an arm towards the doorway. 'Now off you trot and let us get on with our chores.'

'Nothing I'd like more than to trot off out of here,' Drogan said, 'but le Comte de Fouville has ordered me to take your niece, Midwife Héloïse to the church gaol on the charge of misconduct.'

Was that loathing, triumph or mockery on Drogan's face? Perhaps all three mixed together.

My heartbeat quickened and I stepped back from him. 'Gaol? I won't go. You can't make me.' I took the knife again.

'So you really are going to stab me now, are you?' Drogan laughed and clicked his fingers.

Two burly sergeants thudded inside and before I had time to make the slightest move, they each clasped one of my arms.

'Careful of that Devil's charm she wears around her neck,'

Drogan said to his men, 'the eyes can burn a man's skin.'

'What do you mean, misconduct? I'm a midwife and a healer ... proper, God-fearing conduct!' I tried to pull away but the sergeants' grip was fast as iron. I was powerless, whimpering as they bound my arms with rope and dragged me from my cot like a small and bleating animal.

'You can't do this, Captain Drogan,' Isa said, hurrying after us, and trying vainly to release me from their hold. 'I'll speak to le Comte myself if you don't let her go now.'

'Speak to him,' Drogan said in a bored tone. 'See how much notice he takes.'

'You'll pay for this idiocy,' Isa carried on, her blackbird eyes narrowed on Drogan. 'And likely go straight to Hell!'

'And I say to you, old crone,' Drogan jabbed his forefinger at Isa, 'if you want your Devil-niece to eat while she's locked up in gaol so she can't escape her trial, you'd best bring her food.'

'Trial? This is an evil prank of yours, surely?' I twisted and turned, even as I knew it was useless. And the piss I couldn't hold in trickled down my legs.

'That's enough of your yabbering,' Drogan said. 'No point struggling ... we'll take you anyway.'

'Maman, Maman!' Morgane ran across from the barn. 'Where are you taking my mother?'

'Stay with Isa,' I said. 'Maman will be home ... home soon. Don't fret, my sweet.'

In the struggle to shove me into the waiting cart, the sergeants tore my cap from my head. My long hair tumbled free and I felt more naked than if I'd not been wearing a stitch of clothing.

The cart bounced away, across sun-hardened ruts. I looked back at the cot, and the last thing I glimpsed was Isa and Morgane clutching each other.

***

The sun was bright, shadows from the trees dark and light stripes across the dusty road: dark, light, dark, light, in rhythm to the horse's clopping. Bound to the cart with the stink of my pee and the rush of my heartbeat for company, I glanced down at the Vionne, to the bawling lambs separated from their mothers for the sheep washing.

'What's this misconduct charge, Drogan?' I said, giddy with confusion. 'Is it about the milk again? Five and twenty summers, and still you go on about me sharing your mother's milk ... as if there wasn't enough for you; as if that bent your legs. Will you despise me your whole life for something impossible? For your father's death?'

'Nothing to do with your milk-thieving,' Drogan said. 'And you'll find out soon enough about the misconduct. But Maman always said that's what bowed my legs ... what else can I do but believe my own mother?'

'My aunt's told you a hundred times that your legs are bent because your mother wouldn't listen to her and swaddle you properly,' I said, as a hunting hoolet swooped overhead and the horse jinked sideways, almost toppling me over the side. 'And how often have I told you the milk thieving is just ignorant myth ... that the more a breast is milked, the more blood will be turned into milk? Besides, a mother's milk is a gift and should be given freely to any babe who needs it.'

I knew I was gabbling, my tongue rushing away from me to try and mask my terror; something I was well aware Drogan thrived on. I breathed deeply, set my jaw tight, refusing to grant him any more fodder than he already had.

Drogan heaved his wide shoulders in a bored shrug and exchanged glances with the men-at-arms, who were still smirking at the mention of breasts being milked.

There was evidently no point trying to reason with such hare-brained idiots, and I looked to the river again so I wouldn't have to watch Drogan basking in my fear. The sheep, their fleeces scrubbed clean with the greasy yellow soap, were scrambling from the water. Children snatched up the hollering lambs and skittered from ewe to ewe matching up mother and baby, the lambs almost knocking over the children in their urgency to nuzzle.

The washer-men stopped and stretched their backs, holding up their hands and gazing at them as if amazed at their whiteness. The hours of strong soap and sudsy fleece had accomplished what a year of cold water alone could never scrub off.

Further along the road, amongst the sweat-laden farmers weeding the crops—loathsome task between the haymaking and the August harvest—I glimpsed Poppa's son. Holding his long-handled sticks, Farmer Donis looked up at me, frowned and scratched his head.

As bewildered as Donis, all I could do was shake my head.

We finally reached la place de l'Eglise, and the men pushed me from the cart onto the burning cobblestones.

'Why've we stopped here?' I asked, then, as Drogan dragged me before the half-built vingtain wall, I understood. Oh yes, such delight he'd take parading and flaunting his victim to the townsfolk. And to my husband.

'Let me go!' I cried again, my voice sharp with rage; curdled with fear.

'I bet this is your doing, you miserable whore,' I hissed at Alewife Rixende, and spat in the dirt at her feet.

Drogan and Rixende exchanged a wink and a laugh. The sergeants tightened their clutch and I could already feel my skin bruising beneath their fingers.

Wide-eyed, Yolande stared at me from the tailor's shop bench. 'Héloïse, what...?'

'I don't know, Yolande ... I just don't know!' I shrugged, quivering as I took in great, desperate gulps of air.

Sibylle flung open the bakery door. 'What the Blessed Virgin are you doing with the midwife?'

'Taking her to gaol,' Drogan said, his voice bright with glee. 'Off she goes to gaol, to gaol. Off she goes—' he chanted.

'Gaol! Whatever for?'

'Misconduct,' Drogan said.

'But she's got to birth my child,' Sibylle cried. 'I can't have it without her, no I can't!'

'Misconduct?' Yolande cried, 'what does that mean?'

'It means nothing,' I shouted. 'Just a pathetic excuse for Captain Drogan to take his revenge on me for his bent legs; on my aunt because his family has always falsely accused Isa of killing his father.'

'That's impossible,' the usually mouse-timid Ariane said. 'The midwife and her aunt are good, healing women. Certainly not killers.'

I was grateful for their kind words, but they fell on deaf ears, as the sergeants dragged me towards Saint Antoine's church.

I scanned the vingtain site. No Raoul. My head swivelled about like a spinning top—left, right, all over the square. Still no sign of Raoul.

Where is he? My husband would speak up for me; he'd surely save me from this lunatic.

***

Deep beneath Saint Antoine's foundations, amidst niches of the bones of priests who'd been laid in the catacombs for centuries, the men opened a stout wooden door. In the dim lantern light, they shoved me into what must be one of the penitents' cells. It was small and cold with only a pile of filthy straw in one corner.

'Don't touch me, brute!' I tried to smack the gaoler's leathery hand from my breast, as he unbound my wrists, his ale and onion breath making me retch. The other men chuckled along with Captain Drogan as they began to move off.

'Leave me the lantern,' I said. 'At least leave me some light.'

'Why do you need a light?' Drogan said. 'Nothing to see besides the ghosts of those who were here before you.'

The great wooden door closed behind the men. The key turned in the lock, the laughter fading with their steps. Then there was only darkness. Cold, black and stinking of my terror. I sank to the floor. Knees bent up to my chin, I crouched against the cold stone wall, limbs cramped, already aching. I strained to hear the smallest noise but there was only the rustle of creatures through the straw and the pounding of my heart.

'Come back!' I shouted. 'Please, Captain Drogan, come back!'

It was useless, I knew it, so I was surprised to hear footsteps, slow and steady, getting louder. I heard the key turn in the lock, the creak of the wooden door opening.

'You called for me?' Drogan's voice was thick with mock concern, the lantern lighting only his mouth and nose, but I imagined the scornful eyes above. I was certain he was about to laugh, and say: 'Just a joke, Midwife Héloïse. You're free to go.' The kind of joke Drogan would find hilarious.

'Why won't you tell me?' I said, 'what is this misconduct charge?'

Captain Drogan sighed as if the whole ordeal was boring him senseless. He inhaled a long breath before he spoke the words that stopped my heart.

'You'll have to ask your husband that. Raoul Stonemason is the one who brought the misconduct charge ... the one who had you thrown in this cell.'

XXV

The following morning, as Raoul was packing his leather satchel to leave for the vingtain site, an urgent rap came on the cot door. He'd thought it best to return home yestereve, as soon as he'd seen Captain Drogan hauling his wife off to gaol. His little Flamelock would need him, and neither she nor Isa need ever know it was he who'd brought the charge against Héloïse. He was the one truly guilty of misconduct—yes, Raoul did acknowledge that—but he was still certain he'd done the right thing.

He watched as Isa hobbled over from the cauldron in which she was brewing some kind of smelly potion and opened the door.

'What in God's toenails could you want with us now, Captain Drogan?' she said, wiping her hands down her apron. 'Isn't it enough you dragged my niece away from her family on some ridiculous charge?'

'That's what I've come about,' Drogan said, strolling inside uninvited, his burly frame occupying the entire room. 'The misconduct charge has been dropped.'

'Dropped?' Raoul stopped short. 'Why?'

'Well thank the Devil's arse you've come to your senses,' Isa said. 'So Héloïse is on her way home?'

'Can I sit?' Drogan gestured to a stool at the table. Raoul remained silent and so did Isa but Drogan sat anyway, the stool vanishing beneath his bulk.

Dread twisting from his gut like an uncoiling serpent, Raoul watched, wordlessly, as Drogan spread his long legs wide, propped an elbow on one knee and leaned his cheek against his fist. The fingers of his opposite hand drummed on one thigh. It was the confident look of a vengeful brute and Raoul feared he'd been a bird-brained half-wit to trust Drogan.

'And?' Raoul said, not taking his eyes from Drogan as he eased himself onto a stool across the table. 'Explain, Captain.'

'The misconduct charge is being dropped because a far more serious accusation against your wife has since come to light.'

'More serious ...?' Cold beads of sweat slid down Raoul's brow, and he knew in that instant that Drogan had gone back on his promise. He realised the Captain had somehow tricked him.

'Your wife, Raoul Stonemason,' he said. 'Is now charged with heresy, a dissenter—'

'Heresy?' Isa, wide-eyed, stared from Drogan to Raoul, and back to Drogan.

The serpent in Raoul's belly unfurled, stretched its neck till it was rigid, and spat its venom into his throat. The thought flitted through his mind to beseech Saint Etienne for help, but he knew it was useless. There was no avoiding it: Isa was about to discover how and why her niece was locked up.

'A dissenter from a member of our Catholic Church, who disavows a revealed truth,' Drogan proclaimed. 'She was overheard voicing heretical thoughts on the market-place.'

'Héloïse's words, whatever they were, surely weren't spoken in earnest,' Isa said, swiping at grey threads of her hair that had slid from her cap. 'It was only her despair speaking ... the desperation this terrible pestilence has begotten in us all.'

'Le Comte de Fouville first ordered us to burn the cats, then the lepers,' Drogan carried on, as if Isa hadn't spoken. 'But the pestilence remains, which means, so our good priest says, there are still sinners within our midst. And I say a heretic like your niece,' he pointed at Isa, 'and your wife, Raoul Stonemason, is the greatest sinner of them all.'

'And what if her pendant,' Drogan continued, 'the one that burned me, really is the Devil's charm? What if the rumours are true, that she *has* been using that angel of Satan to curse us with the pestilence?'

'What are you—?' Raoul said, the throbbing in his temple so loud and fast he feared his head would explode.

'Don't be ridicul—' Isa started.

'Of course,' Drogan went on, cutting them both off, 'we all knew about the witchery. You and your niece's spells and magic charms, but this heresy is a different thing altogether. Especially when our godly priest is insisting we root out every last sinner to halt this pestilence.'

'This is just another of your pathetic excuses, Drogan,' Raoul said, 'your hatred of Héloïse. You've always tried to make a misery of her life, right from her sorry birth.'

'Besides,' Isa said, 'even if she does have such power, which she certainly does not, why the Devil's black arse would she bring a deadly sickness to Lucie, when she swore an oath on her dead mother's soul to bring life?'

'And so she doesn't run off,' Drogan carried on, still ignoring Isa, 'she'll be kept in the church gaol until her trial—three days hence—by le Comte de Fouville.'

'Captain Drogan,' Raoul said, gagging and swallowing the bitter taste of that serpent's poison, aware he was about to destroy not only his wife, but her beloved aunt too. 'That wasn't what we decided. You promised—for a healthy sum—to keep Héloïse comfortable, with a well-stuffed mattress, clean water and food, and visits from her friends and family. Just until this pestilence passes. That was our agreement.'

'Agreement?' Isa's shrewd, blackbird eyes narrowed, and Raoul flinched from her thorny gaze. 'What agreement, Raoul? What on God's bleeding bones have you done?'

Raoul leapt from the stool and waved his arms about, already desperate to defend himself. 'After Héloïse went to Yolande's pestilence home, then to the miller's,' he said, 'I thought it was the only way to be sure she'd stop trying to treat pestilence victims.'

He wished Isa would stop shaking like that, her face white as bleached bone, her hands tightly clasped as if she was restraining herself from slapping him senseless. 'If you knew how sorry I am, Isa ... I never thought Drogan would invent this new—'

'*You* had her locked up?' Her red-black stare snagged Raoul's breath.

'I was just trying to keep her safe.' Raoul was barely able to get his words out. 'Don't you see? It was the only way I could protect our family.'

He turned to Captain Drogan, who'd been watching him and Isa with an indulgent smile, arms crossed, as if enjoying a humorous mummer's play.

'You and that drunken alewife have always hated her, and this is simply another of your vengeful plots. Now I can see it, plain as the prick on a rutting bull. You only wanted her locked away to make it easier to press this ridiculous heresy charge.' Raoul cleared his throat, which felt thick with the dust of a hundred building sites. 'So since you can't keep your promise, Drogan, what say we keep this between us: how le Comte de Fouville's Captain took a bribe to bring wrongful charges? You keep my sous and I'll cut my losses. But just release her now.'

Captain Drogan stood, and brushed at imaginary dirt on his breeches. 'What bribe, Raoul Stonemason? What sous are you talking about?'

Raoul could barely speak. Sick with nervous rage; with the Captain's gall, the voice that came from him was hoarse and breathless. 'How dare you ...?'

Raoul lurched at him, brought a white-knuckled fist up to Drogan's face.

'Don't!' Isa shouted. 'That's just what the Captain wants, you foolish idiot ... a good excuse to lock you up too.'

Raoul's stare still fixed on Drogan's clear gaze, he inhaled deeply, unclenched his fist and forced his arm back to his side. 'I was sure you'd be good for some easy coin,' he said, 'but as she says,' he flung an arm at Isa, 'I've been a foolish idiot, and I should've seen this coming.'

'Besides, who are the people likely to believe?' Drogan said. 'Our *Seigneur's* own Captain or the husband and aunt of an accused heretic?'

He turned his charming smile to Isa. 'So there's no point you going whining to le Comte, we both know whose arse he'll cover. Now step aside or I'll arrest both of you for obstructing justice.'

'We certainly do know whose arse le Comte covers,' Isa said, her voice heavy with scorn, as Drogan walked through the door. 'Yours and that buggering priest's.'

'Rattle out any tale you want, you stale old hag,' Drogan sneered, 'neither of you can prove a thing.'

Raoul kept staring through the open doorway, long after the Captain had sauntered off. He slowly turned back to Isa, waiting—like a man cringes beneath the punishing whip raised to crack—for Isa's tongue-lashing. He held up a hand. 'I was desperate. Don't you see that? I should never have trusted Drogan, but now it's done I have to think of a way to get her out.'

Isa didn't utter a single word, which seemed worse to Raoul than her fiercest castigation.

He looked down, began picking at a clot of dirt on his breeches. 'I know it's all my fault. If I hadn't brought the pestilence to Lucie with Crispen, Héloïse wouldn't have felt pledged to treat its victims ... would not have put my family at risk. But then again, I might not have brought it ... perhaps it was Merlin Lemarchand. We'll never know.' He knew he was rattling on, blindly grasping at things—clutching at anything—to try and make sense of the whole sorry mess. Tears pricked at his eyes but he swiped them away angrily. 'And if I hadn't gone journeying for work in the first place ... depriving my family of a husband's income and protection ... forcing Héloïse to become so dedicated, none of this would have happened.'

Isa got up from the stool and brushed down her blue kirtle.

'You know what the punishment for heresy is, don't you,

Raoul?' She turned her back to him and walked towards the cot door. 'Burning.'

***

From the Mason's Lodge, Raoul looked towards the old Roman fountain, where the baker stood, seemingly well-recovered from the pestilence.

'It's a boy!' the baker cried, louder than the most fervent town crier. 'I have a son!' Tears coursing down his cheeks, he stretched his arms and raised the little bundle above his head like the prized beast of a hunt.

Shopkeeper-artisans and their families came from their homes, cheering and clapping. Despite his terrible time that morning with Captain Drogan—and the remorse Isa had seared into his own guilt and idiocy—Raoul couldn't help but afford the baker a smile. Eight years waiting for their son, he could only imagine his and Sibylle's joy.

And what joy to be able to see his newborn after surely fearing his own pestilence death—the only survivor besides Yolande!

But Raoul's smile quickly faded, the remorse hammering at him over and over, as a carpenter driving home a nail. What of his own unborn son, locked in gaol with his wife? What desperate demon had possessed him to think of doing such a thing? He kept beating a fist to his breast, trying to bash out the sour air of self-hatred.

To make things worse, he remembered too how Héloïse had so looked forward to midwifing Sibylle's child. He'd heard the excitement in her voice as she told him how hopeful she was that Sibylle would finally carry a child to term. And he'd denied her this pleasure; this satisfaction. How rough of him. No loving husband would do such a thing.

Another thought struck Raoul then: who *had* midwifed the baker's son?

His mind spinning with ways of best approaching le Comte to explain the terrible blunder he'd made and try to get Héloïse freed, Raoul hadn't been able to concentrate on his work all day, continually drawing, then scrapping, his building plans on the Mason's Lodge tracing floor. Somehow, he had to secure Héloïse's release. But whichever way he looked at the problem, inside out, upside down, it refused to fit together like the straight lines and neat angles of his masonry work.

The baker was still calling out to anyone there to listen: housewives, chickens and geese, the clouds in the sky, the hills. His happy cries pealed out over the market-place, echoing across field and valley, and to the east a rainbow haloed the *Montagne Maudite*. Raoul imagined how Héloïse must feel at such heavenly moments: seeing how the birth of a healthy babe brought out the best in everyone. Even in the worst of times.

The baker came striding towards Raoul, holding his new son under an arm like one of his loaves, his grin still wide and silly.

'A miracle, Raoul Stonemason,' he said, thumping him on the shoulder. Raoul smiled, but took a step backwards. Sibylle's husband might be recovered from the pestilence but he was still wary.

The baker carefully laid the baby down on the drawing floor and grabbed Raoul's hand. He flipped it palm-up and began pouring coins into it from his leather scrip. 'However can I pay you enough?' he said. 'Truly a miracle.'

Raoul kept trying to pull his hand away, but the baker's grip was, surprisingly, stronger than his own.

'Stop!' Raoul said. 'Why are you paying me? It wasn't Héloïse who midwifed your Sibylle.'

'But your young Morgane did just as good a job,' the baker said. 'Since that yard-brained Captain locked up your wife, your girl came instead. And a fine—'

'*Morgane* birthed your son?' Raoul said. 'But she's only into her eighth summer. How could she …?'

'No matter,' the baker said, scooping up his son from the floor, 'my boy still came out healthy and perfect.'

And as the baker hurried from the Lodge, as if he had a hundred more people to show off his son to, Raoul saw Morgane coming from the baker's shop. His little Flamelock was smiling—the confident beam of a professional who's proud of a job well done. She skipped across the square, Héloïse's midwifing-basket swinging over one arm.

As soon as the setting sun shot like fire through the clouds and the curfew bell rang, Raoul hurried back to his cot.

***

'Didn't you think to call Isa to come and help you, my little Flamelock?' Raoul said. 'Or Yolande?'

'What for?' From the stool on which Morgane sat, Blanche curled in her lap, she swung her legs back and forth. 'That horrid Captain Drogan put Maman in gaol and since he hasn't let her out yet, there was nobody else to do the birthing. I was on the market-place when Sibylle started her travail ... and couldn't find Yolande. I wasn't about to leave Sibylle on her own, was I?'

Raoul risked a look at Isa, but she remained tight-lipped, still refusing to afford him a single word.

'I knew what to do,' Morgane carried on. 'I just told Sibylle to breathe in and out and that she was doing really well, and the baby would be here soon. And we prayed to Saint Margaret and when she said, "Satan's arse I gotta shit!" I held back the baby's head so it wouldn't tear her flesh. Just as Maman taught me.'

'You did well, poppet,' Isa said. 'But you should have come for me. Sibylle's been fretting like a fly in oil right from when this one took root in her womb. She must've been terrified when she realised your maman couldn't midwife her.'

Raoul felt Isa's accusing glance, heavy and rough as uncut stone.

'But I didn't need you, Isa; my cat helped me for the birthing.' Morgane waved Crispen's wooden carving in the air. 'I laid it in her navel just as Maman does with her angel pendant … told her it would help her babe on its journey, and it did … the little boy came out of Sibylle's womb alive and squealed straight off.'

Despite himself, Raoul couldn't resist a proud smile at his daughter's eagerness to learn; how she was growing into the same efficient and stubborn woman as her mother. His little Flamelock would likely cause trouble for her husband too, but that's also why that husband would adore her.

But just as quickly, his chest tightened again, as if he were suffocating.

Think, think! How to get Héloïse out? No point asking Drogan if he could see her; no reason to give him more pleasure.

'Eight summers is certainly the age to begin your working life,' Isa was saying, 'but still too young to birth a child alone.'

'I'm not too young.' Morgane stroked the purring cat. 'I know everything. I know a babe is made by a man and woman's seed mixing and … and if the seed is hot, and the mother's right breast bigger, it'll be a boy, but if cold and the mother's left breast bigger, you get a girl. And you need the mother's blood to make the fleshy parts. Oh, and God's blessing, of course.'

'You've learned your lessons well,' Isa said, and beneath her frown, Raoul sensed her pride too at Morgane's thirst for their knowledge. So unlike his wife at her age, Héloïse had told him. It must be a relief for Isa to have such a willing apprentice.

'And one day you'll make an excellent midwife,' Isa went on, 'but before assisting at such a wondrous thing, you must be mistress of your own temperament, my sweet. You must learn that a good midwife doesn't feel the pain of the labouring mother. A woman may shriek and weep but the midwife must be both dove and hawk, Morgane—soothing and gentle on the outside, fierce, quick and pitiless on the inside. And you're still a bit young to grasp all of that.'

'What is there to understand?' Morgane said, with an exaggerated shrug. 'Sibylle is well, the baby is well, the father is very happy.'

'Isa's right, my little Flamelock,' Raoul said. 'A good apprenticeship takes seven years. But you did well today, and don't you worry, I'll find a way to get your maman out of gaol.' He clasped her small hand and squeezed it. 'Now what about that bedtime story?'

'Oh, I'm a bit tired, Papa.' She gave a huge yawn and sneezed twice. 'From the birthing, and thirsty ... so thirsty.'

Morgane ran her tongue over her lips and Raoul's heart seized in his chest when he looked closely at her: the beady line of sweat above her lips, her glistening brow. The clumps of rosy rings on her neck and arms.

XXVI

It must've been my third day in this Hell-gaol. But in the hot confines of the constant darkness, apart from the occasional chink of the gaoler's lantern light, there was no telling night from day. And I, who'd been nurtured on the greens of field and meadow, the blues of summer skies and the purples of the westward hills, plunged into a deep melancholy. It hovered about me like the stink of a midden and as my spirit faded, so did my body. If I'd not had the angel pendant's strength and solace, I think I would have already died, and my unborn with me.

And where was Isa with more food? Save for the tepid water and trenchers stained with meat juice the gaoler threw at me, I'd had nothing since the beginning when Isa had come with the shocking news of why Raoul had got it into his witless skull to have me locked up.

In a small nook of my mind, I did understand Raoul's warped logic in having me gaoled; his yearning to protect me and his family. But that didn't mean I would forgive him, or ever speak to him again for going that far. Something was riven between us, lightning forking open a swollen sky that would never fit seamlessly together again.

My husband was dead to me. The thought shredded my heart, but how could I ever trust him again, after such a terrible betrayal?

'He wants to come and see you ... to beg forgiveness,' Isa had said.

I'd told her Raoul could beg all he wanted, I'd never change my mind. And if that wasn't grim enough, Isa then told me about the heresy charge. My words with Yolande on the market-place tumbled through my mind again.

Watch your blasphemous mouth, Héloïse. Pina's heresy accusations … surely told her mother …

It had to be Alewife Rixende's doing, and likely Drogan's too.

I was flailing at the bottom of a black pit, and surely things could not get worse, but still I'd sensed Isa was keeping something from me; something more sinister. And I wanted her to come back and tell me everything; to bring me food. I wanted to hug Morgane—to bury my face in her red curls and see her sweet smile crinkle her freckled cheeks and light up those pretty, two-coloured eyes.

As she and my two deadborn boys had grown in my belly, I'd felt only the delights of carrying a child, but this one just made me feel sick. The hurt, my resentment of Raoul, withered me a little more each day like a plant shut away from sunlight and water.

Beyond exhaustion, but too afraid to sleep, when my eyelids did close I lapsed into vivid dreams that bled into a waking torture. I was trapped in a cage, surrounded by flames. I only knew where the dreams ended—where the fire stopped burning my flesh—and the waking began, from my twitching limbs as the rats tried to nibble my toes.

I squeezed my eyes tighter and in my mind's eye I saw my mother's pale heart-shaped face—how I'd always imagined Ava.

Don't give up, my little warrior … the talisman will help you find a way out.

Her living breath was sweet on my face as her blue-grey eyes looked into mine. Her smile soothed my frayed nerves, her pendant, warm against my breast, as comforting as Isa's hot chicken broth on a winter night. I kissed the talisman, leaving my lips pressed against the old bone and I prayed to Our Lady, beseeching her help.

But it was pointless. Our *Seigneur*, with the people of Lucie's encouragement, would find me guilty of heresy. I would die. I knew it and at the thought of being burned alive, the stench of the charred lepers' corpses flared in my nostrils. The fear struck up such a trembling I thought it might never stop.

Isa was old and likely not long for this life. Who would take care of Morgane? Of the child I carried? But how silly of me—the unborn too, was doomed.

I wanted to scream and hammer my fists at the injustice; to damn to Hell Drogan and Rixende and their hatred for me. Damn my hateful husband too. And damn God, for I was certain—after all this—that He no longer walked beside me; had never walked beside me. I folded my arms about my knees, rested my head on them and sobbed until my throat and tears ran dry.

A shuffling noise outside the wooden door, and a key turning, made me lift my head.

'Time to kiss the gallows post,' the gaoler said, his grin all the more devilish in the eerie lantern light. 'Or hug the fiery stake. Hmm, what will it be, *ma belle*?'

***

Raoul plodded into the cot, feeling as if he held his heart in his hand as he'd done the past three days. But no, his little Flamelock was still alive, though she did resemble Death. She lay limp and still on the pallet beside the hearth, her skin whiter than bone, her eyes dull, her body glistening with the sweat that Isa constantly dabbed at with cloths soaked in their supposedly miraculous rose-water.

His desolation more extreme than any cold, heat or darkness he'd ever known, Raoul couldn't bear to look at her. Nor could he shift his gaze in case it was the last time he saw her chest rise and fall.

If Héloïse is executed, and my little Flamelock dies too, there'll be nothing left to live for. I'd rather die as did our stonemason patron, Saint Etienne. Stoned to death.

'Are they turning darker?' Raoul gestured at the blood roses dotting Morgane's arms and neck. He felt sick himself, waves of it jabbing at his belly like fish hooks. 'I'm sure they're about to turn into the black boils.'

'No they're the same,' Isa said. Since Morgane had caught the pestilence, he'd felt Isa's needle-like gaze soften a little, as if she—as well as his daughter—had almost given up the fight. 'So, are you going to tell me what le Comte said, Raoul, or just keep me guessing?'

'He refused, of course … Christ's precious heart!' Raoul slumped onto a stool, poured a beaker of ale and swallowed it in one gulp. 'Said I had a nerve coming up to his castle and begging for my wife's release when I was the one who'd had her locked up in the first place.' He poured another beaker of ale. 'And I could hardly say I needed her released so she could come home and care for her daughter's pestilence.'

'No,' Isa said, 'or le Comte would've hanged you on the spot for daring to come to his castle from a pestilence home.'

Raoul nodded wearily, the irony of that not lost on him—how he came and went from his pestilence cot when he'd forbidden his wife to do the same thing.

'I've been a fool from the start, Isa. Though for the life of me, I still can't see how else I could've handled things.' He rubbed at his brow, scraped back his thick red mane. 'Le Comte told me if I thought he'd just forget this more serious heresy crime and simply release Héloïse, that I was as mad as her.'

'I'd slice off his balls and throw them to the pig,' Isa said, 'if I had the strength. But there doesn't seem any point, does there Raoul? No point in anything, now?'

Morgane gave a whimper, and Isa held a mug of some strong-smelling herb drink to her lips. 'Sips, poppet. Little sips … good girl.' Raoul could see the sorrow etched into Isa's crinkled face as she eased Morgane back down onto the pallet and turned to face him.

He held up a palm, knowing she'd chastise him yet again. 'I know I'm to blame for this too … if I hadn't got Héloïse locked up, she'd have midwifed Sibylle, and our daughter wouldn't have gone there and caught the baker's pestilence.'

'The baker was recovered, so it mightn't have come from him,' Isa said. 'Or it might. There are so many infected in this town, she could've caught it from anyone.'

'I know, but that doesn't make me feel better,' Raoul said. 'Besides, if Héloïse hadn't taught her daughter to be so strong-willed, she'd never have gone to the baker's in the first place. No, my wife would've done better to teach her about household chores rather than rushing about learning a trade … it's not like we need the income now I'm back home and earning well.'

'You could blame me for that,' Isa said, 'for insisting Héloïse get a trade … for telling her she'd never get a husband, and would need to support herself.'

'Maybe we all share the blame,' Raoul said. 'But blame is useless. We need to do *something* for Héloïse … can't sit by and watch her …' He fell silent, stroking his beard, grappling around for any kind of hope.

'If we could get Héloïse's angel pendant,' he finally said. 'That might help cure—'

'The same talisman you scorned when Héloïse claimed it was protecting her?' Isa said.

'Yes, but things have changed. I'm a mason, anchored in the earthly world. I understand what I can touch, mould or sculpt. Apart from appealing to our patron saint, I've never had time for those otherworldly celestial kinds of myths, and yet I can think of no other reason why Héloïse has been spared the pestilence.' He heaved a great sigh. 'This horror has changed us all. And if the story of the bone from which it is sculpted *is* true, that talisman might well be able to protect us, *and* cure my little Flamelock.'

'Many things are possible,' Isa said, smoothing back Morgane's red hair from her sweaty brow, 'if you believe strongly enough.'

Drowning in his misery, Raoul almost fell from where he sat on a stool when Yolande bustled into the cot, solemn-faced.

Since Héloïse's friend—the one he had denied his wife's care, he did admit that—had survived the pestilence, and everyone was fairly certain a person couldn't catch it twice, she'd offered to sit with Morgane while he and Isa tramped up to the castle for Héloïse's farce of a trial.

'And remember,' Isa said, as Raoul hoisted her up onto the cart seat, 'Héloïse is not to know about Morgane ... not till after the trial, at least. There's nothing she can do, and it'll just make her agony worse, if such a thing is possible.'

XXVII

My legs quaked as le Comte's men led me up towards the castle gate and the battlements that gnawed at the sky like a toothy beast. Denied light for several days, the sunlight blinded me for a moment, but when my vision cleared I saw the usual small crowd that waited there daily for the coin and leftover food le Comte Renault gave out. Not because he was a good noble wishing to help the poor, but in the belief that giving out alms would buy him a place in Heaven.

My guts churned and rose with the huge portcullis grinding upward on its chains; right up to the clutch of vultures perched in the battlement crannies as if waiting there just for pestilence victims to drop. The men-at-arms hauled me inside, and as the portcullis slid back down with a thud, the birds took flight, circling overhead in a great screeching wheel.

In the bustling courtyard, with grim and towering walls surrounding me, my courage faltered yet more. A maid filled pails from a well, chickens squawked, scattering about us, and a pig nosed at the gutters, not even lifting its head in our direction. Grooms carrying hay into the stables turned their gaze, and another maid stared as she emptied a chamber pot into the gutter that ran down into the Vionne.

Poppa and her girls were hanging out bucketloads of sheets, tablecloths and towels. 'Faster now!' Chief Washerwoman Poppa scolded, 'you lazy good-for-nothing wenches.'

Isa's old friend looked up at me, and opened her mouth as if about to say something. Then she pressed her lips into a small but encouraging smile as le Comte's men led me into the Great Hall.

'Bring the prisoner closer, Captain Drogan.' From the far end of the Great Hall, Renault de Fouville gestured with a gloved finger. His beautifully-carved chair was positioned in the centre of a dais and his paunchy frame took up all of it. Père Bernard, robed in his usual black, sat beside le Comte.

Of course I'd been inside *le château de Lucie* before, but this time there were no townsfolk seated at tables celebrating the harvest or Yuletide. There was no music, dancing or fine feasting. This time I was standing before a man who could snuff out my life on a whim.

Fires burned in copper braziers on each side of Renault de Fouville, like those we'd heard blazed around the Pope's throne in Avignon. A fortress of flames against the miasma, prescribed by the Holy One's physician, Guy de Chauliac.

Tallow candles flickered from wall sconces; le Comte was evidently not going to waste good wax candles on my case. The enormous hearth had also been lit, likely as extra protection for the lord and his household against the miasma any townsfolk might unwittingly bring into the Great Hall, though I knew they'd all have been carefully vetted at the castle gates for any sign of the pestilence. In the sweltering June heat, and after the cold and damp of the cell, I felt I'd been hoisted into a furnace.

As Captain Drogan prodded me towards le Comte's dais, the vision of those caged lepers filled my mind, flames licking at ghostly bodies, the crowd screaming for their deaths. But it was me cringing from the snaking flames now. And in that stifling air, malodorous with dung-caked shoes, rank wool, stale sweat and tallow, I found myself struggling to breathe. Or was it my terror that made my breaths catch, as if my throat were barbed with hooks?

I suffered the priest's cold frown, le Comte looking me up

and down as if appraising a horse and deciding whether to purchase it or not. Despite the heat, I shivered as I shuffled forward, staring around me like a doe cornered in the hunt. It seemed as if every person in Lucie was crowded into the Great Hall, murmuring, their black looks shredding me from where they sat on the benches brought in for the occasion. The candle flames curdled their faces, souring the reds, green and browns of their clothes into a single hue of old mustard.

I sought out Isa. She gave me a rallying smile but there was no mistaking the worry etched into the lines of her sun-beaten face or the fear in her eyes. Where was Morgane? I tried to mouth the question to Isa, but she looked away. Why? Out of shame? My terror had stopped me thinking clearly, but it didn't stop me casting Raoul a hateful glare. And I hoped he saw in my eyes what I yearned to shout at him:

How could you betray me like that? What happened to our love … the lost love for which I'm grieving as deeply as death itself?

Still trembling, I forced myself to look up into le Comte's face, dripping with perspiration as if he were carved of the tallow that was melting around him. The *Seigneur's* gaze pierced mine. He already believed me guilty.

'Pronounce the charges, Captain.' He nodded at Drogan.

'The prisoner, Midwife Héloïse, wife of Raoul Stonemason,' the Captain said, barely able to keep the joy from his voice, 'is accused of the crime of heresy. On la place de l'Eglise she was overheard to say: "Haven't we had enough of praying to Our Lord and seeing not the slightest result? Has He given us a reason to believe He is really working for us?" It is also believed that these heretical thoughts provoked God's rage and caused Him to send the pestilence to Lucie-sur-Vionne to punish us.'

Drogan paused for breath, basking in the spectators' rapt attention. 'It is further claimed that Midwife Héloïse, wife of Raoul Stonemason, uses the mandrake root and other unknown herbs and potions of the Devil. That she has a pact with Satan to prey not only on the sick but also on the healthy.'

'Unknown herbs like the datura root?' Isa cried her eyes bright with rage. 'To set and mend your bones? The herbs she uses to safely birth your children?'

'The people will be silent!' Le Comte turned his scornful gaze to my aunt. 'You shall all have occasion to speak for or against the prisoner after the charges have been pronounced.'

'And finally,' Drogan went on, 'she is charged with using a talisman, worn on a leather cord about her neck, as a vehicle of the Devil to curse those she chooses with this pestilence.'

I clutched my pendant, shaking my head wildly. 'N-no, that's a l-lie! No Devil's ch-charm—'

'The prisoner will remain silent,' Renault de Fouville snapped. 'So, the healer-midwife is using her talisman to curse those she chooses with the pestilence—God's punishment for her own sin of heresy?' Stroking his beard, he raised his sword and pointed the tip at my pendant, not quite touching it. The story of its burning eyes must have reached even le Comte's ears.

'That is correct, *Sire*,' the Captain said, and the people struck up an excited whisper.

My head giddy, my every thought misted with terror and panic, I was sure I was about to pass out. I cupped my hands over my nose and mouth, closed my eyes and breathed deeply— in and out, nice and slow. Just as I advised birthing mothers.

Our Lady, give me strength, for only a miracle can save me.

'One at a time.' Le Comte held up an arm. 'If you all persist in chattering together, not a single one of you will be heard.'

'We all know by now that this pestilence doesn't come from Lucie-sur-Vionne,' Isa said, 'and surely not from one single woman, but from the south, even from the far-off Arabian lands. So how can you claim her pendant has the power to curse a person with it?'

'Yes, this pestilence is affecting the whole of France,' Raoul said, his voice more raspy than I'd ever heard. 'Perhaps every country of the world. If you say my wife has cursed Lucie-sur-Vionne, you'd have to say she's cursed the world!'

Why is Raoul speaking up for me now? How dare he, when it's because of him that I'm here, defending my life? It's far too late for remorse!

'This pestilence certainly is not caused by the hand of one single sinner,' Père Bernard said, 'but by the hands of many different ones. And since your wife is the greatest sinner in this town, we can only conclude it is her evil hand that's working here. She is just one of many servants of the Devil who have been sent to give us a foretaste of Judgement Day.'

'And since her only friend, Yolande, caught the pestilence and recovered,' Rixende said, 'that proves she can cure it ... if she chooses.'

My head swivelled about, across the crowd, but there was no sign of Yolande's tall figure. Why wouldn't she be at my trial?

'Are we certain she survived the pestilence?' le Comte said. 'She would be the first I've heard of, aside from the Pope's physician.'

'Since you can see I didn't wake as idiotic as a court jester, Rixende,' Anselme said, throwing the alewife a scornful look. 'I'll confirm my mother did make a complete recovery.'

'I too, caught it and recovered,' the baker said.

With a frown, le Comte muttered, '*Humph!*'

'If only I did have a cure,' I said, trying to will the quaver from my voice. 'I'd give it freely to all. But there's no remedy ... none. Those who recover are just blessed with good fortune.'

'Silence from the prisoner,' le Comte said. 'You will have your turn to speak.'

'The only remedy is to burn the sinner what brought it here,' Rixende said, making the sign of the cross. 'To stop it killing the lot of us. All what she started on those first poor victims in her own cot: that trader with the sorcerer's name and her husband's own apprentice.'

'Merlin Lemarchand already had the pestilence when he brought Raoul Stonemason and his apprentice to Lucie,' Isa said, 'and Crispen might have caught it from his brother, Toubie. It's unfair to say Héloïse caused it.'

I looked into Raoul's eyes, hoping he knew what I itched to shout at him. And at the crowd.

Yes, it's far more likely you, Raoul—rather than me—brought the pestilence to Lucie.

But I refused to stoop as low as my husband had, and said nothing. I just watched the blood drain from Raoul's face, and I knew he'd understood.

'Alesi Stonemason was another of her early victims,' Poncet Batier said. 'We reckon the midwife cursed him with the pestilence so her husband could take the Master Mason job, with its higher wage and status.'

'Hear, hear,' several people murmured.

'There's not a bushel of truth in that!' Raoul cried. 'The Master Mason caught the nose-bleeding pestilence at the tavern. He was nowhere near my wife.'

'Well it's a known fact the midwife practiced witchery on my wife while she was birthing our child,' Poncet Batier said. 'Used her Devil's charm to kill her, and make of my son a changeling. I ain't forgot that, never will.'

'Your wife, Poncet Batier? The wife who was your own daughter, who you callously made with child when she was but a maid herself?' Isa blurted out the words my fear had stopped me saying.

'And that's not the woodcutter's only evil deed,' Poppa said. 'I heard he's been luring poor sick souls into their graves afore they're even dead!'

'The woodcutter is not the one on trial—' le Comte began.

'Bah, what do you know, old crones?' The gravedigger curled a sore-crusted lip at Isa and Poppa.

'I happen to know quite a lot, Poncet Batier,' Isa said. 'I know that while we might accept what Père Bernard says about God sending us this pestilence in divine punishment for our sins, we in our misery will look for a human on whom to vent the hostility we can't vent on God.'

'Stands to reason it must be a woman though,' the blacksmith said, in his ale-garbled slur, 'women being the cause of all man's weakness. Everyone knows a woman's soul is feebler than a man's. And because women are wicked by nature, and weren't made with much sense, they can't control their natural wickedness. They tell more lies too, and are slower in working and moving than a man.'

'That's ripe,' Raoul said. 'The way drink slows your work these days, Pierro Blacksmith.'

'Did not the great Aristotle say,' Père Bernard interrupted, 'that women are basically deformed men? And we all know it was the wicked Eve who first persuaded a man to bite into the forbidden fruit, and so cast out all humanity from Paradise. Woman was the ruin of Mankind,' he carried on with a sorrowful shake of his head. 'As said the great Jean de Meun: "Of honest women, by St. Denis, there are fewer than of phoenixes".'

'Women,' le Comte hissed, staring at me as if he were addressing my very soul, 'are a disease of this modern world. A disease no better than this pestilence.'

Isa gave a great sigh. 'Why is it we are blamed for everything, from the Fall of Man to … to a hedge growing crooked?'

Several women nodded emphatically.

'Mayhap it's not because we're weaker,' she went on, 'but the source of all true power. The source of life?'

'Yes, the source of life!' Poppa said.

'Certainly, one cannot be too careful in dealing with women,' le Comte de Fouville cut in, 'who have a naturally lower capacity for comprehension.'

'My niece has worn that talisman since she was eleven years old,' Isa said, as I tried to will away the terror that had gripped me so that I too might defend myself. But my mind remained darkly empty and I could barely reason, let alone speak. 'So why hasn't Héloïse used it afore?'

'That's right,' Poppa said, 'why would she wait this long to curse the town?'

'God only knows how long it takes Satan to weasel his way

inside a person,' Père Bernard said. 'Perhaps he's taken this long to take root inside your niece?'

'She's been causing evil long before now,' Rixende said, with another hasty sign of the cross. 'Right since we were girls, like she cursed my dear husband with the pestilence.'

'The same dear husband you almost beat to death at every turn?' Isa said.

'Learned all the dark arts from you, didn't she?' Rixende said. 'And not forgetting those rumours about you and your dead sister—twin midwives using that very same talisman for black arts when it suited them: punishing people with deadborns and changelings. Stands to reason you both passed on that magic to Midwife Héloïse, who's now using it for the same thing.'

'The same magic my twin used to get you safely, arse-first, from your mother's womb?' Isa waggled a bony finger at the alewife. 'You should be thanking Ava for saving your life, and your mother's, instead of accusing her of black art!'

'Talking of black arts,' Drogan's mother cut in, 'I believe Midwife Héloïse used them to wash away my daughter-in-law's babe.'

Almost frozen with fear already, Sara's words were splinters spiking even deeper, chiseling my terror to its sharpest point.

Not daring a glance at Catèlena, I took a deep breath, summoned my steadiest voice against the assault of so many pairs of eyes. 'As I explained, Mère Sara, the seed never took hold in Catèlena's womb. I was simply comforting your daughter-in-law.'

'Is this true?' Drogan glared at Catèlena. 'Why didn't I hear of it, wife?'

Catèlena's eyes filled with tears and she gave her husband, and me, fearful glances.

'Because your wife is too terrified to tell you anything,' I said, 'afraid she'll meet the same fate as your first wife, and—'

'Silence from the prisoner!' le Comte barked. 'Our Captain is not the one on trial here, and another word from you and I'll simply abandon this trial and punish you anyway.'

'And she cursed my other two sons with the pestilence,' Sara went on, 'and that after her aunt killed my husband with her poison for his bad knees ... hard it was, bringing up my three boys on my own.'

Isa seemed about to say something, but shut her mouth. We both knew her wolfsbane liniment had likely killed the weaver. An unfortunate accident.

'Catèlena?' Drogan repeated, 'I demand you tell me if my mother's accusation is true? You'll tell me the truth or ... '

Catèlena gave the slightest shake of her head. 'N-no, it's not true.'

I almost cried with relief.

'Let us deal with the charges at hand,' le Comte said.

'Midwife Héloïse is a God-fearing woman and healer,' the baker's wife, Sibylle, said. 'Gave me a special potion to stop my son falling out of me.' With pride, she held up her swaddled babe for all to see. Until now, I wasn't aware Sibylle had birthed her child, and despite my terror and desperation I managed a feeble smile. But who had midwifed her? Isa perhaps, or maybe Yolande. Where *was* Yolande? Unable to speak up for myself, I needed every possible ally.

'*Oui*, a God-fearing woman,' said a labourer whose name I couldn't recall. 'Her talisman protected my own daughter; helped her birth my grandson ... didn't curse her at all.'

'And where's your daughter now?' Rixende said to the man. 'Who was it put your girl in her grave? The midwife, that's who ... cursed both the child's parents with the pestilence.'

She looked around the crowd. 'I ask you all, what use is an orphan with no parents to slap it about and teach it the ways of the world? Just a burden on the rest of us.'

'You'd be the only Devil's servant here, Rixende,' the labourer said. 'Spouting such evil.'

'That be the Devil's truth,' Poppa said. 'The alewife's the one what should be on trial, not our good midwife. I ain't forgot how Héloïse saved my grandson—my Loup—from one of those brigands.' She gestured beside her, to baby Loup strapped to Alix's breast.

'Saved your grandson?' Nica said. 'I don't remember that, but I do recall the midwife using the talisman to curse that same brigand.' She dug her elbow into Alix's side until her sister nodded in agreement.

The Great Hall fell silent for a moment, then chatter broke out again at this new claim against me.

'You know Midwife Héloïse only pretended to curse that fly-ridden turd of an outlaw, Nica!' Poppa said, 'or he'd have dashed baby Loup's head against the wall. We all saw his mind set on that, didn't we?'

Say it, Nica ... the truth!

Not a word, or sound, echoed against those great stone walls, as everyone turned to Nica, all waiting for her to say something. My heart beat frantically again. Nica remained silently defiant, avoiding my gaze. And Poppa's.

'The Devil's arse, what's got into you, girl?' Poppa flung her stout arms, and I began shaking uncontrollably then, beginning to lose my balance as if the floor were slipping from beneath me. But the terror was still strangling my tongue, and I couldn't voice a single word to absolve myself of these sickening accusations.

I fought to push aside my trepidation, and raised my hand like a child in church. 'I request the right to speak.'

Le Comte gave me a curt nod. 'Granted.'

'This accusation ... that I used my pendant talisman to curse Lucie-sur-Vionne with the pestilence is false, *Sire*,' I said, trying to keep the quiver from my voice. 'I swear it on our Blessed Virgin. I'm a healer and a midwife. And as you are, I'm a soldier ... fighting fiercely to bring life, not death.'

I folded my hand over my pendant. 'This talisman is no Devil's curse; no evil charm, but a simple gift from my mother.'

'How can a simple gift burn you then?' Drogan said. He raised a hand, tweaked two fingers. 'I still bear the scar from when I had the bad luck to touch the evil thing as a boy. Isn't that proof enough it's a Satan's charm?'

'Look carefully, *Sire*,' I said, 'you'll not find the slightest scar on Captain Drogan's hand.'

'You think I'm imagining the marks?' Drogan's booming voice matched his burly body. 'That I invented them?'

'Yes,' I said. 'Look closely, anyone—all of you!—you'll find nothing.'

But nobody did because they'd all turned to the priest who had begun to speak.

'A simple gift cannot scald the skin,' Père Bernard said. 'Only a charm with the Devil's powers can cause such burn marks.'

'*What* burn marks?' I felt my head would explode with frustration. 'Ask the woodcutter-sexton if it burned his fingers when he tried to strangle me.'

'When you cursed and killed my wife you mean?' Poncet Batier said, his hawk gaze sharp on me. 'Ah just chuck the Midwife in the Vionne ... and don't forget the stone around her neck.'

'The only power this pendant holds,' I said, holding it up high for all to see. 'Is to help the safe passage of infants into this world.'

I was aware of the raw fear in my voice, high-pitched to make myself heard above their din. I looked at le Comte, and around the crowd, and held their gaze. 'It gives us force and solace to lend to birthing mothers and the sick. It has no evil powers at all, and it certainly cannot cause, or cure, the pestilence.'

I chafed to tell them from where the bone of my pendant hailed, but caught my tongue. That story was not for the ears of Lucie's townsfolk. And certainly not for the priest's.

'Well it is known that midwifing is not an art practiced by respectable women,' Père Bernard said.

'It should be the most respected profession,' Isa said. 'God's witness to new life.'

'More like witness to expelling the fruits of sin,' the priest said, pointing a long thin finger at me. 'And her words, her actions,' he went on, 'only demonstrate that the Devil has claimed her. From the sins of Eve we have learned that women—descendants of that depraved temptress—are the tools of the Devil, always willing to enter his service when he moves their hearts to his cause. She who has been made intractable by the Devil is bringing destruction on us all. What price will God exact of us for refusing to purge the world of this Devil's servant? To you, my lord I say that through the execution of this most evil being we can redeem ourselves in God's eyes, and save the souls of all who have already perished as a result of her damnable heresy, as well as those who will perish in the future. Expunge this heretic from our minds, or we may bring even greater calamity upon our town which has already suffered most hideously at her hand. Consign her to the flames and save the souls of hundreds, or fail to kill her and damn thousands.'

As the crowd broke out in a wild gabble, my gaze flicked to Raoul. His face as red as his hair, he thumped a fist in the air.

'She's no heretic, no Devil's servant,' Raoul shouted, his words echoing as if on a noisy work site. 'As many here today have said, my wife is a God-fearing, skilled and nurturing healer and midwife.'

Still defending me. It's too late, Raoul. Too late.

'Silence!' Le Comte turned his iron gaze on me. 'Midwife Héloïse, wife of Raoul Stonemason, shall be burned at dawn.'

He delivered this last sentence in such a matter-of-fact tone—as if giving orders for his horse to be groomed—that at first I couldn't grasp what he'd said.

But amidst the rising din, his words sank in as darkly as a storm severs the banks of the Vionne. My fate was sealed. My blood seemed to still inside me, and I heard someone start screaming.

'No, no, no!'

Isa or Raoul? Or was it me?

My legs buckled beneath me and I crumpled senseless to the ground.

***

'... burn the talisman with her.' Rixende's voice. 'The Devil's charm she summoned the miasma to prey on us with.'

'... what if the heretic don't die ...?' Pierro Blacksmith. '... claws her way out of the flames and comes back to curse us ... moon is at its highest ... most dangerous?'

'The only sure way is to slice off her head.' Poncet Batier. 'I'll do that ... after she's burned.'

From where I lay on the ground, I breathed deeply, trying to make sense of what was happening above and around me.

Just a terrible nightmare. Any second I'll wake, turn to Raoul, everything melting away as I slide into his embrace... but no, no! There's no Raoul's embrace. No Raoul at all ... but the pain is worse because there is, still, Raoul.

'Who knows what she is or what she could turn into once she's dead?' Drogan said, words I plainly heard. I opened my eyes, saw him—all of them—sideways, staring down at me.

No dream.

'She's not natural ... a non-born that should never've lived from the start,' Drogan carried on. 'So if we burn her instead of hanging her, there'll be no body, and she can't be resurrected at the world's end, isn't that so, Père Bernard?'

Several heads nodded in agreement.

'She's a heretic,' the priest said, dismissing the debate with a flick of his wrist. 'Her soul will fly straight to Hell.'

'I have already pronounced sentence,' le Comte said. 'The midwife will be burned tomorrow at first light. The talisman shall be burned with her, until there remains no trace of either of them.' As if dismissing a fly on his venison steak, he flapped a hand at Drogan. 'Take her away, Captain. Lock her up again.'

Drogan grabbed my arm, pulled me upright, his mouth widening in the evil smile of a torturer who revels in his work.

'You can't execute her, *Sire*,' Isa said. 'Because Midwife Héloïse is with child.'

The crowd fell silent, all of them turning to our *Seigneur*, stroking his beard. The candles flickered, sending quivering shadows across the painted walls.

'Is this true, Midwife, or some pathetic ruse to prolong the inevitable? And if it be true, why did your aunt not say so beforehand?'

'I only just remembered the law, *Sire*,' Isa said. 'It seemed to have slipped my mind … like yours.'

'No ruse, *Sire*,' I said, my hands straying protectively to my belly. 'My child will be born next spring.'

'I don't see what difference that makes?' Captain Drogan said.

'Yeah, burn her anyway.' Rixende crossed herself with gusto.

'It is against our laws to execute a woman with child,' a voice proclaimed from the back of the Great Hall. I looked up to see Physician Nestor, though I was certain he hadn't been here through my trial. I knew le Comte's brother spoke from his physician's conscience rather than for any fondness for me, but I began to breathe easier—to breathe!—a tiny flame of hope flickering in my heart.

As if holding its breath the Great Hall fell quiet again, the only sound the scurrying of small rodents through the rushes.

'The prisoner shall remain in the castle gaol,' le Comte de Fouville finally said, 'until after the child's birth. Then she will be burned.'

'My niece won't survive that long in the castle gaol, *Sire*,' Isa said.

'That would be as good as killing her and her unborn child,' Raoul said. 'Look how wretched she is after only three days in a cell.'

'The prisoner's family will ensure she is supplied with food and drink,' le Comte said. 'Now as I said, lock her up Captain Drogan.'

Through the blur of my shock—the fear once again swamping me—I caught Raoul's tear-filled gaze as the Captain dragged me past my husband and my aunt. My chest clenched as if battling to hold my heart inside me.

'How could you, Raoul?'

'Keep strong,' Isa said in a trembling voice. 'Keep Ava in your mind … she—and the pendant—will help you.'

I shoved Raoul's outstretched hand aside and reached for Isa's. 'Where's Morgane? Look after my poppet, Isa ... like you took care of me.'

My aunt shook her head, tears pooling in the hollows beneath her eyes.

My fingertips almost touched hers, but not quite. Drogan tugged me away.

XXVIII

Rushlights held aloft, Drogan and the men-at-arms shoved me through a heavy door studded with nails and along narrow, shadowy corridors.

Yesterday I'd been alive. Today I faced death. Despite all this dying from the pestilence, I couldn't make myself grasp the reality that I, too, was to be sent to the next world. And what then? Hell ... everlasting torment and torture, like in the church wall paintings? Forced into the flames, my arms flailing as I boiled in the cauldron?

How does a sinner such as me—a condemned heretic—prepare herself? Could I chant the words that might save me from the fires of Hell? I couldn't remember what the dying were supposed to say. Perhaps I'd never known. Besides, God would hardly listen to me now.

Damn you, God! Damn all the townsfolk! The risks I'd taken to care for you all, to birth your babes safely, and you repay me with a death sentence? I should have heeded Raoul's words from the beginning and thought only of myself and my family. This is my own stupid fault. And Raoul's. Damn you again, Raoul.

They hurried me down a flight of slippery steps and into the dank castle bowels. I had trouble keeping my footing but they took no care, striking my head several times against the stone wall. Suddenly they stopped and we were standing at the edge of a large hole.

I peered over the lip to where a burly man with the long and grim face of a bloodhound stood. The gaoler stared up at me, his lantern flame flickering across the beaten-earth floor with its sparse straw covering. Around him rose stone walls glistening green and slimy, a stench of decay tinged with stale piss and shit loitering on the chilly air.

'Please don't put me down there, Drogan, I beg you. However much you hate me, please.'

'I'll give you a choice then,' the Captain said, his grin ghoulish in the shadowy light. 'You can climb down that ladder or,' he looked around at the men, 'we can throw you down. But I'll wager that lying down there with broken arms and legs would be worse than climbing down yourself.'

'I'll go on my own,' I whispered shakily. The men-at-arms unbound me and I descended into that black pit.

'When can my aunt come with food and drink?' I said. 'Le Comte said she could come.' My mind flickered back to the Great Hall; how Morgane hadn't been there. 'And my daughter,' I said, 'I need to see her too.'

'You might get lucky and see your craggy old aunt,' Drogan said, 'but I doubt le Comte will allow that Devil-eyed daughter of yours within a league of this castle.'

'Why not?'

'You don't know?' Drogan shook his curly mop in feigned sympathy. 'Your aunt or husband hasn't told you? Aw, that was sweet of them, not to make things harder … you stuck in that horrid church gaol, unable to take care of your poppet. But I'm surprised they still haven't told you.'

'Told me *what*, Captain Drogan? I have the right to see my daughter.'

Blessed Virgin stop me from driving my fist into his taunting face.

'Not since she caught the pestilence, you don't,' he said.

His words chilled my blood to ice. I couldn't speak or breathe. I sank to the grimy floor.

'Oh yes, your Raoul tried to keep her sickness a secret, but news of every pestilence case—and death—spreads around Lucie like fire, so naturally I found out.'

'I don't believe you,' I finally said, my legs still buckled beneath me. 'This is just more of your evil.'

'Don't believe me then,' Drogan said. 'Someone else will confirm the news soon enough.'

No, no, no! She can't have it ... how, when?

I wanted to shatter Drogan's face into tiny pieces, to yank out wads of those shiny black curls; to hurl at him every curse Isa had ever sworn. But suddenly I had no force to fight him. No voice to rebuff him. I was dead.

***

Despite my grief, my yearning to be gone from my terrible life, I must have lapsed into slumber as the faint glow of a lantern woke me. The wood groaned under a heavy weight as the ladder slid down into the pit, and minutes later I smelled the gaoler's stale breath and saw him in the dim lantern light.

'What do you want with me?' My voice was a shaky whisper, the terror raw. Certain he was going to hurt me, I kicked and struggled from his grimy fingers. Even as I knew it was useless, a last desperate plea for help, I tried to scream. His hand clenched across my mouth.

'Stop struggling, fool,' he hissed, setting the lantern beside him. 'La Comtesse Geneviève's travail has started. Our *Seigneur's* heir will be born this night.' He thrust a bread trencher and a leather flask at me. 'Now eat and drink, hurry up.'

'What business of mine is la Comtesse's travail?' I said, between shovelling bread into my mouth and washing it down with the ale. 'She has her own midwife, from Lyon.'

'The Lyon midwife is dead of the bleeding type of pestilence this very afternoon. Struck her down in an hour, it did. Le Comte says there's no time to fetch another midwife, so he's ordered you to la Comtesse Geneviève's solar chamber. You're to deliver the heir ... *safely.* So there'll be none of your witchery or charms, you hear? Hurry now.'

Why hurry? Why even bother? My husband is already dead to me, and my precious little girl will likely die. So why can't I just die right now and put an end to this grief?

As the gaoler pushed me ahead of him, his lantern lighting our way through the dank passageways that led to every part of the castle, I thought back to Poppa's words.

... hard time carrying the heir. Losing blood ... the midwife's ordered her to bed ....

My pulse quickened. If my midwifing caused the death of la Comtesse Geneviève, or the heir, le Comte would magic up a worse punishment than any kind of instant death ... or a burning stake next springtime: the rack, disembowelment, the heretic's breast ripper.

***

Despite the sweet smell of nutmeg and musk, la Comtesse Geneviève's solar chambers—her sleeping quarters—located high up in the castle were as hot and stifling as the Great Hall had been. Colourful tapestries, patterned but not dramatic enough to upset the labouring woman, hung not only from each wall but were piled high on the floor to keep out the slightest draught. And since someone must know that too much light and air is bad for a woman in childbirth, only one window had been left open, letting in a violet sliver of the summer eve light. The room felt almost womb-like.

'Midwife Héloïse,' I said, lowering myself into a curtsey before the writhing mound of la Comtesse, and tucking vagrant threads of hair under my cap. 'At your service, my lady.'

'Oh let me die, Midwife,' la Comtesse Geneviève sobbed, from her sumptuous bed. Her hair was not in its usual neat coils over her ears, but hanging loose, sticking out from her face like a wild bush. Her face shone with sweat, and her linen tunic was stained with bloody fluid. She clutched the quilted coverlet in one hand, the ampoule of "Virgin's Milk" I recalled her buying from the pedlar at the Spring Fair in the other. 'By the bones of the Blessed Virgin, help me die.'

Her servants stood around her wringing their hands, terrified looks plastered on their faces. They made no move to try and ease la Comtesse's suffering or comfort her, and I realised that childbirth was often easier for the poor. Even those without family lived so close to their neighbours that the cries of a labouring mother would bring other women to her like geese answering a call to flight. Whereas the rich, such as la Comtesse Geneviève, are surrounded by servants too fearful to act as sisters.

Not even lords or physicians are allowed near birthing rooms, but I was still thankful there was no sign of Renault de Fouville or his brother, Physician Nestor.

'Bring me a bowl of water—clean water—to wash my face and hands,' I said to the servants. After three days of hunger, without having washed or cleaned my teeth, I must have looked a fright. And sweating like a hog in that infernal solar heat my grime would stink yet more.

'You won't die, Comtesse.' I knelt beside her as another pain took her up. 'I'm going to help you birth your heir. Now just take nice slow breaths, in and out.'

'Yes I will die.' Her face twisted in pain. 'I know this babe is stuck and will never be born and we will both die and why not now, to end my suffering? Surely you have something in your basket to help us along, Midwife?'

My midwifing-basket! Inside it, I knew what each medicament was, depending on the type of cloth or leather bag, the colour thread with which it was laced, or its scent. I just knew my own medicaments, and I was lost without my basket.

'Have a messenger ride to my cot please,' I said to the

cowering servants. 'And bring my midwifing-basket … and my birthing chair.' One of the maids nodded and scuttled off, evidently pleased to have an errand that would make her seem useful.

The bowl of water arrived, in which I hastily washed my hands, arms and face, then dried with the towel the maid handed me.

'Please, Midwife,' la Comtesse pleaded again. 'Let me go to my Maker.'

'Hush, Comtesse Geneviève, it's just pain and fright making you think like that.' I laid an ear against her belly, my practised skill taking over and helping to quell my own fear. 'The baby's heart beats strongly. You must concentrate on breathing when the pain comes. In and out, yes … that's good.'

I kept checking the heir's heartbeat, and eventually my basket and the birthing chair arrived. The sight of Raoul's exquisite carvings on my chair, the newborns nestled amongst angels, birds and trees, sparked my fury again; flared my desperation for my own child.

I should be at home, Isa and I caring for Morgane … sharing the burden. But instead I'm stuck in this brute's castle, anger's hovering hand ready to snatch me up every time I think of the wrongs that are being done to me.

Dusk surrendered to night, and I gave la Comtesse Geneviève mugwort in warm ale. I warmed oil over the fire and rubbed her belly. I crooned and fussed and gave her raspberry leaf brew and comfrey wine, for a calmer, more rested woman has a better chance of an easier travail. I concentrated on my patient, not resting for a second; not allowing my mind a single idle moment to dwell on my own sweet, sick poppet.

The hours wore on, and when I pressed my ear to her belly again, the babe's heartbeat had slowed. I inhaled sharply. All the comforts of noble coffers wouldn't protect la Comtesse from the dangers of childbirth; she needed spiritual comfort too.

No, Saint Margaret, please don't let the heir die.

Given the crime for which I'd been condemned, I removed my talisman from around my neck with foreboding. 'Will you allow this?' I asked la Comtesse, dangling the pendant over her navel. 'It can help the birth.'

So exhausted was la Comtesse, I think she'd have let me pile dog turds onto her distended belly, and she nodded swiftly. 'Do whatever you have to, Midwife ... whatever will end this torture.'

Shortly afterwards, as I detected the subtle change in the labouring mother's breathing and behaviour, I inserted my oiled hand inside her. Sure enough, there was the tip of the baby's head.

'Get her back onto the birthing chair and support her from behind,' I ordered the servants, as I slapped la Comtesse's great belly and gave her a good shake.

Finally, amidst the noise and stifling heat, I pulled out a hefty baby boy. But instead of bawling lustily, the *Seigneur's* heir was silent, his lips blue, the navel string tight around his neck. La Comtesse Geneviève looked down at her limp child, then up at me.

'What is wrong with him, Midwife? Why doesn't he cry?'

As I hurriedly cut the navel string from the babe's throat, she started up a sobbing and shaking as I'd never seen. The gossips screamed too, and I could feel the shadowy figure of Death creeping into that solar chamber.

I snatched a reed from my basket, began sucking the muck from his air passages. I blew air into his little nostrils. My hands should've been trembling, but were surprisingly steady, as I sucked and blew, sucked and blew.

The baby coughed, let out a cry and turned pink, and that bleak room seemed to brighten, for I'd never known Death to linger after bowing to Life's victory.

The voices of the servants echoed around me, chattering and laughing with relief, as I sealed the navel string with cumin and swaddled the baby.

'How beautiful he is ... how perfect,' la Comtesse said, as I placed him triumphantly into her outstretched arms. 'The most radiant child ever born.'

I couldn't help a small smile, thinking how every mother believes their babe is the most beautiful ever. No matter how bruised or deformed he is from birth, there's no love as compelling and blind as a mother's.

The pain jabbed at my heart again, so sharp I had to press a hand to my breast.

Please don't let my poppet die.

'You are a miracle-worker, Midwife,' la Comtesse said. 'Surely a saint sent by Our Lord to save the life of my husband's heir; to perform such a miracle. Have you ever heard the tale of the princess from Sicily?'

I shook my head as the afterbirth slid into my hands, and I checked closely, ensuring nothing had been left inside her. La Comtesse's bleeding before the birth could have stemmed from the afterbirth peeling from the wall of the womb.

'It was over a hundred years gone,' she carried on, as the servants whipped off her bloodied tunic, and the linen beneath her, remade the bed with fresh sheets and dressed her in clean garments. 'This Sicilian princess produced a son at forty years of age. Forty! Naturally it was thought to be a miracle ... as is this birth of my husband's heir. I thought I was past childbearing age and at the end of my monthly courses,' she said, chattering at such a speed that I thought her delirious with happiness. 'But look at him.' She smiled at the child again. 'A healthy, perfect son.'

She laid her fingertips on my forearm. Startled, I struggled not to jump from her touch.

'Whatever they all claim about you, Midwife, to deliver me safely of this wondrous child, then to bring my boy back from the dead, you can be no Devil's servant. I'll never believe you would curse Lucie-sur-Vionne with this pestilence. Besides, as the death toll keeps rising, it strikes me it would take a far more malign power than one small midwife to exact so much death.'

'This is my work, Comtesse,' I said. 'But I'm very happy for you.'

'And Renault will be elated ... never will I be so prized in my husband's eyes,' she went on. 'I shall flaunt my son in front of them all, and finally none will have cause to whisper behind my back, laughing at me for my failure ... for my husband's ...'

'Yes, you will flaunt your handsome son,' I said quickly, not wishing her to dwell on any dark thoughts of her husband's preference for Père Bernard, and, if I could trust my instinct, Captain Drogan too. 'You can be proud ...'

The words dropped from my lips as le Comte strode into the chamber. Clothed in a black robe shot through with gold thread, red hose and shoes that ended in such long points that at their tips a gold chain led back to the ankles, Renault de Fouville was—as ever—a formidable presence.

'Is it true, Midwife?' he boomed, his grin as wide as his girth. 'You have midwifed me a live and healthy son? I can hardly believe it, after so many years of la Comtesse's barrenness. Let me look at him.' As he took the baby from his wife's arms, the little one struck up a lusty howling.

'And what a strong voice. My son—my heir—will make the fiercest knight.' Comte Renault gleamed like a gilded painting, and thrust the child back into his mother's arms. 'Sounds as if he's a hungry heir, too ... better give him some suck.'

I helped la Comtesse latch the baby onto a heavy, mottled breast, and he quietened as he suckled, mewling when he took a breath.

'Midwife Héloïse did a splendid job midwifing your son, Renault ... there could not have been a more skilled midwife.'

Le Comte turned to me with a startled look as if he'd already forgotten I was there.

'Well then, Midwife, you shall be paid in as many gold coins as you can carry home.' He grabbed my hands and began pouring coins into my cupped palms from a leather pouch.

I could scarcely believe what I was hearing, what was

happening. I looked up with trepidation at Comte Renault, hardly daring to mouth the words. 'Can carry home? What of my ... my sentence, *Sire*?'

'Sentence?' Le Comte frowned as if he hadn't the slightest recollection of consigning me to the flames so recently. 'Do not speak such nonsense, Midwife. That is all in the past ... over and forgotten. Once my wife needs you no more, you are free to return to your home.' He flicked a wrist at me and strolled from the chamber grinning like someone not right in the head.

My hands still cupping the mound of coins, I looked at la Comtesse Geneviève. All I could do was shake my head in amazement and murmur thanks to Our Virgin and to Ava for this miracle.

'Bring food and wine please,' la Comtesse ordered the servants.

When the girls had scuttled away, she pursed her lips and spoke in a whisper. 'My husband is a fickle and untrustworthy tyrant,' she said. 'As you have observed, he is in the finest humour, overjoyed with his heir, and has thus freed you. But I know him, and tomorrow morn he could change his mind on a whim and consign you once again to the flames just as mercilessly. You must flee the castle now, Midwife. Lie low somewhere safe until we are certain le Comte will not reinvoke this ridiculous heresy accusation.' She gazed down at her son again, tracing a finger over his little face, exclaiming as he suckled. 'I shall not lie here with the fear my husband will burn you—giver of life and joy— like some common criminal.'

'Flee ... hide, Comtesse?' I said. 'But I can't, I've had word my little girl is ill; I need to go home to take care of her.'

'Your girl is ailing?' la Comtesse said. 'Then of course, Midwife. You must go to her this minute. But I shan't rest easy ... worrying my husband might have a change of heart.'

'Unfortunately that's a risk I'll have to take, Comtesse.'

Her ladies returned with trays laden with nutty yellow cheese, cake stuffed with dried fruit, and cuts of the best ham.

There were figs and dates and the whitest wheat-flour bread I'd ever seen. A maid poured wine flavoured with the pungent cinnamon and saffron I recognised from the rich merchants' market stalls.

'But before you go, Midwife,' la Comtesse Geneviève said, pushing a goblet towards me. 'You deserve a taste of our best hypocras.'

As much as the wine and food was heavenly, sating my belly croaking with hunger, all I could think of was rushing to the cot, and Morgane, before it was too late.

XXIX

'God's fingernails, Héloïse.' I caught the worry and the surprise, tight in Isa's cursing words, and her small, blackbird eyes. 'When the messenger came for your basket and chair, I guessed you were birthing the heir, but now …? Did you escape, or what?'

'Maman,' Morgane cried weakly, from where she lay sheened in sweat on the pallet. She gave me a weak smile and I dropped to the ground beside her. Isa was sitting on her other side, Raoul on a stool at the table.

Without looking at him or Isa, I looped the talisman over my head and placed it in Morgane's palm, closing her fingers around the old bone. 'This will help, poppet … it will make you better … it must!' I felt strange and hollow—unable to cry, unable to feel anything but an empty place in the pit of my belly.

'Héloïse?' I still didn't look up at Raoul, keeping my gaze on my daughter, my stooped form casting a deformed shadow across the wall. I took one of the cloths Isa had soaked in rose-water, and began wiping it over her fevered brow. 'What …' Raoul went on. 'How …?'

'Ask my husband to leave me alone with my daughter please Isa,' I said. 'Now I'm no longer imprisoned I need to take care of her.'

'Please, Héloïse,' Raoul said, 'I know it was a terrible thing I did but understand I only wanted to protect—'

I held up a palm, still not looking at my husband, and tried to keep my voice steady. 'Isa, please ask Raoul to go to the Mason's Lodge. Or somewhere ... anywhere but here.'

'I admit the greater fault is mine,' Raoul began again, 'but not completely. You have some part—'

'Get him away from me, Isa.' I still managed to keep my voice calm, but felt its panicked edge and I knew if Raoul didn't leave the cot right now, I'd scream and hit him. Kick him hard enough to kill him.

'Mayhap it's best you go back to the Lodge, Raoul,' Isa said, 'just for a time.' Sensing, in her softened voice, some misplaced pity for the man who still dared call himself my husband, I threw my aunt a dour glare.

I heard my husband's heavy sigh, the thud of his boots, and I jumped as the cot door slammed behind him.

I didn't mention Raoul again, as Isa and I sat together beside Morgane. I told her about le Comte's astonishing change of heart, revoking my death sentence. I also told her how la Comtesse didn't trust him to keep his word. And once I'd cleansed my stinking body in rose-water, I barely moved from my daughter's side for the next two days.

I bathed her, and gave her sips of fairy cup brew made from the cowslips she'd plucked from a hayfield. I told her the stories about Ava that Isa had told me, while I fed her thyme-scented chicken broth to build her strength. And I prayed to our Virgin as I'd never prayed before.

The last morning of our vigil, as the first bands of dawn pierced the shutter chinks, I flung them open, and the door, and let the early day's cool freshness wash inside. I stretched my arms, my aching back, and looked up at the sky.

The little white ball of moon still clung to the last straggle of night. Beneath her, a narrow stripe—the same deep turquoise as a blend of Morgane's two-coloured eyes—stretched across the horizon. I watched it grow, lighten to emerald, and topaz.

My daughter's red hair shone bright in the slant of new sun, her freckles pale against healthier cheeks. Her eyes gleamed, and the dark night was over.

But our bliss was thwarted later that same day when Captain Drogan's torso filled the doorway, obliterating what remained of the sunlight.

'Lice of Satan!' Isa cursed. 'What now?'

'Midwife Héloïse, wife of Raoul Stonemason,' Drogan said. 'You're under arrest.'

'Again? You're getting beyond a joke, Drogan,' I said. 'Le Comte de Fouville revoked my—'

'You killed my unborn child,' he cut in, without a trace of the usual mockery or sarcasm.

'She did not,' Isa said. 'I've been treating your wife; smeared goose salve on the bruises you gave poor Catèlena ... set her wrist you broke. I've tried to lift her spirits after you almost beat her to death, Captain Drogan. And for something she didn't do.'

'My wife can deny it all she wants,' he said, 'but I'll wager the stupid cow's lying ... I know she, and you,' he jabbed a finger at me, 'murdered my child before it had a chance at life. My wife committed a crime, so I punished her for it ... as you'll be punished, Midwife Héloïse.'

'To use your own words, Captain,' Isa said. 'You can't prove a thing.'

'No you can't!' I said.

'I don't need to prove a thing.' Drogan clicked his fingers and signalled to his sergeants to bind my wrists yet again. 'And this time,' he said, with a blistering glare. 'You'll stay in that cell till you burn. I won't rest until I've seen your charred corpse.'

***

'Might I ask where you are taking the midwife, Captain Drogan?' From the castle courtyard bustling with workers, I looked up to a window, to the pale face of la Comtesse Geneviève. 'Are you not aware my husband freed her?'

'Yes, Comtesse,' Drogan said with a small bow, 'but she's committed another crime, so she needs locking up again.'

'Well, before you put her to the cell, I need her midwifing services.' La Comtesse's gaze was steady, her voice cool with authority. She gave me not the slightest glance, as if she hadn't a care for me. 'I was just about to dispatch a messenger for her to help me with ... some troubles feeding my son. Send her up to my solar chambers immediately, Captain.'

When I reached her solar, la Comtesse Geneviève was sitting in a velvet-upholstered chair by the window, cradling her son. She might still look drained from the laborious birth, but her finery obscured any weakness in her body. She wore a necklet of amber, her coiled braids decorated with an elegant butterfly-shaped headdress and the cloth of her full, scarlet-coloured gown spilled over the chair in ribbons of burnished gold.

'*Bonjour*, Comtesse Geneviève, I hope you are well,' I said, with a small curtsey. 'At your service.'

'Leave me alone with the midwife, girls,' she said to the maids changing her bed linen and tidying the baby's cradle. 'Just you stay, Maid Delphine,' she said to one of them.

'You're having trouble feeding your son, Comtesse?' I said.

'Oh not at all,' she said with a smile and a flick of her wrist. 'He's feeding perfectly well. Just look at him.' She held the baby out to me. 'And your daughter?' she said.

'Morgane is well recovered ... thank the Blessed Virgin.' Of course I didn't specify from what illness she'd recovered, or they'd have hoisted me out of that chamber quicker than a trout channels the Vionne.

'He does seem contented,' I said, taking the child, unswaddling him. 'His limbs are all moving well too, and he's a healthy colour.' I kept waiting for her to explain. 'So ...?'

'A little rat informed me,' la Comtesse said, touching her finger to her nose, 'of Captain Drogan's new plan to have you imprisoned.'

'I'll deny the charge, as will his wife,' I said, hoping the heat rising to my cheeks wouldn't betray me. I could not go back to that gaol. Would not. 'Captain Drogan has no proof of any crime to his wife's body.'

If poor Catèlena had denied it to the point of almost being killed, I was certain she wouldn't go back on her word now.

'A good midwife like yourself,' la Comtesse said, as I took my time reswaddling her boy, 'performs her work as she deems fit. She should not feel obliged to justify her actions. And, as I said before, I'll not see you executed.'

I still couldn't meet her clear gaze. She knew I'd banished Captain Drogan's seed from his wife's belly; knew it for certain, but she accepted that I'd judged it necessary. Something the law could not. As I placed her son back in her arms, she gave me a knowing smile, and I acknowledged that la Comtesse was far from the small-minded noble I'd once taken her for.

'However, Midwife Héloïse,' she said, latching the baby onto her breast. 'Nothing's changed ... I still advise you to flee Lucie-sur-Vionne for a time. You are right, and Captain Drogan cannot prove this crime, but he does hold a certain ... a certain sway over my husband.' She winced as the baby fastened his lips tighter.

'You really believe I should flee?' I said. 'My daughter is recovered but I'd prefer—'

'And besides Captain Drogan's influence, and his apparent obsession to see you locked up,' la Comtesse cut in, 'le Comte may still reinvoke your death sentence. Go away, I say. Lie low, perhaps only for a week, just long enough for my husband to find a new victim ... someone else to occupy his idle mind. Long enough to know you will be safe when you return.'

'But where would I go?' Yet even as I spoke the words, the perfect place came to mind.

'Delphine is my most trusted servant.' La Comtesse Geneviève nodded at the maid standing awkwardly beside the door. 'Please procure a basket of food, Delphine. And new garments and a cap for my midwife. You must disguise her as one of my ladies.

And don't forget a clean wimple to hide her face as much as possible. Then you shall guide her along the underground passageway that leads to the secret exit beyond the curtain wall. And,' she said, as she put the softly mewling baby to her other breast, 'mention this to no one. Not a soul. Understood?'

'I'll fetch the disguise immediately, Comtesse Geneviève.' The girl curtsied and hurried from the room.

'How can I thank you enough, Comtesse?' I said.

'I am the one to thank you, Midwife,' she said, gazing again at her son. 'You have given me something far more valuable than all the gold in Italy.'

A few moments later Delphine arrived with the clothes and handed me a basket. 'Food for you, Midwife and a blanket, candles, fire striker, cooking pot and other sundries I thought you'd need.'

'Thank you, Delphine, that's kind of you.'

She nodded and helped me into the new chemise and kirtle—rust-coloured, rather than the wise-woman's blue Isa and I wore—and cap. She tied the wimple about my face and neck.

'If I can be so bold, Comtesse,' I said, as Delphine tucked the last snippets of my hair out of sight. 'Could someone let my aunt know where I am?'

'Certainly, Midwife. Where shall we tell your aunt you have gone?'

'Chief Washerwoman Poppa is my aunt's friend. She'll let Isa know I'll be at ... at the place of the Romans.'

Almost singing with joy at my abrupt change of fortune, I turned from la Comtesse to follow Delphine. But as we made to leave the solar, two glowering men stood before us, blocking our way. Drogan's sergeants again. I stiffened, glanced over my shoulder at la Comtesse Geneviève, but sensed she could do no more for me.

'Back to that cell now,' one of them said. 'Captain Drogan's orders.'

***

As the men grabbed my arms, a hooded figure appeared behind them. Like a ghost rising from the twilight shadow, it intercepted the men, muttering something incomprehensible. In that dun castle lighting, I had no idea who it was, but the next thing I knew, my captors were backing away into the shadows and Delphine was tugging on my arm.

'Who was that, Delphine?'

'I don't know, Midwife, but just come now ... hurry!'

Hardly believing what had just happened, I skittered after Delphine and the light from her hissing and sputtering rushlight. The vaulted passageway seemed to go on for leagues, and my legs shook beneath me, my heart beating as wild as the wings of a caged bird.

'Almost there,' Delphine said, pointing ahead into the darkness. The rushlight smoked and flickered as if it might burn out any second.

A man—a castle guard no doubt—stepped from nowhere and Delphine stopped still. I ran into the back of her, both of us almost toppling onto the stony floor. The guard shone his lantern into our faces. I held my breath, not daring to make a sound or a movement.

'Who are you?' His voice heaved with suspicion. 'And where are you running off to at this time, after curfew?' Without a glance at Delphine, his gaze travelled the length of me, settling on my face. He'd surely recognised me as the condemned heretic.

'My sister and I are maids of la Comtesse Geneviève,' Delphine said, clutching my arm. 'But just this very evening, the pestilence lumps have grown in my poor sister's armpits. I too haven't stopped sneezing, and we all know what that means. La Comtesse ordered us from the castle before we infect others ... to leave via this underground route, so as not to encounter anyone.'

'Ask la Comtesse if you don't believe us,' I said with far more boldness than I felt.

But the guard had no wish to check our story. Like everyone at the mention of the pestilence, he seemed speechless with terror. His eyes wide in the lantern light, he backed away, holding up his free arm as a shield. 'Go! Get away from here before we all catch your poison!'

Delphine smothered her giggles as the man faded into the darkness, still shouting, 'Go! Go!'

Moments later, a little further on, Delphine's footsteps slowed. 'Here's the way out, beyond the castle wall. Go from Lucie now, before le Comte changes his mind, or Captain Drogan discovers you're no longer with la Comtesse.'

'Thank you, Delphine. I'll repay your kindness one day.'

One day when this living nightmare is over. If it ever ends.

She turned on her heel. 'Godspeed you, Midwife Héloïse.'

'Godspeed you too, Delphine.'

And she was gone.

I stepped outside, beneath a sky littered with clouds and a moon swollen as a labouring woman's belly. Fireflies, the souls of unbaptised infants, hung about me like a curtain of diamonds and I realised I'd come out on the slope of a hill; the side of the castle opposite the market-place, for I could hear the Vionne River burbling in the darkness below.

Free from the terror of Morgane dying, of that dank and filthy cell and the husband who put me there, and of Captain Drogan, I wanted to leap about and dance. But still so close to the castle, I knew I wasn't yet out of mortal danger.

Holding Delphine's basket in one hand and my skirts in the other, I scurried down towards the river and the Roman road.

Once amidst the thick summer foliage of the Roman way I felt a little safer. I passed no one, and hoped it would stay that way, for there are many kinds of traveller—human and beast—who hunt lonely night roads.

Ragged clouds flirted with the moon, flitting back and forth as if afraid to stay pressed on her too long. And when they did expose the moon, she was so bright I could make out the trains of fish streaming through the Vionne, their bellies shimmering as the current flipped them sideways. The moon made glittery trails of snails' paths too, and fallen stars of the yellow primrose clusters.

Clouds shifted back across the moon's face and darkness surged around me. The trees seemed to hold their breath, every one of them taking the shape of something frightening: a cut-throat holding his knife aloft, a boar set to charge, a wolf crouched to pounce. The cloud peeled away again and I hurried on, anxious to get to safety.

I'd almost reached our magical pool on the Vionne when an owl swooped across my path, silent and pale as the dead. It glided away over the trees. So intent I was, gazing at its graceful silhouette against the moon, that at first I didn't notice the luminous eyes of the fox.

Isa had taught me it was an omen if that symbol of the Devil crossed your path, so I'd grown up fearing the living fox.

A portent that Drogan would banish me again to the dismal gaol cell ... that Comte Renault would send me to the flames?

I swivelled away, pretended I'd not seen the fox, but it pricked its ears and looked straight at me. I held my breath, waited for it to hurl itself at me. The fox turned and slunk away into the night.

In daylight the cave was well-concealed, but at night it was impossible to find unless you knew to start climbing from our pool into which the white river foam tumbled.

I picked my way up the valley wall, the moonlight deceiving my eye rather than helping. Shadows masked holes, solid-looking rocks rolled away beneath my feet and the boulders and bushes I gripped slid from my sweaty fingers.

Panting, I finally reached the cave entrance, shallow as a fool's grin carved on the rock face. Isa had told me that long before her and Ava's time, a hermit built a low stone wall across part of the cave entrance. Over time, dry twigs and vegetation had built up behind it, and I scooped up some to use for kindling. The

June days might be hot, but the night damp would linger inside the cave and I needed to warm my limbs if I was to get some much-needed rest.

I took one of Delphine's candles from the basket, lit it with a flint, and wrinkled my nose at the rancid tallow smell. Using its light just long enough to start a blaze, I fanned the flames towards the cave interior. I had to be frugal with the candles, who knew how long before Isa could come with more supplies. That is, if Poppa managed to let Isa know where I was.

Of course that vile piece of *merde*, Captain Drogan would have his falcon eye trained on Isa, Raoul and Morgane, tracking their every move. And if one of them led him to me, he'd be ready to swoop. But they'd know not to come to the cave too soon; they'd know not to take any chances.

I set stones around the edge of the fire to heat, another of Isa's tricks—hot stones wrapped in sacking make good foot warmers. I took the wool blanket Delphine had also stuffed into the basket and spread it on the ground.

My heavy eyelids drooped with the heat of the firelight that lit up the smoke-blackened, marbled cave walls.

Starved in that bleak church cell. Raoul's betrayal. The terror of the trial and execution sentence. The birth of the heir. Morgane's sickness. My uncertain reprieve and now, having to hide like a hunted outlaw. At the thought of it all, exhaustion engulfed me.

As the first almond-green band of dawn broke clear of the horizon, I pulled my cloak about my shoulders and sank down onto the cave floor. Against the sound of the water trickling over the riverbed boulders below me, and the birds wakening in the treetops, I drifted off.

Summer in the Year of Our Lord 1348–
Spring in the Year of Our Lord 1349
Lucie-sur-Vionne

XXX

The harsh honk of geese woke me with a start, a slice of light pale as whey slanting through the cave entrance. It was my third morning here, and in that moment between sleep and waking I hungered for my cot with its welcoming hearth-fire, its burning lavender and rosemary, and herb bunches drying from the beams.

I pictured Isa tending our garden, the colourful tumble of her rose bushes, the rustle of birds nesting in the thatch, the hens scratching in the grass. The pig would be gorging itself on scraps, blissfully ignorant it was being fattened only for the Michaelmas slaughter. I smiled as the breeze flapped Morgane's braids while she played with Blanche, Raoul sitting on the bench beside the woodpile, sharpening his tools.

From time to time he'd glance up from beneath his shock of red-gold hair and wink at our daughter. Then I remembered that there was no more Raoul and my smile soured. It seemed an age since I'd felt such a moment; a time when my home felt safe and filled with love. A time before the pestilence. Pangs of loneliness jabbed at me, the rage a black swell in my breast.

How dare Raoul, then the townsfolk, treat me so unjustly after my tireless efforts for them? How unfair to be separated from Isa and Morgane, forced to cower in the woods like a common outlaw, my life dependent on the whimsical wishes of a tyrannical lord and his bully of a captain.

I rubbed my calves and stretched my back to drive out the ache from the cold ground. The morning was cool, a pink mist loitering over the silvery spine of river below. I rekindled last night's fire, smoke threading up into the pearly light as birds called to each other across the valley, vying with the noise of water gurgling into our magical Vionne pool.

I ate the last of la Comtesse Geneviève's bread and cheese, drank the wine and made my way down the slope towards the river. I plucked thyme and garlic as I went, and as I bent to pick a handful of wild barley, I stepped into a hole and stumbled, twisting my foot. Everything went black and I slumped to the ground, lathered in a cold sweat.

I breathed deeply for a few moments, gripping my ankle which had started to throb. The pain surging through my body, I cried out as I groped around for a sturdy stick, hauled myself to my feet and limped the rest of the way down.

I sank my ankle into the cool shallows, my only means— without my medicaments—to lessen the swelling, the Vionne grumbling like an old maid, combing underwater weeds into fans of dark green swishing hair. Despite the cool water numbing the pain, the ache of my loneliness and my anger magnified this small injury.

I should be at my cot, free to take Saint John's wort or lime blossom for the swelling … any remedy I need.

I tilted my face, shook my fist at Heaven. 'Damn you, God! Damn you!'

I closed my eyes and waited for Him to strike me. Nothing. But as I looked through the willow trees, and the giant oaks, vines strangling their trunks, I had the feeling someone, or something, was watching me. God? Ava's angel?

Once again those sombre doubts about Our Lord pressed upon me: why were all of us, from Père Bernard at his altar to the richest cloth merchant in his emporium to the poorest farmer in his lowly cot, placing this pestilence in His hands … His *invisible* hands?

Of course no answer came, and as I shook my head in frustration, I spied a clutch of comfrey. A poultice of its leaves would reduce my ankle swelling, and I plucked the purple-flowered plant from its earthy riverbank bed.

Standing in the shallows I splashed water over myself, which brought to my mind those sheep scrubbed so clean when Drogan had first arrested me. Isa's words throughout my childhood echoed in my mind: "All healing begins with cleanliness", and I wondered about humans scrubbing themselves with that strong and greasy soap too; so clean that perhaps it could help ward off the pestilence miasma?

I thought of Morgane speaking with her little friends, Pétronille and Peronelle.

'... *she washes the fleas away, again and again. Maman's always washing me ... she says a clean body and clean clothes means less sickness.*'

Brought up on Isa's strict cleanliness rules, I too had always insisted on clean hair, bodies and clothes. And a clean home. Far more than other townsfolk bothered. Could that be why the pestilence had passed me by? With all the closeness I'd had to its victims I should have succumbed by now. Yet I hadn't.

My fingers folded over my talisman. When I'd claimed to Raoul it would protect me, I only half-believed it, but perhaps it was true, and this little angel really was protecting me, keeping me free from disease so I could care for others?

I finally managed to hook a fat trout, then, still leaning on the stick, I laboured back up the slope. I crushed the comfrey and boiled it over the fire embers and while the herb-seasoned fish roasted, I held the poultice against my ankle.

If only I had some rose-oil, our finest remedy for swelling. It struck me then how many ailments we did treat with rose medicaments: soothing irritated skin, cleaning infected eyes and lifting melancholic spirits. Excellent for stomach sickness, sore throat and headache, it also calmed nerves. It just simply made a person feel well.

I watched an ant crawl close to my injured ankle. She was carrying a crumb of something; struggling to take it back to her nest where it would feed her fellow ants for a day or a week, I didn't know. So intent she was, falling and stumbling under the weight of her crumb, she didn't notice my foot.

I searched the ground for other ants and followed a line of them running to and from a hole. Home, surely. I placed a leaf in front of the ant, which she walked onto, carried it to the hole where the other ants were, and put it down. The ant twitched her feelers and, balancing her precious morsel, walked down the hole. I smiled to myself, feeling as if I'd saved the world.

And as I ate the fish, my mind began to imagine a new concoction; a potion we'd brew up in our cot. My head spun wild with dreams, possibilities, and hope. I couldn't wait to see Isa and tell her about it.

***

I gathered all the fish bones to return them to the river, so—as Isa had taught me—the trout could be reborn.

Learn about the river, the woods and their plants and beasts, and you'll never starve, even in the worst famine or plague.

During the hottest part of the afternoon I rested in a thicket of drooping willows along the riverbank. I ached to see Isa and Morgane, to be back in my cot, my ire at my predicament weighing heavier with each passing, scorching hour. But however I turned the problem around in my mind, I could see no way of returning to Lucie just yet. Comte Renault could change his mind as quickly as he changed his ridiculous pointy shoes, and Captain Drogan would throw me back in that foul cell in a heartbeat.

Still bone-tired from my days in gaol, then caring for Morgane—not to mention the exhaustion just thinking of Raoul's betrayal—it was barely dusk when I curled up on the cave floor. I must have lapsed into a deep sleep, for at first I thought I was dreaming when I heard the noise. Stones, or large pebbles, falling around the cave entrance. *Plock, plock. Plock, plock.*

Someone was hissing my name. My pulse leapt to my throat. I sprang to my feet, and hurried to the cave opening.

During this season of scant rain, the waterfall was only a small stream, but it was still hard to define the noise. Was it the Vionne calling me? Isa had always said I was a child of the river, dragged from my dead mother's womb against its gurgle and rush.

'Héloïse, you up there?'

'Isa!' My heart soared with joy.

'I'm past climbing that Devil's arse of a slope these days, Héloïse; you'll have to come down here.'

It wasn't fully dark yet, but I lit a candle and carefully, so as not to further damage my ankle, picked my way down the slope to the old Roman road.

'I knew you'd come!' I threw my arms around Isa's bowed shoulders, squinting left then right. Not a soul, but in that dusk light, and over the Vionne's babble, it would've been hard to see or hear anyone approaching.

Isa held me at arm's length and examined me from my head to my feet. 'You look well enough. I knew the cave, the woods and the river would treat you well. But you're limping.'

'Just a twisted ankle,' I said, as we sat together on a rock by the woodland road. 'I'm well, just … frustrated. After all I did for them. I risked my life and they tried to burn me! And now I can't go home until I'm sure that ogre Comte Renault won't change his mind and send me to the flames, and Drogan won't keep persecuting me.'

'I could hardly believe our good fortune,' Isa said, 'when Poppa told me la Comtesse intercepted him and helped you flee the castle.'

'Good luck maybe, but for how long?'

'There's every chance this idiotic heresy accusation—and

Drogan's latest murder charge—will soon be completely forgotten,' Isa said. 'With the pestilence raging out of control, people have other worries. Poppa said as soon as la Comtesse is recovered enough from the birth to travel, they'll be off to one of their outlying estates, far from the miasma. Apparently the roads are full of horses, ox-carts, wagons and people fleeing north. But that's pointless, since these days the pestilence is everywhere you run.' She swallowed a mouthful of ale and handed me her flask.

'La Comtesse's travail was long and hard, and she still looked weak when I saw her,' I said, and gulped down some ale. 'She won't be fit to travel for some time.'

'Well for now,' Isa said, 'nobody's allowed in or out of the castle, except those who work there during the day, like Poppa, and the carters bringing supplies. And all those are carefully checked for pestilence signs.'

'Renault de Fouville is a buggering brute of a man,' I said. 'Blaming la Comtesse Geneviève for her barrenness all those years when she as good as told me he barely visited her chambers ... that he preferred the company of Père Bernard.'

'A sin for which our *Seigneur*—and the priest—would hang if it was ever proven,' Isa said. 'Speaking of that miserable old milksop,' she went on, taking her flask and swallowing another mouthful of ale, 'Père Bernard has locked himself in the presbytery ... refuses to give last rites to the dying, or to bury the dead.'

I recalled Raoul's first terrifying words.

People are dying in Florence without last rites; buried without prayers! Can you imagine their fear of that, in their last hours?

'Just when the people need their priest the most, he turns his back on them,' I said. 'And I bet purgatory is getting rather crowded.'

'And there are no more timbers to be had for coffins.' Isa winced, shifting her hips on the hard boulder. 'Families are simply dragging loved ones to their grave on a blanket. At Père Bernard's last Mass, he claimed he'd done all he can against the pestilence: cast out those of simple mind and deranged wit in whom the miasma is supposedly stronger, punished the faithless and tried to punish the heretic—'

'Sodomist swine!' I hissed.

'He says he fears this truly is the Great Dying,' Isa went on, 'and that a travelling friar told him priests in other places are refusing to have anything to do with the dying or dead, so he thinks fit to do the same. He also said that people on the point of death should confess to each other—even to a woman!'

'Women allowed to hear confession, and give absolution?' I said.

It felt as if someone had slapped my cheek. Alongside my steeping outrage, a strange mixture of shock and excitement filled me, as if the world was shifting below me and I didn't know where we'd all stand when it settled. 'After Père Bernard's vicious remarks about women at my trial? And his plea at the beginning for us to stay in Lucie and fight? I bet those words make for piss-poor fodder now.'

'Yes, many have turned against Père Bernard.' Isa turned her gaze upward, the moonlight furrowing the creases that lined her worn face.

'I've been lonely here on my own,' I said.

'I wanted to come straight away ... that first day,' Isa said, 'but Drogan and his sergeants never took their eyes off us. He's furious that la Comtesse helped you flee, though Poppa said she denies it.' She let out a giggle. 'Eyes bulging like a landed fish when he marched into the cot at dawn, threatening to arrest us for hiding a fugitive. They searched the whole place ... even the privy! Leastwise Morgane and I didn't have to pretend innocence, since we were as surprised as he was. But he's set on finding you,' Isa said. 'And if Poppa's not gilded the truth, as I know she can, Captain Drogan *does* have le Comte in his pocket. He knows Renault hankers after handsome men like himself, and he'll use that to sway our *Seigneur*. That's why you have to stay here, Héloïse. Just for a time.'

'But it's so unfair, Isa! So—'

'How many times have I told you? Life is not fair, Héloïse. I know patience has never come easy to you, but bide your time you must.' She squeezed my hand. 'Have faith in Our Lady, in our angel talisman, in Ava, and you'll come out the victor.'

'It seems I have no choice,' I said with a sigh. 'How's my poppet … still …?'

'Fit as a frog, not a single sign of the pestilence, but she misses you … spends most of her time with Blanche. And Raoul—'

'I don't want to know about Raoul.'

'Well all I'll say is your husband's still sleeping at the Mason's Lodge and this morning, when I saw him on the vingtain site, he looked so miserable and hunched over, as if his very heart was weighing him down.'

'More like his conscience weighing him down.'

'He did wrong,' Isa said. 'But so did you, disobeying him. You should ease off him, especially in such terrible times. The pestilence has taken many more in just the three days you've been here … townsfolk and farmers. Poppa's lost everyone—entire family gone except her and baby Loup. Seems the only happy one in Lucie is that greedy Poncet Batier. He's raised his price three-fold for digging graves and since no one else is willing to touch the dead, he's digging like Lucifer himself, those devilish eyes popping out of his skull with the news of every fresh corpse.'

'Do the people still think it's me … my talisman, cursing them with the pestilence, even if I'm no longer in Lucie?'

'Some,' she said. 'Alewife Rixende and Captain Drogan and his mother say you must be working from afar to curse us.'

I rubbed at my aching ankle, thinking back to what had been going through my mind; those vexing questions that had eventually brought a chink of light.

'I've been thinking, Isa, why should this pestilence be either a punishment sent by God, or the evil work of the Devil? What if it's simply an earthly thing, like a hole in a hillside in which I can stumble and twist an ankle? I can't truly believe that God, or the Devil, put that hole in my path to trip me.'

'Most would say God's hand places everything,' Isa said. 'But however you see things, it seems to me we're spending too much time thinking about these unanswerable questions.'

'So if we stopped wasting time searching for impossible answers,' I said, 'stopped waiting for God's punishing hand to fall. What if we looked on the pestilence as an earthly thing, like unwanted garden weeds, and tried to understand how it poisons our blood, then we might come nearer to finding a way of saving lives?'

'You're right,' Isa said with a groan, as she raised herself from the rock. 'We'd do better to get on with weeding the garden. Now, it's time I got home to Morgane.' She handed me her basket. 'Food, ale and candles. And I'll come again when we're certain our fickle *Seigneur* isn't going to change his mind.'

'Oh but I'll find a way to change his mind.'

The voice, coming straight from the tangle of willows, startled me, and Isa and I spun around. In that shadowless gloaming, neither light nor dark, it would have been difficult to make out who belonged to the voice, had I not known Captain Drogan's almost as well as I knew my own.

XXXI

Raoul went to take another swig of ale from his flask, found it was empty, like the other two lying at his feet. He hurled the flask against a wall of the Mason's Lodge, the last ale drops spattering across the castle drawings on the tracing floor—the plans he kept trying, and failing, to draw up.

'Seems I arrived just at the right time, eh, Raoul Stonemason.' From the doorway, one hand leaning against the frame, the other holding a jug of ale, Alewife Rixende nodded at the flasks on the floor.

Oh no, not her again …

'What do you want, Rixende?' he said, unable to keep the slur from his voice. Raoul knew he'd been drinking too much. And playing too much dice. And not working enough. At this rate, neither the vingtain wall nor the castle repairs would ever be finished. But it was so hot, too hot to work, and with the pestilence felling so many workers, the task was even harder. And if Raoul was honest with himself, his mind just wasn't on the job.

'Thought you'd appreciate my company,' Rixende said. 'Since I noticed you been here three days now, all on your lonesome.'

Three days already? Three days since his wife had ordered him from their—his!—cot, then disappeared from Lucie. Naturally he'd heard the market-place prattle: how Drogan wanted to lock her up yet again, but that she'd managed to escape with la Comtesse's help.

He knew Héloïse had gone to the cave; the place she'd taken him when they first met. The enchanted spot they'd first made delicious, forbidden love. A time when Raoul had thought that love as solid as a crude quarry stone, before it had splintered into fragments; fractured at the slightest touch of hammer, chisel and wedge.

Several times he'd started out for the cave, then stopped himself. He knew she wouldn't speak to him; still wouldn't listen to his forgiveness pleas, her wrath still smouldering. All he could hope for was that in time she'd come around. But he so missed her! Couldn't bear life without her ... hated staying alone in the Mason's Lodge every day, every night. He wanted to be home in his bed, in his wife's welcoming arms.

At least Isa had told him of Morgane's recovery. Praise Our Lord! If his little Flamelock had succumbed, Raoul knew he'd have died too. Without her, and Héloïse, there was no reason to go on living.

'Raoul?' Startled, he looked up into Rixende's eyes. Once summer-sky blue, they were now red-rimmed and glazed with a madwoman's glimmer. Her face was haggard—from grief and drink, Raoul thought. But while Rixende might be on the cusp of insanity, and had let herself run to a wreck, she was still a force of seduction any normal man would battle to resist. He lowered his gaze, and braced himself.

'So, *mon cher* Raaaoulll.' One breast was almost bursting from her kirtle lacing. She held the ale jug to his lips and as he drank, he felt the fingers of her other hand groping at the drawstring of his breeches.

'You had enough time to think about it now,' she said, 'how I'd make a far better wife than she ever was—that witch what cursed my husband with the pestilence.'

'There was nothing Héloïse could've done for Jâco,' Raoul said, trying to back away from Rixende's hand sliding beneath his breeches. She held the jug to his lips again, her tongue darting between her two front teeth: in, out; in, out.

He wanted to stop drinking; to push away her clammy hand, but instead he parted his legs a little and let out a soft moan.

Rixende's fingers found his yard, her breaths quickening, the breast popping from her kirtle lacing, and pressing against his mouth. Her hand moved faster, and, before he could stop himself, Raoul's tongue shot from his mouth and licked that fleshy breast, his teeth making little bites around her hard nipple.

'Your yard always this limp?' She sprayed beads of spittle across his face. 'No wonder you only spawned one babe. Never mind, Rixende will get you going, you'll see.'

Through his ale-haze, Raoul saw her lurch upright, spread her legs and push her bushy groin into his face. The hairs, stuck together in whitish clumps, smelt a little like fish gone off, but still he didn't turn his head as she ground her fleshy womb lips against his mouth.

She moved back a step, bent her head and took him full into her mouth. Raoul felt himself hardening, his yard starting to fill her mouth.

She sprang upright again, straddled him and lowered herself down and, with a grin that looked devilish in the dim light, she took his yard and tried to shove it inside her.

An image of Héloïse swam into Raoul's mind: her pale, heart-shaped face, her blue-grey eyes determined, stubborn, nurturing. He inhaled her green smell of the river, and of peace. And suddenly Raoul knew he'd drunk too much; was on the verge of vomiting.

Rixende pushed and forced and pushed, but still Raoul's member stayed soft and limp. A hot wave engulfed him and he felt himself shooting down into Hell, the flames of the eternal fires reaching out for him.

Blessed Saint Etienne, save me!

Rixende jumped to her feet. 'Christ on the cross, what does a woman have to do to get a fuck?' she snarled. 'That useless blacksmith's such a drunk he can't get it up either.'

With a scowl, she shoved her breasts back beneath their

lacings and tugged down her skirts. And as she stamped from the Mason's Lodge, Raoul bent and vomited all over his builder's drawings.

Tears pricked his eyes and he despised himself even more.

XXXII

'God's wounds, Drogan!' Isa said. 'You're really making a bad habit of this.'

Captain Drogan stood astride the woodland road as if it were a narrow lane. 'I knew you'd lead me to her … in the end.'

'Where is it then, whore of Satan?' In one hand, Drogan fingered the rope he held, entwining it through his hands, twirling it as if playing. In the other he held a lantern. 'Your hut … shelter, wherever you've been hiding out, and sleeping?'

'No hut … been sleeping out under the stars.' My defiant voice belied my frantic heartbeat. Instinct screamed at me to run. I thought of my twisted ankle and of my aunt who couldn't run. My simmering outrage bubbled, and spat from the cauldron.

'You won't bind or shackle me again, you spineless brute,' I said. 'And parade me through the town like some beast killed in the hunt. Le Comte has revoked my sentence. You have no proof of the allegation against your wife and I'm within my rights not to return to Lucie with you, Captain Drogan.' I spat at his feet, grabbed my angel pendant and began shaking it at him.

'Héloïse …'

I ignored Isa's warning, knew I was being reckless, but after all I'd suffered, what more did I care? I stepped towards Drogan until I was so close to those almond-coloured eyes that I could see, in his lantern light, the dark bits swell; could feel his quickening breaths as his gaze flickered to my talisman. I kept staring into my enemy's face, forcing Drogan's gaze to meet mine. It did for a second then twitched back to the pendant. A coward's flinch.

I began swinging the pendant a hair's breadth from his face, the luminous eyes glowing in both the lantern light and the new light of the moon. 'You say these eyes burned you once, Drogan,' I said, 'well, so they can again. Burn your whole hand off this time. Your face too. One quick move and you'll be ugly forever. Would Comte Renault listen to you then—*desire* you—with a face as scarred as a leper's?'

I was aware of Isa's rapid breathing, but she kept silent as Drogan reeled backwards, one hand still clutching the rope, the other held up shakily in front of him. 'N-no ... k-keep your Devil's charm away f-from me.'

'Well you keep away from me then.' I kept my voice steady, one hand still swinging the pendant, the other hovering over my belly. 'Go home, Drogan and don't pursue me again. Ever.'

Wordlessly, his eyes gaping with fear, Captain Drogan spun about and began running. 'I hope you burn in Hell,' I called after him, 'for all you've done against me.'

I turned back to Isa. 'Don't you say a word.'

'Well I hope that's choked the wrath out of you,' she said. 'For outrage only eats you up; stops us concentrating on what's most important ... weeding the garden of this pestilence.'

'Let's get back to the cot then,' I said, 'and start now.'

'You still can't come home, Héloïse. Just think, Drogan's convinced you're an evil witch by now, and that the talisman *can* curse your enemies. He'll head straight for the castle and charm le Comte into reversing his decision yet again. Mayhap you scared the Captain off—and, with luck, he'll still not be able to find our cave—but you might well have hammered your own burning stake into the ground.'

***

Time in the cave stretched as long as wetting stretches wool—each drawn-out waking hour of those hot and brassy days. After almost a week Isa hadn't returned, but at least I'd not seen or smelled a whisper of Captain Drogan. Surely if he was coming back for me, or if le Comte was going to change his mind, it would've happened by now.

Today was the wettest since the month of May and in the midst of such ferocious summer heat the misty rain was a relief. It fell all morning from a sky the colour of a dead man's shroud, casting the cave into shadow. Against the rain's patter on leaf and rock, I sat cross-legged on my cloak and thought about my rose-tonic pestilence potion. The more my mind ticked it over, the more eager I was to try it. After all, what was there to lose now?

Mid-afternoon, the wind turned to the north, sweeping away most of the cloud and I stepped outside, straight into mud that rose up around my ankles. It was cool—one of those bleak, windy days that come unexpectedly at the height of summer—and I trembled as I slithered down the muddy slope, and waded into the shallows of the Vionne, grey and chaotic after the rain.

From the dark tangle of writhing eels, I took only one. I could have caught twenty but if I took more than I needed the Vionne wouldn't give freely again. I squatted, using Delphine's knife to slice through the eel's body. A rustle in the willows behind startled me and I spun around to my aunt, her hollowed chest heaving as she hobbled forward.

'What is it?' The panic rose immediately. My hand pressed against my still-flat belly, I hurried towards Isa. 'Morgane ...?'

Thin as a lizard, her skin wrinkled as sheep's wool, and looking every one of her five and forty years, Isa sank wearily onto a wet rock. Her wind-scoured cheeks wore a magenta hue, her knuckle bulges shining as she pushed away the silver hair threads that clung to her brow.

'Good news,' she said between gasping breaths. 'It's safe for you to return to Lucie ... wanted to come this morning, but the rain ... had to wait till it cleared.'

'How are you sure the *Seigneur* won't reinvoke my sentence? And Drogan …?'

'Le Comte de Fouville has left *le château* with his entourage. Poppa said there's not been a word said about you since you fled the castle. And Captain Drogan is dead … from the blood-spitting type.'

'Drogan dead … are you sure?' I began to shake all over.

'Rumour has it his dying words were: "the heretic bitch got me in the end … cursed me."'

'Hardly,' I said, 'but if God really is watching over us, he'd surely strike me down right now, so glad I am he's gone.'

'Oh I'm sure He'll forgive you just this once, Héloïse. Besides,' Isa went on, massaging her hips, 'people have far more to worry about than you. The pestilence has taken many others in the ten days you've been gone. Everyone is afraid it'll get as bad as in the south. They say that in Bordeaux, bodies are piling in the streets, and in Avignon *four hundred* are dying daily, the graveyards so full they're throwing corpses into the Rhône River. At the monastery, all the monks are dead.' She let out a crazy kind of cackle. 'Perhaps this truly is the end of the world.'

'The end of the world … could that really be?' I kept shaking my head at that impossible thought. 'No, Isa, after all this suffering, we can't let it end here! I've had idle time to think about what we spoke of before—treating the pestilence as a garden weed—and I hope I've found a way to stop it spreading.'

'Stop the pestilence spreading? You must be mad, Héloïse. You know there's no cure and—'

'Not a cure … listen to me. When I think about the people who've died in Lucie, none have been silverhairs like you. Why is that, do you think?'

'Because the old ones, such as Poppa and me, must be good fighters of sickness; experienced soldiers in the battle against disease. Or we'd already be in the ground.'

'So I say we arm the children and the young … give them weapons to fight off sickness,' I said. 'What if we mixed strength-building rose petals with other such plants into a fortifying tonic?' I took a quick breath. 'We know that where there's more filth and vermin the pestilence flourishes, so we should also insist on frequent scrubbing with the farmers' sheep-washing soap. People should wash their hands in rose-water, or vinegar, and we must tell them all to wear masks not only when treating the sick but always while this pestilence rages.'

'Satan's hairy yard, but you've got some courage and determination, girl, after how the townsfolk treated you. Now go and get your things from the cave and let's get home ... we'll dry off by the fire with a mug of ale, and you'll tell me about this miracle tonic.'

As I climbed back up the muddy slope, Isa told me more about le Comte leaving Lucie. 'Poppa—who's lost her washer-woman work, poor old crone—said he took Père Bernard away with them too.'

'*Humph*, I wonder why.'

'You should've heard them all the people hissing in the street as they rode out of town. Now the people truly feel abandoned. And Raoul and his workers aren't that happy the vingtain and castle repairs are halted, since our *Seigneur* is no longer around to pay them.'

'Why didn't you bring Morgane to fetch me? I said, still not caring to hear a word about Raoul.

'Oh, she wanted to come, but your budding apprentice had to stay and help Blanche birth her litter of kittens.'

'So at least one male cat escaped the burning,' I called from the cave, smiling as I imagined Morgane eagerly playing mid-wife to Blanche. 'And I'd rather her midwife cats than humans for now ... I still can't believe she dared to midwife Sibylle.'

'And did a cracking job of it too,' Isa said, as I eased my way down the slippery slope again. The wind picked up, pewter-coloured clouds scudding across the hills as I took Isa's arm and hurried her along the woodland road before it rained again.

As we reached the northern boundary of Lucie, my heart

soared once our cot came into sight, the only dwelling besides the charred remnants of the lepers' home on that isolated knoll above the Vionne.

'You're home!' Morgane bellowed like a calf separated from its mother as she skittered towards me, hair and eyes shining, her filled-out cheeks even more freckled. Perfectly, beautifully, well again. 'Come and see Blanche's kittens, Maman ... I mid-wifed her. My cat helped.' She held up Crispen's wooden carving. 'Same as when I birthed the baker's wife; same as the angel talisman helps you with births.'

As I hugged my daughter the tears bloomed, and leaked down my cheeks. I lifted my gaze to the sky, tilted my face to the cool cleansing rain descending from the dun-coloured heavens.

I let the rain wash away my tears of happiness at holding Morgane; the tears of new hope that I might finally do something against this pestilence.

XXXIII

'Since le Comte's left Lucie and there's no more building work, I thought I'd make myself useful here.' Raoul's hoarse voice startled me as I stepped outside the following morning. Isa had told me he was still at the Mason's Lodge, so I was surprised to see him at the cot. 'The fence needs fixing,' he carried on, 'and the roof ... so much needs fixing.'

He started walking towards the barn, where I was preparing Merlinette, and my pulse quickened. 'I'm glad to see you home, Héloïse. I'd like to ... to come home too. But I won't, unless I have your blessing.'

'Well you don't. Now please let me pass, Raoul.' I stepped around him. 'I've got patients to visit.'

'Patients I never should've forbidden you to see.' Raoul's hand grasped my wrist, stopping me from walking on. 'I know that now, but I thought I was doing the right thing, trying to protect—'

'I know,' I said, 'but locking me in gaol was going too far ... really, too far. And I know you begged le Comte to release me but when I couldn't take care of our daughter, you can't imagine ...'

I held my breath as he leaned in close and took my pendant between his thumb and forefinger, careful not to touch the eyes. Although I was certain Raoul had known for a long time there was no truth to that tale.

295

'I shouldn't have tried to stop you going into pestilence homes,' he carried on. 'As you said in the beginning, this angel must be protecting you.' He touched a fingertip to my cheek. I flinched, and his hand dropped. 'When you first told me the story of how your midwifing ancestor came by the angel carving, I didn't believe you. I scoffed at your faith in it.'

'You did, Raoul, and you can hardly try and stop me treating pestilence victims now, since you allowed me to treat our own daughter.'

'I won't stop you any longer, Héloïse. But listen to me ... if your talisman story isn't simply legend—if the pendant does hold special powers to help the safe passage of babes, and to heal the sick, why wouldn't it protect you? After all, you've been so close to those afflicted but the miasma passes you by every time. And my little Flamelock and Yolande both recovered ... your friend and your own daughter. Many would say that's not just down to luck.'

'I'm convinced the talisman does possess powers for easing birth,' I said, 'even if it's only because the women want to believe it ... clinging to any notion in the face of such agonising pain. But guarding against the pestilence? I'm not so sure. Anyway, I have to go.' Apart from my haste to be away from Raoul, I was anxious to visit the patients I had abandoned, albeit unwillingly, and to start brewing the rose tonic.

I hurried away from his outstretched hand, mounted the mare and rode off down the woodland road without a backward glance.

I was still furious at Raoul; I could barely believe he'd asked me to forgive him, but as the summer-fragrant sun warmed my face and neck, the breeze around the farmers' cots sighing and whispering like a chorus of haunted voices, I thought how lucky I was to be alive; lucky my whole family was still living. And even more fortunate that Morgane and Yolande had been amongst the few to survive the pestilence. I sensed an ebb in the tide of my fury; the resentment starting to shrivel like the muddied roads and puddled fields after yesterday's rain.

But as I approached the devastation around la place de l'Eglise, any tentative feelings of peace were immediately quashed.

***

It was the smell of the alleyways coming off the market-place that struck me first. Someone tipped a chamber pot into a drain that was clogged with the corpses of a dog, two chickens and a goose. The cloying odour of rot—the stink of death and human foulness—hung on the hot air, making every breath a gag.

On the market-place, many of the shop fronts were shut- tered, the few open, upper storey windows staring at me like dead eye sockets. Rotting straw, evidently heaped up for days, teemed with a swarm of rats. They tore at the rubbish within, not even looking up at my approach.

It was like exchanging one gaol cell for another, wondering who would be next up for the gallows. Helpless against terrible forces, I could understand why people threw up their hands and said everything was controlled by God. But that would not be my way. Not now. I held a hand over my belly as if that simple gesture could protect my unborn from this horror.

My ears rang, not with the usual noises of Lucie-sur-Vionne: the laughter of children who were no longer allowed to play outside for fear of the miasma air, the chatter of women around the drinking trough, the hiss of geese, the squawk of chickens, the yelp of dogs. The noise too, of the blacksmith's hammer in his forge, the clunk of the butcher's cleaver slicing bloody meat. No, my ears buzzed now with the silence.

When the pestilence first came, the bell of Saint Antoine's went from ringing a few times each day to almost continuously: one long, sad peal for the dead. It became a background noise to our days. But now—since the priest was gone—the bell didn't ring at all. And the silence seemed worse than its constant toll.

I gathered those old sights and sounds into my heart in the

hope that one day they might all be back. Though I sensed nothing would be the same, ever again. Even when the pestilence was gone.

Sibylle appeared at the baker's door as I hitched Merlinette to the fountain post.

'So relieved I was when your aunt said you'd be back with us, Midwife Héloïse,' she said, launching straight into her breathless gibber. 'Glad you were saved too, of course. Look, my little boy's doing well.' She held out her swaddled son to me.

'I'll check him and you in a minute, Sibylle,' I said, 'but first, I'm asking you to wear a mask all the time now. I'll be giving them out to all the townsfolk.'

I also told her—and as many others as I could find that morning—about my washing instructions. And once I'd seen all my patients, as I crossed the market-place back to Merlinette, the shoemaker's daughter sidled across to me.

'I must speak with you urgently, Midwife Héloïse.' Ariane's voice sounded more fearful than usual. 'I've been trying to see you for weeks, but you've been … away.'

'Are you ill, Mistress Ariane?' I tied a mask over her mouth and nose. 'You're pale as the Virgin.'

'Not ill.' She glanced around, but nobody seemed to be listening. 'I'm with child, but I can't have it. You must give me a potion to be rid of it.'

'How many of your monthly courses have you missed?'

'Four maybe … don't remember exactly. But I've felt it moving.'

'Moving already?' I said. 'Then I'm sorry, you can't be rid of it.'

'B-but, I have to.' Her eyes clouded with tears. 'I can't … nobody can know …'

'Is there a special boy, Ariane? One who might marry you and make this right?'

'No! No special boy. The father is … this child is the Devil's spawn.' The girl wobbled on her small bare feet, and I feared she'd faint right into my arms.

'The father is one of those outlaws who attacked Lucie,' she said in a hoarse whisper. 'It could be any of three or four of them, I can't remember … don't *want* to remember.'

Her words were a sword slicing through my breast, more so as Ariane had just voiced my suspicion about my own seeding, and I put my arms around the girl's heaving shoulders. 'Oh, Ariane I'm so sorry for you, my sweet.'

'See why I can't have it? It's a poison growing inside me and I just want the hateful thing out of me.'

'I do see but I still can't give you the potion. It's one thing to bring on the courses of a woman who's a few weeks late,' I explained, thinking of the pitiful, battered Catèlena, 'when the babe doesn't yet have a soul. But something else to cast out a child who's already quickened. This baby has clearly taken hold in your womb, and washing it out now would be difficult and dangerous. You could bleed, or die of any of the foul humours likely to invade your body. So much could go wrong and then I'd need to go exploring … to stretch the mouth of your womb, hazardous in itself for the womb might rise up into your chest and suffocate you.'

Ariane's doe-eyes widened. 'Suffocate me?'

I knew my words sounded harsh, but I had to convince the girl she had no choice but to keep this babe, or I'd risk her seeking out charlatans such as Rixende who, sensing the girl's desperation, would sell her some dangerous potion at a ridiculous price. 'And black bile may flood out and overwhelm your other humours,' I carried on. 'Or the mouth of your womb may never close again. Foul humours could then get into the womb, making it so slippery that future babies would be cast out. A hundred things could go wrong, and the blame would be on me. I would be imprisoned, and hanged. As would you.' I patted her arm. 'A midwife doesn't bring death, Ariane; she brings life … even a life brutally seeded.'

'I'll be cast out from Lucie-sur-Vionne.'

'Try not to worry so much,' I said. 'We'll work something out.

But meanwhile, I must examine you; make sure everything is well with you and the babe.'

The girl gave me a tearful nod and as we both trudged towards the shoemaker's shop, the weight of her misery weighed me down. But my sadness for Ariane was mild compared with my sorrow for her unborn child. I knew what it was to grow up an outcast non-born bastard. Even as I did my best to help the ailing townsfolk and those awaiting births—often for no payment and only insult, and death sentence!—life had so often been a battle. As it had been for Ava and Isa, the bastard twins. I wouldn't wish that heartache and misery on my worst enemy.

My thoughts were cut short as we approached the shuttered door, and the wooden sign of a golden boot, for the smell of rotten apples hit me—that once-loved autumn scent now firmly bound to sickrooms. I threw Ariane a questioning look, but the girl just shook her head as I pushed open the door, knowing well enough what I'd find inside.

Ariane's mother lay whimpering and wasted on the stained and musty rushes. As I got closer, and despite my mask, her stench made me gag—the odour of burned and rotting meat. Sweat and grime matted her hair, blackened dried blood caking her chin and neck. But that wasn't the worst of it. No, worse—if that were possible!—was the wound in her groin. Like a cattle brand, the flesh was singed black as burned meat. The place where the iron had seared was laid open and seeped green, smelly pus.

'Ariane?' I couldn't catch my breath, or take my gaze from this terrible wound. I crouched next to the ghostly girl, who'd slumped on the ground beside her mother. 'Whatever happened to your maman?'

'The blacksmith did it. Two days gone. Fired up his forge and came with his poker glowing red ... buried it into her flesh. Pierro Blacksmith's telling people if he burns away the sores the sickness will vanish with it.' Ariane clamped her hands over her ears. 'I can still hear Maman screaming as he did it ... agony like the fires of Hell must be. I heard he's also poking out eyes so people won't catch the illness through them.'

'Poking out eyes?'

Ariane nodded and I heard a sob catch in her throat. 'He's charging a lot, but I was desperate ... Maman's the only living soul left of my family. Though I don't know how to help her now, and I fear she'll die soon.'

Her mother's eyes opened. They already looked dead, though they shifted restlessly about the hollow sockets until they took me in. The damp brow puckered. 'Look after my Ariane.' Her voice crackled, the almost lifeless gaze moving to her daughter's belly.

'I'll care for your girl as if she were my own,' I said, filling a beaker with ale, to which I added a little poppy juice. I held it to her lips, cracked like the fat on a roasted pig. The mother drank, let out a small sigh and her eyes closed again. I wiped a rose-water-soaked cloth across her face, then her body, avoiding the blacksmith's dark, gaping wound.

'No, Midwife,' Ariane said, as I pulled the sheet up to her mother's chin. 'Take no care of this baby. I can't think of bringing another living thing into this pestilence-poisoned world. And after the way I've seen the townsfolk treat you, especially not a bastard child.'

'You'll change your mind as soon as you feast your eyes on your little one, Ariane. You'll see. Besides, anything you say, your black moods, could harm the baby's growth.'

'Everyone I've ever loved has been wrenched from me. Yet somehow I survive. And that's what I've come to fear ... survival.'

'You must welcome survival into your heart, for the good life you might give your unborn child. Once this pestilence has passed we can all go back to having good lives,' I said, trying to convince myself that one day this might truly happen. 'But for now we need to protect ourselves not only with masks, but by keeping our floor rushes clean and renewed, and our bed linen. Where there's less filth and grime, there's less disease, Ariane.'

Surprisingly, Ariane's babe seemed to be growing well, and I left the shoemaker's, telling the girl I would return shortly. But my muttered words of comfort rang hollow, for I knew the decay, or the pestilence, would take her mother before dusk. Then the girl and her unborn bastard would be completely alone.

***

Back on the market-place, I marched across to the blacksmith's. But the smithy's shop was still closed up, no oily black smoke pouring from the forge, drifting and rolling as it had always done, like a dark fog across la place de l'Eglise. No sign of Pierro Blacksmith either.

'Héloïse!' Yolande hurried from the tailor's ship and kissed me on each cheek. 'I thought … thought.' Her voice trailed off, my friend's face breaking into a smile. 'How did you … how—?'

'I'll explain everything later,' I said. 'Right now I need to find the blacksmith; he's killing people with his hot poker.'

'Yes, I've heard rumour of Pierro's branding iron burns … you'll find him in the tavern,' she said, waving an arm towards Au Cochon Tué. 'Since Rixende lost her husband, he's made a habit of spending all day in the tavern … and most nights.'

'I heard as much,' I said.

'These are terrible times, Héloïse. What's going to become of us all?'

'Nothing, if I can help it,' I said, and as Yolande walked with me to the tavern, I told her about the rose tonic.

'If only you'd thought of this before … my Pétronille and Peronelle might still be alive.'

'Oh Yolande, I don't know if it could've have saved those we've already lost. I have no idea if it will work to help those still alive, but I must try.'

'And I must help,' she said with a firm nod. 'Besides being your midwife apprentice, I'll help you gather ingredients and make this remedy. It will do me good. Something useful instead of sitting at home weeping and shaking my head in despair.'

We reached the tavern and I was surprised to hear so much noise coming from inside. At this time of the morning, people were usually hard at work, saving revelry for later. And, from the drunken state of the rowdy clientele, it was immediately obvious that the Au Cochon Tué was doing brisk business. Most strangely of all though, nobody seemed the least bothered about catching the pestilence.

But it wasn't just the usual tavern merrymaking. Something was different, and as I looked more closely, I realised many people were wearing oddly elaborate clothing: velvet hats sat atop matted and grimy hair, gold-threaded, embroidered tunics partly covered ragged hose, and jewelled shoes sparkled on filthy feet. Two hairy-faced men were prancing about in women's long kirtles and wimples.

'All these people are dressed in garments they would not normally be able to afford,' I said to Yolande. 'Where could they have got them?'

'Poppa might no longer work at the castle,' Yolande said, 'but she still seems to know everything that goes on up there, and she told me that since le Comte left, looters have been breaking in and pilfering whatever they can get their greedy hands on.'

I shook my head in amazement, watching a small pig standing on a tavern table, tearing at a hock of roasted lamb. Several cats—more who'd evidently escaped le Comte's funeral pyre—spat and hissed over fish carcasses. A dog gobbled what looked like a hunk of cheese.

On other tables, several men and women were singing badly, others staggering about. In a corner, a man was throwing up, whilst in another, two girls were baring their breasts at the very drunk looking Pierro Blacksmith. A young girl was bent over a table, a man pounding into her from behind. Several men looked on, cheering, waiting their turn, it seemed.

My stomach turned, and I shook my head.

'Whatever's going on?' I shouted to Yolande, over the din. 'What are they all celebrating?'

'Every day's a celebration now,' one of the castle-building carpenters said, staggering passed us with a lopsided grin. 'One more day the pestilence hasn't killed us.'

'Why not celebrate, when we're all going to die from it sooner or later,' said another, shoving a cup into my face. 'Have some ale?'

'Why worry about what's going to happen next?' the carpenter went on, flinging an arm at me. 'We'll all be dead soon, from the pestilence or earthquake ... rains of fire and frogs, lizards and elephants. Or whatever else God torments us with.'

'Did everyone go mad while I was gone, Yolande?'

'I know it's terrible,' she said, 'but I understand them living for the moment, since they may not be here tomorrow. I fear it might be down to the flight of le Comte and the priest.'

'Yes, the Almighty, God's representative and our *Seigneur*, abandoning Lucie right when the townsfolk need them most. And with all the sergeants and the Captain dead,' I added, 'people seem more unleashed.'

'Look everyone,' Pierro Blacksmith shouted in an intoxicated slur, his red-rimmed eyes glittery. 'The heretic is risen from the dead!'

The crowd burst into laughter as the blacksmith raised his cup, slopping ale across the table. His hair and beard had grown long and unruly since I'd seen him last, his nose more purple and blotched.

'You frog-wit!' Rixende thumped Pierro on the back. 'She escaped the stake, remember?' The alewife turned her rheumy gaze to me. 'Shame ... looking forward to seeing you burn, I was. But once this pestilence is gone and le Comte's back, we *will* burn you. You won't escape the flames while I'm still kicking about.'

'Shouldn't you be shoeing horses, or making nails?' I said, ignoring Rixende and addressing the blacksmith. 'Instead of swindling people out of their hard-earned sous, jabbing your hot poker into them?'

That started up lively chatter and head-shaking.

'And what are you going to do about it if I won't stop?' Pierro said. 'Besides, once the pestilence gets you, a quick end is a blessing.'

'Why drag out the suffering?' slurred a ragged-looking Poncet Batier, his yellowy eyes and spiked hair wilder than ever, the grease-stained beard thick with food crumbs.

'Can't you see Pierro's still grieving for his family?' Rixende said, leaning her head against the blacksmith's shoulder. 'Like most of us here. Now get off with you and let us have our bit of fun.'

'As if I'd choose to stay in your foul tavern a second longer than I have to,' I said. 'I'm only here to tell the blacksmith to stop burning pestilence boils with his hot poker. It won't help ... and will only kill people more quickly.'

'As I said, get off with you,' Rixende lurched at me and whispered in my ear. 'And now you're back in Lucie, you might want to take your husband back into your bed.' She threw me a wink, the tongue darting into the gap separating her teeth.

'What's that supposed to mean?' I said.

'You know what they say, if a man can't jab his hot poker into his wife, he'll jab it into someone else.' She lowered her voice to a croaky whisper. 'And I'll let you in on a secret, Héloïse ... my fleshy forge ain't been short of a fiery iron or two of late.'

XXXIV

'Looks and smells like an alchemist's den in here,' Yolande said. She waved away the fragrant steam that filled our cot, sweetened with the great bunches of mint and lemon balm scattered across the table.

Ariane held up her plant-stained hands. 'And it looks like I'm wearing brown gloves.'

Since her maman's death had left her on her own, I'd coaxed Ariane into coming to live in our cot, hoping to turn her grief-filled mind to more purposeful work. I also wanted to feed up this ghost-girl; to keep my eye on the unwanted bastard growing in her womb.

Morgane giggled, her freckled cheeks pinking, and our chatter fell back in time with the rhythmic *thump, thump* of our knife blades on my table that the plants had turned a glassy green.

I looked around at the lively faces of my helpers—Isa, Morgane, Yolande and Ariane—as we cut, pounded, boiled and infused roots, petals and plants, the hot July breeze sifting the smells through the cot. For the first time since that terrible Spring Fair day when the pestilence swept into Lucie, my heart bubbled with hope that we might survive, and go on living.

Besides the thousands of petals we needed to gather for our rose-water and the fortifying tonic, we wrested from the sun-baked earth nettle for the blood, cress for the stomach and wormwood for the blood and the liver. We also gathered the broad sorrel leaves that would quench thirst, reduce fever and strengthen weak stomachs.

The sun well on its westward arc to the Monts du Lyonnais, I went outside to the privy. Anselme was repairing the fence on one side of the cot, while Raoul fixed the hen-house. Since the vingtain and castle work had ceased, the men seemed to wander around purposelessly, filling their time with these small repair jobs. Some days they even helped us gather, chop and brew the plants.

'Finally, a moment on our own,' Raoul said, as I went to walk back inside. 'Please listen to me. You've barely spoken to me for a whole month, since you came back from the cave. Can't we forgive each other?'

'You're back home,' I said. 'Back in my bed. Isn't that enough?'

'Maybe, if that bed wasn't so cold.' His knuckles whitened around the hammer handle, and I flinched just a little, recalling how cold and lonely my bed had been for the two years he was away in Florence. 'I can't bear it, Héloïse. Besides, all of this wasn't just down to me. You could take some of the blame.'

My hands on my hips, I squinted against the sun's glare. 'I know I was wrong to disobey you, Raoul … to want to treat pestilence victims, and put our family in danger, but how can I trust you again after you had me imprisoned in a stinking cell? How can I ever trust you for anything? And there's still Rixende and her story.'

'*Pfft*, I've told you a hundred times, nothing happened with that sour-faced viper … whatever she says.'

'I just don't know,' I said. 'Don't know what to think about us these days.' I swiped a hand across my sweaty brow, feeling the clammy wetness in my armpits, the tears of sweat rolling down my back. 'But for now, I need to cool off in the river.'

'I could come? We could swim together like we used to … our first summer together?'

I shook my head. Our late afternoons at the Vionne had become, as childbirthing, a women-only ritual.

We left Isa with Raoul and Anselme drinking ale in the shade of the cherry tree, Blanche stretched out beside them, her kittens tumbling about her, and tramped down to the Vionne.

Below the secret cave, where the water tumbled over a ridge into our clear, enchanted pool, we unlaced our kirtles, threw them aside with our chemises and our caps. Far from men's eyes, we lay bare our arms and legs, something only wild or fallen women dared do in public.

We waded into the chilly water, gasping at first then surrendering to it, wrapping our arms about ourselves and cleansing our grimy, sweat-soaked bodies.

'How wonderful to feel cool and clean,' Yolande said, floating on her back, her hands making little flapping motions on the gleaming surface.

'To feel pure,' I said, my long hair flowing loose and free, caressing my body like Raoul's soft hands once did. But that seemed so long ago—as if it might never have been.

'If only we could be rid of this rotting death for good,' Ariane said, as we dragged ourselves from the water and lay on the pebbly shore to dry off. 'If we could always feel this clean and unstained.'

'That's why,' I said, rebraiding Morgane's hair, 'along with our rose tonic and masks, we must keep telling everyone to scrub their bodies and their homes with the farmers' sheep soap, and I'm sure ... I'm *certain* we'll see a halt to the pestilence spread.'

'And a halt, I pray to Our Lord,' Yolande said, as Morgane scuttled off to pluck cornflowers. 'To your rift with Raoul.'

'It's not easy to forgive what my husband did,' I said, watching our poppet crouch down to pick the flowers from which we'd make a wash for sticky eyes. I knew the ongoing cleft between us upset Morgane, so I kept trying to mask it; to pretend our love was as seamless as before.

'When you've lost over half your family,' Yolande said, 'grudges seem silly and unimportant.'

'And when all you've got left is a bastard you don't want,' Ariane said. Her dark eyes glistening with the sun and her tears, she glanced down at her thickening belly.

'Yes, Héloïse,' Yolande went on, 'God would want you to forgive him.'

'Don't talk to me about God,' I said. 'How has He ever helped us? About as much as my husband has helped me!'

***

The inferno of August upon us, I woke one sultry morning to the single sweet note of a bird.

Despite our hard work fashioning and distributing the tonic, and instructing the townsfolk in hygiene, the pestilence had not let up at all. The toll only kept rising, and we'd taken to wearing lavender, rosemary and juniper to mask the ever-present stench of Death.

The bird fell silent, then sang again. The sky was still sheathed in night, without the slightest pearly sliver across the *Montagne Maudite*, but the early breeze had stirred, warning that dawn was close. Another bird, with a different call, answered, then another until a flock of them had struck up a noisy chorus.

From beside me on the pallet, Raoul laid a hand on my arm. 'Listen to the birds singing, Héloïse.'

'Such tiny creatures,' I said, 'their lives so short and fragile, yet they don't need any God, or church sermon to teach them about life. They just know dawn will break, and on they go bravely, facing whatever each new day brings.'

'But they have other birds,' Raoul said. 'They don't go on bravely alone ... as you do, Héloïse.'

'I'm not alone, Raoul, I have many helpers—' I started.

'That's not what I meant.' With a thick finger, he began tracing circles on my gently-swelling belly. I went to brush off his hand, then I felt it: the first light tapping inside my womb. A kick from a tiny foot. A small but precious movement that made my unborn child so real; so alive. My heart leapt into my chest and I caught my breath.

'Oh!' Raoul's face broke into a smile as the baby wriggled again beneath his palm. 'Amazing, isn't it?'

'Incredible, yes.' I got up from the pallet. 'But I need to get to my work now.'

Once we'd broken our fast, amidst the lazy buzzing of bees, Raoul and Anselme helped us harvest the lavender, to dry against pests or mix with lilac for pomanders, and to make oil. Our woad, madder and weld dyeplants were also ready. The flax too, and the hemp from which we'd make rope, and cloth that lasts an age.

Hugging an armful of lavender to my chest, I gazed across the precise lines of Isa's plants, stretching for the sky, reaching sideways or hugging the earth in sprawling mats. So orderly and neat against the chaos of our pestilence-ridden lives. I breathed deeply, inhaling the lavender's clean scent, holding on to the beauty which had made me love every August in the past.

Several hot and sticky hours later I bade Morgane fetch my work-basket. 'It's time we visited our patients, poppet.'

Raoul might no longer object to me caring for pestilence victims, and whilst I still feared catching it myself, at least I worried less about Morgane, almost certain that the pestilence did not strike the same person twice.

Raoul hurried over from where he was chopping firewood. 'I'll hitch Merlinette up for you.'

'Thank you, Raoul, but I can manage on my own.'

'I know you can do everything on your own,' he said, 'but why not give me the pleasure of helping you; of believing you might need me around here sometimes?'

'We mightn't have had Merlinette or the cart when you were away in Florence,' I said, 'but I had to learn to do every other task on my own ... I can't just suddenly rely on you for everything again.'

Raoul shook his head and looked away as I prepared Merlinette and the cart.

***

Morgane and I set off along the woodland road, the grass in the fields so parched there was barely anything for the beasts to graze on, and those that hadn't perished from the pestilence were little more than skin and bone. The farmers must be counting down the days till they could drive their stock to the hay meadows.

But as we rode past the crop fields, there wasn't a single farmer or labourer in sight. How sad not to see the usual rows of men and women moving their scythes across the golden grain-field strips. How unsettling not to hear their banter and shouts. How terrible to see the plentiful harvest lying wasted.

'Why aren't they harvesting the winter corn?' Morgane asked, her voice muffled behind her mask.

All I could do was shake my head as we rode on through that dank, airless heat, the silence broken by the caw of a crow, the bark of a dog, the lonely bray of a donkey. In one pasture, all the cows and sheep lay dead. I gasped at the shock and the stench; at the dark cloud of vultures gorging—uncurbed and fearless—on the corpses. Both of us gagged as we skirted the maggot-riddled body of an ox.

'Oh, Maman it's awful.'

'Yes, poppet, all too awful.'

Beyond the corpse, we came across a group of farmers drinking ale in the shade of an oak tree. 'Why aren't you harvesting your grain?' I asked, halting Merlinette.

'What's the point?' one said. 'We could all be dead tomorrow … or today. Or in an hour.'

'But we'll never survive this winter, with no harvest.'

'We might all be dead by this winter,' he said, 'so why waste time and energy on the harvest?'

I handed them down some of my fortifying tonic and masks, explaining the hygiene instructions. 'This might be our only hope to stop the spread of the pestilence.'

Despite their thanks as we rode away, I was far from convinced they'd follow my advice.

'Is it true, Maman? We'll all be dead by winter?'

'I'm doing my best to avoid that, Morgane, but sometimes it's hard to get people to do what I say. Many still refuse my instructions.'

'Oh but a lot of people are doing what you say,' she said, as Merlinette clopped on. 'Yolande says almost all the people on the market-place are wearing masks now ... *and* washing their hands in vinegar.'

We'd almost reached the road that led down to Lucie's centre when we heard the cries of a baby, loud enough to wake the Devil.

'Who's that?' Morgane said.

'It's coming from Poppa's cot ... must be her little grandson. Stay out here with Merlinette, my sweet.' I stopped the mare outside the cot, and hurried towards the blackberry hedge, through which I'd spied Poppa dragging baby Loup.

'What are you doing, Poppa?' I snatched the naked and squirming baby from his grandmother. 'Look at him, covered in cuts and scratches.'

'Oh, it's you, Héloïse.' She seemed startled to see me standing there beside her, holding her grandson. 'Alewife Rixende says you can protect little ones from catching the pestilence if you drag them through blackberry bushes.' She trudged after me as I took baby Loup into the cot.

'And I suppose she's charging a healthy sum?' I said, recalling those vultures devouring the dead cattle, and I realised that not all vultures are birds.

'Rixende's remedies don't come cheap,' Poppa said. 'But anything that saves us from the pestilence is a bargain, don't you reckon? She's also selling dried rabbit's balls ... says if you rub them on the pestilence boils they'll disappear.'

'Those things will no more save you than any other superstition,' I said, cleansing the child's cuts with rose-water. Busy making the fortifying tonic since my return from the cave, I'd not seen Poppa, and I was shocked at the change in her.

In a shapeless russet kirtle, her head wrapped in a grimy

kerchief, Poppa looked far older than Isa, even though I knew they were born around the same time. Gone was the round, blooming face, which now sagged in hollow clefts, puffy grey bags hanging beneath the once cornflower blue eyes, now greyish and watery. The wisps escaping the kerchief had turned a dun silver. Vanished too, was the quick-witted humour, the beaming smile and the chuckling curses.

'I thought you had more sense than to listen to charlatans like Rixende?' I said.

'I must do everything I can to save Loup.'

I heard the sob catch in her throat, and I laid the baby in his cradle and began to rub Poppa's heaving shoulders in slow, soft circles, my heart aching for Isa's old friend. The pestilence had stolen her entire family, she'd lost her Chief Washerwoman work, and now she had to care for the bawling baby Loup when I was sure she craved only to grieve quietly and peacefully.

'I'm sorry I spoke harshly, Poppa, I just hate to see you wasting your money on that charlatan's useless potions.'

'I knew what Rixende's saying couldn't be true.' Her bleak gaze searched mine, as if pleading for answers. 'I'm just desperate. I've lost every last one of them besides Loup.'

'You're only trying to do your best,' I said, pulling some of my rose tonic and a few strips of cloth from my basket. 'But these will do far more good. You must wear the mask all the time now, Poppa ... wash your hands often in watery vinegar. It's very important if we are to halt this sickness. Now let's see what salve I have in my basket for your grandson.'

'The old witch once told me it's the blackberry leaf what best soothes its own thorn prick,' Poppa said.

'And I have Isa's special salve of just that,' I said.

'Their ghosts are all around me,' Poppa carried on, as I anointed the mess of cuts and scratches, the sweet-smelling ointment scent lingering about Loup's tender flesh. 'Alix, Nica and her children, their old mother, my boys and their father ... all of them crowded in here with me. But when it gets quiet, when I can't hear their voices no more or smell their wax, there's just a ghost-cot with me and the babe. Gets to me sometimes it does, Héloïse ... not that I'm one to complain. Others have it worse. But the nights are long, I must say. It's all just too ... quiet.'

'I suppose Isa's told you I'm very busy these days?' I said, telling Poppa about brewing my rose tonic. 'Yolande comes to help us, and the shoemaker's daughter, Ariane, who's living under our thatch, now but honestly I could do with another pair of hands. That is, if you could spare the time,' I kept on, helping Poppa dress the much-calmed baby. 'And just supposing you did want to help, it would be easier if you and Loup came to live in our cot. I'm certain Raoul will agree it's the best thing ... as he did for Ariane.'

'Live with you and Isa?' The skin around Poppa's eyes crinkled like dead leaves against a winter sky. 'I was born in this cot .... always lived here. Be strange to leave it. But the company would ...' She fell silent, gazing about her cot.

'It'd not be forever,' I said. 'Just until this pestilence passes.'

'Well I suppose we must all do our bit to try and stop this disease of Satan. So yes, Héloïse, I'll come and help you brew your tonic.'

'After Morgane and I have visited our patients, we'll come back for you,' I said, as she grabbed baskets from a shelf and began packing things for herself and the baby. 'And tomorrow morning we'll undress Loup and lay him in the sun. Cleanliness might be the start of healing, but the sun too, is a wondrous healer.'

'So we'll lay the baby outside and have the sun bake him, just like my pies?' Poppa said. The wide smile creased the sadness from her face for a moment. Then it was gone.

'Hmm, baby pie,' I called back to her as Merlinette clopped off. 'Why not? But I'd really prefer your pigeon pie, Poppa.'

XXXV

'What the Devil's hairy arse you doing here, old crone?' Isa's face crinkled into a smile as she flung fistfuls of thyme, garlic and beans into the pottage. 'Come to check up on me?'

'Need to keep an eye on you, don't I?' Poppa said, 'make sure that's not some poison you're brewing up to finish me off.'

'Poppa's come to stay in our cot—just for a time,' I said. 'She's kindly agreed to help us make our medicaments ... you know how busy we are, Isa.' I glanced over at Raoul, to where he was sitting on a stool, sharpening his tools. Of course, it was my husband's place to decide who lived in our cot, but it seemed he didn't object to anything I suggested these days.

'And just look at this hardy boy,' Raoul said, taking Loup from Poppa and placing him on the floor beside Morgane, who was playing with Blanche's kittens. From a high shelf, Blanche opened one eye, checking on her kittens' new playmate.

'Loup will live with us too?' Morgane picked up baby. 'It will be like having a baby brother ... now look here, brother, since the kittens aren't interested I'm going to show you how you came out of your maman's womb.'

Isa, Poppa and I all smiled, watching her guide one of her dolls, head-first, through a cloth circle she'd somehow fashioned from my mask rags, easing the doll's head out as I'd taught her, to stop the mother's skin from tearing. Loup cooed as if he were truly interested, and an idea began to seed in my mind. But now wasn't the time to think about such a thing.

'Well soon, my little Flamelock,' Raoul said, pouring us all beakers of ale, 'if Saint Etienne answers my prayers you really will have your own baby brother.'

I lay a palm against my belly, wishing life into this one. Two deadborn babes almost broke our hearts and now, the binds of our love so thready, a third would sever them completely. Besides, with so many still dying around us, one living babe seemed a lot to ask for.

'Isn't that the finest grandson you ever saw?' Poppa said to Isa.

'Let's have a look at this fine grandson then.' Isa hobbled over, took the baby from Morgane and unwrapped his swaddling. 'Hmm, quite a handsome fellow, aren't you, Master Loup, except you got your grandmother's great ugly feet.'

Isa let out a great cackle as if it was the funniest joke ever, which set Poppa laughing, and I caught a glimpse of the old twinkle in those blue eyes. Isa, too must've sensed how hard it was for Poppa to accept my offer, but she also knew her friend couldn't bear to remain in that cot bedevilled with her family's ghosts.

I'd been shocked at the pestilence's ageing of Poppa, but as I watched her and Isa thumping each other on the back, throwing about the curses and bad jokes of rowdy tavern men, I saw it had taken its toll on my aunt too. Her naturally-tanned skin looked grey and brittle, her shaky hands pushing back wicks of silvery hair that strayed from beneath her cap. Limping about on spindle-thin legs, she seemed like the last withered piece of fruit clinging to the tree.

Poppa pulled hunks of meat from one of her baskets. 'Better throw these morsels of mutton into that stew, old witch ... smells as if it needs *something* so it don't taste of old rope,' she said, wrinkling her nose.

'Mutton you poached from le Comte's land I'll be guessing.'

Isa winked at her friend as she threw in the meat morsels and flavoured the stew with a little oil. 'Seems the whole of Lucie's gone on a wild poaching spree since le Comte left.'

'Ah, people've always poached,' Poppa said, 'especially at this hungry time when we're waiting for the August harvest—which don't even look like happening this year! But true enough, since that craven *Seigneur* of ours abandoned us, nobody's thinking twice about a bit of easy poaching.'

'Not only poaching,' Isa said, patting out the oat-cakes and slinging them to Poppa to string up and dry before the fire. 'I've heard people are breaking into homes where everyone has died … just strolling in and making off with whatever takes their fancy.'

'Like the farmers and labourers,' Poppa said. 'Suddenly I'm seeing them flaunting fancy calf-length boots, belts and hats. And more tools than they'd ever dreamed of.'

'And since all the sergeants are dead,' I said, setting the pottage bowls on the table, 'there's no one to keep the peace. If any of us are to survive this thing—if Lucie-sur-Vionne is to survive—*someone* must bring about order.'

Raoul threw me a warm smile. 'And as well as trying to heal and birth the whole of Lucie, I'll wager I know who's thinking of taking on that job.'

***

Once I'd checked Sibylle and her baby son were well, and handed out masks and cleaning instructions to all those on the market-place who'd accept them, I made my way to Isa and Morgane at our usual spot, selling the flax and hemp.

There certainly were empty spaces where stalls had once stood, fewer people and no acrobats, musicians or other enter-tainers, but the market still bustled with trade. Out of necessity, it was one of the few places people still gathered and, as such, one of the most dangerous.

'Tastiest pies on the market ... get your pies,' a food-seller chanted, swatting away flies with a leafy tree branch. 'Pies, meat pies. Goose and pork pies. Hot and tasty!'

'Furs ... best wolf pelts,' a hunter wearing a hat made from two whole foxes called out. 'Winter will be here before you know it. Get your furs now.'

People shouted and bargained as they'd done before the pestilence, only now they stood further apart. And they wore masks—mine or ones they'd fashioned themselves.

One merchant, selling the bright red wool of Florence, showed off his cloth using two sticks, rolling and waving it as people passed by. Though customers couldn't get too close as he'd placed a boundary of bricks past which their feet were not to step.

'All money to be placed here,' he said, pointing to the bowl of water on the table. 'To cleanse it of the miasma.'

'Buy now,' another merchant urged, 'it may be many moons before we can get another shipment. Stock up while you have the chance.'

'Even in this time of pestilence,' another trader said, 'life goes on, and we all have to eat.'

And buy up the people did: herbs, oils, cloth, cheese and game flew from the stalls as if we were preparing for a siege from the English.

'Five deniers for the lot,' the ragpicker said, as I picked through her pile of rags—cloth I would wash, then cut into strips for more masks, or to use as bandages.

'Not worth more than three,' I said.

'Four deniers, my last offer.' The woman clacked the black stumps of her teeth. I pulled the coins from my leather scrip, dropped them into her grimy palm, and stuffed the rags into my basket.

From a fishmonger whose apron glittered with bloody scales, I purchased two carp, then from a spicemonger, some of the cheaper spices, and lastly a black pudding for a denier.

'Héloïse!' I swivelled around to Catèlena. 'I'm so glad to see you ... I prayed and thanked the Lord when you escaped that ridiculous burning sentence,' the fragile-looking girl said from behind her mask. 'I know my husband disliked you, but you're a God-fearing healer and midwife.'

'I was happy to help,' I said, flinching at the word "God-fearing" as I thought of my rejoicing at her husband's death. A very ungodly thing.

Drogan and his savagery might be gone, but my old enemy still pursued me as if I'd killed him and the guilt burdened me. I kept catching glimpses of him: in the swirling waters of the Vionne, in the hottest blue speck of a hearth flame, in the beams of dawn light cutting through the shutter cracks. And I'd shut my eyes and hold my hands to my belly, afraid his haunting would frighten my unborn child as Drogan had frightened me all my life.

'I don't miss my husband for a minute,' Catèlena said, 'but since the pestilence took his mother, along with Drogan's little girls, it's lonely in the weaver's shop on my own.'

'If the days seem too long, you'd be welcome at my cot,' I said. 'We need every pair of willing hands to make enough of my rose tonic for the whole of Lucie.' I gave her hand a small squeeze, and moved off.

By the time I reached Isa and Morgane, they'd already sold the bulk of our flax and hemp, or exchanged it for grain and oils, a hen to replace the one taken by the fox, and a freshly-killed rabbit. Sold too were all our clothing dyes and many more salves and potions.

'How's Sibylle's boy?' Morgane said, 'the one I midwifed all on my own,' she added proudly, as I shared the black pudding with her and Isa. Since she'd successfully birthed the baker's son, Isa and I both knew there would be no keeping her away from birthing women.

'Feeding, growing and sleeping perfectly,' I said, feeling another kick from my own child, as if he knew I was thinking about him.

'Healthy babes are good for that,' Isa said, 'for filling up your head and your heart with joy ... pushing out all that's black and miserable. And speaking of joy ... or rather joyless,' she went on, with a grim nod at Poncet Batier, headed towards the graveyard with his shovel slung over one shoulder. 'Poppa tells me that greedy gravedigger's been at it again, stealing jewels and clothes from the dead.'

'And not wearing my mask,' I said. 'Likely not washing his hands either. Stay here with Isa, Morgane, I won't be long.' I hurried off towards Saint Antoine's, but the instant I reached the graveyard, I drew back in horror and almost fled.

***

Crows dotted the grave mounds, pecking at the earth. A pig snuffled, its snout buried in the shallow earth, gnawing on a small skull that still had patches of hair attached.

'Get off with you,' I shouted, stamping a foot. The pig lifted its head and stared defiantly at me with bright little eyes. It kept on chewing, strands of the child's hair dangling from its mouth.

'Go, hideous beast!' I flapped my arms. The pig skittered away a little, immediately plunging its snout back into the earth.

In the other direction, a cat prowled among the graves with what looked like a human bone between its jaws, and two thin dogs were snarling over a mottled chunk of flesh.

The hot August wind changed direction, bringing with it that atrocious pestilence stink and I gagged, bent over and threw up the blood pudding. And when all that was left of my belly contents was a foul taste in my mouth, I kept staring at the ground, at the graveyard creatures—the spiders, worms and maggots—feasting on our dead.

I stretched upright, steadying my shaky legs, and as I looked more closely, I realised all the recent graves were so shallow that I could make out shapes beneath a thin dusting of earth: a grey foot, two gnawed fingers, part of a hand. A pair of buttocks. I didn't want to look further, but couldn't help my eyes straying right across the graveyard to the tangle of mangled, rotted limbs; the clots of earth-stained clothing.

I shuddered, thinking back to those early, proper funerals, and comparing them to how we were now burying our dead.

A wolf loped across from the edge of the woods. As it approached the graveyard, it raised its snout and sniffed the air. Then it turned, and slunk away back into the woods. How terrified I'd have been if the wolf had starting preying on the graveyard corpses, but more terrifying still was that the pestilence stink had frightened away such a fearless beast.

My belly rose again, and I swallowed hard to settle it, pressing my mask more firmly over my mouth and nose. Once the sickness eased I looked up again to Poncet Batier, still digging.

'Can't you see the graveyard is full?' I shouted at him. 'You can't bury any more bodies here.'

'Bah! What would a heretic murderess like you know of Christian burials? They should'a burned you by now for killing my wife and child ... for cursing us with the pestilence.'

'I certainly don't call these burials Christian, Poncet Batier. And if you refuse to stop, I'll find a way of getting you stopped.'

'Find a way of getting you stopped ... getting you stopped,' he chanted in a mocking tone. 'And if you don't shut that trap of yours, Devil-servant,' he carried on, 'I'll find a way of getting *you* stopped.' As I turned and bolted from the graveyard his yellowy eyes burned through my back.

XXXVI

𝕭ack on the market-place everyone was packing away their wares, buyers negotiating last-minute bargains, sellers anxious to get rid of their stores. Beside the drinking trough, I turned a wooden crate upside-down, jumped upon it, and clapped my hands for everyone's attention.

'In the absence of our priest,' I cried in my loudest voice, still muffled behind the mask I didn't dare remove, even to speak to a crowd. 'I'd like to say a few things.'

Nobody, besides le Comte Renault de Fouville, the Captain and the priest—and especially not a woman—ever called the people's attention, and they fell silent in mid-chatter. My heart thumping, I took calming breaths as they all gathered around the fountain—just as the Romans would have done all those moons gone, this same fountain gurgling with water from the hills above. That alone gave me courage, despite catching snippets of their mutterings:

'Dunno what a heretic could say what's worth listening to ...'
'... should be burned and dead by now ...'

'When Héloïse was wrongfully imprisoned, then gone from Lucie,' Yolande said, her willowy figure standing taller than most, 'the pestilence remained ... even worsened, so she cannot have been the sinner who brought it upon us.'

'That's true,' said Sibylle, hurrying from the baker's shop cradling her baby son. 'So shut up and let her speak.'

'Yes, let her speak!' Isa cried.

'I'm only asking for a few minutes,' I said, my throat already hoarse, with nerves or fright, or both. I swallowed hard, the bitter taste of vomit still caked inside my mouth.

'Fear works in strange ways,' I began. 'It stops us from thinking clearly. And I've seen that our fear and helplessness of this terrible pestilence has given way to depravity and decadence. Unbridled revelry in the tavern, charlatan remedies, looting from homes and from the castle—'

'Serves le Comte right for fleeing,' Pierro Blacksmith cut in, the only one, besides Rixende, not wearing a mask.

'Only what the *Seigneur* deserves for abandoning his people,' Rixende said, leaning drunkenly against the blacksmith.

'Hear, hear,' shouted several people, waving fists into the hot summer air.

From the doorway of the Mason's Lodge, I caught sight of Raoul. He gave me an encouraging nod and a smile; the same rousing look that had always spurred me on. 'While we may not agree with le Comte fleeing, that's no excuse for this unchristian behaviour.'

I might be questioning my own faith—the workings of God and the Church—but if I wanted to capture the people's attention, I had to defer to theirs.

'Our harvest lies rotting in the fields. The farmers say why bother, we could all be dead by winter. But I say we shouldn't lose hope; we must pray that as other pestilences have come and gone in time, this one will pass too.'

'And meanwhile,' the baker said, 'the harvest should be brought in, so we can eat.'

'And I'm certain we can all help to stop the spread of this pestilence,' I said, pulling my rose medicament from my basket. 'Use this fortifying tonic, wear the mask at all times and wash your hands in a mixture of vinegar and water when caring for the sick, or before eating or preparing food. Sweep out your rushes. Wash your bedding, your bodies, as often as you can.'

'We've been washing our hands ten times a day,' a carpenter said, waving his hands in the air. 'Since you first told us to, and the only thing that's done is give us all chapped hands.'

'Better chapped hands than pestilence boils,' Sibylle said.

'And don't be taken in by worthless charms and spells of charlatans,' I said, 'which do nothing to cure the pestilence, and simply cheat you out of your money.'

'Your just pissed I'm taking away your business.' Alewife Rixende clamped her hands on her aproned hips. 'Any fool can chuck together a few herbs and call it a tonic. Like any fool can birth a child. Likely I got as much experience in that as you, Midwife. And since people know me for an excellent business-woman at the tavern, I could set myself up as a midwife and take away all your business if the fancy took me.'

'Good midwifing takes years of apprenticeship, Rixende,' I said. 'That's why so many mothers and babies die, because unskilled people make things worse.'

'Besides, Héloïse's is not business,' Yolande said, 'she gives out her medicaments freely.'

'Which should be proof enough of her good intentions,' Ariane chimed in. I smiled at the timid, doe-eyed girl who'd never have spoken out in public in the days before she came to our cot.

'Like most of us,' Yolande said, over the people's yammering, 'I'd never have thought something so frightening would happen to Lucie.'

People nodded, mumbled their agreement.

'No one thinks disaster is coming to them,' I said. 'But it does. It came to Jesus … it came to the Israelites and the Egyptians. And many hundreds of years from now, disasters will still come to man, and he'll still be hoping Providence will save him. This pestilence is a grim and grievous trouble, and more sorrow than we could ever have imagined. But many of us still live, and we have to work hard together to try and halt its deadly march.'

'Hear, hear!' The crowd's cries were muffled behind their masks.

'One last thing,' I said. 'From what I've seen, it's clear Saint Antoine's graveyard is no longer able to meet the demands confronting us.'

'Yeah,' the alewife said, and I almost jumped in surprise at Rixende agreeing with something I said. 'Seems the gravedigger's the only one doing well out of this pestilence.' She nodded at Poncet Batier. 'I seen you making off with keepsakes what folks wanted taken to their grave.'

'He's the one making the most sous, at least,' Sibylle said.

'I heard he asked poor Johan Miller for a whole pig to bury his children,' Poppa said.

'And now there is no miller,' Isa added. 'No one to grind our grain ... so we have to spend two hours on the quern stones just to make our bread.'

'Hear, hear!' the women cried.

Poncet Batier fixed his yellowy gaze on the people, his face twisting into an ugly grimace. 'Bah to the lot of ye!'

I could sense this discussion sliding into the usual church service squabbles, so I raised my voice and my arms, to try and regain their attention.

'We need new burial ground,' I said. 'And I suggest opening a pit in Père Bernard's pasture behind Saint Antoine's.'

'And who's supposed to consecrate this new graveyard?' Pierro Blacksmith said. 'With no priest? Or are you suggesting we bury our dead in unconsecrated pits?'

'No!' came the crowd's terrified shouts.

'If Lucie-sur-Vionne isn't to become like the big cities, with bodies piled in the streets,' I said, 'we must shoulder the grim task of burying victims immediately, in whatever suitable ground we can. It may not be the best Christian burial, but packing bodies one atop the other so close to the surface will only increase the spread of the miasma. And,' I took a quick breath, 'make it easier for animals to dig up and chew on our loved ones, which is what's happening right now.'

From the horrified gasp that rose from the crowd, and the mutterings: 'I seen that too ...', 'me too ... ', '... Devil's arse of a stink ...' I was certain I'd made my point.

XXXVII

As much as I sensed most of the townsfolk had taken in my advice on the market-place, I was afraid some would still treat me with the disdain I was so used to, with the added suspicion reserved for condemned criminals. But my heart lifted when Poppa announced she'd be going out the following sunrise with the farmers.

'They've decided to harvest their grain after all,' she said. 'So I'll need to start on my husband and Donis's wheat and rye.'

'What's a washerwoman know about harvesting crops, you silly crone?' Isa said.

'I've seen how they do it,' Poppa said. 'I'll learn fast.'

'You'll be busy for weeks,' Morgane said. 'I'll keep Loup here at the cot so you can work more quickly.'

Isa clapped her hands together. 'Yes, the little one will help Morgane and I plant the turnips. We'll take him to gather nettles and wild onions, and more ingredients for the fortifying tonic.'

Several days later, as I rode Merlinette down to la place de l'Eglise, I saw the farmers had indeed begun the harvest: men swinging sickle and scythe, mowing down the wheat and rye, women following to scoop up the stalks and bundle the sheaves.

It was only mid-morning and their clothes already sweat-soaked, but they'd go on until nightfall, spending every hour of the hot August days beneath that vast, unclouded sky. And since people were continually demanding my treatments, or my presence with a dying loved one, I'd come to understand such bone-weary fatigue, staggering home, like the field workers, only when it was too dark to see.

And as there was no longer priest, *seigneur* or sergeant in Lucie, I doubted the farmers would give over the customary one sheaf of every ten in church tithes. I was sure too, that no cottage or land rents would be paid to the absent le Comte this coming Michaelmas.

Once I reached the market-place, I was pleasantly surprised to see a team of men clearing Père Bernard's meadow behind the church. The new graveyard wasn't quite ready, but Poncet Batier and several other gravediggers—all of them masked— were already at work. Humped lids of grass, yellow as piss, and mounds of raw earth sat in neat lines beside straight-sided pits, which they were placing as close together as possible to save space.

'Seems people are heeding your words,' Raoul said, from the doorway of the Mason's Lodge. 'Others besides me believe in you.' He pointed to the sketches spread over the tracing floor of the Mason's Lodge. 'But you're not the only one who's been busy. Since our cot's become crowded with Ariane, Poppa and Loup living beneath our thatch, and Yolande and Catèlena coming each day to help, Anselme and I thought to extend it ... to build two new rooms.' He stretched out a hand. 'Come, I'll show you my plans.'

I let Raoul draw me into the pleasant coolness of the Lodge. 'True, the cot is becoming crowded,' I said, as he closed the door, then the shutters. 'And soon baby Loup will be running about.'

'I hope you haven't forgotten my son, who'll soon be here too?' Raoul placed a hand against my belly.

'How could I forget? Since you keep reminding me every minute, as does he or *she*, with those hard kick—'

He pressed his lips to mine, melting away my words. His sturdy hands on either side of my temples held me to him, so that I couldn't have shied away even if I'd wanted. I closed my eyes, felt his hand drop to my shoulder, fingers tracing a line down to my breast, caressing, kneading its new fullness. The warmth began in my feet, shooting up my legs, gathering strength until my loins were on fire.

I drew away from him to catch my breath. 'What about those plans of yours?'

'Plans?' He frowned, unlacing my kirtle, and I felt his hardness as he pressed himself against me. 'What plans?'

'For the extra cot rooms.'

He pushing me gently, and I took backward steps until I was standing against one of the walls.

'Ah, those plans.' His breeches slid to the floor. 'But I have a far better plan for right now. I only hope it won't hurt my son in there?'

'Don't worry,' I said, as he held me to the wall. 'He, or she, is protected inside the watery pouch.'

And, as I wrapped my legs around Raoul's muscled back, surrendering to him, I couldn't stop myself from crying out.

***

'Is the rumour true?' The voice came from outside the Lodge, on the square. 'The pestilence has killed them all?'

'That's Rixende,' I said, lacing up my kirtle over my chemise. 'Whatever is she spouting off about now? Killed all of who?'

I retied my cap, poked away hair wisps, and Raoul and I stepped outside to where a small crowd had gathered.

'What's happened?' I said to Yolande who, along with everyone else, was looking at Physician Nestor, riding his black stallion across the square. Père Bernard followed, on an old nag of a horse. And behind physician and priest trudged one desperate-looking girl—Comtesse Geneviève's Maid Delphine, who'd helped me escape the castle.

'Le Comte and his entourage are all dead,' Yolande said.

'Is it true Physician Nestor?' Pierro Blacksmith called out. I was amazed to see he and Rixende were now wearing masks.

Physician Nestor slowed his horse, lifted his gaze to us and waved his cane in the air. 'I confirm, with great sorrow, that the pestilence has taken my brother, Renault de Fouville. His wife, Comtesse Geneviève, their infant son and heir and the servants, aside from one, have also perished.'

'Oh no, not Comtesse Geneviève and her little boy!' I felt the sorrow twisting my heart and clutched Raoul's arm. 'I worked so hard to save the heir ... then la Comtesse worked so hard to save me.'

'Blessed Saint Etienne, so why's Nestor and the priest come back to Lucie?' Raoul said. 'Where the pestilence is surely more rampant?'

'Apparently they can no longer get supplies to their estate,' Yolande said. 'No one to deliver food or anything else. And I also heard that on his deathbed, 'Renault de Fouville demanded he be buried in the brown robes of Saint Francis, so he wouldn't go to Hell.'

'He'll go there anyway,' Raoul said, 'for abandoning his people.'

'And for buggering the priest,' I said. 'Not to mention the wrongs he did to his wife.'

Wordlessly, his head bowed so low that we could see the whole of his tonsure, Père Bernard disappeared into the presbytery. Physician Nestor and Maid Delphine continued on up to the castle.

'Will Physician Nestor be our lord now?' the blacksmith said to nobody in particular.

'Who knows? We might be left lordless,' Rixende said. 'And the heretics will truly take over, poisoning our minds and bodies with ungodly charms and potions.'

'You're one to talk about ungodly charms and potions,' I said, my fingers instinctively stroking my talisman.

Feeling its smooth warmth between my fingers, an idea

sprang to my mind: something, besides the rose tonic, that would surely help to halt the pestilence spread. A bold thought perhaps, but surely worth a try.

Fearful as I was of that forbidding castle, I decided I would ride up there the next day and speak with Physician Nestor.

***

As I rode Merlinette to *le château* in the fierce heat of the following morning, I saw the farmers had finished harvesting the wheat and rye, and had started on the barley and the oats. As usual, the men reaped, the women—including Poppa—bundled. Children followed, gathering stray stalks the women had missed, until they had enough for a sheaf. Other, nimble-fingered children plaited the straw into cords for tying the sheaves. The hot and hard harvest work was almost done, and at least those surviving the pestilence wouldn't starve over the coming winter.

I hitched Merlinette to the post and tramped up to the castle gate. The usual flock of prey birds circling overhead, I pulled the cord that rang a bell up on the battlements. No answer. I pulled the cord again.

After several more attempts, a servant—a new one I supposed—finally appeared. 'What do you want?'

'I've come to see Physician Nestor,' I said, 'please tell him it's important ... and it'll only take a few minutes.'

The servant disappeared, and, after what seemed like hours, Physician Nestor came limping with his cane onto the rampart. He looked even paler, more shrunken than on his return yesterday.

'What have you come here for, Midwife?' the monk-physician called down to me. 'If it's to get me to wear your mask, dry out my hands with vinegar or swallow your tonic, you are wasting your time. And mine. Your treatments are not working ... nothing is working.'

'I know we've not yet seen results,' I said, 'but I'm convinced that we will, in time.'

'The Italian doctors, men trained not in a lowly cot in Lucie-sur-Vionne, but in the best universities in the world, are adamant,' Physician Nestor said with a great sigh, as if speaking to an imbecile. 'The pestilence spreads through the air. You catch it by looking at sick people, or touching them, or breathing their breath. And there is no disputing the Italian doctors are the best, aside from the Arabs. So I believe this mask-wearing business must have come from the Saracens and as such is a heathen practice.'

'And I've heard from the merchants' market-day tales,' I said, 'that Maître Chauliac, physician of the Pope and the King—our country's finest—is really no nearer to fathoming why the pestilence fells some and not others. And that the physicians are all still making the same diagnosis of overheated blood, and prescribing bleeding and diets varying from apples to salted meat and tripes.' I took a quick breath, but the physician made no move to interrupt, or stop me. He seemed so fatigued, I wasn't sure he was even listening. 'But it doesn't seem to matter what they eat, for they can't keep a thing down towards the end. I'm also convinced that taking blood from one who's already bleeding too much—coughing, vomiting and pissing it—only makes them worse.'

'Now that,' he said with a dismissing flick of his wrist, 'is simply an ignorant healer woman's nonsense.'

'But if you say the pestilence spreads through the air,' I carried on, undeterred, 'surely wearing a mask might stop this bad air reaching you? And if it doesn't help, it certainly does no harm. Forgive my boldness, Physician Nestor, but I've come here in the hope we might work together for once, to try and—'

'Work together? Do I have to remind you I am a mourning man, Midwife Héloïse? That I have lost my entire family? I'm not in much of a mind to work at all these days.'

'Oh yes ... yes, I'm very sorry for your loss.' But the physician's drawn and grey face, his hooded eyes, made me suspect it was more than grief ailing him. He didn't look feverish, and I couldn't make out any rosy spots, but I was too far away to be sure.

'Besides, how can you even think that throwing together a few plants and rose petals would cure something as almighty as this pestilence?'

'My rose tonic doesn't cure it, Physician Nestor ... I'm only hoping to stop its spread. And since we know people in the same family catch it from each other, I believe we should be separating the sick from the healthy.'

'Separate the sick?' Nestor said. 'And you propose to separate them to where?'

'To a hospital. Not just one providing nightly shelter for the poor and travellers, but a place where they could be isolated from the healthy while they're being treated.'

'And where would this hospital be, Midwife? Or might you have your husband build such a place?'

'I thought we could use an existing building like ... like this castle. The perfect place, Physician Nestor. That's why I've come to you—heir of *le château de Lucie-sur-Vionne*—to plead my cause. I'd come here daily to care for them, at night even, if need—'

'Please, Midwife, just go away and leave me in peace with my grief. I do not wish to be bothered by your fanciful ideas.'

'The people understand it wasn't me or my pendant that brought the pestilence here,' I kept on brazenly. 'And they are heeding my advice now.'

'Please just go.' He waved me away wearily. 'Your thoughts might have reason, but I am too exhausted by ... by everything, to think. I need to rest.'

'Please, Physician Nestor, will you at least think about ...?'

But he'd already turned from me, and disappeared.

***

Dejected, I trudged back to Merlinette. Beneath the blistering market-place heat, Alewife Rixende was slumped on the hot cobblestones in front of the tavern. Her cap had slid from her head and her white hair hung in sweaty, tangled clumps. As I approached, she lifted a swollen, tear-stained face. But rather than looking at me, her misted blue gaze seemed fixed on something faraway, beyond la place de l'Eglise.

'They're dead ... three of my girls, in there.' She jerked an arm towards the tavern. 'Only Pina left now ... me and Pina, that's all.'

'Oh Rixende, I'm so sorry.'

I sat beside her, placed a tentative hand on her arm, expecting her to fling my fingers off with a curse. But Rixende didn't jerk away; she just sat there, shaking her snowy head.

'Got something in your basket to finish me off too?' she said. 'What do I care about livin' now.' She swiped away the tear leaking down one cheek.

'You still have Pina ... one daughter who needs her mother.'

'That girl's old enough to look after herself,' she said, 'cheeky pigeon she is nowadays.'

'A girl always needs her maman. But for now, we should get you out of this heat.' I helped Rixende upright, still amazed she didn't resist as I cupped my hand around her elbow.

'And let me give you a sedative, won't you? I could help you prepare their bodies for burial too ... if you want?'

I was still expecting a scornful insult, but she gave me a small nod as, together, we shuffled into the tavern. It seemed—like with so many others—the pestilence had beaten the fight out of the alewife too. Or Rixende had finally realised how silly our ongoing battle was, in the face of this far greater war we were all fighting.

'Much as I hate to admit it, you're doing good work in this town,' she said, as we began washing her girls' sweat-dampened bodies, sponging away the waste that Death had expelled from them. 'And I ain't the only one what thinks so ... all with their admiring looks as you come and go from pestilence homes, wiping them down with your rose-water, cleaning up their vomit and waiting for them to die.'

'Not much more I can do,' I said.

'Even heard someone call you Sainte Héloïse,' she said, as we began combing out her girls' hair. 'But I reckon that's taking things a bit far. I mean *you* a saint, of all people?'

'Oh I'm certainly no saint, Rixende! Just a person who hates brooding and prefers to act. But like everyone else I too wake every morning with my heart in my guts, touching my loved ones to make sure they're still warm and breathing. But the only way I can fight those fears is by concentrating on the task at hand.'

'Well, saint or sinner,' she said, as we began to dress the girls in clean smocks. 'You'd best keep away from Père Bernard.'

'Keep away from the priest? But I'm no longer afraid of him, or his accusations.'

'I heard he wants that talisman of yours,' she said, her gaze dropping to my pendant.

'Why would the priest want my talisman?'

'I know my loose tongue tends to wag a bit too much at times, and I might've let slip, you know unintentionally, like ...'

'Let slip what, Rixende?'

'I might've let slip to the priest about it being a ... a holy relic ... or something.'

'Holy relic? Whatever gave you that idea?'

Then I remembered; knew she'd got that idea from my conversation with the pock-marked pedlar at the Spring Fair. I'd revealed nothing about the talisman's true origin, but I clearly recalled Rixende's passing taunt.

Holy relic? More likely the bone of some dumb ass or mangy dog.

The pedlar's warning chimed too, in my mind, and I knew why Père Bernard wanted it.

... religious relics are such pilgrim pullers, the priest would claim it for his church ...

'I know you'd hate to lose that pendant,' Rixende said, 'even if it's no Devil's curse, *or* a holy relic ... but just a silly bit of old bone. Since you've got the grace to help me prepare my girls for their graves, I thought it only fair to warn you to keep an eye on that priest.'

XXXVIII

𝕱inally, after that disastrous month of August—the worst for pestilence deaths—we did see a change. Come the end of the first week of September, when cold north winds banished every trace of heat and swept in the unrelenting wet and leaf-fall chill, there'd been only two pestilence deaths. Then no more for the rest of September: no word of new fevers, coughs, blood roses or black boils. After killing half of Lucie's six hundred souls, the sickness seemed to have vanished as quickly and stealthily as it appeared.

Yes, the miasma was gone. But on its way out, it slunk into my cot and Death—in its final and timeless grip—seized one from my fold.

I thanked the Blessed Virgin that Isa's death was quick. She left us at dawn, as the first slice of light slid through the shutter chinks and the birds took up song. I liked to think that as she breathed in, breathed out … and breathed in, that turquoise light and birds' music, and my kiss on her cheek were the last things she knew.

'I'd prefer to be alone,' I told them—Morgane, Ariane, Poppa and Raoul—when they wanted to help me prepare her for burial. 'There was only Isa when I came into this world, and so it must be as I see her off to the next one.'

Tears blurring my vision, I washed Isa until her rose-water cleansed skin shone like a pearl. I sprinkled a little precious salt over her body to protect her departing soul from the Devil's grip. I dressed her, brushed her hair till the silver glowed shinier than the best minted coin.

I took Isa's scrip from her belt, and gave it to Morgane. 'She'd rather it be used, poppet,' I said, 'than take it with her.'

I wanted to bury Isa at the most beautiful part of the day, so we waited for witch-light. Late in the afternoon, I went outside and sat by the woodpile, next to the back door. Raoul came and sat beside me.

'It's as if I'm losing my mother all over again,' I said. 'I know I couldn't have known of Ava's death, but it's like I've always been aware of that moment: the seconds between Ava's passing and my birth. And as Isa did, I would've tried everything to save Ava … if only I could have.'

'Of course you couldn't have done anything,' Raoul said, and I let him fold me into his embrace. 'And I know—Isa once told me—you blamed yourself for her dying.'

'I did, for a long time … I must've driven Isa mad, saying if it wasn't for me, my mother would still be alive.'

'Remember I lost my own mother while she was birthing me,' Raoul said. 'But I never felt I'd killed her. You, of all people, should know death comes easily to birthing mothers and babes.'

'Yes I know … of course I've always known that,' I said, and it struck me then that Raoul had always understood a lot more than I realised.

I glanced down to the green ribbon of Vionne carving swiftly through the valley after the autumn rain, wending its way to a place I didn't know. A sea, I thought. A place I'd only heard about. But my eyes didn't need to feast on that sea; I just knew it was a wondrous thing.

'Isa kept telling me Ava *was* still with us, in our hearts.' I held a palm over my own, quiet heart. 'But I thought, what use is a mother inside a heart? I wanted to speak to her, touch her … kiss her. And now, after all this,' I said, 'sparing me the pestilence, execution and gaol, I know Ava and her pendant have been with me at every turn … she cherished me as much as any living mother.'

'Isa was the best maman any girl could hope for,' Raoul said, patting a solid hand against my back as the sobs came. 'And you were the daughter she'd never have had … she was grateful for that.'

'Yes, she was.' I rested my head on my husband's shoulder.

'She never did tell me who my father was. I'd stamp my feet and badger her, but she kept saying she didn't know. I think she did, but for some reason wouldn't—or couldn't—tell me. Now I'll never know. But it doesn't matter too much, Isa was all I needed as a child. Then you married me, gave me your name. Morgane came to us, and now …' I felt the child move inside me again.

'And now we have more than any husband and wife could wish for,' Raoul said. His lips found mine and I too was hungry for his.

As the blood-soaked eye of the sun set over the westward hills, shining its golden light on the tumble of Isa's late-summer roses, every tree casting a long, straight shadow, we carried her body to the hole Raoul had dug beneath the cherry trees. No nameless communal pit for Isa, and as for hallowed ground, I knew she'd never cared for, or had much faith, in any earth beyond her beloved garden.

The velvety folds of the hills changing colour and shape with the fading light, the Vionne rushing green and clear, the last of the sun's rays setting the whole water dancing, we lowered her shrouded corpse into her grave.

'Curse you, old witch.' Poppa's lined face crumpled. 'Why did you go and leave me? Now I'm truly alone.'

'We're here, and Loup,' Morgane said, taking Poppa's hand. 'We are your family now.'

Yolande nodded, took Poppa's other hand and the woods became still. Not a whisper of breeze, as if in deference to one who'd spent her life foraging there. Baby Loup was quiet too, even the animals fell silent—Merlinette, Blanche and her kittens, the chickens, goats and the pig—as if in mourning for that great mistress of a humble cot.

'I'll never forget you,' I said, throwing a fistful of soil onto Isa's shroud as the last of the day's warmth pushed down. 'There was never anyone like you in all the world.'

A flock of starlings swished across the dusky sky, their feathers gleaming iridescent like oil on water. And amidst those stars shifting and twinkling high above me as the world tumbled, Isa's soul became a new one, and I knew the angels were already watching over her.

***

With no more deaths in Lucie-sur-Vionne apart from Pierro Blacksmith—who didn't die of the pestilence but drank himself into the ground—we dared to move into the light; to come indoors from that icy pestilence miasma, and bask in the warmth of the fire's golden glow.

We barely rejoiced though, for the losses were too great and our spirits too deeply wounded. Our loss was not just for the dead, it was also for the gap they left—the great hole we didn't know how to fill. But it seemed even the weightiest heart lightened as it dawned on us survivors that we'd been spared. And I'm sure that's how man was made, so that we could go on, and on and on.

'At one time I thought the whole world was going to die,' I said to Raoul. From where I was crouched, weeding the garden, I lifted my gaze to the westward hills, to the fields, and to the *Montagne Maudite* far to the east. 'The pestilence has gone though, and here we are, you and I, like Noah and his wife standing on the top of a mountain after the flood looking out at a new world.'

'Our new world, together,' Raoul said, bending down and

wrapping his sun-bronzed arms about me. 'And if something else comes along to topple us from our mountain, we'll be stronger this time and stop ourselves falling ... falling down.'

'No one can be strong all the time, Raoul.'

'No, perhaps not ... anyway I just wanted to tell you that Anselme and I have almost finished the extra rooms, but we thought to make the cot larger still ... big enough for your hospital, since Physician Nestor refused you the castle.'

'Big enough for a hospital? Well you'd best stop blithering on, and get your lazy arse to work.' I pushed him upright, smacked his backside, and began tugging out the more stubborn garden weeds.

'Just like Isa, you are ... tougher than a ploughman driving an oxen team,' Raoul said, as Poppa bustled through the gate, her basket swinging from one chunky arm, her cloak flapping about her like a kestrel's wing.

'King Edward's daughter, Joan Plantagenet, is dead of the pestilence in Bordeaux,' she said. 'Heard it just now, on the market-place. Only fifteen, she was.'

'So she never made it to Spain,' Raoul said.

I frowned. 'Why was she going to Spain?'

'To marry Prince Pedro, heir to the Castile throne.' Raoul sat back on the bench beside the woodpile. 'The marriage was to ally England and Spain so King Edward could concentrate on his war against us without worrying about interference from the south. But no matter how many times King Edward invades,' he took up his chisel to sharpen, 'we'll never accept any Englishman as our king, even if he does believe he's the legitimate heir to the our throne.'

'Poor Joan,' I said, 'just a pawn in her father's game. She might've lived twenty more years, though with all the children she'd have been forced to bear, she'd likely have died before her time anyway.'

'Such a sad end for a royal princess,' Poppa said. 'But that's not the only thing I heard on la place de l'Eglise. You know what people are calling you, Héloïse? The blood rose angel! Saying your rose tonic and cleaning instructions cured us of the pestilence … that you got rid of the miasma.' She took a quick breath. 'By God's toenails, I can see why though. You do more than care for the sick and women birthing. You comfort them … talk of things they understand, of swelling and fever and pain. You don't confuse them like a physician with jargon about humours and aligned planets, which only makes them feel more stupid and scared.'

'I'd love to think my rose tonic and our hygiene instructions helped stop the sickness,' I said, wiping a soil-streaked hand across my brow, 'but it was more likely just the natural slowing down of disease with this cooler weather.'

'They're also saying,' Poppa's gaze fell to my angel, 'that your pendant's no Devil's charm—no curse at all—but a good luck talisman that helped banish the pestilence from Lucie.'

'I don't—'

'Everyone admires you now,' she carried on, 'but you'd do good to rest sometimes, too. Look at you … that pestilence didn't kill you but the work's worn you down to a wraith. Don't forget that little one needs care too.' She jabbed a pudgy finger at my belly.

'That's what I keep telling her,' Raoul said.

'It's true, I am tired,' I said as Yolande arrived at the cot for her midwifery instruction. 'Only the Virgin could know just how tired. But I promise to take care of this one … to rest now that I can.'

'I'm happy to report that our priest has finally come out of the presbytery,' Yolande said with a smile, 'and is giving Mass again. I've just come from there.'

'I knew that,' Poppa said. 'And what I also know is whereas before, folks would stop Père Bernard on la place de l'Eglise to ask him things, or for a chat, now everyone shuns the man who just skulks about like some defrocked monk.'

'And since the Church and its servants seem to be above the

laws by which the rest of us have to abide,' I said, 'there'll be no punishment for Père Bernard. And I for one can see no reason to seek God's solace in His house, whose workings have shown us nothing but pain, loss and misery.'

'Héloïse!' Yolande hastily crossed herself. 'Haven't you learned from your blasphemous outbursts? Aren't you worried you'll be accused of heresy again?'

'Not a bit,' I said with a wry smile, realising my friend would never think badly of the priest, whatever he did or was rumoured to do; however many times he abandoned his flock. 'I told you before, the pestilence has changed everything and people all over are questioning the workings of God and the Church. And if you think that's heresy we'll just have to agree to differ.'

***

Despite our grief over Isa's passing, our cot was a bustling place amidst the loveliest October weather I could recall. Sunlight flooded us, yellow as fresh butter, the sky a clear blue and no hint of frost in the air. Mauve tides of heather leaned into the breeze, the woods sparkled with shades of green from the emerald moss to the glossy dark ivy, and showers of cherry, amber and gold leaves tumbled to earth. For the first time in so long my heart opened once more to Mother Earth's gifts.

As always, we set about preserving food for the winter. We harvested the garlic, carrots and turnips and gathered the apples. Inhaling their sweet scent, we wrapped the perfect ones in straw and stored them in the lean-to. From the damaged ones, Poppa, who'd taken on Isa's job as cook, made jam, pies and butter. She fashioned apple-ring garlands with Morgane, which they hung from the rafters alongside the herbs, flowers and onion plaits.

We harvested the cabbage, Poppa reminding me of Isa as she cut a cross into each stalk that remained in the ground to protect it from the Devil and bring forth new shoots. And I thought that while Poppa remained in our cot, a part of my aunt would stay there too.

Isa's old friend gladdened our spirits as she brewed ale, while Ariane helped me string and slice the beans and pack them into jars between salt layers. Loup crawled about with Blanche's growing kittens, all of them getting under our feet.

The woodpile went down as quickly as Morgane could collect wood, the fire burning throughout the day and night for cooking and brewing potions, as well as heating. And the steady *smack, smack* of wood breaking beneath Raoul's hatchet held the promise of warmth in its sap.

'Why does rubbing my face and hands with this evil-smelling soap make them clean, Maman?' Morgane scrunched her nose at the great vats of boiling goose grease and mutton fat, with which we would make our soap. 'Why doesn't it just make them black and sandy?'

'You ask too many questions, girl,' Poppa said with a flushed and sweaty grin as she stirred the bubbling fat. 'Just keep stirring.'

Morgane and Raoul hunted juicy hares, which we roasted, salted, pickled or smoked. I took her with Ariane, and often Catèlena—when she wasn't giggling and flirting with Anselme—down to the Vionne where we hooked fish and eels to eat and to smoke. Amongst the willows huddled in whispering groups, silvery leaves quivering, we plucked tawny-capped mushrooms from the woody earth, the gold autumn sun warming our faces.

We gathered rushes from the Vionne, tiny rainbows arching over the water gurgling like a contented baby. I inhaled air that felt scrubbed clean as freshly-washed linen, and felt my soul—after being stifled for so long—breathing once more.

'It's such hard work cutting all the rushes,' Morgane said with a pout. 'Why can't I go home and play with Blanche's kittens and Loup?'

'You think this is hard work?' Ariane gave me a knowing wink. 'Have you forgotten the candle-making job ahead of us? The sweaty, stinky hours we'll spend dipping these rushes into cauldrons of hot tallow, our eyes stinging and our arms scalded and blistered with all that spitting fat?' She smiled and placed a hand on her rounded belly. 'With any luck I'll be too tired from carrying this one, which will get me out of that awful job.'

With a disturbing jolt I realised that was the first time I'd seen Ariane smile. Ever. There was a shift too in her manner since she'd come to our cot. Gone was her stooped, frightened stance, like a pig glimpsing the slaughterer's knife. The sad doe-eyes had brightened and despite the weight of her belly, Ariane stood tall and serene. Her body had filled out too. Gone was the skeleton. And she'd winked at me! I'd not thought that girl even capable of a wink.

I quietly hoped this child was finally growing in her heart.

XXXIX

'Isa always said a good year for nuts meant a good year for babies,' I said, as we gathered our bounty—walnuts and chestnuts—the growing mounds in our baskets stirring my thoughts to hot roasted nuts on the icy winter nights that lurked around the next river bend.

'We'll need a lot of good baby years to replace all those souls the pestilence took,' Yolande said, reaching over and patting Ariane's belly. The girl frowned and said nothing.

'But how can we be sure of a good baby year?' Catèlena said as we tramped from the woods, our nutting-baskets brimming.

'The only way is to ensure more babies and mothers survive birthing,' I said, pulling my cloak tighter against the chill blowing up. 'And I might know a way to do just that.' I looked up at the dove-breast clouds scudding across the hills, feeling I could just reach up and bury my hands in their softness. And I gazed beyond, to Heaven, summoning the experienced minds of Ava and Isa to this new midwifing task that was brewing in my mind.

'What way, Maman?' Morgane said, as we reached the cot, the stiff wind rattling the shutters and trembling the skeletons of bracken and near-naked trees.

'Yes, what *are* you planning now, Héloïse?' Yolande said.

As I made to answer them, the snappy voice of Père Bernard startled me from behind.

'I must speak with you now, Midwife Héloïse.' His face was pinched into the usual frown.

'I'll join you inside soon,' I said to the others, recalling Rixende's warning and guessing what was coming. With fearful glances, they all disappeared into the cot and, bracing myself, I turned to face Père Bernard. As much as I'd have welcomed Raoul's strength and manly presence, and my friends' support, I knew this was another battle I had to fight on my own.

'You'll need to give me that pendant,' the priest said, the wind swelling his robe like a ship's great black sail on a stormy sea. The crucifix and rosary dangling from his girdle shook as he jabbed a spidery finger at my talisman.

'You must be joking,' I said. 'Besides, it's not mine to give away. I'm just its keeper, protecting it for the next in line. Anyway, why would you want it? Not long ago you believed it a Devil's charm; a cursed thing that brought pestilence to Lucie. A thing for which you'd have happily seen me burn!'

'It wasn't me who pronounced the sentence,' the priest said, as if he'd played no part at all, rather than practically convincing le Comte of my guilt. 'And I've now heard said this talisman is a holy saint's relic, so its rightful place is within my church where all valuables are housed … where pilgrims may touch them and be rewarded with miracles.'

'And pay you a healthy sum for the pleasure,' I said, not disguising my distaste. 'But how do you know about this, when you locked yourself in the presbytery for … how long was it? Abandoning your flock when they needed you most, even after vowing to serve, protect and listen to them? I took a vow too, Père Bernard, but did I abandon the sick or those carrying babes? No, I cared for them, risking my life and the lives of my family.' I took a sharp breath. 'I'm sure Our Blessed Lord is displeased by your heartless treatment, as is your congregation, more of whom now stand outside your Church than within. Shame on you.'

The priest's hands curled into fists and his jaw tightened, but on I went. 'So how dare you preach to me and try and take my pendant?'

He unclenched his teeth, but the hunched shoulders—as if he were cold—told me I had unsettled him.

'It's been said this talisman rid our town of the pestilence miasma … and that it's carved from the bone of a saint. That makes it a holy relic, which should be housed within the church. All pieces of sacred Host must be stored in a consecrated place.' He raised his voice a notch. 'You, a heathen, should not be touching or wearing Christ's body.' The priest fixed his dark gaze on me. His nose twitched. His lips flinched.

'My talisman is just an ordinary pendant,' I lied, lowering my gaze and trying not to blench.

'So why are people saying it's a saint's relic?'

'I don't know, Père Bernard, perhaps because they want to believe it. When there's no hope, no cure, nothing left—and especially when their lord and their priest abandon them— people need something to cling to. Anyway, I know you got this crazy holy relic idea from Rixende, but the alewife has lost almost all her family,' I said. 'And her mind, so you'd do better not to listen to her.'

'I'll still have this saint's relic for the church,' he said. 'Besides, you of all people—with your magic potions and charms to cheat people out of their hard-earned sous—must know the truth has little importance. It's what people believe that's important.'

'Certainly I know that, Père Bernard, as well as you do if your sermons are anything to go by. But what if I refuse to hand it over?'

'If I recall,' the priest stroked his chin as if in deep deliberation, as if his was not a well-rehearsed argument, 'your appointment with the flames was never revoked. If you refuse to hand it over, I may have no choice but to—'

'What … invoke my sentence?' I spat the words. 'Have you forgotten that the peace-keepers—the captain and all the sergeants—are dead, along with le Comte who sentenced me? Physician Nestor is the new lord for now, so I don't know how you propose to have me burned?'

I shook my pendant at him and stamped a foot. 'You keep trying to get at me, one way or another, don't you? If it's not ridiculous heresy accusations, it's attempting to steal my talisman. But I'll never let you take it from me.'

'I could easily have a word in the ear of Physician Nestor,' Père Bernard said, his voice thick with malice. 'So easily.'

'And what would the townsfolk think if they knew—for certain—their priest prefers the company of men to women?' I said, rolling my last dice. 'You—of all people—must know sodomy is the greatest crime. You must have heard, like all of us, the story of King Edward's father ... a despicable sodomist killed by a red-hot poker shoved up his arse? It seems to me that the servants of God are greedy hypocrites, no better than men in a brothel.'

'You have no proof,' the priest said. 'As you pointed out, my ... our ... Renault de Fouville is dead.'

'Did I mention le Comte?' I said, with an exaggerated frown. 'I don't recall it.'

'You dare to threaten me?' The priest bunched his hands into fists again, as the wind funnelled down the valley moaning louder than the Hell-damned.

'Spare me your outrage, Père Bernard, you're the biggest coward that ever pissed. I'm sick of your false piety and your evil.'

The priest whistled through his teeth, set his mouth into a grim line. 'Whatever you say, I will have this talisman for the church—holy relic or not.' He lurched at me, one hand reaching out to my pendant.

'You can't touch it.' I reeled from him, a palm protectively over the talisman, the other held up before me. 'Don't you know the eyes scald those who have no right to lay hands on it? That's how we know who can rightly use its birthing and healing powers.' I was amazed again at how freely that falsehood still tumbled from my lips, and how after so long I might easily have convinced myself it was the truth. Perhaps I already had.

'Enough of your rot, and enough of my time wasted,' Père

Bernard said. 'Your husband has sorely failed to discipline you ... he should've beaten you into submission years ago.' In one surprisingly quick movement for a man of his age, the priest lunged at me and tore the pendant from about my neck.

He immediately sprang backwards, dropping the angel to the ground as if it were alive, and shaking his fingers. 'Whoring, heretic bitch, it did burn me!'

'I won't say I told you so.' I bent down to retrieve the muddied pendant, hiding my triumphant smile, but as my fingers curled over the bone carving, one of the priest's black boots stamped down on my hand.

I heard the cracking of small bones, felt a white-hot pain. My head span and black spots danced before my eyes. I gasped, stared back up at Père Bernard.

My eyes filled with tears but I blinked furiously, refusing to let them spill. 'You call me a whoring bitch,' I said, the fingers of my other hand curling around the injured one, trying to squeeze away the agony. 'But you dare call yourself a man of God. You, with a heart blacker than Satan's wings.' I spat a glob of spit onto the boot that had crushed my hand.

'Maman, Maman!' Morgane came running from the cot, red braids flying. 'He's hurt you!'

'Come back inside, Morgane,' Poppa called from the doorway, blocking the path of the others I glimpsed behind her wide girth. 'Your maman can defend herself.'

But Morgane ignored her, and kept running to me. She folded her small hand into my uninjured one, and stared defiantly at the priest.

Without another word, Père Bernard turned and strode off into the tangle of dying leaves along the woodland road.

'Remember, Père Bernard,' I called after him, 'it's not the truth that's important, it's what you *believe* is the truth. Get some salve for that burn, won't you, or you'll be scarred for life.'

Cradling my limp and aching hand, I watched until the priest was gone. The one thing—the only thing—comforting me was thinking of Père Bernard imagining a burn mark on his fingers. The same mark Drogan had imagined when he'd tried to take the pendant from me on the market-place, and again after he'd followed Isa to the cave. Impossible burn scars.

The pestilence had instilled doubt into my mind about the workings of God and our Church. But our priest's most unchristian viciousness towards me now sealed any lingering uncertainty. Whilst I would still pray in church to the Blessed Virgin, and speak to Ava, I vowed I would never again attend a priest's Mass.

As I shuffled into the cot I smelled the first snow in the cold north wind, the green tops of the poplars giving way to its icy breath.

Sensing I didn't want to speak about that terrible scene, nobody said a word. I avoided their questioning eyes as I crouched, and plunged my hand into the pail of cold water, waiting for the pain to ease.

'I'm glad you didn't let him take the angel pendant,' Morgane said, a few moments later, gently applying a comfrey leaf poultice to my broken fingers. 'Because the talisman will be mine soon, won't it? Can it be mine now, Maman?'

'Not yet, poppet, it seems I need the angel a while longer,' I said, as she deftly splinted my hand with flat pieces of wood, and bandaged it. 'But it will be yours soon enough.'

'Is it really a holy saint's relic, like Père Bernard said?'

A shiver caught me. Of course, my daughter must have overheard every word of that terrible argument.

'Don't listen to that priest's *merde*-ridden addle,' Poppa said as she stirred her delicious-smelling chicken and almond milk soup. 'I've had enough of his evil ways.'

Ariane and Catèlena nodded emphatically but Yolande, staunchly loyal, remained tight-lipped.

'I've told you many times, my sweet,' I said, taking her hand in my good one. 'As Isa told it to me, you'll know the talisman's story when you're old enough to understand it.'

'But I'm eight summers now, Maman ... quite old enough to know everything.' As she packed away my work-basket in the lean-to, her serious little voice made me smile, and I had to acknowledge that Morgane *was* growing up so quickly.

'Perhaps you are old enough, my sweet ... almost.'

XL

One grey and cold November afternoon, as I pulled flax fibres towards my spindle—laboriously with a broken hand—a rapping came on our door. We all looked up: Poppa from Isa's loom where she'd taken over weaving new bolts of cloth, Morgane and Ariane from where they sat by the fire making rope from the hemp.

Another knock. 'Héloïse, are you there?'

I opened the door, delighted to see Delphine, la Comtesse Geneviève's maid, crimson-cheeked and rubbing her mittened hands together. Beyond, a messenger on horseback waited outside the gate. 'Delphine! I thought I recognised your voice.'

'You look much better than the last time I saw you,' Delphine said as we exchanged kisses between foggy breaths. 'And so glad I am to see that. I've come because Physician Nestor's ill ... can you come up to the castle?'

'Come up to the castle, me?'

I was exhausted. It was almost a month after Père Bernard had savagely stomped on my hand, and Martinmas was upon us—the season for slaughtering those animals not to be kept over winter: sheep past their wool-giving years, rams past breeding, cows no longer lactating and most of the pigs. Even after the pestilence ravages had left far fewer animals, we were kept busy carving, salting and smoking; tying off sausages and making blood puddings and broths garnished with pork shavings. The fire blazed to smoke the ham, at which Blanche and her kittens leapt relentlessly. Our eyes watered, clothes and hair stinking of smoke, hands chapped from rubbing salt into the meat. With all that work in the mornings and the babe growing in my belly, all I could do in the afternoons was slump down beside the hearth and spin.

'Nestor called for me to care for him?' I said. 'I know there's nobody else in Lucie, but he's never acknowledged my treatments.'

'All I know is he asked for you,' Delphine said, 'and that he's very sick.'

I looked at Raoul, tongue out in concentration as he sketched something in his paper notebook. He gave me a quick nod. 'I'll take you,' he said. 'You won't be able to hold Merlinette's reins properly with that broken hand.'

'I'll meet you up at the castle, Delphine,' I said, grabbing my work-basket and my cloak as the maid hurried back to the shivering messenger and the horse exhaling streams of fog.

'And while I'm waiting for you,' Raoul said, helping me up into the cart. 'I'll go over to the presbytery and wring that swine of a priest's neck.'

'So you keep threatening,' I said, the mare clopping off along the woodland road shrouded in gloaming. 'But stop wasting your time or anger on that useless bit of flea-shit. I surely have.'

'What if he'd hurt our son when he attacked you?' Raoul held the horse's reins in one hand, and placed the other on my cloak, tight across my rounding belly. As always, we waited a moment, both smiling in amazement when the baby moved beneath his father's hand.

'Let's hope this babe is ...' His voice trailed off as if he hardly dared go on, for fear of cursing him ... us.

'I always tell women with child to think the best, not the worst, Raoul. Bad thoughts and moods will affect the baby's health, so stop thinking of such blackness.'

'You're right,' he said. 'This boy will come out pink and

squealing like a piglet. I can see him already; know he'll be strong and already sure of his place in life.'

'He ... or *she*,' I said with a wink.

It was almost curfew, but la place de l'Eglise throbbed with activity. People from the countryside had started coming to Lucie, moving into the empty pestilence houses and fixing them up—outlanders or existing tradesmen who wanted a better spot. Some too, had begun new businesses to replace the ones that had disappeared when the pestilence swept away the owners.

The butcher's wife looked up from the counter where she was chopping a great side of meat.

'Greetings,' she called, wiping a hand across her forehead and leaving a bloody streak. Since so many men had died, it wasn't unusual to see a wife taking over the family business; women doing men's jobs and, I had observed, often proving more astute in dealings than the late husband.

From where she stood in the tavern doorway, Rixende lifted an arm in a heavy, sorrowful wave. Not a trace of the spiteful glare I'd suffered for so many years.

'Stop the horse please, Raoul,' I said.

I stepped down from the cart, and pressed into Rixende's hand sage and violet-oil, which might eventually ease the melancholy that had claimed her when her daughters perished.

'Burning juniper branches can help too,' I said.

'I see you didn't let the priest take it,' she said, her gaze dropping to my angel talisman. 'Good for you ... I knew you wouldn't.'

She gave me a small nod, and a strange glance at Raoul, as Merlinette set off again.

We reached *le château* and from Raoul's tender kiss, as I stepped down from the cart again, I guessed he too was recalling that time I'd stood at the castle gate before my terrifying trial. I waited for it to open, thinking again how quickly, how easily, things can change: on the hatred of childhood foes, the greed of a priest, the caprice of sickness, the luck of the dice. On the whim of an iron-fisted lord prone to fits of mercy. As the baby gave me another hefty kick, I looked back over my shoulder and smiled at Raoul.

But how lucky I am, right now. And it's the right now that counts, for I've learned there might not be a tomorrow.

***

A servant led me to Physician Nestor's chambers, where the monk-physician lay on a sumptuous bed of ermine-furred blankets, his face pale and pinched.

'You came,' he said, his features twisting in pain. 'I'm dying, Midwife Héloïse.'

I had no idea what ailed the physician, but from the look of him—thin as a skeleton, the bones almost poking through yellowed skin, the light already faded from his eyes—Physician Nestor did seem to be on his deathbed.

Why then, had he called me?

I rummaged in my basket for the poppy juice, poured a little into the beaker of wine beside his bed. 'Drink this,' I said, holding the beaker to his bloodless lips.

He gulped it down and closed his eyes. Wordlessly, I remained sitting beside him until, after a time, he opened his eyes and placed a clammy palm over my hand. His touch surprised me, and I lurched backwards, but for all his frailty the physician held his hand firmly over mine.

'God showed mercy to my brothers ... except Renault,' he began, 'when they died quickly on the fields of battle. And He might take pity on me, a fallen sinner, if I confess it all to you now ... might raise me up as He promised on the Last Day.'

I'd never heard Physician Nestor speak like this before—especially not to me—and I feared whatever sickness he had was sending him delirious.

'Just rest,' I said. 'Save your strength to fight the sickness.'

He gave a great sigh and raised his dull gaze to me. 'Spare me your empty hope. I'll not recover, and I cannot leave this world without your forgiveness.'

'But what must I forgive you for?' I said, thinking he must be referring to his disdain of my healing and birthing methods.

'As you know, as all of Lucie knows, I've been a cripple from birth,' he said, motioning towards his inturned foot. 'Never to become a knight like my brothers ... and fight for the King.' He ran his tongue across his lips, which I dampened with a wet cloth. 'Destined only for the church.'

I nodded, still unsure why he was telling me this. But I had learned from sitting with so many dying that most wanted only a friendly ear.

'So when I was in my seventh summer,' Nestor went on, 'my father sent me off to train for the monkhood.' A shaky hand gestured in the direction of the monastery, behind the castle. 'I became interested in herbal treatments and was eventually elevated to the monastery's Chief Infirmarer.'

'Yes, my aunt Isa told me that,' I said, 'then you left the monastery to study medicine at Montpellier University.'

'So proud I was to gain such high physician status,' he said, 'since my family had always thought I was good for nothing. But I digress ...'

He fell silent for a moment, and seemed to be struggling to catch his breath. 'Before ... Montpellier,' he began again, 'I would spend hours in the woods gathering ingredients for my medicaments, as do you ... as did your aunt and ... and your mother.'

'My mother? You knew Ava?'

'I was in love with Ava.' Another few torturous breaths. 'And Ava loved me.'

In love? Something started to awaken in me, like a rushlight gradually illuminating a dark and stuffy room, revealing—little by little—ghosts crouched in dusty corners.

Nestor nodded. 'And if I don't tell you the truth now, I'll be damned straight to Hell.'

Dizzy with the thoughts swirling in my head; with what I was certain he was going to admit, my breaths came out short and sharp. I couldn't speak a word, so I merely nodded.

'From the first day I saw your mother, I was enchanted: her blue-grey eyes, her creamy heart-shaped face ... your face. My heart melted like ... like butter in a hot sun.' His face crumpled as a wave of pain engulfed him and I pressed the beaker to his lips and bade him drink more poppy juice.

'We began meeting in secret and ... and ...' His grip tightened on my hand. 'And when she said she was carrying my child, I did not hesitate to ask for her hand in marriage.' His features distorted in pain again, his breaths so ragged I thought they were his last.

'I told ... told Ava I would gladly rescind the monkhood and spend my life with her, and you. I so badly wanted that, but feared my family, especially Renault, would never allow it.'

Nestor fell silent, and I thought he was going to stop his story right there, but his lips parted like a dying trout's and he went on. 'And Renault did *not* allow it ... he even forbade me to mention Ava.'

'The *Seigneur* would never let you, a noble,' I said, 'marry a lowly bastard girl.'

'Renault yelled at me ... called me a feeble-minded dolt,' Nestor kept on. 'Said love is just another word for lust, falsehood and trickery—the darkest and most evil of all plagues.' He took several rasping breaths before he continued. 'On and on he raged, each insult making me feel smaller and smaller ... my brother had a habit of doing that.

'I always hoped there would be a way,' he added wearily, 'some way I could be with Ava, and you. But it wasn't to be. Aware of my love for medicine, and seeing a way to salvage the family name, Renault quickly packed me off to Montpellier University ... forbade me to return to Lucie or to mention either of you.' He fell silent for a time, pain crimping his drawn features.

'That is why I stayed away from Lucie so many years ...

my studies, then working as a physician in Lyon. But when complications from Renault's war injuries required a personal physician, and he asked me back here, well ... I couldn't resist the temptation to see what you ... what had become of you. And what I saw made me painfully proud.'

He fell silent again, and closed his eyes for a moment.

'I was frantic when I heard your burning sentence,' he began again, 'tried all I could to stop it.'

'You came into the Great Hall,' I said with a nod, 'told them that a woman with child couldn't be burned ... something your brother seemed to have conveniently forgotten. Or he simply didn't care.'

'My brother might have shown the odd fanciful mercy but he was a cold and harsh man.'

He turned from me, gazing out onto the grey leaf-fall evening. 'I am ashamed and dishonoured, Midwife Héloïse. And, in the face of God, my soul is blighted. I cannot escape judgement.'

'Isa must have known all of this,' I said. 'Why did she never tell me?'

'Renault told your aunt that if she said anything, he'd remove you to a nunnery. "Let you rot as a virgin" were his words.'

I heard Isa's words to that young and defiant girl as clearly as if she were speaking to me now.

... lavishing thanks on Saint Margaret for this miracle ... on Ava for not making an angel of you; for giving me the daughter— the midwife apprentice—I'd never dared hope for.

'Yes,' I nodded, 'Isa would've done anything ... guarded any secret to keep me.'

'And now I need your forgiveness,' Nestor said, 'for abandoning her—and you—so you were forced to live your life as a bastard child. I suppose that's too much to ask?'

I stared at him, too shocked by his revelation to arrange a single thought in my head.

'My notary came this morning,' Nestor said. 'It's all down in writing ... in my will ... how I have bequeathed your husband,

Raoul Stonemason, funds to complete the vingtain wall and the castle repairs ... funds to build your hospital.' He took a sighing breath. 'A distant cousin shall become the new *seigneur*. A just and righteous man, have no fear. But this is the least I can do for you.'

'Why have you always despised me then?' I said.

'No!' Nestor's eyes clouded. 'I had to distance myself, to disguise my love beneath disdain ... always holding back from blurting everything out. Because if I did, Renault would have whisked you away to that nunnery.'

'But le Comte had already died when I asked you about using the castle as a hospital,' I said, 'so why didn't you tell me all this then?'

'I had already sickened then and besides, I'm a weak and cowardly man ... it's taken this—my own approaching death— to give me the courage to admit my sins. But know that I have always cared for you ... always. I would never have let you rot in that gaol, or be burned after the birth of your child. It was I who suggested to Renault that you midwife la Comtesse Geneviève ... not that he had much choice of midwife. But I knew la Comtesse to be a good woman who'd suffered my brother's ... my brother, for years ... I was certain she'd help you.'

'So it was you, the hooded figure outside la Comtesse Geneviève's solar? You bribed those men-at-arms not to take me back to the cell?'

He nodded, gripped my other hand, clasped my joined hands in both of his. He held them tight for a moment, then released me.

'I must go back to my cot now,' I said, rising from the bed- side as I saw dusk had fallen. 'I'll return tomorrow.' It might be curfew and time to go home, but even so I just wanted to be gone from this castle. I felt no urgency to spend my father's last days or hours with him. Sitting beside this dying man I'd just learned had seeded me, I couldn't feel or think of a single thing.

His face drawn in pain and sorrow, Physician Nestor nodded and managed a weak smile as I left his chambers.

I walked back across the market-place towards Raoul and Merlinette, recalling my conversation with Isa that first day I'd seen Physician Nestor on la place de l'Eglise.

And if they don't get an heir, what will happen to their wealth? I know not, Héloïse. All I know is what good a person could do with all those riches.

Thoughts too, of my midwifing plans—and the funds I would need—flitted through my mind as Raoul hoisted me up onto the cart and Merlinette clopped away from the market-place.

***

Two days later Physician Nestor was dead. A messenger from the notary came to our cot and officially informed my husband that Physician Nestor had bequeathed to Master Mason Raoul Stonemason sufficient funds to pay his workers to complete the castle repairs and the vingtain wall. Physician Nestor also specified that of these funds, Raoul Stonemason impart to his wife, Midwife Héloïse, monies for a hospital to separate the infirm and dying from the healthy, and to provide care for such persons.

Dumbfounded, I could conjure up neither excitement over this new-found wealth nor grief over my father's passing. I was so overwhelmed I felt only a strange numbness, as if I'd stepped outside my body and was sitting on a cloud, like an angel, watching it all unfold below. I kept gripping my own angel, basking in its real warmth and comfort, instead of those strange and invisible feelings hooked to my father and his sous.

'I knew my father for one day,' I said to Poppa. 'I suppose that's better than not knowing him at all?'

'God's toe-nails!' she said with a great guffaw. 'What do you really care, Héloïse, after the sous he left you? I only wish the old witch were here to see it,' she said. 'How Isa would cry with mirth. Now hurry and pour that wine, Raoul ... let's taste some good castle brew for a change, instead of our thin and bitter old ale.'

XLI

'At least we'll be safe from outlaws now,' Raoul said as we prepared to celebrate Christmastide, along with the completion of Lucie's vingtain protection wall. 'Or if those plundering English cross the Oceanus Britannicus and tramp down here to Lucie-sur-Vionne.'

'Now you just need to build a wall strong enough to stop the pestilence coming back,' Morgane said as she hung ivy from the rafter beams, holly to welcome in the good fairies and spirits, and mistletoe over the door to ward off ill-fortune.

'If only it was that simple, my little Flamelock,' Raoul said.

Despite the ever-falling snow, an endless white blanket across the fields and the Monts du Lyonnais, Yolande and Anselme came to our cot for our Christmastide feasting. We'd also taken in Delphine, until the new *seigneur* was installed in *le château*. Catèlena was here too, sitting cross-legged on the floor with Ariane and Morgane, spinning a top for Loup who squealed as the toy spun before his eyes. Since she's been rid of Drogan, Catèlena's unbattered face seemed continually creased in a smile, as pretty as a blooming peony. Seeing my home filled with such an abundance of warmth, love and laughter, my heart seemed about to burst with happiness.

From Physician Nestor's funds, Raoul paid for musicians to come with rebec, citole and gittern to play, then to help us devour the ducks and geese that turned golden on skewers over the roaring fire, so juicy they sent Blanche and her kittens mad with the leaping, then skittering away shaking their singed paws.

Poppa cooked up stewed beef seasoned with cinnamon and saffron, chicken with almond rice, and pike—that nobleman's fish—in ale.

'Just because we can afford these exotic eastern spices for now,' I said to Poppa, as she closed her eyes, sniffing at the scents of musk, ambergris, nutmeg and cardamom. 'Doesn't mean you have to use them in every single dish.'

'The old witch would never have believed it all, would she?' Poppa said, her eyes gleaming as she turned over almonds, dates and pomegranates, and gazed in wonder at the colourful blaze of lemon and orange peels spread across our table.

Raoul pointed to the pages from his notebook that he'd laid out on the table: the sketches he'd made of the beautiful hospitals of Florence. 'I'd thought to make of this cot your hospital, Héloïse, but Anselme had a better idea.' He nodded to his apprentice.

'Since it's vacant after the pestilence sadly took all the monks,' Anselme began, 'we thought it fitting to turn the old monastery—where Physician Nestor was once Chief Infirmarer—into Héloïse's hospital.'

'We'll start next spring,' Raoul said, and the boy nodded, his eyes bright and eager as always when he and Raoul discussed building work. I caught Anselme's secret smile too ... the one he'd been keeping of late for Catèlena. Through her blush, Catèlena smirked at Anselme.

'And once the hospital's done,' Raoul said, 'I'll be making of this cot a sturdy stone dwelling. Many builders are using stones now. Wood might be beautiful, but stone is the thing ... stone is best of all!' He raised his beaker filled with wine. 'There will be much work for many willing hands.'

'Hear, hear!' everyone cried, and we all raised our beakers.

'I'd like to have work in your hospital, since I have no husband,' Catèlena said, darting Anselme another covert glance. 'I'll need an income.'

'And me,' Ariane said, with a dismal glance at her belly, hanging heavy as a lead noose.

'I'll wash and cook for your patients. That'll make the old witch turn in her grave,' Poppa said with a wide grin. 'Isa never could admit I was the better cook.'

'And you'll have those silks you once spoke of, Poppa,' I said. 'Do you remember what you said when Alix birthed baby Loup? You said: "we can all stop this hardworking life and idle away our days on silken beds, wearing ermine cloaks, listening to beautiful minstrels with great pulsing members, sing".'

I was dismayed to see the eyes of Isa's old friend fill with tears. 'I thought I had nothing back then,' she said, 'but I had the lot. Give one of my fat arms, I would, to have my family back ... just one of them.'

As if sensing her sorrow, Loup grabbed at the folds of her kirtle. She picked him up and cuddled him. 'Oh but I do have you.' She buried her face in the baby's curls. 'Even if you have got my big ugly feet.'

'And what of the beautiful minstrel's great pulsing member?' Ariane said with a giggle, gesturing at the musicians. 'We'll need to find you one of those, too.'

Ariane, so bold and giggling! I could hardly believe my ears as we all exploded in mirth, our laughter ringing through the cot like a minstrel's finest melody.

'But my true Christmastide wish,' Poppa said when the noise died down, 'is to make of this cot—and your land, Raoul Stonemason—the greatest farm in Lucie-sur-Vionne. I might be a washerwoman, but farming's in my blood. Hire me a band of strong and willing workers and you'll see, we'll be the richest farmers in all the country.'

'Your wish is granted, Farmeress Poppa,' Raoul said with a smile.

'Delphine,' I said, 'I promised to repay your kindness. How might I do that?'

'Witnessing the heir's birth made me want to learn your art

of midwifery,' Delphine said. 'I'm sure that birthing must feel like working miracles, so alongside your own daughter and Yolande,' she carried on, her cheeks flushing pink as everyone looked at her. 'I'd like you to teach me to be as skilled a midwife as yourself.'

'We'll start your lessons tomorrow,' I said, with a gleeful clap. 'So you too can work miracles, Delphine.'

'Now Maman has three apprentices,' Morgane said proudly.

'And one day I'll have three hundred,' I said.

Raoul's gaze snapped to me. 'Three *hundred* apprentices? Oh, what's this you haven't told me about, Héloïse?' The green eyes widened, but his tone held not a trace of accusation or threat. And that was enough to spur me on.

'Watching Morgane show baby Loup how he was birthed gave me the idea,' I said. 'I'll use a doll too, and some kind of cloth model of an afterbirth with navel string attached, to teach apprentices the art of midwifery. It would also have a womb, into which the doll and afterbirth could be folded, for carrying it in my basket, you see?' I took a quick breath. 'I'd teach all women carrying babes about good health ... safer childbirth is the only way to replace those souls the pestilence took.'

'That's all well and saintly, Héloïse,' Poppa said, thrusting a finger at my distended belly. 'But have you forgotten your own babe's a comin'? I'll not see you traipsing across the country teaching midwifing or anything else.'

'They'll come to our cot then, after our child is born,' I said. 'I'll provide lodgings as long as the women vow to learn a midwife's skills.'

'But where would they all sleep?' Catèlena said.

'Raoul will just have to build yet more rooms,' I said, with a wave of my hand and a wink at my husband. 'And the cot will be called *L'Auberge des Sages-femmes*.'

Poppa clapped her chubby hands together. 'Not only the richest farm in Lucie, but the *Inn of Midwives* too!' Her blue eyes shining, she looked about the cot as if recalling the small and simple dwelling of Isa and Ava's childhood and how it had changed. And dreaming about what more it would become.

***

Ariane's child came after Epiphany, in the midst of a snow-covered January. Encumbered with my own swollen belly, Yolande and Morgane helped me down to sit beside the pallet where Ariane lay, tears flooding her cheeks.

'I don't want it, make it go away,' she sobbed.

Gushing water and bloody fluid had already made a great stain on the sheet beneath her and as I knelt by her side, and turned up her dress, I saw the top of the baby's head.

'Your little one is already here,' I said, removing my angel pendant and placing it in her hand. 'Squeeze the talisman, it will help with the pain.'

Morgane and Yolande darted about fetching clean linen, cloths and towels, while Poppa heated the kettle and restrained Loup from crawling around Ariane.

'Don't cry, my sweet,' I said, bending up both her knees. It was too late to get her onto the birthing chair, so I had to squat—awkward with my big belly—on the ground before her. 'The baby's coming and all will be well very soon.'

'All will never be well,' Ariane wailed. 'I don't want the bastard. And even if I did, I might die and it would have nobody ... like me.'

'Don't talk,' I soothed, 'and the pain will be less. Just breathe deep.'

'We're your family now,' Morgane said, clutching one of Ariane's hands, 'just as Poppa is. Isn't that so, Maman?'

Jiggling baby Loup on one hip, Poppa nodded, as Yolande and Delphine—who'd come to the cot at the first sign of Ariane's travail—dabbed sweat from the girl's brow and gave her sips of raspberry leaf infusion to help her pain and lessen the chances of bleeding from the womb.

Ariane's eyes widened as another pain took her up. She began pushing, and I guided the head out gently, to stop the fragile skin tearing. The body came, and the throbbing navel cord.

'Don't show me the monster.' Ariane turned her head as the baby girl began breathing with barely a cry, and flushed a beautiful pink. 'Just drown it in the Vionne and be done with it.'

I looked at her lying between her mother's legs—pink and lovely as a rose—a shadow of dark hair glistening on her soft head, her tiny features screwed up as if annoyed at being removed from her warm, watery bed. A little fist folded and unfolded, her legs curled up towards her belly. I'd not seen many births go this smoothly, and after all the pestilence dying, here was a lovely, perfect babe, unwanted. It seemed so unfair and I couldn't help weeping.

'Like your little one, Ariane,' I said, swiping away my tears. 'For a long time, I thought I too might've come from the seed of a nameless brigand. Like Isa and Ava, whose maman—my grandmother—was violated by outlaws in the woods. But my aunt always told me beginnings have little meaning. What's important is a mother's love for her child; how she cherishes and values it.'

The gossips seemed lost for words, and simply nodded. The cot remained silent as I waited for the navel string to stop pulsating. Ariane's eyes were clenched, so as not to catch the slightest glimpse of her newborn.

I gazed outside onto my world: the snow-covered, heather-thatched roofs in the distance, the frozen Vionne. It looked as if someone had thrown a white blanket across the earth to silence it; to hunker down Lucie-sur-Vionne for her long winter sleep. Sleet had churned the old Roman road into a muddy channel, and our wooden shutters creaked like old bones, the midden farting the bad smell of old men.

Once I'd severed the cord and delivered the afterbirth, Yolande and Delphine removed the stained linen from beneath Ariane. They spread a clean sheet and a blanket over her, and Morgane took the little girl in her arms.

'Can I wash her, Maman?'

'Her?' Ariane said. 'A girl then. Poor wretch, she's even more doomed.'

'Héloïse's bastard life was hard at times,' Yolande said, 'but see how well it's turned out. Besides, the pestilence has changed everything. There are so many orphaned children, and I suspect that being a bastard might not mean the same as it did before.'

'People—many people—are thinking differently about God, the Church, priests, bastards and those of low-birth status,' I said with a glance at Yolande. 'Your little girl's life might not be tougher than any other child's.'

'She's very beautiful,' Morgane said.

'Beautiful?' Ariane turned her head a little, but still did not look at her infant.

'Beautiful as the dawn sun rising over the snows of the *Montagne Maudite*,' Yolande said.

'Lovely as a starlit sky,' Poppa said.

'Enchanting as a summer gloaming,' Delphine said.

And as Morgane held the naked little creature out to Ariane, a miracle unfolded before my eyes. The new mother's face softened, and slowly she reached out her arms, and cradled the baby against her. The little one began rooting around for milk and, clearly moved by that helpless, trusting movement, Ariane folded back the blanket and the little girl found her nipple and began to suck.

'She is quite beautiful, isn't she?' Ariane said, as she watched the baby suckle. We nodded, our tears transformed to smiles and laughter.

Morgane took the angel pendant from Ariane and wiped it clean. 'You said I was almost old enough to know its story, Maman. Am I old enough now?'

'Yes I think you are, poppet.' I hooked the little angel back over my head, sending silent thanks to my talisman, and to Ava, for helping us through this birth. For banishing the strife from a new mother's heart.

XLII

Our hoods pulled snug around our faces, extra blankets shrouding our cloaks, Morgane and I sat on a snow-shrouded log in the misty garden. It seemed a fitting place, beside Isa's grave—the only place where my aunt could listen, and ensure I was telling the tale properly, as she'd told it to me. As Ava and Isa's mother had told it to her twins.

'I've told you of Saint Margaret,' I began.

Morgane nodded. 'The one we pray to for a safe birth.'

'That's right, my sweet. Well, it's said Saint Margaret was the daughter of a pagan priest of Antioch.'

'Antioch?'

'A place in Pisidia ... a far-off land across the sea, where Margaret turned into a Christian, which made her father drive her from their home. She became a shepherdess and there was a Roman prefect called Olybrius who found her very beautiful.'

'What's a prefect, Maman?'

'A very important person in the times of the mighty Romans. Remember the people Papa told you about, who made camp here in Lucie-sur-Vionne? Those who built the road that leads to our pool on the Vionne, the crumbling fountain on la place de l'Eglise and the great aqueducts to take water from the hills all the way down to Lyon? The same people who mined for gold in our cave?'

'Yes, I heard the tale at the Midsummer Eve feast yesteryear.

The storyteller told us the Roman slaves cut those caves from the mountains and worked inside the tunnels, searching for gold. They made shrines and vases and jewellery. And used it for coins, too. And that's how Lucie-sur-Vionne was named,' she went on. 'After the Roman soldier, Lucius. Like the villages of Julien-sur-Vionne and Valeria-sur-Vionne too.'

'Clever girl, you remember everything. So, when Margaret would have nothing to do with Olybrius, he charged her with being a Christian and had her tortured and imprisoned.'

'A real barbarian, that Olybrius ... like horrible Captain Drogan and le Comte, who wanted to burn you at the stake.'

I nodded, trying to block all memory of that dank gaol cell; the terrible burning sentence, from my mind. Our lives since the Spring Fair, in fact. 'While she was imprisoned, Margaret met the Devil in the form of a dragon, and it swallowed her. But, with the cross she was carrying, Margaret tickled the dragon's throat and he spewed her out, alive.'

'Alive?' Morgane frowned. 'That sounds impossible.'

'Well, poppet, it is a legend. But because she was delivered safely from the dragon's stomach, she's known as the patron saint of women in childbirth—to deliver babies safely from their mother's womb. And, to finish the story, after many attempts to kill her, Margaret was finally beheaded.'

'Poor Margaret.'

'And this angel talisman,' I said glancing at a crimson autumn leaf—the only one it seemed that had escaped winter death— fluttering onto Isa's grave, 'is supposedly carved from one of Saint Margaret's bones.'

'And the eyes are the colour of a dragon glowing in the dark?' Morgane's mismatched ones gleamed with excitement.

'Is a dragon blue and green then?' I said.

'It's whatever colour you want it to be ... you know that's what Papa told us. But if the pendant comes from a faraway land, Maman, how did you and Ava and Isa get it?'

'That, my poppet, is the exciting part of the story.' I took her mittened hand in mine. 'Isa told me many tales, but the one I love best is about Eleanor of Aquitaine, a beautiful and powerful queen who lived many moons ago, and who went on a crusade to Antioch.'

'Why would she go on a crusade?'

'To help her Uncle Raymond, prince of Antioch, fight against the Saracens. But there were other reasons for people to go on crusade, like the lure of looting precious objects from the enemy.' I inhaled, and breathed out a long foggy puff. 'The story goes that sometime after the crusade, the midwife attending Eleanor when she birthed one of her children—we don't know which one, for she had ten—was a kinswoman of ours; yours and mine, Ava and Isa's. It was a difficult birth but the child survived and Eleanor was very grateful—'

'As la Comtesse Geneviève was grateful when you birthed her son safely?'

'Just like that, poppet.' I felt another stab of sorrow for la Comtesse and her young son.

'Eleanor told this ancestor—this midwife—that she had something that was useless to her. Perhaps, if she'd taken it wrongfully from the Saracens during the crusade, she was feeling remorseful, nobody knows, but she said this object could be of great value to our kinswoman, as a midwife.'

'Our angel?' Morgane said.

'She told the midwife this bone angel was very old,' I went on with a nod, 'and that it came from Antioch, and was sculpted from a bone of Saint Margaret. She said it would give her powers to help birthing women.'

'And power to burn those who aren't supposed to touch it,' Morgane said.

'No, poppet, it can't burn anyone. Some simply believe it can, just as we convince those giving birth that the pendant can help them bear their child more easily and safely. The talisman placed on their swollen bellies or folded in their fist comforts and reassures them, as it does me when I wear it.' I rubbed it between my thumb and forefinger, feeling it warming my skin, cool despite my mitten. 'But the truth is, it may not possess any special powers at all. What's important though is what people believe ... in what they place their faith. Their trust and hope.'

I almost mentioned the Church and God, but held my tongue. When she was of an age, my daughter would make up her own mind about Him, Heaven, Hell and priests' sermons. I shivered, pulled my cloak tighter around me.

'So the dragon story may not be true, Maman?'

'Perhaps it's true,' I said, my arm circling Morgane's shoulder and drawing her closer to me. 'But maybe it's only a legend that makes a good fireside tale. You can believe what you think is real.'

I stared through the thick fog at Isa's garden and her silvery plants asleep for the winter. Or dead, never to be resurrected. 'You need to have faith in something, poppet ... get strength from something, be it Our Lord, the Blessed Virgin, a mother or aunt gone to the other side. Or a bone-sculpted talisman you'll pass on to your daughter.'

'How many daughters might wear it, Maman?'

'We'll never know, my sweet. But I hope its journey will go on long after you and I have left for the next world ... with all its secrets safe inside the old bone.'

XLIII

Spring came with its sudden changes that give and take life: one day mild, beckoning the tender tips of shoots from the moist earth, and giving off the fragrance of new growth, the next a dawn frost that seared the new growth to death.

But of course most of the shoots did open, buds swelling into unblighted bloom. The ewes began lambing and the sight of those tiny creatures springing on all fours, glad to be alive, their fleeces so white against the lush new grass, moved me.

As Master Mason, Raoul hired tradesmen and labourers for the monastery and castle repairs, providing work for many. These workers brought their families from outlying villages to Lucie-sur-Vionne. They occupied vacant pestilence homes, or if they were from Lucie, their new wages allowed them to build better ones. Better homes and better lives, from the Fouville wealth—in coin and in exchange for meals.

It was during one of the lambing season nights, with a blizzard sweeping in from across the Monts du Lyonnais, that I felt the first twinge of my travail. The throws were not yet intense—only a pain low in my back—but they niggled enough to stop me sleeping. I clambered down the loft ladder and paced about the hearth.

My fingers pressed into my back, I breathed in and out—just as I taught others to do—in rhythm to the gentle snores and snuffles of those asleep in my cot, their sounds almost lost to the noise of the wind pummelling the cot as if trying to slink into the crannies of the old walls.

Between two pains, I pushed aside the oilcloth at the window. The blizzard had calmed and the stars were mirrored in a new blanket of wild snow that glittered on ice-crusted fields. Which star was my mother, and which my aunt? I picked out the two brightest ones. Sure they were Isa and Ava, I smiled up at them. They twinkled back down at me, walking hand in hand in the moon's bright light.

Several hours on, as my pains hardened and sharpened, dawn broke cold and blue, one of those perfect mornings so welcome in early spring. The first sliver of sun pushed its way across the horizon of the *Montagne Maudite*, the soft pale light on the rim of the earth announcing a new day. A sparkling morning made for new beginnings.

'Is it really coming?' Raoul bounced on the spot as excitedly as Morgane. 'I'll care for it just as much if it's a girl,' he said, slipping one hand beneath my chemise and running it over my taut belly.

'I know,' I said, between two painful throws. 'And if it's a maid, just think, I might be carrying the very first stonemistress?'

'Stone*mistress*? But that's impossible, only boys—'

'Nothing's impossible, Raoul, if you want it badly enough.'

He kept looking at me, grinning like a lunatic one minute, frowning and fearful the next. 'You always say birthing is a woman's—and a child's—most dangerous journey ... you'll be safe won't you, Héloïse, you and the little one? I couldn't bear it if ... if you were gone from me again.'

'You won't be rid of me that easily, Raoul Stonemason.' I laughed, taking his rough hands and folding them around my talisman. 'Can you feel its power ... how it warms your skin?'

'Yes ... yes I can!' Raoul said, his green eyes wide and bright in surprise.

'Believe in it, or in whatever you can—your patron Saint Etienne?—and we'll all survive this.' I kissed him more tenderly than ever and ran my hands through his corded hair. I filled myself up with his heavenly smell of sweat, stone and hard work. And his love, to help me through this perilous journey. 'Now you'd best get gone from the cot for—'

'For a birthing room is no place for a man,' Morgane cut in. She clapped her hands to call to attention Poppa, Delphine, Ariane and Catèlena. How lucky I was to have so many eager and comforting gossips. I looked at Catèlena, and she didn't have to say a word, her yearning for a child so clear in her eyes.

'You and Anselme will have many children, after you're wed at the next haymaking,' I said with a smile and a squeeze of her hand. 'Children who'll be cherished by two loving parents.'

'I know,' Catèlena said. 'I'm just impatient to be a mother.'

'That's enough chatter, Maman,' Morgane said. 'Just concentrate on your breathing.' She turned back to the gossips. 'And I'll need clean linen, boiled water and fresh straw,' she ordered.

'And fetch Yolande,' I said. 'Delphine and you can't birth this baby on your own.'

'You're always saying how well I've learned my lessons, Maman. I'm sure I could do the birth on my own … just like Sibylle's boy. And Delphine's been learning everything so quick—'

'Listen to your mother, my little Flamelock,' Raoul said, slinging his leather satchel across a shoulder. 'Come with me, we'll ride Merlinette down to the market-place and fetch Yolande. And I'll be at the Mason's Lodge,' he said with a grin, 'since I'm banished from my home.'

They all skittered about, fetching the birthing chair from the barn and my midwifing-basket from the lean-to. They clanked the kettle onto the trivet to boil, and pulled clean linen from the wooden chest. The throws strengthened, as if great hands were gripping my sides, squeezing me. The pain stabbed like a knife, burned like a flame, but when it ebbed, there was only warmth and drowsy comfort.

Like the wells in autumn and spring, I was overflowing.

Streaming through me was excitement tinged with fear, anticipation and trepidation. So many feelings all at once, I was breathless and my pulse quickened. Between two throws, I removed the talisman from where it nestled against my heart, and furled the bone-sculpted pendant in my fist.

As the unforgiving pains took me up, and my child and I set out on that most treacherous road, I squeezed my angel: that shard of Saint Margaret's bone; the token so ancient, so skillfully worked, so safely kept. I prayed for the saint to protect us both.

Raoul opened the door to leave with Morgane, and on the gust of cold clean air that whipped through the cot and shifted the lavender, rose and thyme-scented rushes, Ava's whispery voice swirled inside.

Are you ready, my warrior ... for this next battle of your life?

'Yes, Ava,' I said. 'I am ready.'

Glossary

Banalités: Until the 18th century in France, *banalités* were payments enforced for use of a lord's facilities: mill to grind grain, wine press to make wine and oven to bake bread.

Courses: Menstrual period.

Ell: Unit of measurement approximating the length of a man's arm from the elbow to the tip of the middle finger.

Fife: A high-pitched transverse flute.

Gipon: Originally a tight-fitting tunic worn next to the shirt and buttoned down the front, it came down to the knees and was padded and waisted. Later in the century the gipon became shorter, and it was replaced by the doublet in the 15th and 16th centuries.

Gittern: Obsolete medieval stringed instrument resembling the guitar.

Gossips: Special female family, friends and neighbours chosen by an expectant mother to be with her during her labour. Under the midwife's direction, they might support the woman in whatever position she chooses to give birth and provide encouragement and support.

Lute: A stringed musical instrument having a long, fretted neck and a hollow, typically pear-shaped body with a vaulted back.

Montagne Maudite (Cursed Mountain): old name for Mont Blanc.

Murrain: An antiquated, umbrella term for various infectious diseases affecting cattle and sheep such as anthrax, foot-and-mouth disease and streptococcus infections. Some of these could also affect humans, and also referred to an epidemic of such a disease.

Physick: Obsolete form of physic (medicinal drugs).

Privities: Old word for "private parts".

Queek: Game played using a large, checkered cloth and spread on a hard, smooth surface. Children would toss pebbles onto the board, calling out in advance whether the pebble would land on a light colour or a dark colour.

Scrip: A small bag, often hung from the belt and made from leather, to carry food, money, utensils, etc.

Solar Chamber: A room generally situated on an upper storey of a castle, called the Lords and Ladies Chamber, or the Great Chamber, and intended for sleeping and as private quarters, or a sitting room.

Spindle: A slender rounded rod with tapered ends used in hand spinning to twist and wind thread from a mass of wool or flax held on a distaff.

Throws: Labour pains/uterine contractions.

Windfucker: Common kestrel.

Strawberry tongue sickness: Scarlet fever.

White plague: Tuberculosis.

Yard: Penis.

Author's Note

CHARACTERS

All the characters in this novel are fictional. Even those with real-life counterparts such as Guy de Chauliac, King Philip and Eleanor of Aquitaine, have had their personalities changed to meet the story's needs.

Eleanor of Aquitaine did go on crusade, but I must apologise to her memory for portraying her as a thief on no grounds whatsoever other than the purpose of my story. The actions I accuse her of are fictional, as is the story of the bone angel talisman itself.

BLACK PLAGUE

Rumours of a terrible plague that had supposedly arisen in China had reached Europe by 1346. No serious concern was felt in Europe until the trading ships brought their pestilence cargo into Messina while other infected ships from the Levant carried it to Genoa and Venice.

The plague arrived in France via Marseille in early 1348. Carried along the coast and inland via the rivers, it spread westward from Marseille through the ports of Languedoc to Spain and northward up the Rhône to Avignon. It reached Narbonne, Montpellier, Carcassonne and Toulouse between February and May. Between June and August it reached Bordeaux, Lyon and Paris, before crossing the Channel from Normandy into southern England.

Guy de Chauliac, the Pope's physician in Avignon in 1348 and himself a plague victim who recovered, diagnosed two strains of the disease. The first, which modern physicians recognise as bubonic plague, spread by contact, is characterised by the buboes (swellings) in the groin or armpits. Chauliac (as well as my characters Yolande, the baker and Morgane) contracted and recovered from this type. The second, which he recognised as more deadly, was characterised by chest pains and spitting blood. This—the pneumonic plague—recognised by modern physicians as spread by respiratory infection, was extremely infectious. A third type—the septicaemic form which Guy did not recognise—was fatal within a few hours since the bloodstream infection was so severe that other symptoms did not have time to develop.

The actual plague bacillus, *Pasteurella pestis*, remained undiscovered until the nineteenth century. Living alternately in the stomach of the flea and the bloodstream of the rat (the flea's host), the bacillus in its bubonic form was transferred to humans and animals by the bite of either rat or flea.

Called the Black Death only in later recurrences, the plague was known during the first epidemic simply as the Pestilence or Great Mortality.

In October 1348 King Philip VI asked the University of Paris medical faculty for a report on this affliction that appeared to be threatening human survival. After careful thesis, antithesis and proofs, the physicians ascribed it to a triple conjunction of Saturn, Jupiter and Mars in the 40th degree of Aquarius, which had occured on March 20th, 1345. However, they acknowledged the presence of effects "whose cause is hidden from even the most highly-trained intellects." This verdict of the Paris masters became the official version.

I wanted to write about the Black Death because it was a very real catastrophe. The people truly believed the world would end. But society—although stretched to its endurance limits—did survive. And like the years following WWI, the years after the

Black Death were ones of enormous social change. Women took on traditionally male professions for the first time, many of them thriving. Feudalism and the power of the Church were greatly weakened. Many could no longer worship a God who had destroyed so many people. Poor families grew wealthy as land was now in great supply and labour was hard to come by.

FRENCH LANGUAGE

The language spoken in this region in 1348 was Franco-Provençal. However where I have used foreign words in the text I opted for modern-day French to avoid confusion to readers.

HOLY RELICS

Objects believed to be a physical part of a religious figure such as a saint, the Virgin Mary or even Jesus. Relics ranged from bone fragments to a tiny piece of the cross or objects modern minds may find absurd such as a hair from the Virgin's head or a drop of her milk.

In the Middle Ages many people believed that relics held heavenly powers. To touch one would provide a person with spiritual blessings, divine protection and miraculous cure from illness.

Since there were so many churches and cathedrals some relics were certainly not authentic, but they all had a story and all were treasured, assuring the church of a steady stream of visitors. Most churches charged a fee to view the holy object, and religious communities relied on relics for a large source of their income.

Relics could also be bought individually by those who could afford them and this trade became so popular that a counterfeit industry thrived during the period. In such an uncertain world, people often sought the protection of a religious relic, which they would carry with them at all times.

Many highly-venerated European relics had been brought

from the Holy Land by the Crusaders. These relics were especially revered as they came from Jesus's birthplace and were strongly associated with the Holy Family.

MIDWIFERY

The midwifery procedures in *Blood Rose Angel* are as accurate as historical records will allow. The obstetric and medical conditions suffered by the characters are as authentic as I could make them. Women usually gave birth sitting upright on a wooden birthing chair with a horseshoe-shaped seat to allow the midwife access and to provide room for the baby to pass through.

Eclampsia: The condition that killed Midwife Héloïse's mother, Ava, defined as the onset of seizures in a pregnant woman already suffering from pre-eclampsia. Pre-eclampsia can occur any time after the 20th week of pregnancy, and until 6 weeks after delivery. Signs and symptoms of pre-eclampsia include severe headaches, blurred vision, upper abdominal pain, vomiting, high blood pressure, protein in the urine and sometimes facial swelling. It is thought to be due to a problem with the placenta but nobody understands exactly what.

Ergot: A fungus that lives on rye. Controlled doses of ergot have been used since the Middle Ages to induce abortion and to stop maternal haemorrhage after childbirth. It has saved the lives of countless women and is still used in some form or other today to prevent or treat post-partum haemorrhage. Midwife Héloïse gives this (her angel powder) firstly to Jehanne when her labour has stopped, to induce uterine contractions. She then gives it to Catèlena, to induce an abortion. The ergot alkaloids can also cause hallucinations, irrational behaviour, convulsions and even death, and Isa teaches Héloïse to be wary of it for '... *it can bring madness, death, and evil tramping in its wake.*'

Changeling: A changeling was a child considered to have been swapped either in the womb or after birth by fairies. Jehanne's stillborn suffered from myelomeningocele (spina bifida) and hydrocephalus. Such inexplicable birth defects were often put down to the "evil eye" or the midwife practicing "dark arts".

ROSE TONIC

For the purposes of this story, I have based the rose tonic that Héloïse concocts to attempt to stop the plague spreading on the "rose pills" of Michel de Nostredame, one of the most fascinating personalities of 16th century France and better known by his pseudonym, Nostradamus. On completion of his medical and astrological studies at the University of Montpellier, Nostradamus took to the countryside with his medical and astrological books and assisted with the care of bubonic plague victims. He prescribed fresh air, clean water and bedding and the removal of corpses, and ordered the streets to be cleaned. Each morning before sunrise, he oversaw the harvest of rose petals which he dried and crushed into fine powder to make his "rose pills". Patients were advised to keep the pill under their tongues at all times without swallowing them. Historians, medical men and biographers attribute Nostradamus's success primarily to his great self-confidence and the courage that enabled him to enter plague homes. Nostradamus believed the plague was spread by contaminated air and that clean air protected people, but perhaps his success lay in the fact that fleas, which transmit the disease from rats to humans, were repelled by the rose pills' strong smell, so at least the healthy didn't catch it. Whatever the reasons, Nostradamus was reputed to have saved thousands from plague in Narbonne, Carcassonne, Toulouse and Bordeaux.

VINGTAIN

During the 14th century, the Lyonnais villages built these fortifications to protect themselves from the *tard-venus:* heavily-armed and well-trained troops demobilised after the Treaty of Brétigny in 1360, who attacked the civilian populations of villages and towns. The Treaty of Brétigny was signed between England and France at Brétigny, a village near Chartres, France, and is now seen as having marked the end of the first phase of the Hundred Years' War (1337 – 1453).

***

To learn more about the history behind the stories of *The Bone Angel* series, follow my blog posts at: lizaperrat.blogspot.com

Acknowledgements

With grateful thanks to the writers and readers who helped shape this novel: Barbara Scott-Emmett, Gillian Hamer, Jane Hicks, JJ Marsh, JD Smith, Catriona Troth (Triskele Books); Marlene Brown, Kari Chevalier, Chris Curran, Jane Davis, Tricia Gilbey, Gwenda Lansbury Claire Morgan, Pauline O'Hare, Lucy Pitts, Debra Prichard, Zoe Saadia, Claire Whatley, June Whitaker; C.P. Lesley for reading and for her historical expertise; Pamela Bennett and Bernadette Vogel for checking the midwifery parts; Courtney J. Hall for her help with the blurb; Marie-Thérèse Lorcin (*Docteur es-lettres Maître de conférences à l'Université Lyon II*) for interesting discussions on her knowledge of this region in medieval times; Jean-Marie Robles: http://www.rhone-medieval.fr/; Cécile Jomain, history teacher, *Lycée Agricole Edouard Herriot, Domaine de Cibeins, Misérieux;* Sarah Preston (International Press Officer/Community Manager at Guédelon Castle: http://www.guedelon.fr/en/) for her expertise; Brad Steele (master mason and carver) for his stonemason expertise; Lorraine Mace for editorial advice; Perry Iles for his editorial and proofreading expertise; JD Smith for her cover design; and finally to my family for their patience and understanding.

Thank you for reading a Triskele Book

If you loved this book and you'd like to help other readers find Triskele Books, please write a short review on the website where you bought the book. Your help in spreading the word is much appreciated and reviews make a huge difference to helping new readers find good books.

Why not try books by other Triskele authors?
Choose a complimentary ebook when you sign up
to our free newsletter at

www.triskelebooks.co.uk/signup

If you are a writer and would like more information on writing and publishing, visit http://www.triskelebooks.blogspot.com and http://www.wordswithjam.co.uk, which are packed with author and industry professional interviews, links to articles on writing, reading, libraries, the publishing industry and indie-publishing.

Connect with us:
Email admin@triskelebooks.co.uk
Twitter @triskelebooks
Facebook www.facebook.com/triskelebooks

Other novels by Liza Perrat

Spirit of Lost Angels
Book 1 in *The Bone Angel* series

Available now as print and e-book.

Amazon: myBook.to/SpiriteBook

Smashwords: https://www.smashwords.com/books/
view/161707

Kobo: https://store.kobobooks.com/en-us/ebook/
spirit-of-lost-angels-1

Nook/Barnes & Noble: http://www.barnesandnoble.
com/w/spirit-of-lost-angels-liza-perrat/1111399033?e
an=9782954168104

Her mother executed for witchcraft, her father dead at the
hand of a noble, Victoire Charpentier vows to rise above her
impoverished peasant roots.

Forced to leave her village of Lucie-sur-Vionne for domestic
work in the capital, Victoire suffers gruesome abuse under the
ancien régime of 18th century Paris.

Imprisoned in France's most pitiless madhouse — *La
Salpêtrière* asylum — Victoire becomes desperate and helpless,

until she meets fellow prisoner Jeanne de Valois, infamous conwoman of the diamond necklace affair. With the help of the ruthless and charismatic countess who helped hasten Queen Marie Antoinette to the guillotine, Victoire carves out a new life for herself.

Enmeshed in the fever of pre-revolutionary Paris, Victoire must find the strength to join the revolutionary force storming the Bastille. Is she brave enough to help overthrow the diabolical aristocracy?

As *Spirit of Lost Angels* traces Victoire's journey, it follows too the journey of an angel talisman through generations of the Charpentier family. Victoire lives in the hope her angel pendant will one day renew the link with a special person in her life.

Amidst the tumult of the French revolution drama, the women of *Spirit of Lost Angels* face tragedy and betrayal in a world where their gift can be their curse.

Spirit of Lost Angels listed on "Best of 2012" sites

http://darleneelizabethwilliamsauthor.com/
blog/2012-top-10-historical-fiction-novels/

http://abookishaffair.blogspot.fr/2012/12/best-books-of-2012.
html

http://thequeensquillreview.com/2012/12/10/
holiday-picks-from-the-queens-quill/

Shortlisted Writing Magazine Self-Publishing Awards 2013

http://lizaperrat.blogspot.fr/2013/06/spirit-of-lost-angels-
shortlisted.html

Winner EFestival of Words 2013, Best Historical Fiction category

Recommended at the 2013 Historical Novel Conference in "Off the Beaten Path" recommendations

http://thequeensquillreview.com/2013/06/26/the-mammoth-list-of-off-the-beaten-path-book-recommendations-brought-to-you-by-our-hns-conference-panel/

Indie Book of the Day Award, 13th July, 2013

http://indiebookoftheday.com/
spirit-of-lost-angels-by-liza-perrat/

***Spirit of Lost Angels* Editorial Reviews**

'... I LOVE, LOVE, LOVE when a book sucks me in and is so engrossing that I get ticked when I have to put it down. As a reader, it made me feel as though I was being written into the pages of the book. ... those who refuse to read indie-published books lose out on dynamic novels and this book is definitely an example of why I feel that way. I would not be surprised if this is a book I find in the collection of a large publishing house in the future ...'... Naomi B (A Book and A Review): http://abookandareview.blogspot.fr/2012/11/spirit-of-lost-angels-by-liza-perrat.html

'... how well written and detailed the book is as the author clearly outlines the path of a commoner's life and the hardship of Victoire's life from childhood to adulthood ... very intriguing ... an historical book about enduring, accepting, regret, love, loss, family, hope, coming home, and an angel pendant that held it all together for each of the women who wore it ...' ... Elizabeth of Silver's Reviews: http://silversolara.blogspot.fr/2012/07/spirit-of-lost-angels-by-liza-perrat.html

'... impressed with Perrat's knowledgeable treatment of the role of women during one of France's most tumultuous times, as well as the complexities of insular village life ...' ... Darlene Williams:

http://darleneelizabethwilliamsauthor.com/hfreviews/spirit-of-lost-angels-by-liza-perrat-historical-fiction-novel-review/

'The writing is superb, the sights, sounds and smells of a city in turmoil is brought vividly to life ...' ... Josie Barton: http://jaffareadstoo.blogspot.fr/2012/08/author-interview-liza-perrat.html

'... a tale to lose oneself in ... persuasively combines fact and fiction in this engrossing novel. The peasants' fury, the passion building up to the Bastille storming, and the sense of political explosion are just a few of the vivid illustrations ...' ... Andrea Connell: http://thequeensquillreview.com/2012/10/10/review-spirit-of-lost-angels-by-liza-perrat/

'... a truly astounding book that will have you reaching out to the characters, feeling for them, and fiercely cheering them on ... engrossing, absorbing and you won't be able to put this down. ... a book not to be missed ... perfect for fans of historical fiction ...' ... Megan, Reading in the Sunshine: http://readinginthesunshine.wordpress.com/2013/04/05/spirit-of-lost-angels-by-liza-perrat/

'... escapist fun — Francophiles will want this one and those who enjoy historical fiction that doesn't focus on royals ... great fun for the summer read.' ... Audra (Unabridged Chick): http://unabridged-expression.blogspot.fr/2013/05/spirit-of-lost-angels-by-liza-perrat.html

'... brings to life the sights and sounds of 18th century France. Her extensive research shines through in her writing, from the superstitions of the villagers to the lives of the more sophisticated Parisians.' ... Anne Cater (Top 500 Amazon reviewer): http://randomthingsthroughmyletterbox.blogspot.co.uk/2012/09/spirit-of-lost-angels-by-liza-perrat.html

Wolfsangel
Book 2 in *The Bone Angel* series

Available now as print and e-book.

Amazon: myBook.to/WolfsangeleBook

Smashwords: https://www.smashwords.com/books/
view/363451

Kobo: http://store.kobobooks.com/en-US/ebook/wolfsangel-2

Nook/Barnes & Noble: http://www.barnesandnoble.com/w/
wolfsangel-liza-perrat/1117076332?ean=2940150281158

Seven decades after German troops march into her village,
Céleste Roussel is still unable to assuage her guilt.

1943. German soldiers occupy provincial Lucie-sur-Vionne,
and as the villagers pursue treacherous schemes to deceive and
swindle the enemy, Céleste embarks on her own perilous mis-
sion as her passion for a Reich officer flourishes.

When her loved ones are deported to concentration camps,
Céleste is drawn into the vortex of this monumental conflict, and
the adventure and danger of French Resistance collaboration.

As she confronts the harrowing truths of the Second World
War's darkest years, Céleste is forced to choose: pursue her love
for the German officer, or answer General de Gaulle's call to
fight for France.

Her fate suspended on the fraying thread of her will, Celeste
gains strength from the angel talisman bequeathed to her

through her lineage of healer kinswomen. But the decision she makes will shadow the remainder of her days.

A woman's unforgettable journey to help liberate Occupied France, *Wolfsangel* is a stirring portrayal of the courage and resilience of the human mind, body and spirit.

Indie Book of the Day: http://indiebookoftheday.com/wolfsangel-by-liza-perrat/

Josie Barton (TOP 500 AMAZON REVIEWER) Best books of 2013: http://jaffareadstoo.blogspot.co.uk/2013/12/books-in-my-year-2013.html

Wolfsangel Editorial Reviews

'A heart-stopping novel of love, betrayal and courage which will leave you shaken and profoundly moved.' ... Karen Maitland, bestselling author of *Company of Liars*.

'... one of the best books I have ever read.' ... Kimberly Walker, reader

'... captures the tragedy of betrayal and the constancy of hope. It brings home to the reader that choices made in youth, cast deep shadows. A superb story that stays in the mind long after the final page.' ... Lorraine Mace, writer, columnist and author of *The Writer's ABC Checklist*.

'A beautifully laid-out spiral of unfolding tragedy in German-occupied France; a tale of courage, hardship, forbidden love and the possibility of redemption in times of terror.' ... Perry Iles, proofreader.

'Once I picked this up I found it nigh impossible to put down ... Loosely based on the tragic events of Oradour Sur Glane in 1944, this novel doesn't pull any punches and will remain with the reader for a long time.' ... Lovely Treez (AMAZON TOP 500 REVIEWER): http://www.lovelytreez.com/?p=778

'Wolfsangel is a powerful story that has stayed with me since finishing the last page. Wow.' ... Megan ReadingInTheSunshine (AMAZONTOP100REVIEWER): http://readinginthesunshine. wordpress.com/tag/wolfsangel/

'... an absorbing, well-researched and well-written novel ideal for anyone who enjoys reading historical fiction and like Liza Perrat's previous novel, Spirit of Lost Angels there are courageous female characters at the heart of the storyline.'... L. H. Healy "Books are life, beauty and truth." (AMAZON TOP 500 REVIEWER): http://thelittlereaderlibrary.blogspot.fr/2014/06/wolfsangel-liza-perrat.html?spref=fb

'... reviewed for Historical Novel Society ... entertaining play on the familiar theme of love in the twilight of politics and honour and grippingly dramatic. The prose and the writing are beautiful, the central character conflict and the outcome are very satisfying and the book is a solid achievement.'... ChristophFischerBooks (AMAZON TOP 500 REVIEWER): http://historicalnovelsociety.org/reviews/wolfsangel/

'... a fascinating, forceful and extremely well researched novel that will thrill historical fiction fans. Liza Perrat writes elegantly, with feeling and authority.'... Lincs Reader (AMAZON TOP 100 REVIEWER): http://randomthingsthroughmyletterbox. blogspot.fr/2013/11/wolfsangel-by-liza-perrat.html

Bibliography

Many fictional and factual books, films and other material were useful in creating the atmosphere of *Blood Rose Angel*

Jane Sharp, edited by Elaine Hobby: *The Midwives Book or The Whole Art of Midwifery Discovered*

Nina Rattner Gelbart: *The King's Midwife: A History and Mystery of Madame du Coudray*

Giovanni Baccaccio: *Decameron*

Monica H. Green, editor and translator: *The Trotula–An English Translation of the Medieval Compendium of Women's Medicine*

Marjorie Rowling: *Life in Medieval Times*

Joan Evans: *Life in Medieval France*

Geoffrey Brereton, translator: *The Chronicles of Froissart*

Frances and Joseph Gies: *Life in a Medieval Village*

Frances and Joseph Gies: *Marriage and the Family in the Middle Ages*

E. R. Chamberlin: *Life in Medieval France*

Barbara Tuchman: *A Distant Mirror–The Calamitous Fourteenth Century*

William Langland: *Piers Plowman*

John Hatcher: *The Black Death–The Intimate Story of a Village in*

Crisis, 1345 – 1350

William Naphy & Andrew Spicer: *Plague–Black Death & Pestilence in Europe*

Norman F. Cantor: *In the Wake of the Plague*

Malcolm Hislop: *Medieval Masons*

Ian Mortimer: *The Time Traveller's Guide to Medieval England: A Handbook for Visitors to the Fourteenth Century*

About the Author

Liza grew up in Wollongong, Australia, where she worked as a general nurse and midwife. She has now lived in rural France for over twenty years, working as a medical translator and a novelist.

For more information on Liza and her writing, please visit her website: www.lizaperrat.com

or her blog: http://lizaperrat.blogspot.com

Facebook: https://www.facebook.com/Liza-Perrat-232382930192297/

Twitter: @LizaPerrat

Pinterest: http://www.pinterest.com/triskelebooks/

Google +: https://plus.google.com/114732287937883580857/about

For occasional book news and a free copy of Ill-fated Rose, short story that inspired The Bone Angel series, sign up http://www.lizaperrat.moonfruit.com/signupw

72650171R00253

Made in the USA
San Bernardino, CA
27 March 2018